Ending in Cadence

To those who feel alone...

I promise that you're not

Pintura

Rising Salvation

The Golden Field

The Scrapyard

Residential Area

Athletic Fields

Vainder Headquarters

Infinity Forest

Artmith

Shopping District

University

Business District

Shadow Village

N
W   E
S

CHAPTER I

Ash

The echoes of drums beat through the cemetery. I strike the drumsticks rhythmically, playing the familiar marching band cadence that sounds like hail ricocheting against metal pans. Family members cloaked in black flank both sides of the open grave, and the casket holding my grandma lowers into the earth.

My mom said it would be a nice tribute to her if I played at the funeral. I wasn't all that close to my grandma, and she wasn't interested in spending time with us until my younger sister, Jenny, was nine. By then, I was already ten, and I was more focused on video games and comic books than learning how to sew. But for the next seven years, my sister and I would spend the summers at her house on the top of Grindle Street. This will be the first summer we won't.

"That was a lovely ceremony," my mom says as we make our way back to our cars. "I'm glad you played today." She smiles softly at me, placing a gentle hand on my shoulder.

"I'm glad I played too," I say as we reach my car; an olive green Chevy Malibu that is about five years past its last leg. The trunk squeals open and I place my snare drum and sticks inside.

"You and your sister are going to grandma's to pack up her things, right?" my dad asks. He fidgets with the silver watch on his wrist, eager to get away from the cemetery.

"Yeah, we'll head straight there. Wren is coming over to help," I say, mentioning my childhood best friend that I paid to help move some of my grandma's heavier things.

"That's nice of him," my mother says, not knowing about the allowance I slipped him last week in English class. She and my father walk across the street to their car and head toward home.

"How much did you pay Wren to move grandma's things?" Jenny asks, knowing Wren and I haven't spoken since sophomore year of high school. Nearly two years, and we haven't said a word to each other.

I get into the car and dig my keys out of my pocket, my fingers fiddling with the bronze key chain of a snare drum. I put the key in the ignition and the car wheezes to life.

Jenny fishes a small piece of paper out of the pocket of in her black dress, but I can't tell what it says.

"What makes you think I had to pay Wren?" I shoot my sister a side glance and she rolls her eyes, shoving the piece of paper back into her pocket before I can ask about it.

Even though I haven't spoken to Wren since I was a sophomore, he was the first person I thought of to help. I'm not sure what happened between us. We were inseparable for all of middle school, but once we got into high school, things changed. Wren and I just… *drifted*.

As I steer my old clunker down the rocked road, the dusty radio in the dashboard spits out a mix of electric guitar and deep bass. My sister and I crank our windows down, letting the hot, soon-to-be summer air flood the car. Only two more weeks until my graduation. It'll be a mix of closing projects and final exams, but once it's over, there will be nothing in between me and Coastal University.

I roll out of the cemetery and onto the main road, heading toward Grindle Street, where my grandma's house now sits abandoned. It may seem a bit rushed to be moving her things out, but her passing didn't come as a surprise. She was diagnosed with a late stage of lung cancer seven years ago.

It's honestly a miracle she fought it as long as she did. We've been putting her things in boxes for months, and the sooner we get her house on the market, the faster we'll be able to sell it. That's what dad says anyway. Today, we'll move all of those boxes and clear out the second level. Including my grandma's art studio. A room I'm forbidden to enter. Until now, I guess.

The car weaves around the winding road, up toward the iron gate surrounding the property. Tall, thick forest to my right and salty Pacific waves to my left. Prime real-estate here in Southern California. No neighbors and an ocean view. If I wasn't sure the house was haunted, I'd almost suggest we keep it in the family.

I glance at Jenny and, as our grandmother's house comes into view, her eyes glisten with tears. My grip on the steering wheel tightens at seeing her upset.

I clear my throat and turn down the radio. "How are you doing, Jenny?" I ask, hoping I'm not overstepping some invisible sibling wall she's put up.

As far as siblings go, we're pretty close. She's only a year younger than me, and growing up, I was the big brother she came to for everything. That's rarely the case anymore. She can take care of herself now, but sometimes, I still try to be the big brother I was to her when we were little.

I press the grey button on the remote to open the black iron gate and pull the car into the main circle drive.

"I don't need my big brother to comfort me," Jenny mumbles, popping open the door before I even come to a complete stop. She grabs her bag with a change of clothes from the back seat and quickly wipes away the tears in her eyes.

And there's the wall I knew she'd put up. I huff a heavy breath.

Gravel from the driveway crunches beneath Jenny's feet as she heads toward the tall, white doors at the front of the house. A large paint-chipped porch surrounds the old, orange-bricked home that towers over us. The wooden stairs creak beneath my black dress shoes as I follow her, my own change of clothes in hand. I unlock the door with the spare key my grandma entrusted to me and prop it open.

"Let's change first so mom doesn't yell at us for ruining our only nice clothes," I say, choosing to ignore Jenny's earlier comment.

She forces a chuckle and heads to the bathroom that's off of the living room. Once we've changed into faded t-shirts and shorts, the heat is more bearable. I swap my dress shoes for tennis shoes and I'm almost able to forget I was at my grandma's funeral. If I weren't packing up her things right now, that is.

"We can start loading boxes into my car," I say, tossing our bags into the backseat. "Wren is bringing his truck, and we can load the bigger items there."

"Mom and dad are renting the moving truck this afternoon, right?" Jenny asks, leading me into the living room where dust hangs in the beams of sunlight.

"Should be," I say and let out an exhausted sigh, looking at the mounds of boxes. "This is going to take all day."

"Better to do it now than when summer vacation starts," Jenny mumbles, picking up the first box her eyes land on.

I shrug my shoulders, knowing she's right. I guess my final chemistry lab report will have to wait until tomorrow to be written. *Hell, I've put it off for a month now. What's one more day?* I organize the boxes in the room, finding the lightest ones to leave for Jenny. The heavier ones, full of lamps and old candles, I take two at a time to save myself a trip.

Marching snare drum for four years has helped to build some muscle. By no means am I an athlete, but I'm not your typical *band-nerd* either. I take pride in the fact that I'm at least in the drumline, though my love for the arts stems deeper than just band.

Acting is my true passion, but I'd never admit that to anyone.

Drumming is my *future*, but I know I could be great as an actor. I had the lead in the play last fall, beating Josh Wallace for the part. He was so upset he actually asked the director to recast the play. But I hardly talk about that play anymore. I auditioned as a joke and that's what everyone thinks acting is to me. *A joke.* And I let them think it because a drummer is mysterious. A drummer might get asked to prom. A boy who loves acting...

I like my lone place at the lunch table in the corner. I like being the kid in the back of the practice room that keeps the beating rhythm of the song alive. I'm used to the whispers and the wandering eyes on days my classmates want to notice me, and I'm also used to feeling invisible on the days they don't.

As I take out the last box that will fit in my car, I hear the humming of a truck climbing the driveway. Wren hangs out the window of his chugging, light-blue truck, waving one arm wildly at me while trying to steer with the other.

I shove the last box into my back seat and squeeze the door closed. I step back and tilt my head, waiting for the door to pop back open. After I'm sure it will hold, I meet Wren as he climbs down from his truck.

"Thanks again for coming to help," I say.

Wren drops from his truck, his worn, white tennis shoes blending in with the rock driveway. Jeans that are two sizes too big, passed down from his older brothers, are ringed with permanent grass stains. I crack a smile when I see the emblem of his favorite superhero on his black shirt.

Now I remember why we stopped being friends. Because Wren is so... *Wren*. He's one-hundred percent himself. He found his crowd of friends—other kids who wore superhero shirts—and I kept to myself. The mysterious, brooding drummer everyone whispers about.

"Sure thing. Thank you for the crisp Ben Franklin," Wren says, waving the hundred-dollar bill I gave him in the air before shoving it back into his pocket. It was an early graduation present from my aunt and uncle that I'm sure I'll miss later this summer. "I texted you and Jenny to see if you wanted anything from the gas station."

"Sorry, we left our phones in my car—"

"Hi Wren!" Jenny yells, leaning out the living room window, watching us climb up the front porch.

"Hey Jen," Wren calls. When Jenny falls back inside, I catch Wren flattening down his blonde ruffles.

"Please tell me you're not still crushing on my sister," I say underneath my breath.

Wren's hands freeze on his head before falling limp to his sides. "Of course not," he tries to cover, but the truth is written on his face.

I roll my eyes and huff a laugh. Of course he is. He's liked Jenny since we started being friends in middle school, but it's a lost cause. This fall, we'll both be leaving for college, and Jenny will start her senior year at Weston High.

"Should we start with the couches, or go look at what else is upstairs?" I ask when we enter the living room.

"I guess we should look upstairs," Jenny says, smacking a piece of tape down on a ripped cardboard box. "This stuff should probably go on the moving truck."

We follow Jenny out of the living room and deeper into the house. She swings through the kitchen to see what else is here. We've already removed most of the silverware and dishes, and the long wooden dining table definitely won't fit in Wren's truck.

At the back of the house, a dark brown staircase climbs to the second floor of the home, a light red carpet running down its center. On the second level, we walk through the two guest bedrooms and find them still full of dressers and lamps. We haven't touched the items in the drawers and closets since the last time we stayed in this house.

"Let's start here, I guess," Jenny says, moving toward the room that used to be hers.

I send Wren down to the study to grab some spare boxes and begin to empty the bedside table in the room I used to stay in. I pile comic books and notebooks full of sketches on the bed, flipping through them as I go. I've never been an artist, but my grandma was certain she could teach me. She loved art and swore she was a famous painter in a different life. While she painted fields of flowers, I drew wrinkled monsters destroying cities.

The comic books aren't even mine. I borrowed them from Wren so I'd have something to base my drawings off of years ago. He's probably forgotten, but I guess I can return them now. Better late than never.

When Wren comes back upstairs, I have him pack what I've piled on the bed.

"Hey, these are mine!" Wren says, snatching the top comic book off the pile.

"I meant to give them back."

"This one was my favorite!" he exclaims, picking up the next comic book.

I refrain from saying they're all his favorites.

I move to clear off the dresser, leaving Wren to marvel at his favorite thing; his comic books. Most of the items on the dresser are trash; an old toothbrush, an empty can of deodorant, chewed gum squished back in its silver wrapper. Under an empty water bottle, I find a stack of faded sheet music from last year's band performance.

"Wren, look at this," I say, handing him the music.

"Oh, I hated last year's piece. The second movement was the worst," Wren says, taking the music from me.

Wren is first chair trumpet player, truly the best in the state. Well, maybe not in the state, but he likes to tell people he is because he beat the *actual* best trumpet player in the state at Solo and Ensemble last year.

"Trash or?" Wren says, leaving the question in the air and waving the papers in his hand.

"You can pitch it."

"Are you boys finished, yet?" Jenny asks, leaning against the doorframe, a single cardboard box in her hands.

"Yeah, just about," I say, pushing some more wrappers from the dresser into a trash bag.

Wren and I follow Jenny down to his truck and throw our boxes in his backseat to save room in the truck bed. "We still have grandma's art studio upstairs," Jenny says, trailing off.

Right, the art studio. Jenny and I were never allowed in there. If grandma wanted to show us what she was painting, she'd bring it downstairs, but under no circumstances were we *ever* allowed to step foot in her art studio. I don't blame her, though. Knowing Jenny and me, we definitely would have broken something and ruined one of her prized paintings.

The three of us wander back through the old house, the rooms slowly becoming emptier, and we climb back up to the second floor. We file down the narrow hall, past the two guest bedrooms, and a single bathroom, to the sealed door at the end of the hallway.

My eyes trace the intricate swirling designs on the wooden frame. Jenny lays her hand on the golden brass knob and suddenly stops.

"What is it?" I ask, watching her hesitate.

"I don't know, it just feels weird to be going in there," Jenny mumbles, the years of lectures keeping her from turning the knob.

I place my hand over Jenny's and give the knob a quick twist. Jenny wretches her hand away as if the doorknob is hot iron and, ever so slightly, the door creaks open.

"Well, better you than me," Jenny says, pressing her back to the wall to let me pass. "If grandma decides to come back and haunt someone, it'll probably be you."

I laugh at her remark and push through the wooden door. The floor beneath my feet changes from cracked, dark brown planks to a polished tan. Light bleeds in through the giant dome window above, a sudden shift from the dimly lit hallway.

"No wonder grandma could spend hours in here," Jenny says with a breathy voice, scanning the large room.

Paintings hang from the floor to the ceiling, all around the circular room. Grey drop cloths are thrown across the center of the floor, an easel propped open on top of them. The art is gorgeous, many of the paintings I don't even recognize. She's painted just about everything I can think of; rolling green hills, snowcapped mountains, and foaming blue oceans.

"Grandma really was so talented," Jenny says softly.

After the amazement of the art studio wears off, the first thing my mind registers is now we have to move all these paintings out of here.

"Guess we better take them down," I say, reminding Jenny and Wren of why we are here.

Starting with the paintings at the bottom of the wall, we carefully lift them up from their hooks and carry them one by one back down to the main foyer of the home. We stack them there and wait to ask mom what she wants to do with them. I figure she could probably try to sell them. I bet someone would pay a lot of money for some of these.

Most of the paintings are just bare canvases, soaked with rich colors. My grandma even signed every single one of them with a small *ART* in the corner. Yes, her initials spelled art. *Alice Raze Turner.* Maybe she was a famous painter in another life.

While my sister and Wren work on the front of the room, I move behind the easel and take down some of the paintings hidden in the back. Instead of making a trip downstairs for every single painting, I decide to take them off their hangers and stack them on the floor so I can carry them down together. Jenny scolds me and says I should really be more careful with our grandmother's paintings, but after the sixth time up that staircase, I don't really care if one of the thirty flower paintings gets a little crushed beneath the other canvases.

I scan the empty wall, the places where the paintings once hung darker than the rest of the wall. A chill runs through me, the discoloration reminding me of ghosts. If paintings had them.

I cross over to the last artwork on my side of the room, noticing this one hangs encased in a giant, golden frame. My fingers press against the soft canvas, tracing the lines of the paint. It's different from the other scenes my grandma painted. It's an aerial shot of somewhere I can't place. There's a roaring waterfall, a large blue lake, golden fields, lush green jungle, and a jagged metallic city humming in the corner.

I run my fingers along the swirling metal of the frame that surrounds the canvas. The bottom right corner has a piece of metal that's come loose from the frame and I rotate it left and right, curious about the broken corner.

The painting is nearly my entire arm span and I stretch to wrap my fingers on either side of the frame. I push up on the painting, lifting it from the hanger, and stumble backwards. Knocked off balance from the massive weight of the artwork, I lean forward and the painting flies from my grasp, landing on the ground with a loud *thump*.

"Ash, I told you to be careful!" Jenny screams, crossing the room with fierce strides.

I don't register her yells. My eyes have landed on the bottom left corner of the painting, where the letters *ART* have been gently brushed on every other canvas, but not this one.

"That's weird. Grandma didn't sign this one," I say when Jenny reaches me.

Her fuming face relaxes and her eyes look down at the massive canvas. She crouches lower to examine it.

"Look at this!" Wren calls from behind us. He walks backward, carrying a human dummy used for sculptures.

"Watch where you're going—" I start to say, but Wren trips on the grey cloth beneath the easel and falls backward, bumping into Jenny.

Jenny flails her arms out, trying to catch her balance. She rocks forward, falling onto the large painting, and then vanishes *through* the canvas.

One moment she's there and the next, *she's gone.*

For a second, I freeze, staring at the space where Jenny just was. No matter how many times I blink, she doesn't reappear. She's just... *gone.*

"Jenny!" I yell, reality unfreezing me.

"What just happened?" Wren asks, his voice raising two octaves. He stumbles to his feet, throwing the dummy he had been carrying to the side. "Did your sister just fall *through* that painting?"

I lose my words in my throat. Not knowing what else to do, I lift the normal-looking painting up to peer under it. Tan wooden floor beams stretch beneath it, nothing out of place. I drop the painting to the ground and stumble back from it.

"Jenny?" I yell out again and turn around the room, thinking my mind must be playing tricks on me.

Wren and I pause, hoping that Jenny's voice will call back to us, but the still air in the room tightens in our throats. My eyes land back on the painting in the golden frame. *Did my sister fall through it?* Of course not, you can't fall *through* a painting. And yet, she did.

Slowly, I walk toward the fantasy painting and kneel next to it. Wren joins me at my side, his eyes wide. I lift my hand and hover my fingers inches from the canvas. Carefully, I lower them toward the painting and instead of touching the dried paint, they pass through in a blur, and a cool breeze tugs at my fingertips. I yank my hand back sharply, and Wren gasps at my side.

"This can't be real. That's not real!" Wren snaps, trying to deny the magic that is happening before his eyes.

"I—" I start to say, stumbling for my words. "I'm sure there's some kind of explanation."

"It's *magic*. Like in the comic books," Wren whispers crazily.

"This isn't one of your comic books!" I yell, the anxiety in my veins making my words come out harsher than I intend.

After a breath of silence, Wren leans in and puts his face over the painting. "Jenny! Jenny, can you hear me?"

After another drawn out silence with no response, I say, "I don't think she can talk back to us."

"Well, what do we do?" Wren asks me, a sweaty panic glistening on his forehead.

I swallow, knowing exactly what I'm going to do. I've spent my entire life protecting my little sister. Whether it was bullies at school or a bee sting, I always take care of her. This is no different.

"I'll have to go in after her," I say.

"Not alone, you're not," Wren says, surprising me with his declaration.

"No, you need to stay here and get my parents," I offer.

"You've lost your mind if you think I'm going to go tell your parents that you both fell through a painting in your grandmother's home on the day of her funeral." Wren shakes his head hard, more terrified of confronting my parents than throwing himself into a painting.

I contemplate it for a second and then nod, agreeing. "Together, then?"

Wren nods and readies himself as if he were about to take off in a race. "We just... jump in?"

I lower my hand back into the painting to confirm that it still passes through the canvas. "I think so," I say, my nerves stealing the end of my words.

"On three then," Wren says and we count aloud.

"One... two... three."

Together, we dive into the painting.

CHAPTER 2

Emma

A shrieking shrill almost knocks me down the mountain of old computer parts I'm balanced on. I scurry to the top of the junk mound and snap my head back and forth, trying to find its source. There, up in the sky, hurdling toward the ground, is... *a girl?*

I blink hard, not believing the sight. Above her, the grey clouds swirl in a dark cyclone, looking very ominous spitting the girl into the sky. She vanishes from sight, hidden behind the rolling hills of the wheat fields. I expect a loud crack or thud, but nothing comes.

I turn around on my pile of scrap parts to see if anyone else heard anything, but the junkyard is deserted. *Right, no one wants to work on a Sunday if they don't have to.*

I slide down the hill, pushing broken computer monitors and keyboards out of the way. My jumpsuit pant leg comes unrolled, and I almost trip on the heavy burlap fabric. I snap it back into a loose cuff and continue on, slinging my satchel across my chest.

I run toward the exit of the junkyard, punching my employee card at the fence before heading toward the Golden Field. Toward the falling girl.

The junkyard I work in lies outside the wall surrounding Artmith, the roaring city I call home. I'm guessing no one from inside the wall had seen or heard the screaming girl. I'm sure Patrol trucks would already be crawling every inch of these fields if they had.

"Hello?" her young voice calls out.

When I get close enough to see her, I drop to my knees, peering through the waist-high wheat. She looks like a normal girl, but how was she *in the sky*? Tears ring her eyes and her cheeks are flushed bright red. She's breathing hard, a hysterical panic taking over. Just when I'm about to show myself to calm her down, a deep roar yells out overhead.

I crane my neck toward the cyclone and see two more people falling toward us. Just when their bodies should *splat* on the ground, they abruptly stop, hovering inches above their deaths, and then the air lets them loose and they fall flat on their stomachs.

"Ash!" the girl says, helping one of the boys to his feet.

He's taller than her, his brown hair blown wild around his face. My chest swells as I scan him from head to toe, unable to keep myself from admitting how attractive he is with his sun-kissed skin and muscles beneath a bright white shirt and dark shorts.

"Jenny, are you okay?" Ash asks, looking her up and down to make sure she is, in fact, alive.

"Fine," she says, her senses coming back to her. "Why did you jump in after me? You should have gone and got mom and dad!"

"And told them what?" he asks her. "They just buried our

16

grandmother. I wasn't about to go tell them you fell into one of her paintings."

The other boy, who had been silently staring at his hands and glancing back up toward the sky, finally finds his voice. "Where are we?" His blonde ruffles are practically standing straight up. He's equally as attractive but in a different way. His features are softer than Ash's, kind and inviting.

"How am I supposed to know, Wren?" the boy named Ash snaps, running a hand through his wild, brown waves that reach his jawline. The muscles in his arm flex through his worn, white short-sleeved shirt, a stark contrast against his tan skin.

He seems to have an idea because his worried face becomes more serious and he reaches for his back pocket. Whatever he's hoping is there, isn't, and his face pinches together as the panic returns.

"Please tell me one of us has a phone." He says each word very carefully. Jenny and the boy they called Wren look at each other and then back to Ash.

"I left mine in your car," Jenny breathes out the words.

"Mine is in my truck," Wren adds.

"Dammit," Ash huffs. His blue eyes dart around the field, panicked, until they lock on mine. "Hey!" he hollers.

Shit. I look around, trying to calculate my escape, but it's no use, they've already seen me. Reluctantly, I stand up in the tall grass.

Ash seems to read my hesitation because his next words are said deliberately slow. "We aren't trying to hurt anyone. We just want to know where we are."

I look up at the swirling grey clouds, and then back to the three in front of me.

"You're in Pintura," I say, and watch their faces scrunch in confusion. "Why did you fall from the sky?" I counter, pointing up above us.

"We fell through this painting," Ash says, not believing the words he's speaking

"You fell through a *painting*?" I ask. I let a beat of silence pass, thinking there may be more he's going to say. When he doesn't elaborate, I gawk. "What kind of joke is this?"

"It's not a joke," the girl, Jenny, says. "He," she growls, pointing at Wren, "knocked me over and I fell through a painting and into," she pauses, searching for a word. "What did you call this place?"

"Pintura," I repeat and she nods her head sharply.

"And I fell into Pintura." She says the name of this world with as much disgust as she can muster.

"Do you know how to get out of here?" Ash asks, closing the space between us. "We need to get back to Weston, California."

"Cali-*what*?" I ask, his words sounding like jumbled noises.

"California. It's in the United States. Surely you've heard of that," Ash says, growing impatient with me like I'm some sort of uneducated child.

"Afraid I haven't," I say, a defensive wall building around me.

"Seriously? Where on Earth is this place?" Ash looks at me bewildered, but finally a word he says sticks out to me.

"Earth?" I ask, my voice curling up, trying to suppress a laugh. "You're from *Earth*?"

"Yes? Of course we're from Earth," Jenny says, tossing her jet-black ponytail over her shoulder. "Are we not on Earth anymore?" she asks, and her voice shakes with the question.

I can't help it. Laughter escapes my mouth. *Earth?* These losers are really going to try and convince me they not only fell *through* a painting, but are from *Earth*?

When my laugh suppresses, I see their shocked and worried faces haven't changed. They peer at me seriously.

"Please, we need to find a way out of here," Ash says softer and I shake my head in disbelief.

I pause and really take them in for the first time. They don't look like they're from another world. They seem like normal kids to me. Maybe their clothes are a bit nicer. The quality is like nothing I've ever seen before. It's a smooth, soft fabric with clean edges, but the boy named Wren has a crazy picture of an odd-looking person printed on the fabric. Ash has a weird check mark on his shoes, a different cloth material that stops at his ankles.

None of this means they're from another world. It means they probably have money, which I don't. If I play along, maybe I'll get something in return.

"I don't know who you think you are, but you can drop the act." The three of them glance worriedly between each other. "I'll take you to someone who can help," I finally offer, backing away from them. "But I don't believe a word you are saying." I turn and head toward Artmith, knowing there's only one person in the entire city that may actually believe these hooligans. Let's play along and see where it gets me.

"So, who are you?" Ash asks, jogging to fall in step with me.

I give him a side glance before answering. "My name's Emma."

"Emma," he repeats.

"My friends call me Em," I add.

"Oh, Em then," Ash corrects himself.

"I don't believe I said we're friends," I joke, but he thinks I'm serious and his cheeks burn pink.

"Well, *Emma*," he says, over emphasizing my name, "I'm Ash and that's my sister Jenny, and our friend Wren."

"I know," I say. "I heard you three screaming all the way from the scrapyard."

Ash looks me up and down, taking in the dirty navy jumpsuit I'm wearing and my worn satchel. "Is that where you work?"

"Sometimes," I say, keeping my answer short. My fingers curl around the strap of my bag, tugging it closer to my chest.

"And when you're not working there?" Ash asks.

"Well, I only work when I want to or need to," I explain. Ash gives me a confused glance. "I guess that's not how it works on *Earth*," I say and throw up some air quotes around the fictional planet.

"Why don't you believe me?" he asks genuinely.

For a second, I feel bad for making fun of his story. "Everyone knows Earth is the fictional world in that card game," I say, the name of the childhood game escaping me.

"It's not a fictional world," Ash says defensively.

I raise my hand to cut him off. "Save it, pretty boy. No need to convince me."

The corners of his mouth twitch up at my comment.

"Where exactly are you taking us?" I hear Wren ask from behind me. Jenny and him seem to think I might bite if they get too close. *Good call.*

I notice their wide gazes have found Artmith, the jagged metal buildings towering above the sheet metal wall. If this really is all just an act, they're doing a good job at it. I take on the role of tour guide and play along.

"That's Artmith," I say, gesturing to the topsy-turvy city I call home.

"Interesting architecture," Ash says, considering the city. "Why the wall?" he asks.

"It keeps the vainders out." The iron gate currently stands ajar, letting us travel inside the city with no restriction. "Vainders are nocturnal, so we don't have to worry about them during the day," I add. We're taught about vainders at birth, but if they want to pretend they have no idea what I'm talking about for their little game, I guess that's fine.

I see Jenny give a worried glance to Wren, who looks like he wants to scream every time he sees his shadow.

"The University is this way." I wave them to my left.

Busy people run along the dirt roads. Jenny almost gets run over by a parade of bicycles. The three of them gaze through the clouded shop windows as we pass the bustling businesses.

"I think we time traveled," I hear Wren whisper to Jenny and I roll my eyes. First, they want to tell me they're from Earth, and now they're considering adding time travel to the mix.

"This is where you'll find your answers," I announce as we turn onto University Boulevard.

Unlike the dirt streets we just walked down, this one is paved with a dark red paste. Tall golden lampposts lead up to the main entrance of University Hall. If this were a world with kings and queens, this would be as close to a castle as you could get. University Hall has three grand stories with four towers at each corner. Slick, black metal siding acts like an armor for the building.

We make our way toward the school and past students gathering on the porches of the homes along the boulevard. Their frilly dress and ornate hats look like costumes. I've never been one to appreciate the latest fashion trends in Artmith. Probably because I spend every waking moment in this navy jumpsuit at the scrapyard.

One of the many perks of studying here is you get to stay in these elaborate mansions on University Boulevard. My shack in Shadow Village would look like a piece of junk next to these buildings.

Good thing I like junk.

"Do you go to school here?" Ash asks when we walk up the grand marble-slab staircase.

I huff a laugh and toss my head from side-to-side. "That's a complicated question," I say. "You ask a lot of questions, by the way," I add, pushing open the heavy steel doors.

"You have a geography professor that will help us?" Jenny asks, trying to find out where I'm leading them.

"A history professor, actually," I cluck back to her.

"Close enough, I guess," I hear her mumble. "Especially if we did time travel."

Wren gives a worried hum of agreement.

We walk across the main foyer of University Hall, our footsteps muffled by the deep maroon carpet. Large paintings of past Presidents of the University hang on the wall, guiding us deeper into the school. Classrooms line the hallway, their doors pulled shut for the break. When we reach the grand staircase at the end of the foyer, I lead the three of them to the side of the staircase and pull open a wooden door. "After you," I say.

Wren whispers to himself, "A classroom under the stairs?"

"Who's there?" an old lady's quivering voice yells from the back storage room.

"It's Emma, Professor Sim. I brought some friends with me," I call back to her, closing the door behind us.

There's a faint *thud* from the back room and Wren flinches. "What was that?" he whispers loudly.

"Oh, that's where she hides the dead bodies of students who don't pass her class," I tease.

Wren's face drains of color, his brown eyes so wide his eyebrows vanish into his golden curls.

I chuckle to myself and say, "Only joking, Wren."

He doesn't relax any.

Professor Sim waddles from the storage room and shuffles some papers on her desk into tidy stacks. "What can I do for you, Emma and her friends?" She looks up at us, peering through her small, circular glasses that are balancing on the tip of her nose.

"Well, you see," I say, leaning my hip against her desk to gesture at the three pranksters. "These three tell me they're from Earth and need help getting home."

There's a silence that fills the room and I wait for Professor Sim to laugh as I had. She squints her eyes, my words slowly processing through her wrinkled head.

"Earth?" she repeats, confused. "Like... Like from the..."

"Yes, like from the game," I finish for her.

"What game?" Wren asks, his voice very sharp. His anxiety hasn't gotten any better and, for a second, I think he may start crying.

Maybe I shouldn't have made that joke about the dead students. Fragile thing.

"You know, I just might have it!" Professor Sim says, chuckling to herself. She waddles back into the storage room and Wren's face pales again.

"Ash," Wren whispers, eyeing the door as if to communicate some kind of escape plan in case little old Professor Sim comes back to kill them.

"Wren, relax. She can't hurt you. She can barely walk," Ash whispers.

I debate about going to Professors Sim's defense, maybe play up the joke from before, but I decide not to. The joke isn't funny if he thinks it's true.

"Here it is!" she calls back to us and reappears at the doorway. She returns to her desk and takes a deep breath, tired from all the walking. I glance at Wren, still shaking like a wet dog. Pathetic.

Professor Sim holds up a black velvet bag, slowly unties the golden rope, and pulls it open. She places her thin hand in the bag and pulls out a thick deck of cards, wider than her grasp. I recognize their deep maroon color with gold writing. She fans the large cards out on the desk and Ash, Jenny, and Wren lean in to get a better look.

"This is Ending in Cadence."

Chapter 3

Ash

I'm still trying to wrap my brain around the fact that we aren't on Earth anymore. An easier explanation is that Emma is simply uneducated, or perhaps delirious. But then there's the fact that I just jumped through a painting, and the architecture here is different… but not *unworldly*.

Maybe I shouldn't even waste my time with this silly idea of a card game. It'll be faster to just find a map or maybe a train station. Someone else in this city could be more help to us.

I pick up one of the large cards. It's thick, like cardstock, with a matte finish. The backs of the cards have different shapes printed in a metallic gold. Little shiny triangles border the edges of the card with two golden circles linked together in the center. When you move it, the light reflects off the metallic designs and makes it look like they're shifting on the card.

I turn the playing card over and read what it says. At the top, printed in a clean, golden ink, is the title of the card. *The Starting Rock.* Below the title is a small description that sounds like a riddle.

BEFORE YOU BEGIN
COLLECT YOUR TOKEN

YOU MUST LOOK WITHIN
WHERE YOUR PASSION IS OPEN

GOLD CAN BEGIN THE JOURNEY
BROWN WILL FILL THOSE THAT ARE EMPTY

I flip the card over in my hands a few times before laying it back on the desk. "So, what does this have to do with us getting home?" I ask, glancing between Professor Sim and Emma.

The girl who found us seems on edge, like she has more important things to do, but her curiosity is keeping her here. I don't particularly like the glances she gives Jenny or how she's playing with Wren's obvious anxiety.

"The point of the game is to win challenges," Emma explains, and Professor Sim nods along while she stacks the cards together. "The person who wins the most points unlocks the key to Earth."

"So, we play this game and, once we win, we can go home?" Jenny asks.

"No, it's not real," Emma says sharply. "There is no Earth. It's pretend."

"But there is an Earth and we came from it," I say desperately.

Emma rolls her eyes at my proclamation and tucks a loose blonde curl behind her ear. She's shorter than me, and I almost miss the dismissal on her faint-freckled face.

"Teach me how to play." The air in the room seems to still.

Emma looks at me teasingly. "You think if you play this game, it'll take you back to Earth?" She lets out a dry laugh and scoops up the playing cards. "Professor, do you mind if I borrow these?"

Professor Sim laughs a little to herself and then says, "Oh, no. You kids can have them." She hands Emma the black velvet bag the cards came from and waves us toward the door. "Emma," Professor Sim calls once we've crossed the room.

Emma turns, her long blonde hair swishing around her shoulders.

"Will I see you on campus next term?" Professor Sim asks.

"I don't think so," Emma says, her eyes losing their normal shine, and she leads us from the classroom and toward the exit of the school.

We follow her out of the grand entrance and onto the front quad of the school grounds. She has us sit in the shade of a large tree and begins to shuffle the cards. Emma studies me for a second before shaking her head as if she's wondering why she's still here.

"Usually only two people play. I can deal us all in, but it'll be a relatively short game," Emma says.

"That's okay, we can watch," Wren offers and Jenny nods, agreeing.

"Okay. Well, this is how the game works," Emma explains, flipping over one of the cards. "I'll deal the cards between Ash and myself. When round one begins, we turn over our top card. There's some riddle about the challenge title at the top, but that's not important. The number at the bottom is what actually matters. That determines how difficult your challenge is."

Emma pauses, lifting up the black velvet pouch the cards were in. She reaches inside and pulls out two small, clear bags. One with green marbles and the other with red.

"The green marbles go in the main bag," Emma says, pouring the five green marbles into the black velvet bag. "You add the red marbles based on the number on your card. So, for example, this card is number two. So, I'd add two red marbles to the bag." Emma drops in the two dark red marbles and gives the bag a little shake. "If I pull out a green marble, I pass the challenge and keep the card. If I pull out a red marble, I fail that challenge and the card goes to the discard pile."

"It's just a game of luck," Wren says, wrinkling his nose.

"Aren't all games?" Emma says, shrugging her shoulders. "When the game is over, you add up all the numbers at the bottom of the challenges you won. The person with the most points wins this." Emma pulls up on a pocket sewn to the outside of the velvet bag. She reaches in and takes out another playing card, except this one is a shimmering gold. I lift my hand to see it, but Emma snatches it back.

"You have to win first," she teases.

I press my lips together to keep from snapping at her. This isn't a game to me. I *need* to get home, and that sounds like my key. For a second, I let myself think of *home*. How long have I been gone now? Half an hour? Mom and dad will be heading to grandma's with the moving truck, and we need to ensure we're home before they get there.

"Well, then let's play. We're kind of in a hurry," I say, still considering my other options if this proves to be a waste of time.

Emma scoops up the playing cards, shuffles them a few more times, and deals them faced down between us.

She blinks at me with her wide blue eyes, a smart remark on the tip of her tongue, but she doesn't say it. Instead, she says, "Round one. Flip."

We both flip our cards and read our challenges.

Mine is *The Starting Rock*, the card I had picked up off Professor

Sim's desk. A small number one is printed on the bottom. Emma hands me the bag of green marbles and I add a single red marble. I shake the bag and reach my hand inside. When I pull a marble out, I reveal it's a shiny green.

"So, you keep the card," Emma says, taking the bag back. She fishes out the red marble to reset the odds. "But that'll only give you one point in the end," she adds with a sly smirk.

We continue playing the game and drawing out our marbles. Some challenges we win and others we lose. As far as I can tell, there's no real pattern.

"All right, last round. What's your score right now?" Emma asks.

"I have nine," I say and glance at Emma's stack.

"Seven," she says, biting her bottom lip. "Okay, flip."

In unison, we turn over our cards. A smile splits on my face. *Two.* I lean over and see Emma's card is an eight. Tough chances of getting a green marble with eight red ones in the bag, but if she does, then she'll add eight points to her total score.

"You can go first," Emma says, handing me the velvet bag.

With the odds in my favor, I pull out a green marble. "Eleven," I say, shaking the card in the air and adding it to my pile. "Good luck," I add and hand her the velvet bag.

Emma places all eight red marbles into the pouch until it sags beneath the weight. She gives the bag a quick shake. As I suspect, Emma pulls out a dark red marble.

"Figures. No one ever wins on this card," she mumbles and tosses it into the small discard pile.

"So, I win?" I ask, fanning my cards out in front of me.

"You win," Emma says and hands me the golden card. "Here's your key to Earth."

I take the card gently in my hands. It's an invert of the regular cards. The designs are a deep maroon. Triangles line the edges of the cards with two circles linked together in its center. I flip the card over. At the top, in maroon font, it says *Key to Earth*. Pictured on the card is a jagged piece of wood. It looks like a chunk of tree bark.

"This is supposed to take me home?" I ask, flipping the card in my hand.

"If Earth were real," Emma mumbles, packing away the other playing cards. "That's what I was trying to tell you, Ash," Emma says, and now her voice is more serious. "It's just a game." Her blue eyes study my puzzled face.

"Let me see it," Wren says, taking the card. "How was the painting set up at your grandma's?"

"It was flat on the ground," I say.

"But you dropped it, right?" Wren jumps up like he's solved a mystery. He stretches out his arms and lets the card flutter to the ground. He sinks to his knees in the manicured lawn and hovers over the card. Slowly, he raises his finger and lowers it.

I take in a breath, hoping and praying his finger passes through the top of the card. *Please let this work so we can go back home and leave this weird experience behind us.* Maybe, somehow, even forget this ever happened.

Unfortunately, his finger hits the solid card and I drop my head in disappointment.

"There has to be something this card can do," Jenny says, snatching it off the ground.

Emma lets out an exhausted sigh.

"Oh, maybe we need to be in the field where we landed," Wren says, jumping back up.

I nod. It's a stretch, but maybe it could work. At this point, I'd do anything. "Let's try it," I say and stand up, brushing the grass off my shorts.

"That's going to be kind of hard," Emma says, stretching to get to her feet.

"Why's that?" Jenny asks, narrowing her eyes into an almost glare.

"The gate closes at 5:00 p.m.," Emma says.

She tilts her wrist, showing us her watch reads 4:55 p.m.. *Is it really that late in the afternoon?* Mom and Dad will be at Grandma's within the hour! I thought we had more time.

"We can get there before the gate closes," Wren argues.

"And what happens when you go out in the field and your card trick doesn't work? The vainders will have you for dinner," Emma responds sharply.

"They won't re-open the gates?" Jenny asks, but Emma is already shaking her head.

"Never have before. And I really don't think they will for three strangers claiming to be from Earth."

A stiff, silent air passes and Emma's watch clicks to 4:56 p.m..

But what if we go out there and it does work? We could be home in a couple of minutes.

4:57 p.m..

But if it doesn't work, we're surely dead if the vainders are real and if all that Emma has told us is true. Though, if we wait until tomorrow and it doesn't work, we might as well be dead. If I ever make it back, my parents will kill me for disappearing for so long.

4:58 p.m..

"Ash, what should we do?" Jenny asks, her light brown eyes begging for me to fix this like I always fix everything for her.

4:59 p.m..

"It's too late now," I mumble.

"You can try it tomorrow," Emma offers. "Here, you can keep the cards, too."

She tosses the velvet bag to me and I catch it. I glance back at her and see her blonde curls walking away. "Wait!" I call after her. She turns and questions me with her blue eyes. "Where are you going?"

"Home?" she says, like it's a question.

"Where are we supposed to go?" Wren asks, understanding we're about to be left alone out here.

Emma is quiet for a moment before striding back to us, and her face sets in a glare. "Stop playing games with me!" she snaps and her voice has suddenly turned very defensive. "I don't know who put you up to it, but I'm done playing along. I'm tired of this joke—"

"Emma," I cut her off. "I'm not lying to you. Clearly you know what Earth is. *You're* the one playing games with *us*." I see her jaw tighten, steel eyes narrowing.

"I never should have wasted my time with you lunatics. If you don't believe you're in Pintura, fine! Not my problem. Go find someone else to annoy!"

My mind races, trying to think of some way I can prove it to her. Maybe that's what she wants me to do and then she'll stop this crazy charade. I reach into my pocket and pull out my car keys. "These are the keys to my car, back on Earth."

When Emma's eyes land on the set of keys, they widen, eyebrows raising in curved arcs.

"I'm guessing you don't have cars *here*," I say tentatively, acknowledging that I haven't seen anything like that since we arrived.

"The Patrol do," Emma says, and her voice grows panicked. "Did you steal those from a Patrol officer?"

"No, they're mine," I say and lift the bronze drum key chain.

Emma is already backing away from us. Showing her my keys was the wrong decision. "I don't want anything to do with you or the Patrol or whatever game this is!"

"Emma!" I call after her, but she's already spun on her heels and is striding across the green grass of the university lawn, her worn satchel bouncing at her hip. Her blonde curls disappear into the glow of the setting sun, leaving us all alone. Lost in a place we know nothing about.

CHAPTER 4

Emma

I blow out a frustrated breath, feeling my cheeks burn with embarrassment. They just didn't know when to stop, did they? I've been the center of enough jokes to know when to walk away.

As I stride down University Boulevard, the girls lounging on their porch swings watch me closely. Hair curled and lips stained red. I notice none of them were in my elective study lectures. Because they're here on their parent's money. They don't care to even try. Those are the girls who are never the center of the joke. Me, a scrawny seventeen-year-old scrapyard kid, is always the one everyone targets.

I pry my eyes away from their pastel homes and narrow my focus to the streets of Artmith coming up ahead. I flip open my satchel and sift through the bag's contents. I'm a little behind schedule now, but I still have time to try and sell a few things.

My fingers run over the edge of my first bargaining chip and I set my feet in the direction of the Weights Ring. Narrow alleys pass in a blur as I slide through the metal city. I know these back streets too well to waste my time on the main roads where the foot traffic is far too heavy this time of day.

The further I get from the university, the better I feel. Eventually, the memory of the three from "Earth" fades away. I keep pushing it deeper and deeper into my head, hoping I can forget the meeting ever happened. The sight of Ash's car keys still hangs in my eyes. I swallow a growing nauseous wave. If he really is tied to the Patrol in any way, then I made the right decision walking away from them. If the Patrol found out what I was doing... What I was selling... I could kiss my life away.

I want to turn three sales today, but I know that'll be hard to achieve, now. The rich are less likely to meet at night. They'll think I'm trying to trap them and steal their precious yatz. Since we just received this month's citizen allowance a couple of days ago, they'll think that's even more likely the case. And rightfully so. I've had my fair share of run-ins with the street rats that make their earnings by emptying the pockets of the few idiots who walk the streets alone and unprotected.

I drive my feet faster against the dirt alley, trying to out run the setting sun.

Artmith is unusually noisy today. With summer break just beginning, the conversations on the main streets echo louder than normal through my back alleys. I catch glimpses of the happy crowd mingling in the town square, the bubbling fountain flowing over a sharp flower sculpted from sheet metal, and a cast of theater performers in glittering jumpsuits.

My feet slow when I see a group of girls from my class beaming outside a storefront window. These are the girls that are my age, the ones I went to high school with—not the older girls I had seen on University Boulevard. These are the girls I'm supposed to be friends with. If only I knew what a friend was.

One of them gasps and points to something in the corner of the window. The afternoon sun gleams brightly on the set of silver paintbrushes on display.

I hear one of the girls say, "Those will be perfect for your art elective next semester!"

Another adds, "You should get them! It's not too early to already be preparing for next year."

My throat burns as my stomach does a somersault. I pull my eyes away from the girls and continue to trudge down my alleyway. I'll never know the luxury of attending the university full-time or shopping for supplies for my studies. I'm lucky I was able to take an elective my senior year that the high school waived for me.

Tall, metal buildings rise around me as I make my way out of the Shopping District of Artmith and into the Business District. Skyscrapers full of offices for everything you could think of surround me, but I don't give them a second glance. I'll never know what the insides of these buildings look like. Without a degree from the university, I'm destined for retail, agriculture, or scrapyard work.

Or finding illegal ways to fill my pockets. Like I'm doing now.

I roll my shoulders back and shake my head hard. I *like* scrapyard work. This isn't something that's worth getting upset about. Especially when I've spent years accepting what my future will be. And on top of that, I like the illegal work I do as well—as odd as that probably sounds. Creating things and selling them on the black market gives the inventor in me an outlet.

Finally, I reach the other side of Artmith, just north of where my home is in Shadow Village. A short ring rises out of the dirt ground, made of cinderblocks that are spaced out at the end of the alley. Twenty guys spread across the dirt floor. Their white shirts are damp with sweat from the summer heat. Deep green pants hang like loose fitting waves. They take turns lifting the heavy steel bars and disks, deep grunts chorusing together.

I lean against the side of one of the buildings that casts a dark shadow over the alleyway and wait for Roz to notice me. I've learned my lesson the first time I ventured here to try and make a quick sale to these muscle heads. Don't interfere with the lifting. Roz runs the ring and he'll buy from me for his men.

I find the ring's owner standing atop one of the cement blocks. The sleeves of his white shirt are ripped away and a long scar glows on his right shoulder. Not a common injury for weightlifting, but I know better than to ask questions.

After a moment, his green gaze finds me in the shadows. He jumps down from his block of concrete and strides over to me.

"I almost thought you weren't coming today," he says, sliding into the shadows with me.

"I was a bit preoccupied," I feed him my excuse quickly, my eyes looking anywhere but his clenched face. My heart thumps just a bit faster, on edge in his presence. I hate making sales to him. He could hurl me through the air with one hand. If I ever make an enemy out of him, I won't last long.

"All right, get on with it, girl. What do you have for me?"

At his cue, I reach into my bag and grip the cool, metal bottle. When I pull it out, Roz's eyes narrow, not impressed by what appears to be a normal water bottle. Something I'm sure he has plenty of. Until his eyes land on the machined cap. I jump into my sales pitch that I practiced this morning in my clouded mirror.

"I have a couple of things today," I start, handing him the aluminum bottle. "First, the drinking bottle. I redesigned the twist on cap to have a straw."

Roz's fat fingers run along the thin neck of the bottle where the metal cap twists on and then they glide up the cap and to the copper tube I engineered on as a drinking straw. It's not one of my best pieces, since I'm still fairly new to welding.

Roz grunts when his eyes land on the top of the straw. "A good idea, but it spills now." The meathead turns the bottle over in his hands as if to show me the straw's opening. Already prepared for his rejection, I extend my other hand, a rubber cap balanced on my palm.

"For extra, I'll include the seal."

He glares at me, not appreciating my sales tactics. His giant fingers pinch the rubber cap and he slides it onto the end of the copper straw. When it makes a perfect seal, he grunts in approval.

"All right, girl, what else do you have?"

I pull out my final piece for him today, a pocket made out of an old sock, tethered to a metal clip. "May I?" I ask, extending my hand for the bottle.

He hands it back to me and I slide it into my makeshift pocket, clipping the metal ring around the loop on my jumpsuit.

"A carrier for your bottle," I explain, raising my hands to show off the new fashion piece. "And, it'll keep your drink cold for longer periods of time."

Roz's eyebrows raise, and he nods excitedly. "Very nice," his bulging throat croaks out.

I try not to laugh or roll my eyes. This is hardly nice, but I know what to sell to these men. I unclasp the bottle and hand the contraption to Roz who clips the carrier to his green pants.

"How much for the whole thing?" he asks as he peers down at me. For good measure, I see the muscles in his arms flex, as if to remind me he could snap my neck as easy as he can breathe.

"For everything, twenty yatz," I say and cross my arms, trying to convince him I'm not the least bit afraid of him. This is my fourth sale to the men of the Weights Ring. I know what prices to ask for now, and I can tell he wishes I was still offering him the measly ten yatz price tag.

"You're getting more expensive," he grumbles, but he fishes his leather wallet from his back pocket. "I'll pay for this one now. Come back next week and I'll order more for the rest of the guys." Roz practically throws the two red paper bills at my feet before leaving the shadows of the alley and returning to his post atop the concrete cinderblocks.

I scoop up the money and stuff it inside my bag. Before anyone notices the transaction, I fall deeper into the alleyway and move toward my next customer.

CHAPTER 5

Ash

This isn't happening. This isn't real. I'm simply asleep right now. I'll wake up soon and this will go away. This isn't—"

"WREN!" Jenny screams, and Wren's rambling silences.

My eyes are still trained on the horizon where Emma had faded from sight. I think part of me is hoping if I just stare long enough, the scene around me will change. And after a while, it does. The university and red paved boulevard go fuzzy, and now I could be watching any vibrant sunset back in California. But when Jenny yells at Wren, I blink fast and our unbelievable situation comes flooding back into view.

There's a tight grip on my arm and I turn to see Jenny clutching onto me.

"Ash. What is going on? You don't believe her, do you?"

My mouth falls open, but my words are delayed. "Jenny, we fell *through* a painting. I don't know what to believe."

I see tears build at the edges of her eyes and her bottom lip curls in.

"But I'm going to figure it out," I add, and pull her head against my shoulder. "I'll fix this, Jenny." I know that's my job as her brother.

"I'll help too!" Wren pipes up.

Jenny turns toward him so fast I almost fall over from her sudden absence. "I think you've done enough!" she snaps and Wren's face pales in the presence of Jenny's anger. "You *had* to push me into that painting," Jenny grumbles, rubbing the loose tears out of her eyes.

"Jenny, he didn't mean to." I go to Wren's defense, but all I get is a glare from my sister.

"I'm sorry," Wren says weakly. His hands begin to shake and he shoves them into the pockets of his jeans to hide the tremor. I know Wren would *never* have done this on purpose. Jenny knows that too because, instead of yelling at him again, she just rolls her eyes.

"If we're going to get home, we need to stop standing around," I decide, my first plan forming. I tie the black velvet bag of cards around my wrist. It's the only lead we have right now. I'm not sure what use they will be, but better to have them just in case.

"What's your idea?" Jenny asks.

"Well, someone here will know where we actually are, or confirm Emma's story. So, I suggest we start looking for help. Ask questions and maybe someone will have a map."

Jenny and Wren nod, but I know none of us are all that eager to venture into the crowds of a city we know nothing about.

"No matter what, we stick together," I add as we start to walk across the university grounds and back toward the busy streets Emma had led us down on the way here.

As we go, I try to keep reminding myself that this isn't some other universe. That girl was obviously crazy. I mean, we did find her spying on us in that field.

Once we turn off of University Boulevard, and onto the dirt roads that run through the city, we're immersed in the hectic, loud crowds.

The colorful outfits overwhelm my eyes. Frilly dresses and topsy-turvy hats for the women, eccentric suits for the guys. Heeled flats, black dress shoes, and a sense of community that feels almost nostalgic.

I suddenly feel very out of place in my sneakers and athletic shorts.

"Wren, what did you mean when you said it looked like we had time traveled?" I ask, suddenly thinking the idea of time traveling would be a better explanation than crossing worlds. It *does* kind of look like my grandma's closet exploded onto the street. Perhaps even older than that. Like her parent's photographs that used to hang on the walls in her living room came to life.

"It's like the 1940s collided with Space Zone," he says, mentioning the title of the dystopian comic books we used to read as kids.

I nod, seeing the resemblance. It's a dystopian 1940s. So, not time travel but... maybe still Earth?

The buildings are constructed with pieces of jagged sheet metal, their boxy signs hanging heavy above the doors. I can't help but piece together all the things I've seen—the field, the forest, the city—and realize how similar it is to what was painted on the canvas we fell through. *Could that have been an actual painting of this place? How is that even possible, and why did my grandma have it?*

"Let's start there," Jenny says, pointing across the street to a sign that reads *BILLY'S SALON* with a red and white florescent tube twirling at the edge of the sign. A group of women walk out of the frosted glass door, hair curled so tight it barely hits their shoulders.

I take the initiative to lead us through the bustling crowd and push my way inside the store.

"How can I help you, young man?" a very cheery voice calls as soon as I'm inside. A round-bellied man leans against the glass counter. Metal scissors and a faded can of what I'll guess is hairspray stored inside. "Looking to shorten those waves?" he asks when I don't immediately answer him.

I feel like my body is on sensory overload. There are too many things to take in; the black and white tiled floor, tiny leather swivel chairs, three stations for cutting hair, each with a woman in a large, lacey dress, their hair in florescent curlers, and the unmistakable scent of hair gel.

I shake my head, hoping to loosen the smell of hair products from my nose. "Um, no," I finally force out and step up to the counter.

Jenny and Wren hang a step back from me and I see them squirming, as if feeling as out of place as I'm sure we look. The man loops his thumbs through the straps of his black apron and he squints his eyes at me, thick eyebrows bunching together.

"We're actually lost," I say, trying to find the easiest way to explain this. "Could you tell me where we are, or maybe show me the map on your phone?"

The man's eyes lift over my shoulder to a plastic box phone that hangs on the wall. *Okay, no cellphones here.*

"You're in Billy's Salon, talking to Billy himself," the man grunts out like I should have known that.

"I meant this city. What is it?"

"What are you talking about, kid? It's the only city!"

Suddenly, the man begins to chuckle, his belly bouncing up and down and his face turns a bright cherry red. "What do you mean, *what city*? You're funny kid!"

The three women on the tiny leather swivel chairs laugh and the whole room begins to spin around me. Fear and frustration heat my cheeks.

Once his laughing subsides, Billy wipes loose tears from the corners of his eyes. I'm at a loss for words. I don't want to directly ask if we're on Earth. Before I decide what to say, the man points toward the door.

"Either pay for a haircut or get out, kids. I can't waste my time if you're not paying customers."

Then, he shuffles away, swiping up the little metal scissors as he goes, and approaches the last station. I look back at my sister and Wren, and the two of them nod toward the door. Clearly no luck here. Maybe the next place will be more helpful.

But it's not.

We continue to hop in and out of shops all down the main road. The General Store, Darry's Diner, and the Drug Store. Each one leaves a crowd of people laughing at us, looking to each other like we are aliens, or worse, trying to get us to buy something or they'd call the Patrol.

I remember Emma mentioning the Patrol when I showed her my car keys. Whenever someone threatens to contact them, I take it as my cue to move on. Whoever they are must be similar to the police back on Earth.

I cringe at that thought. I'm starting to think this place may actually be in a different world, and I can feel my denial weakening.

CHAPTER 6

Emma

I n the absence of the water bottle I sold to Roz, my satchel hangs flatter against my hip. Still, it's weighed down by the next two sales I want to make today. I peek inside the tan bag as if to remind myself where I still need to go this afternoon.

First, Billy's Salon. It's back on the northern end of the city. I actually passed it on my way to the Weights Ring, but I wanted to get my meeting with Roz out of the way first. I hate having those sales hanging over my head. Billy will be a quick exchange. He's expecting me and he already knows what I'm bringing him. He's a consistent customer, and I can always rely on him to throw ten yatz my way.

My eyes scan the faces that bustle through the main streets of Artmith, looking to see if I can swing a quick bonus sale this afternoon, but I'm not liking my chances. I carry common items with me, just in case I can corner a lady who wants a new bracelet or a husband looking for a gift for his wife. The streets are packed today, the perfect opportunity to make a sale and be hidden from the onlooking eyes in the chaos of the crowds. Unfortunately, no one appears to be approachable today. I shrug it off and assume it's because everyone just received their monthly citizen allowance. They can afford the higher prices the jewelry stores will ask for. I do my best sales at the end of the month when everyone is trying to find the best bargain.

The tall industrial buildings thin out as I leave the Business District of Artmith and reenter the Shopping District.

Shorter square buildings with reflective sheet metal siding line the streets. Neon signs and artfully twisted iron label the stores, inviting the eager buyers to their doors. Most people are traveling on foot, but a few speed past the crowds on bicycles.

The clicking of metal spokes announces one approaching behind me and I step out of the way just in time as the boy speeds by. Yelps from other women and their husbands ring out as he paves a way through the crowd.

After my meeting with Billy, I'll make a quick stop at the Penny Arcade to deliver Mr. Milo's custom project. He's been waiting a while for me to get this done, but I hope that doesn't affect the price he'll pay for it. I always go to him last and as late in the day as possible. If I get there right before they close, I have a better chance at avoiding my ex-boyfriend, Jake, who works the front counter at the arcade.

Heat races up my neck at the thought of him. It ended a month ago and, bless the stars above, I haven't had to talk to him since. A couple of stolen glances, but that's it. I'm in and out of the arcade before our eyes ever meet or heated words are spoken. It wasn't a clean breakup, and it certainly wasn't a mutual decision.

When the red and white post outside of Billy's Salon comes into view, all thoughts of Jake spin away.

I cross the busy dirt road, sliding in between billowing dresses and giving my apologies to the ladies I cut off. My quick feet bounce through the crowd and I bound up the stairs into the salon.

"Emma! You made it!" Billy's booming voice exclaims as the door swings closed behind me. My heart pounds a bit in my chest after the brisk walk here, and I try to steady it.

Billy stands over a woman sitting in the first station, quickly untwisting the last of the rollers in her hair. I can tell I'm late today because she's the only customer still here. Usually, when I come by the salon, every station is full with paying customers.

"Sorry I'm late today." I try to sweep it out of the way before he can say anything about it.

"Oh, don't worry. The roads are packed today. The first real day of summer has everyone out and about." Billy unwinds the final curler and the woman runs her fingers through her hair, admiring his work.

I give a weak smile and nod. I could tell him that my tardiness has nothing to do with the crowds because I stick to the alley, but if he wants to give me an excuse, I'll take it.

"The first days of summer always bring out the weirdest people," the woman pipes in as she stands. Her mint green dress swishes around her feet. Billy laughs at her remark and some kind of acknowledgement to a joke only they understand passes through the air. Billy looks at me and sees that I must not know what she could have meant.

"We had the weirdest group of kids come in today," he explains as he walks the lady to the door. She gives him a red wad of bills before slipping outside.

"They asked me what city they were in." Billy lets out a billowing laugh that makes his round stomach shake.

My skin prickles at the story. Immediately, the three pranksters I had encountered in the Golden Field outside the wall come back to me. "Who were they?" I ask, trying to play an innocently curious girl.

"These two boys and a young lady. I didn't recognize them and I don't know if it was some kind of joke or game they were playing. What a ridiculous question."

I let out a short *hum*, hiding the fact that I had a similar encounter with the same three people. *Why would they bother Billy with their game?* It's one thing to play a prank on a naïve scrapyard girl, but an adult? Especially one as well respected and loved in the Artmith community as Billy seems strange.

"You didn't know the kids? You know everyone in Artmith," I slip the words out smoothly.

I must agree, I didn't recognize them either. They would have been in my class at school, but I don't particularly know my classmates. None of them wanted to be my friend or get to know me so I stopped paying any attention to them a long time ago.

Billy's eyes squint, his chubby face folding around them. After a minute of deep thought, the barber shakes his head and relaxes his face. "Nope, I've never seen them before. Must have their parents cutting their hair, because I'm the only barber in Artmith." Billy says his last words with a sense of pride that reminds me why I'm here. To illegally sell him my engineered products, not gossip about three kids who have nothing better to do than play mind games with those around them.

I shrug the story away and Billy and I walk toward the glass counter so I can show him what I brought.

"I hope it's more curlers," he says just as I dump a handful of the metal rings on the glass top. He sighs with relief and pulls them closer to him. "Thank goodness. The last batch you gave me has been getting weaker. Not as strong a curl as the ladies like."

"I can bring them more often if you need," I say, knowing our current agreement is once a month. With summer arriving to the city, he's going to be busier. The metal curlers are old springs I find in the junkyard, but I was able to manipulate them to hold pieces of hair in tight curls.

Billy nods to himself, considering the idea. "Let's do every two weeks for a while."

"I can do that," I quickly agree, always happy to do more business with him. "Ten yatz for the curlers," I add, giving him the price we had agreed on months ago.

Billy unfolds the wad of bills the woman had slipped him and hands me one red bill. I take the money and tuck it into my bag. "That's all I have for today. Did you need anything specific for next time?" I ask after sealing my satchel.

Billy shakes his head and leads me to the door at the front of the store. "That should be it. Thanks, Emma. Stay safe out there." Billy pauses as he pulls open the door to his salon and the loud conversations from the overflowing streets filter toward us. "Like I said, some weird people come out during the first days of summer."

I give him a tight smile and dip my head. "I'll keep that in mind." I bounce down the stairs and back into the rolling waves of people flowing through the Artmith streets. My satchel swings against my hip, one last sale nestled inside. Next stop, the Penny Arcade.

CHAPTER 7

Ash

A chorus of bright cheers breaks my train of thought and I look up from the dirt clouds I'm creating with my dragging feet to see a group of kids run into a building on the corner of the intersection.

As we near the building, the sound of more cheers fills the casual chatter of the streets I've grown used to. *Penny Arcade* is written in curly metal letters above the double doors that are pulled open to the summer day outside. We've tried our luck with the adults. Maybe we were just talking to the wrong people. With one glance at Jenny and Wren, we silently agree to go inside.

The Penny Arcade is dark, and it takes my eyes a minute to adjust to the dim lights overhead. A midnight blue carpet runs under my shoes, and it feels like walking on sand to my numb feet. I didn't realize how long we'd been at this. We're probably a couple of miles deep into this strange city.

The sound of gears clinking together in different pitches ricochets around the room. I see the metal box frames of the games lining the walls of the arcade. They don't have the electronic screens that I'm used to. No sound effects or blinking lights. Just a bunch of metal gears and marbles that twist together as someone manually operates the game.

I can't help but continue to think Wren may be on to something with his time travel idea, but now that we've been here for a while, I know it's more than that.

"Welcome to the Artmith Penny Arcade!" a tall man in a stiff black suit says. He walks past us and into a room at the back of the arcade. *Manager* is carved in a metal tag on the door.

Balanced on a stool behind the front counter is a boy who looks like he'd rather be anywhere else today. His green eyes drift to the ceiling, blonde hair tucked behind his ears. I walk up to the counter and he looks at me like he already knows I'm going to ask him a ridiculous question.

But the words I've spoken all day about being lost and wanting a map are erased in my mind. Instead, the man's words take their place and I think I may be sick.

"Did he say *Artmith*?" I ask the boy behind the counter.

He squints at me and stands up, rising a whole head above me, and I realize he's probably two years older than me.

"Yeah, so?" he barks back.

Artmith.

I look at Jenny and Wren and see they recognize the name, too. That's what Emma said this city was called. If she was telling us the truth about that, then what else was she telling the truth about?

"You sick, kid?" The boy leans back from me and I shake my

head, though I feel the clammy sweat gather on my neck.

We really *aren't* on Earth anymore. We're in a world called Pintura, standing in a city called Artmith, with no way home.

I know my next words will earn me a crazy look, but I force myself to speak them anyway.

"You wouldn't happen to know a way to Earth, would you?"

"Shut up, kid, I don't have time for this," he huffs, falling back on his stool.

I bite my tongue and hold back the words of desperation that want to fly from my mouth. I'm not sure blurting out that I'm from Earth is the best thing to do. I saw where that got me with Emma.

The boy behind the counter unfolds his crossed arms to point at the velvet bag that is still tied around my wrist. "Earth only exists in the imaginations of the kids who still play that dumb game. If you haven't noticed, Penny Arcade games are the future." Jake—I realize based on his nametag—gestures around us as if to remind me where I'm standing.

I step up and lean against the counter, suddenly the feeling of desperation blinding me. "Do you have a map of Artmith? I think I may be lost."

"*I'd say,*" Jake mumbles and leans forward to grab something from under the counter.

I exhale, thinking I may finally be making progress here, but instead of a map, he slaps three gold tokens on the counter.

"The only thing you're getting from me is your complimentary game tokens. First ones are on us. Unless you're not here to play."

My heart sinks. "I—I'm not," I say and trudge over to Jenny and Wren.

My sister's lips are pressed so thin her mouth has vanished. Wren, while looking just as nervous, keeps glancing to the games around us and the pure amazement at seeing something like this is controlling his attention.

"That guy's not going to be any help," I sigh to them. "No one here is." And I can't help but think I may have driven away the one person who was willing to help us.

"Ash, are we really in a different world?" Jenny whispers, her eyes glancing at Jake over my shoulder.

"I think Emma was telling the truth," I say. "Think about it, Jenny. We fell *through* a painting. We are in a different world, but we're going to find our way home." I add my last words before the fear I see rising in her cries out.

The dread of moving on to the next store to continue our search of a way home weighs heavily in Jenny's eyes and I feel it ache in my muscles. "Let's take a break for a minute. I don't know if I can get laughed at again," I decide, and we find a leather booth in a quiet corner of the arcade.

Jenny rests her head on the back of the seat and closes her eyes, the exhaustion from today catching up to her. I take out the Ending In Cadence playing cards and spread them out on the glossy tabletop. This is the only thing tying us back to Earth right now. Maybe I can find something here that I didn't see before.

Wren sits next to me, fidgeting with the loose threads on the knees of his worn jeans until, finally, I say, "Wren, you can go play the games if you want."

His serious gaze that had been watching a group of teenagers land a top score on one of the Penny Arcade games snaps to me. "Oh, I just didn't think this was the right time…" he trails off.

"It's okay, Wren. We're not going anywhere soon." I sink back into the leather booth and slide the cards around under the yellow lights.

Wren doesn't need me to tell him again. He jumps to his feet and practically runs to Jake, who gives him the three tokens he had set on the counter earlier.

Wren tentatively hovers behind the group of teenage boys, trying to see how they're playing the game. The guy in the center must have just beat his old score, because he thrusts his arm in the air, his fist the size of Wren's face. He stands straight up, almost taller than the machine, and looks over his shoulder at Wren like a fly that's annoying him. The giant glances at the two other teenage boys that flank his left and right, shorter, stockier versions of himself, and he gives a non-verbal cue to move. The three trudge to a booth across the arcade, still watching Wren closely.

Gosh Wren, don't go and embarrass yourself now.

I lean forward on the table and look down at the card game, not wanting to watch Wren waste his time.

The Starting Rock card keeps grabbing my attention. It's the first of the cards that I had picked up in Professor Sim's classroom. I slide it side-by-side with the gold *Key to Earth* card, but I don't see any connection or clue between the two.

I wish Emma were still here. Maybe we played the game wrong or maybe there's something in the history of the game that could help us.

Suddenly, I very much want the girl with the blonde hair and navy overalls to walk through these doors. I wish I would have believed her from the beginning. But that doesn't change the fact that she doesn't believe me. And do I blame her? It sounds crazy.

I fell through a painting. Please help me get home to a world you believe to only exist in a children's card game.

God, we're never getting home.

I squeeze my eyes closed, panic and frustration flushing my cheeks and beginning to tighten my throat. Through the sound of my blood pumping in my ears, I hear Wren's childish voice travel through the arcade. "I did it!"

I look over at him and see he's pointing to a scorecard that ticks up on a roll of numbers. Maybe I shouldn't have underestimated him so quickly. First try and he's already landed the high score.

Suddenly, the toothy grin on Wren's face falls and I see the three teenagers from earlier walk up to him. The biggest of the group shoves Wren back into the machine and there's a loud *bang* that echoes through the Penny Arcade.

"Who the hell do you think you are?" the large boy growls.

Wren starts shaking and cowers under the larger guy's massive shadow.

"Who walks into *my* arcade and beats *my* high score on the first try?"

"My... My name is Wren..."

"Leave him alone!" I yell, running across the arcade and coming to Wren's rescue.

The boy turns slowly. He looks me up and down once and then his fist collides with my nose. I scream in shock. There's a series of cracks across my face. My hands fly up and warm blood trickles down my upper lip.

"What the hell!" I look up at the beast of a boy. He flexes out the fingers of the fist that just crushed my nose.

"Ash!" Jenny squeals.

"What's going on back there?" Jake asks from the front counter.

But I don't hear either of them, their voices falling away as the teenage boy curls his hand into Wren's shirt and then hurls him to the ground.

"The only way he beat my score is if he cheated! Do you know what happens to cheaters?"

"I... I didn't cheat," Wren stammers.

I fall back a step as the giant leans toward me.

"You still want to stand up for a cheater?"

"He didn't cheat. Maybe you just suck!" The words come immediately as more blood runs into my mouth. I wipe it away with a hand I hope isn't shaking.

What happens next is too fast to comprehend.

The metallic smell of soda hits me in the face. One of the shorter boys drenches me and the other pours his on Wren. My eyes burn with the sugary syrup and I squeeze them shut, aggressively wiping it away and then the giant's fist collides with the other side of my face and I hit the ground, itchy carpet scratching my hands. Wren grunts in pain next to me and I open my eyes just in time to see the giant kick Wren in the stomach three times.

"Okay, okay! Break it up!" Jake calls out, and then the older boy is standing over Wren and me.

I expect him to yell at the teenagers who attacked us, but instead of kicking them out, Jake jabs his thumb at me. "Get out."

"I didn't do anything!" I have to gasp for the words, my jaw throbbing with each sound I make.

"No cheaters. You're lucky this is all Beast did to you."

The giant boy—Beast—gives us a smirk that makes my blood burn beneath my skin.

"Out!" Jake says again.

I stumble to my feet, my head still dizzy from the blow. I pull

Wren upright, and he moans against the sudden movement. Sticky soda covers our faces, hair, shirts, and hands. A bit of my blood mixes in with the brown syrup. Jenny hurries to our side, the velvet bag of cards in hand, and we trudge toward the exit.

The last thing we need to do is cause an even bigger scene.

As we near the front of the arcade, I pause, blinking fast, trying to decide if she's really standing in the entryway or if the Beast hit me too hard.

But when she finally steps inside, the light from the afternoon sun falling away, I see it's Emma.

Her blue eyes are wide, scanning the three of us. I wonder if she ever thought she'd see us again. I'm sure she didn't expect it to be like this.

"Back here today!" A voice calls and I see it's the manager leaning out of his office, directing his words toward Emma.

Her hands curl around the strap of her bag, pulling it closer to her side. She forces herself to walk and slides past us.

"You guys sure know how to make friends," she says under her breath, and then she disappears into the manager's office and Jake is telling us to get out again and my feet start moving, taking me back to the streets of Artmith.

I squint against the sudden bright sunset that glitters across the metallic buildings along the street.

"Are you okay?" Jenny is gripping both of my arms, forcing me to a halt in front of her. My head pounds with her words and I feel the blood run from my nose.

"I'm fine," I say and squeeze my eyes shut at the piercing pain in my ears.

"We're drawing attention to ourselves," Wren wheezes out, arms tightly hugging his stomach.

I look over Jenny's head and see the faces of the thinning crowd turning our way. We need to get out of sight before someone tries to approach us. I don't know why, but I have the feeling that if the Patrol finds out there are people from a different world walking these streets, we'd be in trouble. I pull Jenny close to me and push my way across the street, Wren falling in step behind us. I seek out a narrow alley across from the Penny Arcade and we slide into the shadows.

Out of the summer sun, a chill creeps across my skin, and I feel lightheaded, my ears ringing in the absence of the loud conversations on the main street. My hands find the side of the metal building and I try to keep myself on my feet. *Damn, did he have to hit me so hard?*

"You should sit, Ash," Jenny says, and she helps me lower myself onto the dirt alleyway. My legs all but give out, and I slump back against the building. My sister's hand is under my chin, tilting my head toward the sky.

The sound of something ripping apart echoes in my pounding ears. I tilt my eyes down and see Jenny has torn a strip of fabric off the bottom of her shirt, just like I've seen her do many times before with her old soccer camp shirts.

"Hold still," she instructs and presses the balled up fabric against my nose. My eyes clench shut at the throbbing pain that spreads across my face. "Keep pressure on it," she says, lifting my hand to replace hers. "I've had my fair share of nose bleeds on the soccer field from girls head-butting me."

Her words are meant to comfort me, but all they do is remind me where we *are*, and where we *aren't*.

"Wren, you okay?" Jenny asks, turning her attention away from me.

"Yeah," he groans out not very convincingly.

"Let me see," she says softly.

Over the ball of black fabric pressed against my nose, I see Wren roll up the end of his shirt, a deep bruise already blooming under his ribs.

"Can you breathe normally?" Jenny asks, and I detect the faint sound of fear creep into her voice.

"Yes," Wren says, sighing heavily and his words are stronger this time. "Really, I'm fine. Ash got the worst of it." My old best friend's eyes connect with mine and I see the regret hanging in them. "You didn't have to stand up for me." His gaze falls as he adds, "Thank you."

"I knew you didn't cheat," I mumble, my words getting muffled by the cloth pressed against my face. I know I should tell him that I did it because of the friendship we had, that some subconscious part of me went to his rescue, and that I'd do it again, but instead I just say I knew he didn't cheat because that's an easier explanation.

The last rays in the late sunset glisten in Jenny's eyes, and then they fall away. Darkness fills Artmith. All this time I may have been frustrated or confused, but I haven't been scared. Not until those final moments of daylight sink away, and now, night engulfs this strange world, and I *am* scared. I want to be home. I want to be anywhere but here.

I can feel the fear radiating from Jenny and Wren, just as frightened by the idea of us in an alleyway at night in a place we know nothing about.

"Ash, what should we do?" Jenny asks, and the girl who took charge of making sure Wren and I were okay vanishes, needing her big brother again. "I know you have a plan. I can see it on your blood-covered face," she adds when my eyes meet hers.

She's right. I picked this alleyway for a reason. I do have a plan.

"We wait here for Emma to come back out of the Penny Arcade," I say and turn my head to peer across the street to where the Penny Arcade sits with its doors still pulled ajar. "She's the only one who even listened to our pleas. When she comes out, we'll try to convince her again."

CHAPTER 8

Emma

M r. Marlo, the man who owns the Penny Arcade, gestures to a chair across from the desk once I enter his office. I'm still caught on the fact that I just saw those three from Earth again. I shake away the thought. No, they aren't *actually* from Earth. But, man, they looked *awful*. I'm kind of surprised a pinch of joy didn't find it's way inside of me at the sight of them. After the joke they played on me this morning, it's the least the universe could do to them. But I didn't feel joy. I felt sorry for them. I felt like charging the kid who beat them up and giving him a taste of a fist to the face. The idea is laughable. Yes, me fighting someone is exactly what I need to add to this ridiculous day.

"Emma?"

I look up at Mr. Marlo and see he's studying me carefully. I realize he must have said something, and I missed it.

"What did you want to show me?" he asks.

I nod and pull my satchel onto my lap. Right, the real reason I came here. It's rare that I try to sell Mr. Marlo anything. He's not like the guys at the Weights Ring or Billy at the salon. He's a more well respected man who has the Patrol in his good graces for opening an arcade that keeps the kids out of trouble. But I know this is where I can charge the most for my inventions.

I flip open my bag and pull out a plastic jug. I place it on his wooden desk and he slides it closer to himself. His eyes are drawn to the shiny plastic lid, the red glossy finish reflecting in his eyes.

"Do you have a game token?" I ask him. Without taking his eyes off the container, Mr. Marlo pulls open a drawer to his right and flips a golden coin onto the desk.

I pick up the token, twisting it between my fingers, and then line it up with the slot I had cut in the red lid. "This device will count how many coins you put in it," I say. As I slide the coin through the opening, the spiral counter rolls forward and it now reads *0001*.

"And when we take tokens out?" Mr. Marlo asks, but the instructions are already on the tip of my tongue.

"Roll it back," I say simply and rub my finger on the counter to pull the *1* back to *0*, and now the dial reads *0000* again.

"Perfect! Thank you, Emma!" Mr. Marlo exclaims, and the tension in the air ebbs away.

I let out a silent sigh of relief and extend my hand for the payment we agreed on. Mr. Marlo doesn't hesitate to lay *twenty* red bills in my hand. 200 yatz. Ten times the amount I get from the men in the Weights Ring. Almost a third of my monthly citizen allowance. I try not to snap my arm back and stuff the money safely inside my bag.

If he knew what this meant to me... I pause at the thought. I'm sure he knows exactly what this means to me, otherwise I wouldn't be selling him these items in private.

Mr. Marlo seems to be thinking the same thing because his next words are awkward in the air between us. "Emma, I really do appreciate what you've designed for my arcade, but this is a dangerous business you're trying to run."

"Thank you, Mr. Marlo," I say and stand quickly, hoping to avoid this conversation altogether.

"Emma, if you need the money, I'd be happy to offer you a part-time job working the front desk," Mr. Marlo offers, rising to match my sudden movement.

I force a thin smile across my face. "That's very kind of you, Mr. Marlo, but I do this because I love inventing things. This is my passion. Plus, I have my job at the scrapyard."

Mr. Marlo must hear the forced compliment in my voice because he lets the conversation fall away as he dips his head slightly. "Very well. I'll reach out when I need something else."

I thank him again for his business and slide out the back door of his office. It's our agreed route for me to take so I'm not detected leaving through the front, in case any Patrol are here with their kids, or are doing their rounds. That and the fact that I don't want to have to see Jake. I successfully avoided him on the way in here, and I don't want to add a conversation with him to the incredibly weird day I'm already having.

When I push open the metal door on the back of the arcade, I see that night has fallen while I was talking with Mr. Marlo. I slip into the alleyway and quickly add up my earnings from today. A total of 230 yatz. Not bad for the start I had this afternoon. I seal my satchel and set my feet in the direction of Shadow Village, eager to get off the streets before any more trouble can find me.

The crowds that were shopping this afternoon have cleared and a lot of the businesses have already pulled their doors closed, locks turned tight, with dark windows reflecting my face. Artmith is not the kind of city you walk around in at night. Street rats aside, the vainders come out at night. And even though we have a wall of metal surrounding the city to protect us from the creatures, no one runs the risk of being out later than they have to be.

I only sell at night when I'm in a real pinch for money. Thankfully, that's not the case today.

I've almost cleared the street where the Penny Arcade sits, when a girl's scream rings through the thin night air.

My feet freeze.

I quickly slide into the shadows and hold my breath, trying to hide from whatever *that* was. The sound came from behind me, back toward the Penny Arcade.

She screams again, and this time, two boys' voices ring out. "Jenny!"

The name makes my heart pause. *No. No, this isn't happening. Those idiots are still out here? Why would they do that?*

"Ash, help!" she screams, and my feet turn in the direction of her voice.

No. Go home. Do not go back there. You do not want to get into any trouble.

But my fleeting thoughts aren't enough to stop my conscious from marching myself toward the commotion. I follow the sounds of Jenny's screams back to an alleyway that's across the street from the Penny Arcade. I hang at the edge and survey the scene.

The silhouette of a street rat at the other end of the alley causes me to suck in a sharp breath. I can smell the sewer water on him from here, his long, black hair glistening in the moonlight. The man is two of Jenny tall and he presses his chest to her back, his arm locked around her neck.

"Where's your money?" he growls, and his tongue flips on the words like a lizard. *God, I hate the street rats.* My fingers slide into my satchel.

Ash and Wren are on their feet, hands out defensively, trying to talk the street rat down.

"We don't have any money," Ash pleads.

The street rat grunts at that and his grip on Jenny's throat tightens. She cries in desperation to get away from him, her fingers clawing at his grip. The street rat raises his arm and lifts Jenny off the ground. The air squeezes out of her throat.

"What about now? Do you have money now?" he barks at them.

"Let her go!" I yell, finally stepping into the alley.

Wren and Ash turn around, eyes wide and their mouths hanging open. I pull my hand from my bag and reveal my safety horn. I press down on the nozzle, as if it was a can of spray paint, and an ear-piercing wail cries through the air.

The street rat drops Jenny and falls back a few steps, black eyes flipping between the four of us before he turns and scurries back to his sewer hole. I lift up my finger and let the sound fade away.

Jenny's deep breaths fill the stunned silence, and Ash and Wren quickly run to her crumpled body. She gently massages her neck, her breathing finally slowing.

I want to make sure she's okay, but I think I've done my part. I turn around in preparation to leave them behind when suddenly, Ash's voice calls after me.

"You saved us."

My feet pause on the dirt road as a cold hand reaches for my arm, gently turning me around. I don't know why, but for some reason, I thought, if he really is from another world, that it would feel weird to be this close to him, but... Ash doesn't seem all that different from me. I fold to the force, surprised by how light his touch is from his muscled arms, and meet Ash's shocked gaze. "Thank you," he says as an afterthought.

It's the closest I've stood to him, his long fingers still resting on my arm. I'm reminded of how attractive he is. Wide eyes glowing with moonlight and brown waves of hair blown wild around his sharp jawline.

I try to shrug off his comment and say, "You really shouldn't be out here at night."

He seems to be hurt by my words. He lets his hand fall away, the absence of his gentle touch leaving me a bit off balance. "We don't have anywhere else to go," he says, and it looks like the words actually pain him.

"Because you're from Earth," I add to his broken statement.

His eyes seem to brighten. "You believe me?"

"I—" but my words catch in my throat.

No, I didn't believe him, but... No person in their right mind would be out here at night. The Patrol ensures every citizen has a place to live, or they become a street rat—by choice, I may add. If they have nowhere to go, then that means they really aren't from Artmith. They have on strange clothes and I did see all three of them fall through the sky.

"I do," I say, and I realize that I *do* believe them. But if they're from a different world, that's something that can only be explained by magic. Magic I know my world thinks died a long time ago.

Ash actually smiles at me when I say it. He looks crazy, blood stained to his cheeks, his clothes still soaked with soda, and a crazed grin spreading on his face.

"Oh, thank goodness," Wren says from behind Ash. I look over Ash's shoulder and see he's helped Jenny to her feet. She looks stronger now that she's regained her footing.

"Do you know somewhere we can go for the night? Like a hotel?" Jenny speaks up.

I press my lips together, thinking my words over before I say them. "I can find some room at my house."

"I'm sure your parents wouldn't be thrilled with us staying," Ash says, but I shake my head.

"I don't live with them anymore. It's just me."

Ash tilts his head and I can tell he's taking me in again, knowing I'm no older than he is.

"We should go now, though. Before the Patrol shows up to investigate the alarm I blared," I say and shrug the strap of my bag higher on my shoulder.

"Okay, thanks," Ash says, and I don't miss the surprise and relief in his words.

I silently pray to whoever may be listening that I don't regret doing this.

CHAPTER 9

Ash

For the first time since we arrived, I actually feel like we're moving in the right direction of home. Emma leads us through the dark streets, making sure to keep our pace quick and in as much moonlight as possible. She still grips the air horn that scared away the man who tried to rob us earlier.

My thanks to Emma for saving us and offering to at least try to believe us feels too small. I don't think she realizes how much it means to us, *to me*, that she's willing to help.

All in all, Artmith doesn't seem that different from any other city back on Earth. I'd say there's a clear separation between the upper class and the lower class, with very little in between. Their way of life is definitely not as advanced as ours, but they have the essentials. Everything's a little rough around the edges, with the dirt streets and jagged skyscrapers. I kind of like it.

"So, why do you live on your own?" I ask her as we walk. I swing the black velvet bag with the playing cards around my wrist, the marbles clicking together inside.

"Well, that's just how it works here. When you're twelve, you start fending for yourself. That's when the Patrol begins to hand out your citizen allowance."

"Patrol?" I prompt her, wanting to finally learn more about this group of people.

"That's what we call our law enforcement," Emma says. "When you turn twelve, they give you a monthly allowance until the day you die. It's enough for food and a place to live. If you need any more money, you have to work for it."

"So, you moved out at twelve?" I ask and glance down at her. Blonde hair frames the sides of her face, hiding her from my curious eyes.

"No, I actually just moved out a couple of months ago. I got tired of my parents taking *my* allowance to pay their rent so they could use *their* allowance to buy clothes and fancy wines."

"It's an interesting system," I offer, contemplating it. "It allows you to be very independent."

"That's the point," Emma says, leading us down a thin alley with tall buildings soaring overhead.

"So, are you not going to study at the University because of the money?" I ask.

"You sure do ask a lot of questions, Ash," Emma says, glancing at me.

"Sorry, I guess I do that when I'm nervous," I admit, embarrassment heating my cheeks. "Being in this world that I know nothing about has me on edge."

She processes this and says, "You really are from Earth? You're not lying to me?" Her voice curls up, as if she promises this is the last time she'll ask me.

"I promise, Emma, I'm not lying," I say again, meeting her sideways glance.

"Well, I hope I can help you get home, then," Emma says softly and then leads us down another alley that runs between two topsy turvy skyscrapers. They sit so close together my shoulders touch both buildings.

"You live back here?" I say, not sure how a house could fit.

"It's a shortcut," Emma explains from in front of me.

We come out of the alley and onto a dirt road. On the other side, rows and rows of homes pepper the barren landscape. The first thing I notice is how short they are. They only go up to my shoulders. Most have scrap metal bolted down as a roof and tattered clothes hanging in the windows to act as curtains.

"Welcome to Shadow Village," Emma says.

I glance over my shoulder, back toward the skyscrapers, and see the night shadows they are casting over the homes.

"I'm guessing that allowance isn't much," I say under my breath.

Emma leads us down a twisting path between the small huts and says, "Just enough so you don't die."

She walks up to a dark grey home that is in just as terrible condition as the rest of them. The roof is a red, wavy, metal slab, and the windows are boarded shut. She goes to the crooked door at the front of the home and fiddles with the lock on the door. It's a dial lock, like I have on my locker at school.

After she enters the combination and pops the lock off, she pushes open the door and I see that there are stairs leading down into the dirt.

That explains why the buildings are so short.

"Come on in," she says and we follow her into her home.

It's a simple square. The dark grey cement walls are bare. The floor is made of wooden planks. There's a sagging couch in one corner, and a kitchen in the one diagonal from it. It's complete with a refrigerator and an oven that look like they probably don't work.

"Bathroom is through there," Emma says, pointing toward an opening in the wall where a bed sheet hangs instead of a door.

"You *live* here?" Jenny asks, not trying to hide her disgust.

"This is my home," Emma says, not taking any offense at her remark. "Are you guys hungry? I can make us something to eat. Do you want beans or rice?" she asks, prying open the cabinet door that hangs by one corner.

"Beans sound good," Wren offers, and he plops down on the couch, making himself comfortable. Any fear he had earlier seems to have vanished, his goofy personality back in place.

Jenny is a bit more cautious; afraid she may break anything she touches. She busies her hands with fixing her ponytail, pulling the black strands tight against her head.

"Thanks for helping us," I say when the silence in the home makes me feel uncomfortable. I move to the kitchen counter and open the can of beans for Emma. Her can opener doesn't have a knob to twist, but an odd metal crank. I wonder if it's something she picked up at the scrapyard.

"Well, life was getting a bit boring," Emma admits.

I hand her the open can and when she takes it, her eyes linger on the blood that's still dried to my skin. My nose finally stopped bleeding, but I've definitely looked better.

"You should probably clean up." Emma sets the can down and

gently pulls me toward the sink, her fingers brushing my wrist so lightly I think I almost imagine their touch.

She turns on the faucet and soaks a black cloth. Once it's wet, she steps back and nods to the water. "Wash your hands."

I do and watch the blood lift from my skin and circle down the drain. The whole image is a bit haunting and I see Emma's face tense, her faint-freckled cheeks paling a bit. Once my hands are clean, she leans forward and turns the water off. "Let me see how bad Beast messed up your face," she says, and I turn to look at her. The smile tugging at my lips makes an aching pain spread across my jaw.

Emma lifts the warm cloth to my cheek and, with gentle strokes, she wipes away the blood. She moves slowly, trying not to apply too much pressure where the Beast's fist made its mark. I tuck in my chin and dip my head for her, my gaze locked on her crystal eyes as they study my face.

"There will be at least one bruise," she says, the warm cloth tracing a spot under my right eye, just next to my nose. Her gaze locks on mine and she sees I'm watching her closely. The blue of her eyes appears deeper in the dim light of her home, and I see them brighten with her next words. "Don't worry, no permanent damage, I'm sure."

"I'll try to thank him for that later."

Emma shakes her head, and starts to rinse the cloth in the sink, ringing out the blood and scrubbing it with a bar of soap. "I don't think the Beast is someone you should seek out. I do have clothes you can change into," Emma adds as she hangs the cloth over the edge of the sink.

"I don't want to impose," I say quickly. I'm thankful for the offer, but I don't want to take anything from her. From one look around her house, I can't help but think she must have very little.

Emma ignores me and moves to a wooden chest next to the couch. The black iron hinges groan as she opens the trunk and she fishes out a pile of items.

"These were an old friend's," she says as she tosses a plain blue shirt to Wren with a pair of worn green shorts. The set she hands me is similar; a white shirt with black shorts. The material reminds me of khakis.

"Will your friend mind us borrowing these?" Wren asks, looking at Emma as she crosses back to the open trunk.

I see her laugh a bit to herself. "No, I don't plan on ever speaking to him again." Her hands dive back into the wooden crate and she pulls out a pink, frilly blouse. "Is this your style?" Emma turns her question to Jenny, who looks like she may die at the thought of wearing that shirt.

"I'm good with what I have on," Jenny declines. "I knew better than to get into a fight at the arcade."

"Your shirt is torn, though," Emma says, nodding at the raised hemline.

"That's actually how some people wear their shirts back on Earth," Jenny explains, and Emma seems concerned at the idea, but she doesn't say anything more. She tosses the pink blouse back into the trunk and drops the lid. Wren and I change in the bathroom while Emma returns to the kitchen to continue cleaning the washcloth she used on my face.

Emma offers to wash our clothes in the sink, but I tell her I can do it. While I work on squeezing the soda from Wren's old jeans, Emma moves back to the stove. She clicks it on and places a chipped black pot on one of the burners. When she turns the can of beans over the pot, they slop inside, still in the shape of the can.

"Taste better than they look," she adds when she sees I'm watching her. She uses a wooden spoon to break up the brown mush. "So, what's life on Earth like?" Emma asks me.

"You mean you *actually* believe me?" I tease.

"Just wondering what other stories you can make up," Emma says, glancing up at me through the blonde strands of her hair. "You go to school?"

"About to graduate high school," I say, the chemistry paper I never wrote hanging in the back of my mind.

"Me too," Emma says. "Actually, I just finished my last day yesterday."

"So, how do you know Professor Sim if you aren't a student at the University?" I ask.

"I've been doing some extra studies," Emma explains, continuing to stir the thinning bean paste.

"Extra studies in history?" I ask curiously.

"History of technology," Emma corrects. "And an introduction course in mechanical engineering."

My eyes widen and Emma sees my surprised expression.

"Yeah, that's the reaction most people have," Emma laughs.

"I think that's great, Emma," I say, trying to hide my raised brows. Her cheeks flush a light pink.

"I just needed an introduction. I don't plan on continuing classes."

"Why not?" I ask.

"Don't need it for what I want to do," Emma says, the beans beginning to bubble.

"Which is?" I ask. *Wow, this girl really makes you work for an answer.*

"Afraid I can't tell you that." Emma clicks off the stove and takes a stack of bowls out of the cabinets. "Dinner's ready," she calls over her shoulder to Wren and Jenny.

We ladle mushy beans into bowls and eat our dinner. Emma and Jenny fill the two chairs at the slanted table, and Wren and I sit on the floor across from them. The beans aren't that bad, actually, but I'd much rather have any of my mom's home-cooked meals. My chest tightens when I think about what they must be feeling right now. Showing up and finding all of us missing. I bet they're worried sick.

It's probably only 9:00 p.m., though. Maybe they're still holding out hope that we turn up. They could just think one of Jenny's friends picked us up to get dinner. Yes, I'm sure that's what's happening. But even if it's not, I can't get upset. I have to keep myself calm so I can find a way home. My eyes land on Emma, watching her finish off her bowl of beans. We're so lucky she found us. She scrapes out her last bite of beans and her eyes land on my stare.

"What?" she asks after swallowing.

"Why can't you tell me what you need the engineering classes for?" I ask curiously.

Emma slouches back in her chair. She lets out a sigh and shakes her head. "I guess since you aren't from here, it wouldn't hurt to tell you my secret."

I lean in, crossing my arms over my knees.

"I work in the scrapyard, sifting through the piles to recycle them. Sometimes, I find some useful parts and I steal them. Then, I fix them or engineer something new and sell them on the black market to earn some extra money."

"What do you make?" Wren asks curiously.

Emma slides her chair back and crawls under the table. She runs her small fingers down the crack between the floorboards and pries one of them up. She pops two more from the floor, revealing a gaping black hole. Stairs with a thin coating of dusty dirt peek out. Emma slides down into the hole and then resurfaces moments later.

"Here's what I'm working on right now," Emma says, spreading out her parts on the table. "I try to keep it simple. Easier to sell that way." She picks up a pair of uneven scissors, one blade much longer than the other. "Found these halves and put them together. Billy may swipe these up if I tell him some story about how the different sized blades cut better," she says, mentioning the barber we spoke to this morning.

"These colored cups weren't even broken," she says, picking up a small green glass cup next. "Perfect size to hold a light bulb. Easy colored lights, though I've had some problems with the glass being too heavy and the light falling from the ceiling. Better if it's used on a lamp." She picks up the final item on the table. It literally just looks like a pair of safety glasses with flashlights taped to either side.

"Night vision glasses," Emma says. She puts them on and her eyes double in size. "These are still in the prototype phase, but I really like them."

I catch Jenny roll her eyes and try to suppress a laugh.

Emma takes the glasses off and shoots Jenny a stiff stare. "Science not your thing?"

Jenny's face pales.

Emma doesn't miss a beat, but I get the feeling this isn't the first time someone has laughed at her.

"I think they're really cool," Wren speaks up, filling the silent tension.

"Why don't you just open your own shop in town instead of selling them on the black market?" I ask, recalling how Emma described it.

"Maybe one day I will, but that'd require me to have a degree from the University. The Patrol has all kinds of regulations on how businesses can be run. I need the money now and this is the fastest way I can get it." Emma piles her items back up in her arms and returns them to her storage room under the floor.

"Why do you hide them down there?" I ask when she resurfaces.

"You never know who could be peering in your windows or stopping by for an unexpected visit," Emma says, returning the floorboards to their places and closing the hidden basement. "I have to be really careful about spending the money I get from selling these parts. The Patrol keeps tabs on everyone to make sure they only spend enough to cover their allowance and recorded earnings."

"What happens if they find out what you're doing?" Jenny asks, and I assume she's trying to get a better understanding of this world

"For this," Emma says, considering it a minute, "probably just a citation warning at first. They may terminate my allowance after that."

"And without your allowance, you couldn't pay for food or your home," Wren concludes.

Emma nods and says, "Without my allowance, I'd be dead. We all would, that's the point of it. It gives the Patrol all the control."

"Are you sure vainders even exist?" Jenny asks, shifting the conversation. "Or is the wall and curfew just another way to control you?"

"I guess I've never seen a vainder," Emma admits. "But I have seen enough people come back the next morning torn to shreds to not question it."

"So, what time will the gate open tomorrow?" Jenny asks.

"6:00 a.m. usually."

I glance down at the shadowed face on Emma's watch. 9:30 p.m..

Eight and a half hours of waiting. It's hard to imagine that my grandmother's funeral was only this morning.

We help Emma clean up dinner. Even with how unappetizing the beans looked, we all emptied our bowls.

"No beds here," Emma says, drying off the last bowl. "I usually sleep on the couch."

"We can just take the floor," I quickly interrupt. I don't want to be any more of an inconvenience to her. Partially because she's already done so much for us, but also because I know if she decides to stop helping us, we'll have no one here to turn to. Except maybe Professor Sim.

"Okay," Emma says, stacking the bowls back in the cabinet.

She walks into the living room, stopping by the door to clip the dial lock in place before pulling out some blankets from a basket next to the couch. I try not to gawk at her choice of security. Emma hands us each a blanket with a pillow from the sofa. We spread out around the room and settle in for the night.

Wren and Jenny busy themselves with talking about what we'll do tomorrow if the card doesn't work, and what we'll tell my parents if it does work. I try to tune them out because I know I'll never fall asleep if my mind starts running through the endless what-ifs.

I think Emma senses my restlessness because she leans over the end of the couch and says, "Before you saw me in the field this morning, I heard you mention your grandmother. Something about it being her painting that you fell through?"

I'm not the least bit surprised that Emma didn't miss a single detail. I don't know if it's the exhaustion weighing me down or the fact that my mind is on overload with all that I've learned today, but I remain numb to the fact that this morning was my grandmother's funeral. "We were cleaning out her house when we found the painting," I explain, the words coming easier than I thought they would. "Today was her funeral."

"I'm sorry for your loss," Emma says gently.

"It's something we were prepared for. We're lucky we had the time that we did," I say, my voice threatening to crack as the emotions I've been trying to suppress begin to build in my throat. I think Emma can sense that, because she changes the conversation.

"What do you do on Earth?" she asks.

"What do I *do*?" I ask, confused by what she means.

"Yeah, I'm a scrapyard worker who sells engineered tools on the black market. What do you do?" She peers at me over the couch cushion, probably waiting for me to tell her that I fight space monsters or lead an army of androids.

"Nothing that exciting, really," I admit, shamefully staring at the ceiling. "I play the drums," I offer and glance at her. That's always my first *tell-me-about-yourself* answer.

Emma nods, interested. "Is that, like, a job on Earth?"

"Not really," I say, embarrassed. "I am getting a scholarship to play in college, though," I add, trying to redeem myself. "I'll be going to Coastal University in the fall."

"What are you going to study?" Emma asks, resting her head on the couch.

I let a long silent pause settle. "I'm not sure," I eventually admit.

"Well, what do you want to do with your life?" Emma asks the question my mom has been asking me my entire senior year.

"I don't know, yet. You have an interest in engineering, but I don't have anything like that. I just play the drums."

"That's all you do?"

"Well, I take classes in all the normal subjects. My grandma tried to teach me to draw, but I'm not that great at it, and I like to act a little."

"Oh, you're an actor?" Emma asks, interrupting me.

She's actually interested in me being an actor? I didn't even mean to say that last part. I never talk about that anymore. I was just looking for anything to say that might interest her.

"That's a great job! Do that," she says.

I laugh and scan her seriously excited face.

"That's hardly a real job. I'd never be a successful actor."

"Oh, it's a really important job here in Artmith," Emma says. "The Patrol pays them loads of money. They say actors are a great source of entertainment and they help keep people happy. The Patrol loves anything that will keep the citizens here happy."

"Really?" I ask and Emma nods.

"They always have shows going on downtown. And a lot of them get turned into movies. I've only seen a few. My money is better spent elsewhere, but the plays are all free to attend. I like to go every once in a while. It really is a nice distraction."

Emma rolls onto her back and stares at the ceiling.

A silence falls in the room and I think Wren and Jenny have talked themselves to sleep. I never really thought about being an actor full-time. I've never told anyone how much I actually like it.

"I'm a drummer," I say, breaking the long silence. "That's what I'm good at. Acting is just a hobby."

It's the same thing I told my parents when they thought I'd given up drumming to be an actor when I landed the lead in the play. They were worried all the money they'd spent on drumming lessons would be wasted, and there's no way I could go to college without my drumming scholarship.

"Ash." Emma's voice is soft.

"Yeah, Emma?"

"You can call me *Em* if you want."

I smile, a small laugh escaping me. That was the nickname she had mentioned when I first met her. "Does that mean we're friends now?" I ask, knowing she said only her friends get to call her that.

"Yeah, I guess so," Emma says, rolling over on the couch and turning her back to me.

CHAPTER 10

Ash

"**R**ise and shine!"

My tired eyes crack open and I roll onto my back. Emma is standing next to the front door, leaning against its frame. The velvet bag with Ending in Cadence is tied around her wrist and a black backpack hangs off one shoulder. The living room is still dark, the sun not up yet. She's dressed in another pair of navy overalls, the hems rolled to rest on top of her worn leather boots.

"The gate will be opening soon," she adds.

The idea that I could be home in a matter of minutes sends a rush of adrenaline through my veins. I rise and slide my feet into my tennis shoes, pausing to glance down at the white shirt and black cargo pants Emma gave me last night. It feels odd to be wearing things from both worlds.

"Let's go," I say, pulling a drowsy Wren to his feet. Neither of us hurries Jenny along. I've lived through too many cranky mornings with her screaming at me to know that wouldn't be the best idea. Especially today, when all of our emotions are tied together by a fragile thread. Slowly, Jenny gets up and stretches out her tight muscles. She pulls her hair into a clean ponytail and puts on her tennis shoes, the only one of us to be completely dressed in clothes from Earth. We cross over to Emma and she lays a tentative hand on the doorknob, her still sleepy eyes meet mine.

"I don't want you guys to get your hopes up," she says gently, "but I'm not sure how to tell you not to hope."

"We can only try, *Em*," I say, using the nickname she approved last night. "It's the only idea we have right now."

She nods her head and then pushes the door open. "All right, then let's go. Keep your heads down when we get to the gate, just in case some of the Patrol are still there."

Emma slips the lock on the outside of the door when we leave and leads us into the grey early morning light. It leaks through the tall buildings that tower around us. A low fog is floating over the other shacks. We twist through the maze of homes in Shadow Village and move through Artmith silently, none of us talking, even though I know our minds are moving at a hundred thoughts a minute.

When we get to the gate, I see its iron bars are already pulled open; no Patrol in sight. After we pass over the threshold, Emma speaks up. "I need to go to the scrapyard first. Barry will be expecting me today. It's on the way, so it'll just take a minute."

Emma leads us toward the yard, and I see the tall wheat field growing closer. I blink quickly, amazed at the beauty of Pintura. I hadn't taken the time to really look at it when we arrived, too shocked to notice anything.

The field sits nestled between a forest to our right and a large rocky mountain to the left.

The mountain's tan rock stretches high into the sky, a rushing waterfall pouring from its peak into a large lake. It looks exactly like the painting we fell through. I tilt my head up, the grey clouds still twisting in the haunting cyclone above.

"Is that normal?" I ask.

Emma lifts her head toward the sky, squinting against the morning light. "Umm, I don't think so," she says, shrugging her shoulders.

"It was like that yesterday, too," I mumble.

We approach the chain-linked fence of the scrapyard and Emma fishes a plastic card on a lanyard from her backpack. She walks up to the box that hangs at the entrance and slides the card through it.

An older man leans against the fence, his shirt tight around his dark skin. "Need today off?" he asks.

Emma returns the card to her bag. "Yeah, I turned three sales last night," Emma says. "Thanks, Barry," she adds, and turns to lead us away from the scrapyard, not letting Barry respond.

"What was that about?" I ask.

"Barry lets me clock in, and I turn my sales money into payments from the scrapyard," Emma responds.

"I'm pretty sure that's called money laundering, and it's illegal," Jenny says, her mood considerably worse in the early morning.

"I'm guessing you all have more money than you know what to do with," Emma quips.

"We don't have the same regulations you have," I say, trying to stop the argument before it turns into something more.

We reach the field, the tall golden grass meeting my knees. With high steps, we hike to the spot where we landed yesterday.

"This is it," Wren says.

"Here's the card." Emma's voice is skeptical as her pale hand slips it out of the velvet bag.

Wren takes the playing card, twisting it in his hand and the morning light reflects off the gold print. Wren gently places the card on the ground, falling to his knees next to it. "Do you think we need to say something?"

"Like a magic password?" Jenny asks, wrinkling her nose. "We didn't say anything before."

"Okay," Wren says, still unsure. There's a stretch of tense silence before Wren adds, "Maybe we should try to do it together."

Jenny drops to her knees and lightly knocks Wren back from the card. "Oh, just move." Jenny quickly stabs the card with her fingers, causing it to dent a bit in the center. "Solid," she says.

I expect my heart to drop or a nauseous wave to flood through me, but neither happens. I'm not all that surprised. I knew it wouldn't work, but like Emma said, I just didn't know how to tell myself not to hope.

"Back to square one," Jenny mumbles, flipping the card over to Emma.

My gaze returns to the twisting clouds and my thoughts drift to my parents. That's it. They'll surely be losing their minds this morning. No point in worrying about them, it's inevitable. Now, I just need to worry about getting out of here. I pick my brain for any ideas on how to do that. I think about everything that Emma has told me about this world. The only thing hinting toward home is this card game.

"Can I see the game?" I ask Emma, sadness cracking my voice.

"Yeah," Emma says gently, noticing I'm getting upset. She pulls the bag off her wrist and tosses it to me.

"Maybe we're in the wrong spot," Wren says, jumping around Jenny to pick up the golden card. "Let's try other locations."

Jenny and Wren begin to mindlessly wander around the field, dropping the card and tapping it with their fingers.

I walk away from Emma and sit in the tall grass, stretching the bag open. The cards fall out and I shuffle through them for some kind of clue. I set down the stack, keeping the card with the number one in my hand. Gently bending and fidgeting with the corner, I stare intently at the six-lined riddle printed on it. I stare so hard that the card becomes blurry, frustration heating my cheeks.

Why can't this be easy? Why can't I just go home? Why can't something just tell me how to get out of here?

Wait.

My vision clears, the frustration fading away. My eyes quickly fly across the words on the card. I spread the other cards out in front of me, seeing the different riddles printed on their matte finish. *They are telling me.*

I scoop up the cards and stumble to my feet, my heart beating faster.

"Em!" I say, running to where she's currently laying on the ground. Her eyes trace the grey clouds above her head. "I figured it out," I say, dropping to my knees.

She props herself on her elbows. I don't give her a chance to ask me anything before the words race from my mouth.

"The riddles on the cards are instructions."

Emma squints, not convinced.

I pull her all the way up into a sitting position and hand her the cards. "They're instructions," I repeat. "And these numbers aren't points," I add, gesturing to the bottom of the cards. "It's the order we need to follow the instructions in."

Emma is quiet as she flips through the cards, absorbing my theory. Her nervous blue eyes flicker up to me, her hands dropping into her lap.

"I don't know, Ash," she begins to dismiss my discovery.

"No, that's it!" I say above her comment, my excitement taking over.

"These riddles talk about crazy challenges," Emma speaks her thoughts aloud.

"Challenges we have to complete," I interrupt her. "It's a literal game. Pintura is the game board."

Emma tilts her head, trying to consider it.

"Look at this," I say, putting the cards in numerical order in her hands. "They kind of flow together. The Starting Rock is number one."

"And the marbles? What do they mean?" she counters.

I pause and consider this. "They're a decoy," I decide. "Something that's in the fake game to keep people from thinking the cards could be something more."

Emma is quiet for a long time and I notice her eyes have turned their focus from the cards to the ground beneath us. A glossy haze fills their blue depths, and I see she's deep in thought. I dampen my lips and wait for what she'll say. I know how crazy this probably sounds, but something inside of me buzzes in response to my idea.

Finally, Emma speaks, raising her head to look at me. "Portals to another world could only be explained by magic."

I shift my weight off my knees and nod. "Magic is something in movies and books back on Earth," I say. "But ever since we fell through the painting..."

"Magic has always been real, here," Emma says.

I had trailed off from my thoughts, but with her confession, I feel my senses tighten. "There's magic here?" I ask, shocked. "You didn't believe I was from Earth, but your world has *magic*?"

"It's complicated," Emma says, and she begins to aimlessly shuffle the cards with her nervous hands. "Magic has been dead for a long time."

"Well, how did it work? Maybe that's the answer we're looking for," I prompt her, wishing she would have said something about this last night.

"We're taught that our world is made up of magic. That the dirt beneath your feet, the land we stand on, is a living entity that holds a kind of power no one has ever understood." Emma snaps the cards, trailing her fingers down their edges. "But the world has been dormant for so many years. I don't think anyone living can attest to that even being true."

Again, I look up at the cyclone of clouds twisting over my head. "I think we're seeing that magic above us," I admit.

Emma follows my gaze toward the clouds and I see a sense of awe fill her face. "I stopped believing in the stories about magic when I was little," she says. "I attested the history they taught to science. Something my brain understands."

"But now?" I ask, and we pull our focus back to each other.

Emma's crystal blue eyes shift as she takes in every inch of my face. "Now I don't know what's crazier; that you're from another world or that magic has returned to mine."

"I think both are probably hard to process," I say, and she nods. "But they're both true, and I think these cards are how we get to the portal that can take us home."

Emma looks at the cards in her hands once more, skimming the riddles and trying to read them as instructions instead of pieces in a game. "We can try it," she finally offers. "It's more promising than their idea." She gestures to my sister and Wren, who are still wandering around the field.

"Guys, we figured it out!" I call to them.

Jenny and Wren share a quick, excited glance before jogging back to us. I show them the cards and explain my theory. Emma tells them about the magic her world is rumored to have and overall, I see that both Jenny and Wren are skeptical.

"What if we just do the last challenge?" Jenny asks.

"You can't cheat," I say, already convinced this is how it has to work. The outbreak we had at the arcade yesterday is still fresh in all of our minds. I have a feeling cheating at this game would earn us more than a beating from the Beast. Especially if it's powered by an ancient magic that's been awoken after who knows how many years.

"We're going to need to collect some supplies before we get started," Emma says, fully jumping on board with me.

"You're going to keep helping us?" Jenny asks, surprised Emma would want to after claiming to not believe us all day yesterday.

"Why not?" Emma says, shrugging her shoulders like it's no big deal.

I study her for a moment, taking in the girl who had no idea who we were less than twenty-four hours ago. She's suddenly ready to jump on board with this farfetched concept of a card game being instructions to a portal. This *is* a big deal, and I wonder why she's so quick to want to help.

Now that we have the cards, and understand they are the instructions to finding the portal, she should probably go back to her work at the scrapyard. But what if we start this game and need information about Pintura or how this world and its magic work?

Wren and Jenny hesitantly flip through the cards, and I softly punch Wren in the arm. "Come on. Let's *actually* play Ending in Cadence."

There's an exchange that passes between the two of us. We haven't played a game together in years. We've hardly shared more than a nod in the hallway and a quick exchange in the band room. I didn't realize it until now, but I really miss having Wren around.

When the moment passes, Wren nods, handing me the cards. "Let's try it," he says and I throw a victorious punch into the air.

"Okay! What should we do first?" I turn to Emma.

"If these cards are actual challenges, we're talking about completing impossible and dangerous tasks. First, we'll need some supplies," she says. "Then, we can start with the first card." Emma throws her bag over her shoulder and waves us to follow her. "Let's go, team!"

We follow Emma back through the field and past the gates of Artmith.

"First stop, food and water," Emma says, leading us into a small shop on the corner of the main dirt street.

We grab different granola bars and fruits. Jenny finds Wren, me, and her backpacks in the back of the store. They're an army green cloth material that buckle closed. I grab an arm full of glass water bottles, immediately noticing the difference from the plastic I'm used to back home, and we all meet at the front of the shop. Once all the items are on the counter, I realize how expensive this will be, and of course, they won't accept any of the crumpled dollars I have in my pocket.

"We could probably put some of this back," I say, picking up one of the bags.

"Don't worry about it," Emma says, pulling out a wad of red bills. "I just got this month's allowance."

The lady working the register takes the money and we scoop up our supplies. When we get outside, we divide the food and water, storing them in our bags.

"Don't you need to save that money for food and your home payments later this month?" I ask, but Emma shakes her head.

"I'll figure it out. This is more important." She lays a hand on my arm, her touch soft on my skin. Again, I have to wonder why she wants to help. Her blue eyes hold my gaze before she steps back. "Next stop, some medical supplies."

I expect her to lead us to one of the tall steel buildings, assuming one of them is probably a pharmacy or hospital, but instead she leads us away from the city.

"What kind of medical supplies?" Jenny asks as we head toward a street lined with cookie-cutter two-story houses, a jarring difference from the shacks in Shadow Village.

"Well, you can't go on an epic journey without some safety equipment. Band-aids, wraps, pain medicine," Emma lists off.

"And where are we getting these supplies?" Wren asks, gesturing to the houses around us.

"My mom," Emma says, her voice stiff. "She's a nurse, so she has a stockpile of that stuff."

We stop outside of a two-story home. A white picket fence wraps around the property. Silver stones lead up to the porch. We follow Emma to the bright red front door. For a minute, Emma debates whether she should ring the doorbell or just go in. After she thinks about it, she decides to just enter the house, pushing open the unlocked door.

"Mom, it's me," Emma calls down the entrance hall.

"In the kitchen," a voice rings from the back of the house. Not knowing what we should do, we decide to continue following Emma. "Finally decided to stop by?" the voice asks as we walk into the kitchen.

The polished hardwood floor running under my feet is a big difference from the cracked boards in Emma's house. Glossy white cabinets hang from the walls. Emma's mom stands over a cutting board, chopping carrots, and her red nurse's uniform is vibrant in the neutral room. The resemblance between Emma and her mom is obvious. Her mom's blonde hair is shorter, but her blue eyes are just as bright.

"Oh, you brought guests," she says when her eyes reach me.

"Friends from school," Emma quickly lies.

"Ah," her mom says, putting the knife down and wiping her hands off on a towel.

"You're prepping dinner?" Emma asks, trying to start a conversation.

"Yes, I'm heading into the hospital soon. My shift starts at eight."

Emma lets out an uninterested hum.

"So, what do you need?" her mom asks, scraping the carrots into a sealed container. Somehow, she knows Emma wouldn't be here if she didn't need something.

"I was just going to grab some band-aids. I was in the area and figured I could pick some up. Is that okay?"

Her mother's curious gaze moves from Emma to us, her eyes lingering on all of our matching green backpacks. She purses her lips, knowing there's something Emma isn't telling her. She decides she'd rather not know and nods her head.

"Help yourself." Emma's mom hurries around the kitchen counter and heads toward the front door. She stops in the hallway and glances back at us one last time. "Are you sure you don't need anything else?"

"Nope," Emma quickly snaps.

"It was good to see you," her mom adds over her shoulder, and then closes the red front door behind her.

Emma lets out a tight breath, her tense shoulders visibly dropping.

"Your mom seems nice," I offer.

"She does her best," is all Emma says, and she leads us down a set of stairs toward the basement.

Storage shelves are packed to the ceiling of the tight space with various medical supplies. Emma hands each of us some bandages and wraps. She also finds some painkillers in the back.

"That should be good enough," Emma concludes, and we return upstairs.

"Why'd you tell your mom we were friends from school?" Wren asks and Emma has us sit at the dining table.

The dark wood flashes my reflection across its glossy finish, and from what I can see, I look frightening. My hair is a mess and—

"The less she knows, the better," Emma says, drawing my focus up from the table. "I'm willing to entertain the idea you may actually be from Earth because I saw you falling from the sky. She wouldn't have believed that, and I really don't want to get into it with her."

"So," Jenny says, leaning against the table. "Let's see this first card again."

Emma pulls out the cards, obviously wanting to change the conversation from her mom. She slides the card across the table. "*The*

Starting Rock," Emma reads aloud.

"*Before you begin, collect your token. You must look within, where your passion is open. Gold can begin the journey. Brown will fill those that are empty,*" Jenny reads the riddle.

"So, the starting rock is real. I've seen it," Emma says. "I was told some parents made it for their kids to use when playing the game, but if that's the real stone..." Emma trails off, and I know she's struggling to give in to the fact that this may be a real game and that we are dealing with actual magic.

"Let's just worry about the tokens first," Emma decides, shaking her head.

"So, it says we need to collect our tokens where our passions are open," Jenny speaks her thoughts aloud. "Does that mean we'll find our token where our passions are at?"

"I thought it might have something to do with a passion fruit," Wren says, his brows tightly furrowed. "Like within a passion fruit."

"I think you're taking it too literally," I say and Wren relaxes his brow, lifting his intense focus.

"What do you think?" he asks me, moving his brown eyes up from the card and meeting my gaze.

"I think Jenny might have the right idea," I admit and slide the card across the table to get a better look at it. "That would mean each of our tokens will be somewhere different because we all have different passions."

"Let's start with mine," Jenny offers. "Do you have soccer here?"

Emma shakes her head, but once Jenny explains what soccer is, Emma says they have a form of it that kids play.

"The fields aren't far from here. Just up the road," Emma says.

"Okay, we'll go there and see if we find any kind of token," Jenny says, pushing herself up from the table.

We pack the cards back into their velvet bag, and Jenny and Wren hurry toward the door. My movements seem to have slowed, my mind feeling like it's swimming in syrup.

"What's wrong?" Emma asks when she sees I haven't moved from the table.

"If we go out there, and there isn't a token, we'll be back at the beginning again," I say softly. The idea of this not working seeps into my thoughts. "Em, this has to work," I say, and meet her caring gaze.

"It'll work, Ash," Emma says confidently, leading me toward the door.

"Do you actually think so?" I ask, stopping in the narrow hallway.

I turn and face Emma, pressing my back against the wall. Her blue eyes are clouded as she considers it.

My breath catches in my throat when a beam of light streams in through the front window and makes her blonde hair glow. A piece falls over her shoulder and I have the strangest sensation to reach out and tuck it back for her. I'm not sure where these thoughts come from, why they suddenly cloud my head, but it's like time stops, the situation we're in fades, and it's just me and her. As if only her and I could exist in a moment as simple as watching the light warm her blonde hair, letting myself think about how beautiful she is—

Emma lets out a sigh and pushes the blonde curl behind her ear, pulling my focus back to reality and keeping my mind from wandering further. "I want it to work," she finally says, her eyes meeting mine, and I wonder if she can see on my face where my thoughts had drifted. "At first, I didn't care because I thought you guys may just be crazy, but now…" She pauses, her eyes searching me, tracing every inch so slowly time feels like it stands still again. "I want to help you," she breathes, her lashes fluttering and breaking the moment that built between us.

Emma moves toward the front door that Wren and Jenny have left open. Something about Emma's eyes searching my face, the way the sunlight glistened on her blonde hair, made my throat tighten, and I surprise myself with the sudden emotions I never would have thought would come over me at a time like this. Emma, a girl from Pintura, found a way to make my heart beat faster.

CHAPTER II

Emma

I lead the three *possible* lunatics from Earth toward the playing fields at the end of the road. On the bright green grass, kids run around kicking a brown lumpy ball. I glance at Jenny and see her face has brightened a bit at the sight of the field.

"Any idea what we're looking for?" I ask the group. Their silence is my answer. "Okay, then," I say and start to close in on the field. "Let's walk around and see if anything sticks out to us."

I start by walking the perimeter of the field, using my foot to push the grass to the side. Wren takes to climbing a few evergreen trees at the corners of the field. Either because he really thinks the token will be up there, or maybe he thinks it'll give him a better view to find it. I'm hoping it's the latter, but with Wren, I guess you never know.

Ash mirrors my movements on the other side of the field, keeping his eyes peeled for anything out of the ordinary. At one point, he thinks he's found something, but it's only a worn piece of brown leather that had been ripped off the ball.

Jenny gets as close to the game as she possibly can, looking like she's itching to run out there with the kids. I think this may be a lost cause after all.

"Hey, we're playing here!" a kid yells.

I snap my head up from the grass and see Jenny running through the players to the center of the field, her torn black shirt exposing her stomach. Without giving it a second thought, I run out and join her. She crouches over a patch of dirt and digs her fingers into the mud. A tiny flake of gold shines back. When she pulls the object from the mud, an excited scream escapes her mouth.

"This is it, right?" She shows it to me, like I'm supposed to know what the fictitious tokens look like.

I examine the small gold triangle pendant in her hand. It does resemble the little triangles that border the cards. Before I can answer her, the group of kids circle around us.

"What's that?" one of them asks, the triangle reflecting in her wide eyes.

"Nothing," Jenny says, clenching her hand closed in a tight first around the token.

"It's on our field," the girl says, her curious tone switching to moody anger.

"I said it's nothing," Jenny repeats, stepping back from the kids.

"Just get back to your game," I say. I pick up my pace, grab Jenny's wrist, and hurry from the field before anything else can happen. If this really *is* a token, and Ending in Cadence *is* instructions to a portal, we don't want anyone else trying to figure it out.

"Did you find it?" Ash asks when we hurry past him. He falls in step with us as we walk further away from the fields.

"Nope, didn't find anything," I say intentionally loud enough for the kids behind us to hear. I tuck my hands into the pockets of my navy overalls and steal a glance over my shoulder. The kids have abandoned their game and are digging in the spot Jenny pulled up the golden token.

"Then why are we leaving?" Ash asks.

Jenny shoots him a look that only a brother and sister could understand because he stops asking questions and just follows our lead.

When we pass the tree at the end of the field, Wren falls from its lowest branch and we huddle near the trunk. Jenny lets her tightly grasped fingers fall open and the muddy, golden triangle shines back. Wren's hand covers his mouth when his jaw drops open. My excited eyes find Ash. He looks at the token in disbelief. The corners of his mouth turn into an open grin. His eyes flicker up from the token to me.

"This is real," he says softly.

"*Probably* real," I correct.

He gives me a look that says *whatever you say*, and the corner of his mouth tugs up with the soft shake of his head.

"If we find another token, just like that, *then* it's real," Wren says, regaining his voice.

"How'd you find it?" Ash asks his sister.

"When I moved onto the field, I caught the light hitting it at just the right angle," Jenny explains.

"Do you think that has anything to do with how the magic of your world works?" Ash asks, turning his eyes up to meet mine.

My mind feels like it's in a void because I honestly have no idea.

"Maybe," I offer, but I shake my head in disbelief. "Like I said before, I don't know anyone alive that's seen an act of magic. Lord Neko is the only person capable of communicating to the world."

"What does that mean?" Jenny inquires, and I realize how crazy my last statement just sounded.

"By the power of his position, Lord Neko is able to talk with the world, or the part of it that has its abilities," I explain. "People all over Artmith meet with him to ask that he send requests to the world to heal loved ones or bring amounts of wealth to those who fall out of it. But I never paid much attention to any of that. Those requests have always seemed to fall on deaf ears. As far as I know, the world has never responded to the Lord or his messages. The world hasn't responded to anyone in a long time."

"Except now," Ash says, his voice sounding a bit distant.

"Except now," I agree.

"Well, Wren and I are both in band. Music is our passion. We should find our tokens next," Ash says. "Do you know where we should go, Em?"

"The University has a band," I offer. "We can start there." I hope my voice hides the tremor that crashes through me. That's the last place I want to go, but for something as important as finding a portal, I think I can push through the memories that linger there.

I lead them away from the fields and toward the University. Jenny twirls the golden pendant in her hand, still not believing this may be real. I can't believe it either.

"You should put that in your bag so you don't lose it," Wren offers.

Jenny does, but still keeps a protective grip on it, pulling her bag tight against her shoulders. When we get to the University, I lead them past University Hall and toward the other academic buildings on campus. Tucked away in the back is a small, square building. Its sides are marbled granite. The old wooden doors creak open and I lead them into the rehearsal space to my right.

When I enter the room, a nauseous wave unsettles me. I don't think I was ready to come back here just yet. I spent too much time here with my ex-boyfriend to be able to ignore the memories this room holds.

Jake Holland, first chair saxophone player and a freshman at the University, stole my heart last fall. I never felt like the kids my age ever understood me. When I started taking my elective classes here, I met Jake. The first person who didn't think I was weird for enjoying engineering or for being a little anti-social. The night I walked in on him kissing Tammy Lake in this very band room plays back in my head and my heart pounds as if I were living it again. Tammy Lake, of all people. A tall, blonde, business major. Slacking off in school on her father's money. The kind of person Jake and I talked about hating. The kind of person who's always making fun of me. And the worst part of it all, was that Jake didn't even freak out or try to deny it.

"Well, I guess you know, now. We're over, Em," his voice still echoes in the room.

Em, the nickname he made for me. The only friend I've ever actually had.

"Em, are you going to help us look?" Ash's blue eyes come into view.

"Yeah, sorry," I mumble and start pacing the room with them.

I try to push Jake and Tammy out of my head and focus on finding Ash and Wren's tokens. It's not worth my time to think about them anymore. Especially when I have something as important as a portal to Earth on my mind.

Could you imagine the technology or engineering behind that? Or even more spectacular, *the magic.*

Ash searches the back of the room where the drums are. He turns over the snare drums and runs his hand along the golden cymbals. Wren sits where he says the trumpet section normally is. He goes on about how much he misses band, and then he and Ash get lost in a conversation about some song they played at their last concert.

"Focus," Jenny groans, coming up from under a row of chairs. The boy's conversation falls quiet, but I watch Wren's eyes light up.

He stands and hurries across the room to a wall of barred lockers. Wren runs his hand across the middle row until he finds one that's unlocked. He lifts the latch and pulls out a dark brown leather case.

"You shouldn't mess with that. That's someone's trumpet, Wren," Jenny says, hurrying to his side.

Wren ignores her and flips the two front latches, opening the leather case. He pulls out the shiny trumpet and flips it over in his hands.

"There's nothing there. Now put it back," Jenny hisses.

Wren begins to push down on the three piston buttons at the top of the trumpet. Suddenly, there's a little rattle that comes from inside the horn. Wren tips it forward and shakes the instrument until something falls out and taps across the floor.

"Oh, it's real now!" he yells, and drops to his knees, scooping up whatever had fallen out of the trumpet. He stands and shows us the little triangle token.

"How'd you do that?" I ask.

"What do you mean?"

"One second there was nothing there and the next, it was inside the trumpet."

"I don't know, it just appeared," Wren says, flipping his token over in his hands. It matches Jenny's perfectly. "It's magic," Wren concludes.

"I'm still hesitant to believe that magic is real," I admit.

"Really? And what do you call us falling through a painting and ending up here?" Jenny asks.

I'm quiet, not sure *what* to call it. All my life I denied the whispers about the history of Artmith. I thought the worshipers of the land had lost their minds. Wren holds the token up and it reflects in the florescent lights.

"It's a definite match," he says. "This *is* real!" he repeats, his voice growing with excitement. I look down at the bag of cards around my wrist. Are these actually instructions to a portal? Earth is *real*? How has no one discovered this before?

"Have you found yours, Ash?" Jenny turns, ponytail flying side-to-side.

He lets out an exhausted huff from the back of the room. "I don't see anything," he complains.

Together we check every inch of the room and double check everything that has anything to do with drumming, but come up empty-handed.

"Ash," I say, my voice breaking the frustrated silence that has fallen over the room. I have an idea of where his token may be, but I bite my tongue. I don't want to say it and be wrong.

"What is it, Em?" he asks, his voice lifting with hope. Bright blue eyes look at me, begging me to tell him that I found the token.

"What if your passion isn't drumming?" I offer. "What if it's acting?"

Jenny lets out a cackle of a laugh, and Wren looks at me like I'm crazy.

"Yeah, right," Wren says. "This guy lives and breathes the drums."

While Jenny and Wren think the idea is ridiculous, Ash seriously considers it. His eyes trace the pair of drumsticks balanced in his hands.

Ash told me last night he liked acting. I got the feeling then that he may like it more than he lets on, probably for this exact reason; afraid his sister and friend would judge him.

"Where do you think we should go?" Ash asks hesitantly.

"The public theater in town is the only place I can think of," I offer. I've only been there a handful of times to watch the free shows, but it's our best bet.

"Ash, you get the lead in one play. That doesn't make acting your passion," Jenny says, crossing the room to her brother.

"Well, the token's not here," Ash says, frustration filling his voice once more. He throws the drumsticks back into the box he pulled them from.

"Let's just try it," I offer.

Jenny rolls her eyes. "Whatever. If we're going to go, then let's do it."

I turn and head toward the exit, racing to leave the memories in this room behind me. When I speed out of the rehearsal room, taking the turn so fast I nearly trip over my own feet, I run directly into *his* hard chest.

"Shit, sorry," I breathe and stumble back. "*Jake,*" I gasp, his name flying from my mouth when my eyes meet his green gaze. I take another step back, trying to put some distance between us. Tammy hovers just behind him.

Jake *and* Tammy. My heart tightens, a burning nausea creeping up my throat.

"Hey, Em," he says coolly, and the sound of my name on his lips makes my vision turn red.

Once the shock settles, I build up a stiff wall. "I don't think you get to call me that anymore," I say through a tight jaw.

His face hardens and his eyes move from me to the three behind me. "What are you guys doing here? Hopefully not looking for another fight."

Of course, they met Jake at the arcade last night.

"We never cheated," Wren speaks up, but he slips behind Ash.

Jake shakes his head, and it looks like he's about to dismiss us altogether, until his eyes widen, studying Ash's clothes.

"That's my shirt!" Jake points his finger toward Ash, the white shirt I gave him last night having belonged to my ex-boyfriend.

Dammit, of course this would happen.

Ash looks at me, now understanding where the clothes really came from.

"That's all mine," Jake continues, realizing Wren is also wearing his clothes.

"If you wanted them, you shouldn't have left them at my house," I speak up, pulling his attention back to me.

"You didn't give me the chance to come and get them," Jake quickly retorts, but I'm not going to stand here and engage with him.

"And you know exactly why I didn't!" I raise my voice and Jake's face falls, taken aback by my words. He knows exactly what I mean. If he didn't have his tongue down Tammy's throat, maybe I would have returned his stuff. "We're leaving," I add, and step around him to head toward the exit. Jenny and Wren quickly follow, keeping their heads down. When Ash crosses Jake's path, Jake puts a hand up to stop him.

"From one guy to another, don't waste your time with *that* one," Jake says, scanning Ash up and down.

Ash's jaw visibly tightens, but he keeps his words inside. He pushes Jake's arm down and walks around him.

"See you later, *Em*," Jake taunts.

I cringe at my name coming from his mouth again, but I keep putting one foot in front of the other.

"Hey!" Ash yells, turning around to face Jake, who still stands outside the rehearsal room.

"Ash," I hiss at him, but he ignores me.

"She told you not to call her that."

There's a moment of stiff air forming in the narrow hallway, and when Jake steps toward us, I know we need to go. *Now*. My hand latches around Ash's wrist and I pull him outside. We take large, hurried steps away from the building and catch up with Jenny and Wren. I glance over my shoulder and see Jake watching us from the doorway. He doesn't follow, but his narrowed stare watches us until we turn out of view.

"You and the arcade guy have history?" Ash asks when he guesses we're out of earshot.

"Yes, Jake Holland," I answer shortly, hating that I have to speak his name. "Of course he had to be there. And with Tammy of all people."

"What happened between you two?" Jenny asks, her stare burning into the side of my face.

My cheeks flush hot with anger. "Ex-boyfriend," is all I say and my words are dry in my throat.

"Hey," Jenny says, dropping her voice as she and I fall a step behind the boys. Her eyes are wide with sympathy, and I can tell she sees just how much pain rakes through me at the thought of Jake. "You deserve better than him."

"How can you say that? You don't even know what happened," I ask, surprised by Jenny's response.

"I don't need to know what happened," she says with a shrug. "Girl code and all."

"Girl code?" I ask, wondering if this is something from her world, or something I don't understand because I've never had close friends.

"Yeah, girl code. No matter what, I've got you, Emma." Jenny throws an arm around my shoulder and gives me a quick hug from the side. "Friends stick together through this stuff."

My mind catches on that one word, narrowing in on it with laser focus. *Friends...*

Before I can say anything more to Jenny, she drops her arm and rejoins Wren and Ash's conversation, which has drifted to food. After spending the morning looking for Jenny and Wren's tokens, it's past noon. We each pull out one of our granola bars and eat as we walk. It may just be my imagination, but Wren and Ash seem more uncomfortable in the clothes I gave them.

I try to shake the thought of seeing Jake, but I can't stop the wave of memories from flooding through my brain. I sat next to him in my introduction course to Mechanical Engineering the first day. Immediately, he had latched on to me, saying he'd be happy to tutor me in the class since I was the youngest—the only high school student that wanted to take it as an elective course. Most of the kids my age took art appreciation or business ethics, but I took the hardest elective possible.

The memories of fall nights wrapped in the crisp autumn air burn my throat. We had studied together on the quad, and he walked me home, all the way to Shadow Village, every single night.

Jake took me to the band room for the first time last winter. I remember the snow crunching beneath my boots as we raced for the warmth of the band room, and he played his saxophone for me for the very first time. I had been consumed by his talent, his number one cheerleader.

After that, we spent every night there; him playing, and me pretending to do my homework while I'd listen to him play. I confided in him about feeling alone and misunderstood by my peers. I told him things I hadn't ever dared speak aloud before then.

And last month, as spring warmed Artmith and the snow from one of the coldest winters I'd ever seen finally melted away, I walked into the band room and found his mouth on Tammy's.

She's not even *in* band. She wasn't in our classes. I have no idea how Jake even knows her, and somehow, he knew her well enough to kiss her. To kiss her like he had never kissed me.

Tears burn my eyes and I curse under my breath as I wipe them away. *Stop thinking about this. You have to stop thinking about it.*

It's only been a month, but it has been the hardest four weeks I've lived through. My loneliness doubled and my heart hasn't quite stopped aching. I tried to throw myself into my work at the scrapyard, my inventions, but somehow, I always end up thinking about him.

Jenny bursts out a laugh at something Wren says and I look at the three of them walking beside me, pointing to things in the city that I don't even notice anymore.

Finding the three of them in that field yesterday was the first time in a month that I didn't feel alone in Pintura.

CHAPTER 12

Emma

I lead us through town and we turn down a maze of dirt roads. As we move further into the city, they change to cobblestone paths. Nestled in the heart of Artmith is the public theater. The white marble sides of the building stretch into the sky. Flakes of gold in the stone reflect the sunlight. Usually, the theater remains open all the time unless there's rehearsal for an upcoming show.

I pull open the heavy doors and lead us into the vestibule. A dark red carpet runs under our feet and warm, yellow lights burn above our heads.

"Auditorium is this way," I say, waving them past the dark ticket booths.

The silence on the other side of the door confirms that there's no one here right now. Slowly, I push open the doors and fumble into the dark auditorium.

"Are you sure we can be in here?" Wren whispers into the dark.

"We're fine," I say and slide my hands along the wall until I find the light switch. When I click it on, the small lights along the rows of seats glow softly. Plush red stadium chairs stretch out to my right and left. The wooden stage stands on display in front of us.

"I'll look for the other lights," I say and walk along the side of the room. The soft seat lighting will make it hard to find anything.

Jenny searches the chairs to the right and Wren tries the left. Each of them flips down a seat and runs their hands along the backs in case it could be hidden there. Ash moves toward the front of the auditorium, like a magnetic force is pulling him down the center aisle. He hoists himself up onto the dark wooden stage, arms flexing beneath his weight.

I climb up a staircase and into the left stage wing. I run my hands along the black wall until they fumble on another switch. This time, a buzzing spotlight warms above the audience. The ray of white light grows brighter and streams down on Ash.

He stands center stage, his shoulders pulled back, looking out into the audience. The rays from the stage lights catch on his dark brown hair and muscular arms, pulling out their sculpted details through his shirt. With the bright light, you can't see anything in front of the stage except for the glowing beams cascading a blanket of white around the auditorium.

His face sets in a serious and dreamy haze. Looking at him, there on the stage, makes me want to *see* him perform. I can tell the passion for acting is written all over his face. For the first time since they arrived in Pintura, Ash looks at peace.

I stand on my tiptoes and stride onto the stage as if I'm wearing tall heels, and I'm ready to see him put on a show.

"My Royal Highness, how extravagant you look in your uniform," I say in the oddest accent I can muster.

Ash flashes his serious stare to me and I fall into a low curtsy. I peer up from the gesture and the corners of his lips pull into a smile.

"What are you doing, Em?" Ash asks through his growing grin.

Still in my curtsy, only letting myself break character for this instance, I whisper, "Play along."

"Em—" Ash tries to shut down my stunt once again, a warm blush spreading across his face. I find it charming that the boy who fell from the sky yesterday is embarrassed.

"That's Lady Em, to you," I correct, rising from my curtsy, taking another step toward Ash, before diving back into an even deeper curtsy. "My Royal Highness, how extravagant you look in your uniform," I try again, repeating my line from earlier.

Ash lets out a soft chuckle, and after another second passes, he finally says, "Why, thank you," snapping into a deep bow and becoming his own character.

I pull out of my curtsy and smoothly glide toward him. I extend my hand and say, "May I have this dance?"

Ash stands straighter, acting like a king. "It would be my honor," he says very formally.

One of his hands finds my waist, the other closing around my palm. I place my other hand on his shoulder. We step around the stage, taking large strides. His warmth seeps from his hand to my waist, and I feel myself growing more comfortable at his touch. No longer finding it weird to be so close to someone from another world.

We fill our heads with imaginary music, and Ash softly hums along to it. The stage lights make me feel like we're the only two people in all of Artmith right now.

Suddenly, Ash steps back from me, still keeping his hand in mine, and signals for me to twirl. He gently twists me around, pretending I have a large ball gown on instead of navy overalls. When he pulls me back toward him, my feet quickly spin me into his arms, and then he dips me back.

The air races from my lungs as my head falls back, blonde curls reaching for the floor. Where the perfect moment should freeze, it doesn't.

Ash loses his balance, dropping to his knee. I let out a short squeal, landing on my rear. Ash's strong arms quickly wrap around my back when we fall, keeping me from hitting my head.

A laugh escapes us both and his body shakes against mine. I try to search for a witty comment. Something to say about his acting or dancing, but when my blue eyes meet his stare, there are no words that come to mind. Our faces are just a breath apart. I can see the golden flakes in his eyes, surrounded by the purple rim of the bruise that looks awfully painful. I have the strangest urge to run my fingers through his thick, dark hair. My gaze sweeps across the light brown freckles on his sun-kissed skin, wanting to count each one of them. I lose my breath at the sight of his wide smile and bring my gaze back to his blue irises.

The scent of a warm summer day clings to him. I can smell the metallic aroma of Artmith on him too, but beneath that is something I don't recognize. It's foreign, and I realize it's from his world. It smells like salt, and fruit, and a woodsy plant I can't put my finger on.

A tingling spreads across my skin, all the way down to my toes. His eyes lock on my gaze, and just when I think we've been frozen for too long, I see something in his stare change. His eyes move slightly to the left, looking at something on the ground.

Ash's arms unravel from my waist and I prop myself up on my elbows. I glance over my shoulder at what pulled his attention from me and find a golden triangle token shimmering back. He quickly scoops it up, examining it.

"Guess acting is your passion," I say, my words finally coming back to me. They're breathy and my voice sounds nothing like itself.

This pulls his gaze from the token to me, and an awkward air settles. "That was some dance," Ash says softly, his voice thin like mine.

My face burns, and I don't think it's from the bright stage lights overhead. Too many emotions for me to sort out right now crash through me, and I desperately try to ignore them.

I pull myself to my feet, ignoring Ash's comment, and raise my hand to the light, shielding it so I can see out into the audience. Jenny and Wren are still crouched over a set of seats, not noticing the show we had put on.

"We found it!" I call from the stage, my voice echoing and getting swallowed up in the enormous auditorium.

I spin around to head off the stage when Ash is suddenly standing behind me. "Did something just happen?" he asks, wide eyes sweeping my face.

The corners of my mouth pinch too tightly with my forced smile. "No, nothing happened," I say with as much indifference as I can form before stepping around him and heading toward the staircase in the wing. I try to move quickly, ready to leave that exchange with Ash behind us. I'm not sure what came over me.

Ash follows, and by the look on his face, I know he's pushing that moment away too; both of us not sure what to make of it and preferring to just forget it happened.

Nothing happened.

When we reach Jenny and Wren, they hold out their matching tokens, excitement buzzing in the air.

"I can't believe it was actually here," Wren says softly, looking up at Ash.

"Do you really love acting that much?" Jenny questions, her voice not as gentle as Wren's.

I don't think she means it to be harsh, but utter shock and confusion sharpen her words.

Ash shrugs, clearly not sure how to explain how much he must love acting. "Maybe the game didn't want two tokens so close to each other. Wren's had to be in the band room, but mine had a second option," he says, dismissing the importance of this moment. Jenny and Wren seem to accept his explanation, knowing it's far easier to believe drumming is still most important to Ash than to question what he clearly doesn't want to discuss. After a moment, they all look at me.

"We need to find yours," Ash says.

"I'm not trying to go back to Earth," I say.

"Yeah, but you need a token if you're going to help us with the cards," Jenny explains.

"I don't know," I stammer. *What if I can't find one?* I don't want to hold them up. Something about the three of them being from Earth and finding these tokens makes me feel like they're in a special elite group I'm sure I don't belong to.

"Come on, Em," Ash says, pushing my shoulder playfully, loosening any lingering tension.

"Your passion is engineering, right?" Wren asks, moving to store his token in his bag. "It'll probably be at the scrapyard."

"No," I say, letting out a sigh. "*If* I have a token, it'll be at the COT."

"Well, lead the way," Ash says, gesturing toward the door.

Reluctantly, I lead them from the theater and Ash and Jenny put their tokens in their bags.

"So, what's the COT?" Ash asks when we come out into the afternoon sun.

I head toward the tall industrial buildings that rise above Shadow Village. "It's the Center of Technology," I explain.

"And your token will be there *because*," Ash prompts me, waiting for me to fill in the blank.

"Because that's where all the engineers work. I've only dreamed about it my whole life," I admit.

"So, if you got your degree, you'd work there?" His side-glance traces my profile.

"If I could pass all the exams to get the degree, yes," I say. "They work directly with the Patrol, since a lot of their inventions have to do with running the regulations the Patrol sets for us. The Patrol and the engineers share the COT as their headquarters."

After weaving through the tall buildings, we come to a stop outside a jet-black tower. It has three tall legs that stretch toward the sky, forming an abstract, futuristic pyramid. It won't be as easy to get in here.

"Any ideas on where we should go?" Jenny asks, taking in the building.

"I shadowed an engineer here this past semester when I took my elective courses at the University," I explain and lead them down a narrow alley along the building. "We can get in back here, but we can't be seen once we're inside."

"What happens if we're caught?" Ash asks, dropping his voice to a whisper as we near a steel door that's propped open by a grey cinderblock.

I was hoping Zane would leave the back entrance open. He always forgets to close it after his breaks.

I turn back, sending a serious gaze their way. "We can't get caught," I order, not wanting to discuss the consequences trespassing into the engineering and Patrol building will have.

We slip in through the side door on one of the steel legs and I start gliding across the bright white tiles. My feet move quickly, guiding us as fast as I can toward the design room. The path there is still in my head and I trust my feet to take me there. I double check every corner or hallway we turn down, but the building seems to be abnormally quiet today. The elevator is too much of a risk, so we climb the narrow staircase all the way to the engineering floor.

When I see the long stretch of clear plexiglass coming up ahead, I start to let myself relax. The double swinging doors don't lock, so I push my way into the room, glancing around to make sure we're alone. The design room is divided into two sections, one being rows of boxy computers and the other being a small testing lab.

Afraid someone may hear us, we don't speak and instead, split up, scanning for the golden triangle token. I check by the computers first. I spent most of my time over here, helping Zane draft new designs in a 3D model. When I come up empty handed, my heart dips. I knew I shouldn't have come looking for the token. As much as I'd love to be a part of this group and their world, I don't belong. I'm not special like they are.

Ash, Jenny, and Wren ruffle through the drawers on the other side that have weights and tools inside. Ash slides the bottom drawer closed, turning to give me a sympathetic look.

Something different happened when they found their tokens. *What was special about those moments?* Jenny was running onto the soccer field, Wren was pressing the keys on the trumpet, and Ash was acting like a king. They found their tokens in moments where they were *doing* their passions. My eyes land on the 3D printer in the corner of the room, the only place I haven't looked.

My feet lead me over to it, feeling heavier with defeat. I peer into the tinted plastic cover, scanning the empty tray. Tentatively, I lift my hand to the monitor and tap the screen to life. The lights inside the printer respond, buzzing to a neon blue. It's *still* empty. Just when I'm about to back away from the printer, a dark shadow on the tray begins to lift and mold before my eyes. My fingers fly to the clasp and I pull open the printer. Lying in the center of the tray is a *gold triangle token.*

My hand actually shakes as I reach in and lift it. When I feel it's cool, metal finish in my fingers, my mind registers that this *is* real. This *is* mine. Magic may have truly returned to Pintura. I turn and show it to Ash, Jenny, and Wren. I widen my mouth and give an airy, silent scream. Ash and Wren do an air high-five and Jenny gives me two thumbs up.

Looking at them, genuinely excited for me, makes it even harder to believe this is real. I actually have *friends.* I'm really a part of something. Something that's bigger than my illegal engineering business and my job at the scrapyard.

The slam of a door out in the hall makes my heart hit the floor, the blood in my veins freezing. The color drains from their faces, wide eyes looking at me for what we should do. Out of instinct, I drop to the floor and crawl to the wall underneath the plexi-glass windows, hoping whoever it is can't see us down here.

Ash, Jenny, and Wren follow my lead and press their backs against the wall. We hold our breaths and wait as the footsteps grow louder. It's a group of people, the sounds of the different shoes mixing together.

"They should be back soon, right?" I hear a voice ask.

"Yes. We should report to the meeting room. They're going to have a lot to discuss," a woman says.

"What do you think it is?" the first voice asks.

"I think we're looking at a bigger problem than a storm," the woman answers, her voice just outside the design room.

Their shadows stretch through the windows and across the floor. I watch as they slide through the room, waiting for them to move out of the hall. The shadows slip away and the footsteps fade until silence returns to the building.

"Let's go," I whisper, and the three of them nod in agreement.

My feet take off again, flying over the white tiled floors all the way back to the propped open door in the alleyway. I stumble out into the thick afternoon heat, my legs numb from nerves. I almost can't hold myself up.

"That was the scariest thing I've ever done!" Wren yells as soon as we're out of the building.

"Told you we'd find your token," Jenny says.

"We should move before someone sees us," I say, breathing hard from our race out of the building. I slide my token into my backpack as we sneak away. We come out of the alleyway and I take them toward the large fountain in the center of the city. A gathering of people splash in the fountain or lay at its edge; either off early from work or just too financially secure to have a job.

"What's next?" Ash asks me.

"Next, we need to go to the starting rock," I say. "I think I know where it is. I mean, I didn't know it might be the *real* rock until today, but I bet it is."

"So, you believe?" he asks, lips twisting into a smile.

"I *may* believe," I offer, but the energized nerves buzzing inside me scream otherwise.

I do believe. I want to believe that they are my friends. I'm ready to believe that I can be a part of something as epic as discovering a portal to Earth.

"Where's the starting rock at?" he asks, eager to keep moving.

Now that we know the cards may in fact be real instructions, I'm also eager to see what will happen next.

"It's out in the Infinity Forest," I say and start heading past the fountain and toward the gates that surround Artmith. Now that I have my own token, I feel even more a part of this journey. My steps are quicker and my heart pumps harder. But when the gates come into view, my heart almost stops beating altogether.

Rows and rows of Patrol officers are marching into the city.

"Best to stay out of their way," I mumble. I drop my head and file to the edge of the street where the other civilians have been escorted. We fall behind the larger crowd and watch the Patrol move into Artmith.

Their uniforms are a tight, black mesh. Red helmets cover their faces, making them even more terrifying. Never cross anyone in the Patrol. It's the first thing everyone is taught. Their black boots crunch the dirt beneath their feet. They move together in unison, heading toward the COT. Thank the stars above, we just missed them.

Once they've cleared the street, I start moving toward the gate again. When I see the iron bars rattle shut, I stop in my tracks. I flip my wrist and my watch glows *5:00 p.m.*.

"We're too late." I glance at Ash, worry settling on his face. When he sees I'm staring at him, he tries to hide it.

"It'll have to wait until tomorrow, won't it?" he asks.

I see the disappointment in his eyes. This means it's another night here. Another night away from his family. I'd almost be willing to face the vainders if I didn't have any common sense.

"I'm sorry," I say, even though they aren't the words I meant to speak. "Yes, first thing tomorrow," I add.

Without saying much else, I lead them back toward my home. The only thing I can think about is the weight of the cards in my bag. The heavy stack telling me that this journey will be many more nights.

CHAPTER 13

Emma

The next morning, we wake at dawn and head to the starting rock. They didn't complain about having to eat beans again for dinner. Wren even made a point to say that they were better the second time. Ash seemed distant for most of the night. I'm sure he was thinking of home.

Jenny and Wren completely ignored the fact that Ash's token was at the theater. I wondered if it weighed on Ash at all. I was too afraid to ask because I didn't want to acknowledge the energized moment we shared. After I gave it some thought, I decided I just felt that way because I had seen Jake earlier. Maybe something about the encounter with Jake made me subconsciously look at Ash as a boyfriend, especially after he stood up for me. But even if that was true, Jake never made me feel like *that*. Like the way Ash did in the theater…

"Your hair looks great like that," Jenny says, running her hand down the single braid she did for me this morning.

I glance at her and smile as we pass through the iron gate. She still wears the torn black shirt, the hem barely reaching the waistband of her shorts. There are words I want to say right now. I want to thank her for braiding my hair, for wanting to be my friend, but I'm not sure what those words would be. I've never had friends before.

"Will there be other people at the rock?" Wren asks, peering around Ash's shoulder. Both of them traded in the set of clothes they wore yesterday for the ones from Earth, now that they were clean and dry.

"Not today," I say, forcing words past my nerves. "Finals are today," I explain.

"You don't have any?" Ash asks, speaking for the first time this morning.

"Last year students have already taken their Completion Exam instead of finals." There's a silence that settles in the air as we make our way closer to the Infinity Forest. As soon as the silence expands around us, the nerves come back, so I try to make the conversation continue and hope the nerves go away.

"Do you have finals?" I ask.

"Should be taking them right now."

Great. I shouldn't have brought up their home, but something on Ash's face lightens and he lifts his head a little.

"I guess I won't have to take those now." He almost laughs through the words.

"I'm sure we'll have to make them up," Wren says.

"They'll probably be revised, though," Jenny offers.

"Yeah, we could come back and be ready for college," Wren says, nudging Ash.

"Man, I can't believe college is so close."

The three of them continue to talk about what they may be missing out on back on Earth. Some things they're happy to miss, like finals. Others, they're a bit upset about. They say it's called a Graduation Ceremony, where everyone comes together and congratulates them on completing their classes. Jenny isn't upset because she'll be graduating next year, but I wish I had something like that. The whole thing sounds so exciting, and I wish they didn't have to miss it. I just got a pat on the back from my favorite teachers, a stiff handshake from the principal, and a folded piece of paper with my test results saying I had passed. No speeches, nothing with my classmates. No music or parades, no gowns or sparkling caps or confetti. No photos, no memories, and no family.

We make it through the Golden Field and reach the edge of the forest that hangs to the right of Artmith after about an hour. We break into another round of granola bars and head into the dark mass of trees. It's still early in the morning, so the weak sunrays barely break through the thick canopy of green leaves overhead. The forest hangs in a grey morning haze and I'm careful to stay on the narrow path flattened out by the many other kids who've ventured to the starting rock.

The three of them do seem a bit out of their element, always looking in the direction of snapping branches.

"How far is it?" Jenny asks me.

"A couple of hours. We'll get there right before noon," I say.

"That's pretty far from here. Kids really come all the way out here to play at the rock?" Wren asks, and I shake my head.

"Honestly, it's more known as a hideout. A place they go to get away from their parents. I mean, I was never really a part of those get-togethers. Especially after I started taking extra classes at the

University." What I mean to say is, after I started seeing Jake, I stopped seeing anyone my age.

"Oh, kind of like Lover's Lake," Wren says, turning to Jenny, whose cheeks shift to a bright pink. She lets out a low hum, not saying anything else.

"Lover's Lake?" I ask, my voice tilting up.

Ash nods and says, "It's this place in California, where we live. Everyone goes there on dates."

"That's supposed to be romantic?" I ask. "Wouldn't you want your own spot? Not one that everyone uses."

"I've never been there," Ash explains, dismissing the idea altogether. "I've heard it's nice, though."

"So, graduation and Lover's Lake. What else do you have back home?" Almost as soon as I ask, I regret it. The three of them go on for *hours*. Apparently, Earth is bigger than I ever imagined, with all kinds of places and people living there.

They talk a lot about California. Jenny tells me all about soccer and her teammates, and how she's going to play in the Olympics one day. When I tell them I don't know what that is, they go into an entire new round of stories.

My favorite to hear about are the cities. They make them sound so magical. The bright lights and flying machines. It's technology I never would have thought existed. Pintura is small enough to go anywhere on foot. It may take an hour or two, but you can get there. The Patrol are the only people who have automobiles. I've seen the big boxy vehicles every once in a while when there's an issue in town.

They tell me they left their phones in their cars when they were packing up Ash and Jenny's grandmother's things or else they'd show me them.

"This is the kind of money we have," Wren says, pulling out a green paper rectangle. It's much softer than the thick, red bills we use.

"Who's that?" I ask, pointing to the face staring back at me.

"Mr. Ben Franklin," Wren says, taking the bill back and putting it in his pocket. "He's on every one-hundred dollar bill."

"One-hundred," I say, considering it. "Is that a lot on Earth? That would be a lot here."

"Yeah," Ash says. "That's pretty similar, then."

They tell me about other inventions they think I'd like. Most of it sounds made up, honestly. But that doesn't mean it's impossible. I store some ideas in my head of things I could try to make from the scrapyard.

It's late morning now and we should only have a little bit further. When I make that announcement, they start walking faster, taking off in front of me.

"Watch where you're going!" I yell up to them, their backpacks bouncing on their backs.

"Emma, you'd love the national parks we have back home," Jenny calls back to me.

"Jenny, you hate hiking," Ash nags her.

"I don't—" Jenny starts to say, but lets out a scream so loud hidden birds in the trees take flight.

She stumbles back into Ash, knocking him and Wren to the ground. Jenny trips over their fallen bodies and tumbles off the trail and down a steep hill. A stray branch scratches her face and arms and she lets out another scream. I run up to Ash and Wren and see what scared Jenny.

A long, black snake is slowly uncoiling from a branch, his slick black body stretching all the way to the ground.

"Help!" Jenny screams from the bottom of the hill.

"Shhh," I hiss back to her. "No one move," I say. I try to keep my voice even so I don't startle the snake.

Frozen where we are, we watch the snake come down onto the path and slither away, deeper into the forest. Once his other end disappears into the underbrush, I take off down the hill for Jenny. Ash and Wren are close behind me, crashing through the fallen branches and leaves.

"Are you okay?" I ask her when I find her laying on her side in a thick bush.

"Is it gone?" she asks between terrified, shaking sobs. "Yes, it's gone. Are you okay?" I ask again, pulling her from the bush and sitting her up. Her face is damp with tears and her dirty hands are shaking.

"Gosh, I hate snakes," she almost shrieks, but another wave of shaky sobs has her gasping for breath.

"Calm down, Jen," Wren says, wrapping an arm tightly around her shoulders.

"Let's clean you up," I say and pull out some bandages and a bottle of water.

I use the water to wash away the mud that coats her knees and arms. I try to wash out the cuts on her hands and face before putting on the bandages, but she keeps flinching away.

"Hold still, Jenny," Ash says, helping me finish washing her cuts.

Once we get all the open wounds covered with bandages, Jenny has finally calmed down and stopped crying.

"Ready to keep going?" Ash asks her.

"How about you drink some water first," I say, handing her what's left of the bottle I had used to rinse her hands. She sips on it and leans into Wren, who's still trying to comfort her.

"How much further?" Ash asks me.

"Not too far. We're just about there," I say.

Once Jenny finishes the water, we help her up to her feet. Immediately, she lets out another cry of pain and drops back to the ground.

"My ankle," she says through gritted teeth, fresh tears threatening to seep out of her tightly closed eyelids.

I hadn't looked at her ankle. Ash slowly pulls off the shoe on her right foot and she winces in pain. When he pulls down her black sock, I see her ankle is a deep shade of purple.

"That's not good," I admit, and her eyes fly open with worry.

"What's wrong?" she cries.

"Sorry, I didn't mean to worry you," I say.

When she sees the discolored ankle, she mumbles something under her breath. She's an athlete and by how she described soccer, she's probably had her fair share of ankle injuries.

"I hope it's just twisted," she says, wiping away the escaped tears. "Can I have some wraps?"

I hand her the ones from my bag and she makes quick work on her ankle. It's too swollen to get the shoe back on, so Jenny puts it in her bag. We slowly pull her back up because she claims she'll be able to walk on it, but it's obvious she won't be able to make it more than ten steps.

"Let me carry you, Jen," Wren offers, grabbing Jenny to steady her before she falls again.

"I'm fine, Wren." Jenny tries to push him away.

"Even if you could walk, which you can't," Wren adds, "You may step on something and make it worse."

"He's right, Jenny," Ash says and I see the look of defeat cross her face.

"Oh, all right," she huffs.

Ash takes Wren's backpack and combines it with his own while Jenny loops her arms around Wren's neck and he hoists her onto his back.

"Maybe you should go back to leading," Wren offers, nodding at me.

We hike back up the hill and continue on our path. Wren and Jenny share a hushed conversation and fall back a few steps from Ash and me.

"Sorry Jenny slowed us down," Ash admits to me when he thinks Jenny and Wren can't hear us.

"It's okay," I say, quickly brushing it off. "I'm terrified of snakes, too."

"Really? You seemed so calm back there." His blue eyes search my face to see if I'm lying or not.

"It's not my first run in with them out here. Usually, they stay clear of the main paths," I explain. "But with finals and school wrapping up, I'm sure it's been awhile since someone was out here."

We're quiet for a moment, and I realize Ash is staring at me. Those thoughtful, sky-blue eyes locked on my face. The bruise beneath his eye has already started to fade.

"What?" I prompt him, suddenly aware of the loose pieces of my hair that are flying free from the braid and surrounding my face.

"Do you like living in Artmith?" he asks me.

I squint my eyes, confused by his question. "I don't think there's any other choice," I say.

"It's the only city in Pintura?"

"That's it. Pintura isn't that big. There's Artmith, the Golden Fields, the Infinity Forest, and Rising Salvation."

"And at the edge of all that? What's out there?" Ash asks, genuinely curious about my world after we spent most of the morning talking about his.

"Nothing," I say and shrug my shoulders. "It's a dead end in all directions. A complete drop off into a black nothing."

"This world just sits on a piece of land in the middle of a black-vast-nothing?"

"Yep. We're all that's here," I say and watch him as he processes this. "It's not like Earth, where you can go to all these different places and change where you live."

"I think you'd like Earth, Em," Ash admits suddenly.

I advert my eyes from his. I bet I would like Earth. The technology sounds like something I could only ever dream about. The options and places to visit make my head spin. And, of course, Ash would be there. Jenny and Wren, too. But Pintura is my home. That's where I live.

We crawl over some fallen tree trunks and into a round clearing with short grass.

"We made it," I announce with an accomplished sigh and lead Ash to the center of the clearing.

A round rock grows from the dirt beneath it. Large and smooth, it arcs up into the perfect half-egg shape. Indented all over its surface are tiny triangles. Maybe a hundred of them. Jenny and Wren come into the clearing, finally catching up.

"This is it," I say and wave them over. I search for the card in the velvet bag and reread the riddle.

YOU MUST LOOK WITHIN
WHERE YOUR PASSION IS OPEN

GOLD CAN BEGIN THE JOURNEY
BROWN WILL FILL THOSE THAT ARE EMPTY

I look up from the card to my three friends and shrug my shoulders. "I think we just place our tokens here."

We pull off our bags and remove our golden tokens. One by one, we place them into one of the triangle indentations. Ash goes first, and when his token slides in perfectly, we share a sharp gasp. Wren and Jenny add theirs and finally, I press mine into place. The rock hugs the token tightly. I step back and we wait for something to happen.

"Shouldn't we know if it worked?" Jenny asks, snapping her head between us.

"Read the card again," Ash says, and I read the riddle aloud. "Brown will fill those that are empty," he repeats the last line of the riddle, clearly the one thing we must be missing. He runs his fingers over the remaining triangle indentations. "Our tokens are gold. Maybe we should have found brown ones for the other holes?"

"But I don't know where those would be," I say.

I notice Jenny silently staring at the palms of her hands, still a little brown with dirt. *Brown.* Her eyes meet mine, sharing the same thought. I drop my gaze from her to the soft mud below our feet. The dirt here is slightly wet, like clay. Dirt that's a part of a world where magic is rumored to exist at its core.

"We have to fill the other holes with mud," Jenny says, dropping to the ground next to the rock. She scoops up a handful of the wet dirt and starts filling the empty triangle indentations with the brown paste.

"That way, the game knows how many people are playing," I say, joining her.

Ash and Wren share a skeptical glance, but soon join us and help fill in all the other holes.

"Last one," Jenny huffs, filling in the final cavity.

We stumble backward and for a second, the world continues to exist as it always has, until time seems to freeze. Every bird in the neighboring trees falls silent. The wind dies down and thickens around us, like everything is being pulled to a stop.

The ground beneath our feet starts to shake, a sudden jolt of movement in a world as still as death.

"Something's happening!" Wren yells out the obvious, his mouth spreading into an open grin.

The starting rock shakes and slowly turns itself into the ground. Its half-oval shape sinks into the dirt until its flat side faces up. The ground becomes steady again, and in a slow crescendo, the world around us buzzes back to life.

We close in on the now flat rock and read the carved words.

ENDING IN CADENCE HAS BEGUN
FOLLOW THE CARDS TO UNLOCK THE KEY TO EARTH

CHAPTER 14

Ash

T *his is real.* All of it. Pintura, Ending in Cadence, and this journey. I wanted to believe it when we found the matching tokens. I mean, what were the odds? But when the ground began to shake after we put in the tokens and the mud, that's when I knew.

We completed our first card. For a second, I'm so unbelievably relieved and enthused. When Emma dumps out the rest of the cards to find our next challenge, my heart drops. There are so many of them, and we need to complete them *all*. It will probably take days, weeks honestly. I thought that would scare me or upset me, but it doesn't. Yes, I'm worried about how my parents are reacting right now, but at least I know how to get home. I know what I need to do to fix this.

The second card is named *The Linked Star*, and it's about finding a certain constellation or something. It's clear that we can't start that challenge until tonight. We hike back through Infinity Forest and toward Artmith, not wanting to linger too long outside the wall that protects the city. Wren continues to carry Jenny with no complaint. I offer to give him a break, but he says he doesn't mind. Jenny, on the other hand, has her face set in a scowl the entire time. Though, I don't think that was anything against Wren. More likely, it's because she hates the idea of not being able to take care of herself.

This whole world—Pintura—is really growing on me, though. I find that I'm becoming a lot more relaxed here. Things are definitely different. The government, or Patrol, has a lot more control over its people. The idea of magic is definitely unusual.

Some things are the same though, or similar at least. The school and society, for example. I think we could have ended up somewhere a lot worse. I also just keep thinking about how lucky we are that Emma found us. She really *is* something else, though. I've never met anyone like her before.

Just that thought reminds me of our moment in the theater. I really thought about *kissing* her. I don't know what it was, but something about that moment, maybe it was her acting, wide blue eyes, or infectious smile that drove my emotions.

I think it could also be that she's the only person I feel has ever understood me or listened to me. No one else has ever considered my love for acting to be real. *I* didn't even think to consider it. I was confident my token would be in the band room, but I was wrong. Somehow, Emma may already know me better than I know myself.

"How's your ankle?" Emma asks Jenny as Wren lowers her onto the couch in Emma's small home later that evening.

"It's better," Jenny lies, wincing as she repositions herself across the worn cushions.

"After dinner, you can take more medicine for the pain. I'll get you a pack of ice for the swelling," Emma offers, moving toward the kitchen.

Once Jenny is comfortable and has a bag of ice on her ankle, we sit on the rough wooden floor boards in front of the couch with the cards spread between us. Emma puts a pot with beans on the stove and we wait for them to heat up.

"Let's go over the cards so we know what we're getting into," Emma says. There are eight cards in total. We are on number two, so I scoop that one up and read the riddle again.

LOOK ABOVE TO THE STARS
TO FIND WHERE YOU MUST GO

THE CIRCLES LINK ON THE CARDS
WILL LEAD YOU WHERE IT HANGS LOW

IF YOU TAKE WHAT THE STARS PROVIDE
BE PREPARED TO LEAVE SOMETHING ELSE BEHIND

A couple of things stick out to me at first. I'm hoping the mention of the stars is literal. I turn the card over in my hands, examining the linked circle design on the back. Maybe once we see the stars, the mention of the linking rings will make sense.

"Clearly, we'll need whatever is at this new location for card three," Jenny says, having read the card over my shoulder.

"What's card three say?" Wren asks as Emma picks it up off the floor.

She squints as she reads the riddle. "Something about a gift from the stars that we have to follow."

Wren and I scan the rest of the cards, all of them being a wide variety of puzzles and codes. My eyes keep being drawn to the last golden card. My key to getting home.

The beans in the kitchen let out a large pop.

"They're probably ready," Emma mumbles, dropping the third card and hurrying into the kitchen. She comes back over, handing us each a steaming bowl of beans.

We agree that once it's dark enough outside, we'll try to see something in the stars. If it's within the wall, we'll go to it tonight. I glance at Jenny on the couch. I hope it's close and not too far away because I don't know how far she can go on her ankle right now. If it's on the other side of the wall, we'll have to wait to go until tomorrow morning. That may be a good thing, though. It'll give Jenny some more time to rest.

After the day we've had, I devour the bowl of beans in a few bites, hardly even tasting them. Though, they already don't have much flavor.

"What food do you miss the most?" Emma asks me.

I had leaned back against the couch, closing my eyes. I crack one open and glance her way. I close my eye again and consider it.

"I could go for a cheeseburger right now. With ketchup and lettuce. Lots of pickles."

Wren lets out a muffled moan, imagining the meal. "That's the first thing I'm going to do when we get back. Order a big cheeseburger," Wren says, stacking his empty bowl in mine.

Jenny lets out a shallow laugh.

"What?" Wren asks defensively.

"I can't believe that's the first thing you want to do," Jenny says, rolling her eyes from the couch she's lounging across.

"What would you do?" Emma asks.

"Go see my parents so I can tell them I'm okay," Jenny says, like it's the only acceptable answer.

"Ash can do that," Wren says. He leans back and points a finger at Jenny. "I'm taking you out for a burger right when we get back."

I glance up at Jenny and she lets out a soft laugh, avoiding eye contact. I shift my stare between the two of them. Did Wren just ask my sister out on a date? And did my sister not immediately turn him down?

"Want to help me clean up?" Emma asks, nudging me as she stands.

"Sure," I say, scooping up the empty bowls. When we head to the kitchen, Wren and Jenny continue to talk in a soft conversation.

"So, are those two a thing?" Emma whispers over the rushing water from the sink.

"Not that I know of," I say, drying off the bowls as Emma hands them to me. "Before we came here, Wren and I hadn't spoken for years," I add.

"You seem close," she offers.

"We were," I admit.

"Why would you stop being friends with someone who obviously means so much to you?" Emma asks, and her eyes study me.

I wish I had an answer for her, but I can't think of a reason I'm proud to say.

"I only ask because I've never had a friend. Losing him as yours doesn't make much sense to me."

"We just drifted," I lie to Emma and myself. "That's what happens."

We're quiet and Emma stares at me, waiting for me to say more.

"What?"

"What's the real reason, Ash?" Emma asks, reading through my rehearsed excuse.

I sigh, and my stare drifts to the other walls in the kitchen. "Wren is just so," I start to say and then press my lips together. "He found his group of people. I didn't fit or *want* to be a part of that," I explain.

"You isolated yourself," Emma says softly. "I can understand that."

"Maybe that's what this whole mess is about," I say. "Maybe this is what Wren and I needed to restore our friendship."

Emma smiles at that. "I'm glad you fell through the painting, then. Everyone needs a friend."

I look at the girl in front of me, feeling like I'm seeing her for the first time. The overwhelming world of Pintura fades away and I just see her, living alone in Shadow Village, no mention of friends or anyone she knows besides that jerk, Jake. And he doesn't seem like someone she seems to want in her life. I don't know what happened between them, but I can't say I blame her. He hasn't made the best first impression on me.

I know what that's like, to feel like you are on your own. I know how lonely she must feel and it makes me want to say something to make her not feel so alone.

"We're your friends too, Em," I whisper, nudging her.

Her smile grows, and an echo of laughter that escapes from Wren and Jenny bleeds into the kitchen.

"I could see it," Emma says, glancing over at the two of them. "Wren and Jenny."

Instead of following her gaze or contemplating the same thing, my brain wonders if Emma could see *me* with *her*. Before I can let myself process the thought, there's a thunderous knock at the door.

"PATROL!" a deep voice shouts from outside.

Emma's face pales and the bowl she was rinsing slips through her wet fingers, shattering in the sink.

"Uh, one second!" Emma stammers, whispering curses under her breath.

She drops to the floor and crawls under the kitchen table. Her wide eyes meet mine and she says, "You should hide. Just in case." Emma rips the loose boards in the floor up and gestures for us to go below the house.

My stomach twists, the beans not settling with my rising nerves. Wren scoops Jenny up in his arms—grabbing all three of our backpacks in one movement—and hurries into the underground room. Emma's blue stare connects with mine for a second before I lower myself to the top step. The boards fall back into place and I'm surrounded by black. Slivers of light leak through the floorboards and I can just make out the room above.

I hear Emma move quickly to the front door, pulling it open.

"Good evening," she says and I can hear her voice shaking from here.

"Is everything all right?" a muffled, robotic voice asks. "We heard something shatter."

"Yes, I just broke a bowl while cleaning the dishes," Emma replies. "Is there something you need?" she asks and I hear her voice steady out, gaining back some control.

"We need to search the premise," the deeper voice that had announced the Patrol says.

"What for?" Emma immediately questions. There's a pause and then I hear Emma shuffle backward. "I'm sorry, that was rude of me. Of course, come in."

I swallow hard, imagining the army of Patrol members we had

seen yesterday; the slick red helmets and stiff suits. The chorus of boots marching above tells me there must be four or five of them. Out of the corner of my eye, I can barely see Jenny shaking against Wren's tight grasp. In my head, the only thought I'm processing is *please don't find us.*

The Patrol marches above and I catch flashes of them through the floorboards. Same intense uniforms as before. Their helmets make their words come out robotic through a speaker system. The sound of slamming cabinets echoes along with the scratching of furniture sliding across the floor. More than once, the kitchen table slides across the boards above my head.

Emma walks into view, positioning herself over the exposed floorboards of our hatch. A taller man, dressed in a white button up and black slacks, steps next to her.

"Sorry if this is of any inconvenience to you," he says, his deep voice matching the one I had heard earlier. Though, now, his words seem softer.

"You can tell me what this is about, Zane. Maybe I can help."

His eyes dart around the room, confirming the other Patrol members aren't listening.

"We're searching for trespassers," he says in a harsh whisper. "People are in Artmith who don't belong."

Emma may have some talent at being an actress, after all. Her reaction is perfect. Not too shocked and not underwhelming. It's the right amount of curious that someone like Emma would have.

"Really? What kind of trespassers? Someone came from outside the wall?"

Zane slowly shakes his head, still watching the other members of the Patrol. "You've noticed the clouds in the sky, right?" he asks.

Emma's face changes, considering this before nodding.

"Well, we think people from another world have traveled here through a portal. It must still be open, because the sky hasn't changed. By our records, they've already been here for days. They could be anywhere inside the gate."

"Is that even possible? Portals to other worlds?"

Zane studies Emma and then shrugs his shoulders. "I ran some numbers with the energy in the sky and the velocity of the clouds, and gave them to Lord Neko."

Emma seems to flinch at the name. It's familiar to me and I recall that's who Emma said communicates with the world's magic.

"That was his conclusion. Maybe it's happened before. I wasn't told much else. We'll be tightening curfew, just in case. The gates won't open until nine now."

"Why do they have you, an engineer, out here with the Patrol?" Emma asks.

Zane pulls out a white syringe with a long needle. "If we find them, I need to administer this."

"And that is?" Emma asks, her question hanging in the air.

"A sedative to keep them from running," Zane says, being very cryptic.

"Sir," a robotic voice calls from the living room.

Through the cracks in the floor, I watch Zane's head snap from Emma toward the voice. The Patrol member who spoke steps into view with the ice pack that Jenny had been using in his hands. Zane, returns the syringe to his pocket and takes the ice pack, looking it over and considering it for a moment.

"Are you not feeling well?" he asks, meeting Emma's stare.

"I was a little feverish earlier," she quickly explains.

Zane presses a hand to her forehead and Emma tries to hide her squirm at his sudden touch.

"I'm feeling better now," she adds.

Zane doesn't respond and I watch his eyes shift toward the sink.

"Did you have guests over?" he asks and he crosses out of view.

"What?" Emma asks, following him toward the kitchen

"That's a lot of bowls for one girl," I hear him say.

"Oh, I just let them pile up in the sink. I should really get better at keeping up with them."

There's a pause in their conversation and my heart beats in my ears to fill the void. Eventually, I hear Zane call out, "Did you find anything else?"

"Nothing, sir," a few robotic voices reply.

Zane's footsteps thud across the floorboards as he moves toward the front door. His form sinks further away, almost out of sight, when Emma steps forward and says, "Zane, what will happen to them when you find them?"

The world inside of Emma's little house freezes. She shouldn't have asked that. *She shouldn't care.*

Zane turns slowly, the confusion at her question spreading on his face.

"I mean, is this going to be handled as a public matter, or will I need to keep this to myself?" Emma tries to cover, and I think Zane may believe her.

"It's a public matter," Zane finally answers. "*When* we find them, Lord Neko wants them captured and questioned. They could be dangerous invaders coming to seize Pintura. I've heard rumors that Lord Neko will execute them to keep the truth of the portal hidden."

His words drain the blood from my face so fast I stumble back and

Wren reaches up to steady me before I can knock anything over. Zane's words stick with me long after I hear his footsteps leave the house and long after the door closes behind him. It wasn't a matter of *if* they find us, but *when*.

In the dark room below Emma's home, I find Wren and Jenny's wide stares. We're wanted trespassers. The Artmith Patrol is searching for us, and they want to *kill* us.

I hear Emma pacing above us for a long time after they leave. I think about going up, but I wait for Emma's signal. The longer the waiting stretches out, the sicker I begin to feel. She just keeps pacing back and forth across the house. She's probably contemplating going and getting Zane. Now, she knows the stakes. She can't help hide trespassers. She'll be an accessory to this and from what Emma says, the Patrol is not forgiving. If we're caught with her, she'll be executed as well.

I know she must be thinking this, too, as she continues to pace back and forth.

Eventually, her footsteps quiet. The thin rays of light that seeped through the floorboards go out, leaving the house in complete darkness. I hear the boards click together as she pulls them up and her face swims into view, illuminated by a single candle.

She lowers herself and the candle onto the stairs. Slowly, she makes her way down and sits across from us in the dark basement.

"I don't think they left behind any bugs," she says and I'm caught off guard by her words.

"You're not turning us in?" I ask, and her wide blue eyes meet mine across the flame.

"Ash, of course not!" she says like I was crazy for even considering it.

"Emma, if they catch us with you, you'll be in trouble, too," Wren says.

"They won't catch us," Emma says stiffly.

"Emma, they probably will," Jenny says weakly.

"They won't—" Emma starts to say, but I cut her off.

"You don't know—"

"No!" Emma snaps and my words get caught in my throat. "We're a team. We're doing this together, and what we're doing is working. We can't stop now." Emma stares deep into me, and I feel every word she is saying. She wants to be a part of this. She really does care about us.

"So, you were looking for recording devices upstairs?" I ask and she nods, breaking her stare from mine.

"Yes, but I don't think they left any. I just wanted to be sure before I came down. I've drawn all the curtains and turned out the lights in case they come back. We can go up now." She stands and helps us into the dark kitchen.

We sit in a circle in her living room, as far from the draped and boarded-up windows as possible.

"I heard him mention the new curfew. That changes things a bit," I say.

"Yes, we won't get to leave as early, but I think that will be to our advantage," Emma says. "Now, when the gates open at 9:00 a.m., everyone who works outside of the wall in the scrapyard or in the fields will be rushing out at the same time. It'll be easier to sneak out."

"Do you think they know what we look like?" Jenny asks, but Emma shakes her head.

"It didn't even sound like Zane knew how many people he's

looking for. But just in case, we'll try to cover your faces. I have some scarves and hats that should help."

"We need to do this as fast as possible," I say.

She nods. "We already are."

"No, I mean, we have to before they find us. Once we go back home, we can close the portal and they'll know we're gone. Until then, they won't stop looking."

"Then I suggest we start figuring out where our next card is leading us," Emma says, pulling out the number two card.

Emma leans out the front door first, scanning the dirt streets of Shadow Village to confirm no Patrol officers still linger close by. Once she gives us the all clear, we quietly slip outside and sit along the side of the back wall. The tall industrial buildings conceal the area in complete darkness. Up above, the stars brightly shimmer behind the twisting grey clouds.

"The circles link on the cards will lead you where it hangs low," Emma quietly reads part of the riddle.

I glance from the back of the card to the pattern of stars above. "There," I whisper and point out in front of us. The constellation stretches out past the wall and hangs in the middle of the Infinity Forest. There, two circles of stars link together, just like on the back of the cards.

It's really far away, though, and we're already going to have a delayed start. I can see the fear on Jenny's face. She's not going to enjoy another day of snakes.

We sit here a bit longer, putting the location to memory, because tomorrow morning we won't have the stars to guide us.

"We should go back in," Emma whispers so quietly I have to wonder if I really heard her or not.

We slide back into the house and Emma starts laying out our blankets and pillows. Keeping the lights off, we walk around the small house with only the flame of the single candle as our guide. I move into the kitchen where three bowls still sit on the counter and the fourth's shattered remains fill the sink. I put the three intact bowls away and carefully fish out the broken pieces of the last one.

Emma joins me, helping with the remaining few pieces of painted glass. She places the lit candle on the counter, helping us see the bits of broken glass better.

"Sorry about your bowl," I say.

She shrugs her shoulders. "It's okay. I'll find another at the scrapyard. And I have plenty here already."

We're quiet for a moment and I study her face in the fading candlelight as she scrapes out the last little pieces of the bowl.

"About earlier, in the theater," I say, pausing as she turns to me, so close her arm brushes my chest. The words I want to say are right there, on the tip of my tongue. I want to tell her I almost kissed her. I want to tell her that I *want* to kiss her, but I can't get the words to form. My heart just beats harder and harder, and I wonder if she can hear it.

"There's nothing to say, Ash." She finally fills the void I left and moves around me to throw away the last pieces of ceramic. She spins back and gives me a soft smile.

There *is* something to say, though. I want to say it, but in the dying light, I think I see it on her face. I think she may know. I think, maybe, she feels it too.

The flame finally flickers out and the shadows swallow Emma. There's a creak in the floor beneath her invisible step, the only sign that she moves toward me. I feel her arms first, as they wrap around my neck. She pushes herself up on her toes, laying her head against my chest. I surprise myself when I don't hesitate to wrap my arms around her waist and pull her into a tight hug. It makes me wonder when the last time the mysterious boy in the back of band room *hugged* someone.

Her hair is soft against my cheek, the metallic scent of Artmith clinging to her, and a bit of something citrus, like oranges.

Emma shudders against me, squeezing her arms tighter around my neck and I barely catch her muffled cry. In this moment, I feel the fear inside of Emma. She acted brave before with Zane questioning her, but now, in the dark, where no one can see, she finally lets the fear take over, and I feel every bit of it. I pull her even closer to my chest, determined to take all that fear away, because it's my fault she's in this mess. I regret ever involving her. She was just trying to help us and I will never forgive myself if she gets hurt.

"It's going to be okay," I whisper softly under her hair.

We stay like this a moment more before Emma nods against my chest. "Ash," she says, pulling back, but staying close enough that her breath tickles my neck.

"Em," I say. I lift my hand in the dark and find the side of her face. The blonde curls hang loose as usual. Carefully, I push them behind her ear, like I wanted to do yesterday at her house, and she presses her cheek into my palm.

"Thank you," Emma says, and then she steps away from me. I hear her footsteps move toward the couch and she settles in for bed.

I stand there in the dark kitchen for a minute, not quite sure what she was thanking me for. Maybe it's for the hug and the encouraging words. It felt like she was saying so much more with those two words, though. She said so much and so little all at the same time.

CHAPTER 15

Ash

T he first thing I see the next morning is my face plastered on the sides of the buildings in Artmith. I'm everywhere, and Jenny and Wren's faces are there as well. They aren't clear pictures, but very good sketches.

"I guess they *do* know what we look like," Jenny says, her voice muffled by the red scarf pulled up over her nose. Her, Wren, and I all wear an assortment of jackets, scarfs, and bandanas to cover our face from wandering eyes.

Out of instinct, I try to pull the hood tighter against my head, making sure to tuck in all of my brown hair. Emma guesses Professor Sim must have given our descriptions to the Patrol. I want to assume it was Jake, but then I'd be giving him the credit of putting all the clues together. Since they haven't taken Emma into custody, I assume Professor Sim didn't mention anything about her knowing us.

When we reach the iron gates, it's the only sign of hope right now.

A large, angry crowd has gathered, waiting for the gate to be opened. A lot of them are infuriated that they're missing out on time they could be earning money. It's easy for us to slide into the center of the chaos and camouflage into the crowd. I think they may want people to present identification when they go through the gate, but once it's open, there's no way to stop the flood of people.

The feet around us rush forward and we keep close to the mass of strangers and charge through the open gate. Patrol members on either side of the gate yell for some order to be restored, but the crowd is too loud. We head straight for the field, hoping to get some coverage in the tall wheat. Once we're away from the crowd, and the Patrol's focus is elsewhere, we pull back our hoods, unwrap the scarves and bandanas from our faces, and shove all the extra garments into our backpacks.

"Let's keep moving," Emma instructs, taking large strides toward Infinity Forest.

The scared and fragile girl from last night is well hidden this morning. Emma is back to her usual spontaneous self, not showing any fear. I look ahead of us, at two tall trees that reach higher than the rest of the forest. They're the only markers I have of where the stars had lined up last night.

As we close in on the forest, I hope that maybe the stars weren't as far away as they seemed. Jenny hobbles next to Wren, demanding to walk instead of being carried. She's faced her fair share of injuries from playing soccer, so I wouldn't expect anything less from her.

"Tell us about Artmith, Emma," Wren asks once we've entered the forest. The trees provide a shaded canopy and we try to stick to any worn trails to make the hike easier for Jenny.

"What do you mean? Like our history?"

148

"Yeah, how did this all come to be?"

"You'll have to forgive me, but history was my least favorite subject in school," Emma deflects. "This is what I know. Our current ruler is Lord Neko. Before him it was his father, and before him, his father."

"So, rule is passed down through the sons?" I ask, trying to compare it to how a royal family may operate.

"Well, it's an elected position, but it always stays within the Stelling family," Emma says, pulling out one of her granola bars as she continues explaining. "We used to live out here among the vainders a long, long time ago. They were ruthless, never understanding the terms of allies or peace. There are lists and lists of wars between us and the vainders. Far too many for me to ever remember. Eventually, we fought them out of the area now known as Artmith. The wall was built and we settled the area. Once we learned that the vainders are nocturnal, it was easy for us to venture out here for supplies. A lot of books say the Lord who ruled at the time was able to communicate with the world and, in an alliance to achieve peace, was granted access to its magic. That was hundreds of years ago, and no one can be sure that ever actually happened."

"Do you like Lord Neko?" Jenny asks once Emma pauses to take another bite.

Emma scoffs in response. "He's all right," she eventually says. "He's too controlling. The regulations enforced by the Patrol are getting more and more ridiculous. But I get my allowance on time every month. I'm able to do my job without too much hassle. It's not really his fault that I can't afford to go to school."

"Have you met him before?" Wren asks.

I'm trying to decide if he's genuinely curious or if he wants to know if the person who ordered for our execution will be willing to reconsider when they arrest us.

Emma gives a toss of her head that says she really doesn't know how to answer. "Yeah, I've seen him at some important public announcements. But he's always wearing his uniform. It's the same as the rest of the Patrol, but a gold helmet instead of a red one. Besides those masked meetings, he's never out in the public. His father wasn't either, and I wasn't born yet for any rulers earlier than that."

"So, Lord Neko can communicate with the magic in the land?" Jenny inquires, and Emma nods.

"It's a power granted to every ruler. They are supposed to be blessed when they take the position as Lord, and then they'll have the ability to converse with the world around us," Emma says, speaking through a bite of her granola bar.

"Well," I start to say, my mind piecing together all of the information Emma is telling us, "I assume Lord Neko has nothing to do with the magic powering the portal or our game if he wants us caught."

Emma nods as she swallows. "Lord Neko doesn't control the magic, he can just communicate the need for the people of Artmith. The magic has its own mind, its own ability to wield its power."

We're all quiet for a minute and I continue to save away what I've learned about Pintura and the Lord that wants me executed. All I can hope is that Lord Neko doesn't try to communicate our capture to the magic in this world. Or at least, I hope the world refuses to grant his wish.

A stream to our left trickles in the lingering silence, croaking frogs and a chorus of birds going about their day as normal.

"What's your favorite part about Pintura?" Wren asks, steering us away from Lord Neko and filling the lag in the conversation.

I expect Emma to have an immediate answer, but she doesn't.

"I'm honestly not sure," she finally admits.

I think about pushing the question further, because I'm genuinely curious too, but I see Emma's face has darkened at the thought. I suppose it is concerning that there's not one thing about this world that she likes.

"What about Earth? What's your world's history?"

Before I can stop her from asking, it's too late. Wren rambles for the rest of the morning about how our world came to be. History is Wren's other love, right behind music and comic books. He could go on about the American Revolution or the World Wars forever. Emma seems to enjoy every second of it, though I highly doubt it. She asks a lot of questions and loves hearing about the different decades.

"I think that's enough, Wren," I say gently when I'm not sure I can take it any longer.

"Oh, but I haven't told her about the California Gold Rush," he says, sounding so disappointed.

"Oh, gold?" Emma sings, continuing to challenge my thoughts on whether she's actually enjoying this. Then Wren goes off again and there's no use in stopping him. He only pauses his story for a minute when we have to climb over a fallen tree that blocks our path.

The sun has shifted from burning the left side of my face to the right, and I know it's past noon now. Three hours of walking. How far have we gone? Six or seven miles maybe, and still nothing.

The arches in my feet ache with every step. I have no idea how Jenny can possibly withstand the pain she's in. I wipe the sweat on my forehead and glance over at her. She's finishing off her water bottle, swallowing some more painkillers.

I tilt my head back at the burning sun, having no idea how Wren could be surviving in his worn, oversized jeans.

I know we're running out of time as the sun keeps tracking overhead. If we're going to make it back to the gate by five, we're going to have to turn back soon. At most, we'll have one more hour in this direction.

"Em, I think we need a new plan," I say, speaking over Wren, who has gone on to talk about space travel.

Emma glances down at her watch, confirming my suspicions. "Maybe we should split up. We'll cover more area. We've got to be close, maybe just a little off to the right or left."

"Emma and I will go this way," Wren offers, pointing to the right. "I'll tell you all about the solar system."

"Okay, we'll meet back here in an hour," Emma agrees. She turns and follows Wren, their voices fading as they get further away.

"After you," Jenny says, motioning for me to go off to the left.

For about as close to thirty minutes as I can guess, we search the woods, but find nothing. Eventually, we decide to turn back, still hoping Emma and Wren are having better luck.

"How's your ankle today?" I ask, knowing Jenny would never say she's hurting.

Her wince of pain catches me by surprise. "It really does hurt, Ash," she admits weakly, her breathing thin.

"You've done too much walking today," I gently scold, and she nods her head, agreeing.

When we come out into the clearing where we left Wren and Emma, it's empty.

"Sit down and get some rest," I say, though I can see the dread of the hike back to Artmith written all over her face. No small amount of rest will make that any more bearable. Nonetheless, we both sit in the shade of a tree with a thick, wrinkly trunk. If only we could be out here while the stars are visible. It'd be so much easier to find the marked location.

Before I can give it anymore thought, Wren's voice faintly grows nearer.

"Oh, if you think that's cool, let me tell you about the Indian ruins. They're fascinating."

How can Emma put up with that? The two of them emerge into our small clearing. My eyes find their empty hands, first.

"You didn't find anything either?" I ask, and both of them shake their heads.

"We need to head back. We're barely going to reach the gates before 5:00 p.m.," Emma says, letting out a long sigh.

"Jenny's not going to make it," I tell them.

"I'm fine," she says defensively, but her limp is so bad she nearly falls back down.

"This might sound crazy," I say hesitantly. Their eyes flick to me. "What if we stayed out here tonight?"

I expect them to yell at me or call me an idiot for even suggesting it. The three of them are so in shock by my request, they're actually silent. Before they can find their words of dismissal, I continue to explain my idea.

"It'll be easier to find the spot with the stars visible. Jenny will never make it back to Artmith on that ankle. I doubt we could hike to the gate in four hours, and when we get back, how are we going to get inside undetected? You just think we'll fall into another angry crowd by luck?"

My claims make sense, I know they do, and still Emma *laughs* at me. A deep laugh that shakes her whole body. She bends over, not able to control her laughter. Her eyes actually water with tears from laughing so hard. When she finally stops her outburst, she says, "You're joking, right?"

When I don't respond, she looks like she may kill me herself.

"We are *not* spending the night out here."

"Em, it's the best choice," I argue.

The fear I had felt last night when I held her in the dark surfaces in her eyes.

"Ash," her voice is so shaky I think she may burst into tears. Real tears this time, not those fueled by laughter. "You're an *idiot*. We'll die if we stay out here!"

"And we'll die if we go back and get caught!"

"For all we know, we may not make it back in time with Jenny's injured ankle," Wren jumps in, surprisingly defending my plan. "Then we'll be nowhere near the right spot and still locked out."

Emma is quiet for a long time as she paces around the trees. "This is a stupid idea," she finally says, stopping to direct her comment at me.

"It's the only way we're going to complete this challenge," I say.

She bites her lip, trying to stop her mind from agreeing.

"Even if we go back and get through the gate without getting caught, we're still going to fail. Tomorrow, we'll only get this far again, before we have to turn around."

Emma must have been fighting the same realization, because she slowly nods her head.

"We're really going to have to stay out here," she says softly, working through the idea aloud.

"Nothing left to do but wait," Jenny offers, but it's not helpful.

"Want me to tell you about those Indian ruins?" Wren cautiously asks Emma.

She shakes her head. "Not right now, Wren. I need a minute." She turns and heads away from us, into the surrounding woods.

Out of instinct, I step forward to follow her, but Jenny blocks my path. "You should probably just give her a minute," she says.

I nod, understanding this is probably something Emma just needs to wrap her head around. It's a shock to her. She's spent her whole life being told to never stay out here past five. Always make it back to the gate or you'll die. This decision to stay out here is going against everything she was taught to do.

I try to give Emma space. I eat and drink some water. Wren and I continue to hike around the area with no luck, but once the sun starts to set and Emma hasn't returned, I don't care what Jenny says.

"I'm going to go find her," I mumble to Jenny and Wren. They look like they may protest the idea, but don't. I head in the direction Emma had gone earlier. I call her name a few times, but there's no response.

Don't worry, she wouldn't leave us now.

When I hear the sound of a small creek up ahead, I sprint toward the noise. She has to be there.

Sure enough, there she sits at the water's edge. Her leather boots are flipped over next to her and her bare feet are dangling in the water below, the cuffs of her navy overalls rolled up to her knees. I freeze at the edge of the trees. Maybe I should just leave her alone. I know where she's at and that she's okay. I should just go back to our camp and wait for her to return on her own.

Before I can make up my mind, a bird in the trees above gives away my location. It sounds an alarming call to the neighboring tree, which is filled with birds that answer its siren. Emma snaps her head over her shoulder, her red puffy eyes landing on me.

For a moment, we stay like that, staring at one another as the birds above continue to call out their warning. Finally, she turns away from me and looks back down at the rushing creek below. Now that she's seen me, I might as well stay.

I cross over to her and take a seat on the creek's bed.

"I'm sorry if I'm intruding. I was worried when the sun started setting and you weren't back yet," I admit. I mean for my apology to make her feel better, but she looks like I've hurt her. She presses her eyes tightly closed and takes in a deep breath. She lets out the thin stream of shaky air and opens her eyes, but won't meet my stare.

"I didn't mean to upset you more," I try to apologize again. Perhaps not saying anything would be better.

"It's okay," Emma says, finally speaking to me. Her voice is so rough. It sounds nothing like her usual bright, sarcastic self. She clears her throat and her voice edges on almost normal. "I've just been trying to get my head straight. If I'm going to be out here, I can't be scared."

"It's okay to be scared," I say softly. I don't know why, but I reach over and grab her hand, lacing our fingers together.

She squeezes my grasp, and I'm reminded of our embrace last night. How she had waited until it was dark to let her fear surface so that no one could see her.

"I just always feel like I have to be so brave," she says, kicking her feet in the water.

"Why is that?"

She tilts her head up to the sky, organizing her answer. "I used to get picked on a lot when I was little, but if I made them think I didn't care, they would leave me alone. I've never had friends, and my parents have never been interested in me either. My mom wants me to be a nurse and my dad wants me to do research, but I want to build things. For as long as I can remember, I've spent my whole life constructing a brave, defensive wall to hide behind." Emma's head falls and her blonde curls cover her face.

"Whoever was picking on you was clearly jealous," I say. I untangle our fingers and lift my hand to pull her hair back over her shoulder, revealing her damp cheeks.

She humors me with a dry laugh, but shakes her head, disagreeing. "No one was jealous of a girl who wanted to spend her time in the scrapyard."

My chest aches at her words. I don't know how anyone could see Emma and think of her as a scrapyard girl. Even then, what's wrong with that? I find *I* may actually be *jealous* of *Emma*. She gets to do what she loves every day. The Patrol may have tight regulations, but her society has a sort of freedom built into it.

A confession builds inside of me. I don't know if it will make Emma feel better, but I want to tell her all the same.

"Em, I'm scared too," I admit, and she finally looks up at me.

Even though this was my idea, she doesn't look mad at me for saying I'm scared. She doesn't seem worried that the person she's looking to comfort her is also afraid. She looks relieved to know she's not the only one who feels this way.

The howl of a neighboring wolf causes Emma to jump into my side, clinging to my arm.

"Sorry," Emma quickly says, moving away to stand up. "Gosh, I'm so jumpy already."

I notice the woods around us have started to darken, and the howl is a quick reminder of what time it is.

"We'll see the stars, complete the card, and head straight for the gate. The closer we get to Artmith, the less likely we are to encounter vainders," I say. "Focus on that. We'll do this as quickly as we can. It'll be over before you know it."

Emma takes another deep breath and nods. She puts her shoes back on and we make our way to our camp. Out here, night seems to fall twice as fast. Maybe that's a good thing. The stars will be showing soon.

When we get back to our clearing, Jenny and Wren have positioned themselves up onto the trunk of a fallen tree. It leans against another tree, creating a tall ramp.

"We thought we'd be safer to wait up here," Wren calls down from the slanted tree. "Maybe vainders can't climb."

Emma and I join them on the trunk of the tree, carefully balancing on its curved surface. I expect Wren to continue his history lesson with Emma, but his nerves have finally cut him off. Out of everyone, Jenny actually appears the calmest. It's probably because her ankle is emitting so much pain she can't even think about how nervous she should feel.

The grey light of the forest dissolves into a very dark black. "Nine," Emma says, the watch on her wrist illuminating her features as she reads the time.

I look up and see the dark silhouettes of the treetops above. I hadn't thought about them blocking the stars.

"I'll climb up and see if I can find anything," I offer, though my voice shakes at the idea of having to move.

On wobbly legs, I hoist myself along the fallen tree until I reach the top that leans against its sturdy support. It's hooked nicely in an area of thick branches, making it easy for me to pull myself up higher into the next tree. I almost glance down, but I'm afraid if I see how high I am, I may lose my balance and fall.

Instead, I keep climbing until I get to a point where the leaves are thin enough for me to see the stars. I whip my head around quickly, trying to see where the linked rings are. Somehow, it almost seems like there are no stars at all above our clearing.

Then I see our marker and I blink hard, not believing it. The linked point is completely across the forest. It's probably another three miles away. There's no way we are that far off. I turn to my right and left and confirm that I'm centered between the two taller trees I used as markers last night. I'm right where the stars should be.

They must have moved.

I concentrate on their new location, directly to the right of our clearing, and climb back down the branches. If we hurry, we'll be there in an hour. I'm frustrated that they moved, but I try to stay positive. At least we know where to go. No wonder we couldn't find anything today.

When I land on the ramped trunk, I call down to the group. "You guys are going to hate this, but the stars moved."

"Ash," Emma's voice calls back to me in the darkness.

It's not the frustrated groan I was anticipating. It's shaky and broken. As I slide along the slanted tree, I make out her dark figure crouched on the trunk, looking down at the ground.

I freeze in my spot, balancing nearly ten feet above the forest floor. Beneath me, seven sets of black, glossy eyes stare back.

CHAPTER 16

Emma

The vainders are everywhere. I count seven, but I'm sure more are on the way or lurking further back. My mind races, trying to find something to compare them to, because I've never seen one in person. They tower two of me tall, dark black fur coating their legs and arms. A metal torso raises and falls with their fast breathing. Steel claws slowly slide out from their hands, small rays of moonlight glinting off the deadly points. And their faces. The closest thing I can compare it to is a wolf. Beady black eyes and a long, wrinkly snout. One, nearest the tree, pulls back its gums and shows its sharp metal teeth, like little blades.

A cyborg wolf stands ready to tear me to shreds.

Their arms are long, giving them the option to walk or crawl. A low growl grows through the pack and they circle around the tree we're perched on.

"What do we do?" Wren whispers.

For a second, I let myself look away from the vainders and I see that Ash, Wren, and Jenny are staring at me.

"No one make the first move," I whisper and we hold our ground.

Maybe they'll move on. Maybe Wren was right and they can't climb.

Maybe I'm as stupid as I sound.

I train my eyes on their hands with steel claws and swallow. They'll be able to climb. I know they will, so then what? I need to decide fast, because one of them is moving to balance himself on the end of our fallen tree, slowly making his way up the ramp, one small step at a time.

Finally, I snap. *We have to move.*

"Run!" I scream up to Ash and we race up the slanted trunk, into the neighboring tree Ash had climbed.

The vainders below erupt in yapping and harsh barks, so loud they make my head shake. The fallen tree bounces with the sudden stomping feet. The vainder behind us starts moving faster, closing in on us.

We clutch the neighboring tree trunk, looking down to see three more vainders' snapping jaws.

"Jump, Ash!" I say and point to the branch of the tree next to us.

Ash doesn't hesitate, and he leaps across to the closest branch. He runs down it, toward the other tree's trunk. It bounces and sways like a trapeze bar, but he keeps his balance. Wren and Jenny follow, and I bring up the rear.

"Just keep going, Ash!" I scream into the void of branches and dark green leaves. I whip my head behind me and see we're losing the vainders that try to climb the trees. Their incredibly large, furry arms and legs are too heavy for the branches. They make their movements awkward and I watch them get tangled in the trees.

The vainders on the ground, though, keep on our trail. Their noses tilt up, staying our scent. We jump through three more trees before I hear Ash call back to me.

"Em, I don't think I can make this one."

"Ash, you're going to have to," I holler, looking back at the vainders heading our way.

I hear him mumble some words of hope and then he jumps across a clearing in the trees, flying through the sky like I had seen him when he arrived in Pintura.

And then his hands grasp the branch, arms from years of drumming flexing under his weight. I let out a sigh of relief, and he pulls himself up to his feet.

"Jenny, you should go next," Wren says, helping Jenny position herself on the edge of our branch.

"You can do it, Jenny!" Ash calls from the neighboring tree, waving her over.

She bends her knees and jumps as far as she can. Her hands hit the branch hard, and she tries desperately to cling to it, but either from the force of her impact, or her lack of upper body strength, she can't hold on, and she falls toward the ground. Jenny reaches for a lower branch, slowing her fall, but still not being able to latch on.

There's a loud *thud* when she hits the forest floor and Ash and Wren scream at her to get up. Against their pleas, she doesn't move. Curled over, she gasps for breaths after the hard impact. Her short, black shirt is pulled up, revealing the cuts and red skin from her fall. A howl rings out and I know the vainders on the ground are about to reach us.

"Jenny, get up!" I scream with the boys.

She tries to pull herself to her feet, but keeps collapsing. She's too disoriented from the fall. I turn back toward the vainders and see one black figure is just a hundred feet away, closing in fast.

When I spin back around to look down at Jenny, I notice Wren is gone. I lean forward on the branch and see that he's climbing toward the ground.

No, no, no. This is all going wrong.

Before anyone can do anything, the leading vainder leaps into the clearing and lands over Jenny, examining the withering girl on the forest floor. I hate that my first instinct is to cry. The vainder shoots its long, razor claws out and raises his arm, ready to slice her into pieces.

"You leave her alone!" Wren yells.

He leaps toward the vainder, his hands landing on a branch. Wren swings himself forward, kicking the vainder in the back. The monster flies forward, letting out a horrible screech.

Wren drops to the ground and rushes to Jenny. They need to get out of there. They need to move.

The rest of the vainders reach them and the one Wren kicked recovers to his feet. He jumps toward Wren, throwing him off of Jenny's body.

Even in the dark forest, there's no hiding the sudden splattering of blood.

I don't know if it's the vainders, Wren's actions, or the blood, but something finally clicks in my head, telling me to *fight*. I reach into my backpack and pull out the wooden spear I'd been carving all afternoon at the creek. My hands grip it tightly and I hold it above my head.

In a second of hesitation, my eyes snap up to the tree across from me. To the wide-eyed boy who's looking at me like one of these creatures might be behind me. Sheer shock and fear have Ash locked in place, but the sight of me with my makeshift wooden spear positioned over my head snaps him awake.

"Em!" he screams across the tree tops, leaning forward on his branch, but it's too late.

With one quick breath, I let out a warrior scream and jump from the branch. As I fall, the air flies back against my face, blowing my blonde curls in wild ripples. With a hard *thunk*, I land on the metal back of the vainder that attacked Wren, driving my spear through his furry neck.

He screams in pain and whips his head back and forth, trying to knock me off of him.

One hard twist to the right and I fly off, my spear still tightly gripped in my hands. The injured vainder stumbles a few feet to the left before collapsing on the ground. He cries out to his pack, black blood pooling around his head, until he finally stills in the moonlight.

I hurry to my feet and spin around in a circle, ready for the next attack. One tries to lunge forward. I let out a grunt and swing my spear hard, cutting his arm. He whimpers and stumbles back.

There's a moment that passes with me breathing hard and staring down the tentative vainders. And then they retreat. Slowly at first, taking small steps backward, and then they fall on all fours and race away. I'm not sure why they retreat. I have to wonder how long it's been since the vainders fought humans, or the last time one of their members was attacked. A nauseous wave rumbles under my skin. They aren't retreating. They're going to get more vainders. When they come back, we can't be here.

There's a hard *thump* behind me as Ash hits the ground.

"Wren!" Jenny cries. I realize she's been screaming his name through my attack, but I haven't registered it until now.

Ash runs toward Wren's crumpled body, and his hands grasp Wren's shirt.

"Wren! Wren!" he cries, pulling Wren up against a tree.

Wren's face is already pale, his eyes heavy. The smell of blood is so overwhelming I can taste it in the air. A large gash stretches across the front of his shirt. The fabric is soaked, sticking to his chest.

"Oh, gosh," Ash says, taking in a thin breath. "Wren, don't die. Please don't die."

Ash starts crying and Jenny wails at his feet and I'm so nauseous, I keel over. I just want to run away from it all, and in this moment, I realize the only thing I want right now is my mom. I want her to hold me and I want to be safe in my childhood room. *Oh mom, what should I do? What should I do?*

My mom!

"Pick him up!" I snap at Ash, who looks at me through deep sobs. "Pick him up right now! We have to get him to my mom. She's a nurse. She can help him."

"Em, the gates—"

"Pick him up, Ash!" I scream, cutting him off.

He gives me a sharp nod and then scoops Wren into his arms. Blood smears all over Ash, but he doesn't seem to notice. I drop to Jenny and pull her to her feet. She's shaking so badly I don't know if she can even stand up, but she has to.

"Jenny, I know you're scared, and I know your ankle hurts, but you need to run with me. Can you do that?"

Jenny lets out a deep breath, wipes the tears from her cheeks, and nods.

"We'll follow you," Ash says, and I sprint through the woods.

It doesn't take long for my throat to start burning and my heart to threaten to explode in my chest. *Don't you dare stop running. Don't stop.* The thought of the vainders coming back definitely scares me enough to keep me moving, but the real force pushing me forward is the sight of Wren slowly dying in Ash's arms.

It took us three hours to hike this far this morning, but by sprinting through the woods, I feel like we cut that time in half. But no matter how fast we run, I never feel like it's fast enough. I have to stop a couple of times, my heart beating so hard I can't even breathe. When I stop, Ash yells at me to keep going. When Jenny stops, I push her forward, and when Ash stops, Jenny and I both drag him along. The three of us work together as a team to get Wren back to my mom as fast as possible.

When we finally get out of the woods and through the field, I see the gate. I actually see two or three gates, my vision playing tricks on me. I think I'm still running, but my feet feel sloppy.

"Emma, the gate's this way," Jenny says when she realizes I'm leading her down to a different part of the wall.

"The gate is locked, Jenny, but there's another way," I say, but can't finish my sentence.

We reach the solid wall and I run my hands along the slick metal. *I know it's here.* My head pounds and my vision is blurry, but I know I can find the loose metal. I spent too many late nights in the scrapyard to be able to miss it.

Sure enough, the metal gives under my hand. The loose section folds in when I throw my shoulder against the wall. I slide between the jagged tear and help Jenny and Ash through the wall. I push the metal back into place and start heading toward my old house.

166

"Wren, we're in Artmith," Ash whispers.

I look back at Ash. Wren's tired eyes open and he slowly looks around at where we are. Ash seems to think this is a good sign, but all I notice is how glossy his eyes look and how thin and raspy his breathing is.

The white picket fence comes into view first. I hurry through the gate and up to the red front door. I know it's locked, but I try it anyway, twisting the brass knob back and forth. I shake the door, but it won't budge. I raise my fist and pound on the door. My hand throbs, but I don't let up. I just keep striking the door over and over. I don't even hear the locks click on the other side or acknowledge that the windows to my right have filled with light. When my mom pulls open the door, her white nightgown held closed with her hand, I almost fall into the house.

"Emma Delany, what in the world—" my mother roars, until her eyes move to Jenny standing behind me, her hair in a tangled mess. Then her gaze slides to Ash beside me, Wren in his arms, blood covering both of them.

For some reason, now is when the tears come. Through my sobs I say, "He's hurt, mom. Please, we need your help."

She leans out of the door and checks to see if any of the neighbors saw us come. "Get in here," she hisses, pulling me by the collar of my shirt.

Jenny and Ash shuffle in behind me and we follow my mom into the living room. In the dim light from the lamp next to the couch, Jenny, Ash, and Wren's faces are exposed.

"Emma, I can't help you," my mom says sternly, surely recognizing them now.

"But mom," I say, shocked by her response.

"The Patrol was here last night looking for you," she says, pointing her disgust at my friends. "I will not be a part of this."

"But the vainders—" I stop when her eyes widen with anger. I don't think I have ever seen my mother so angry.

"You were outside the gate?" she screams. "What is wrong with you?"

"Mom, he's going to die!" I shriek so loud my throat feels like it's ripping apart. I gasp for air and a shaky sob escapes me. Wren takes in another tired breath, weeping into Ash.

My outburst seems to have sobered my mother's anger. She presses her lips into a thin line and looks from me to Wren. Since the Patrol came by last night, I'm sure she knows when they find us, we'll be executed. Wren would die either way. I know she's on our side when she says, "Okay, take him to the basement."

Relief floods through me, and I almost fall over. "Thank you," I say, but my mother raises a hand to cut me off.

"I don't know if I can save him," she says sternly. She drops her hand and nods. "But I will try."

My mother leads the way to the basement and we follow behind her. She pulls a string that's tied to a light bulb and the basement glows into view.

"Place him here," she says, patting a steel table in the center of the room.

The number of times I sat on that table while she put band aids on my scraped knees or took my temperature run through my mind. Now, a dying boy lies on that same table and I just want to scream at the world for being so horrible.

With Wren laying under the light, his injuries look much worse. The cut from the vainder stretches diagonally across his entire torso.

There is so much blood I can't even tell what color his shirt actually was. My mother grips the fabric and rips it open along the cut, fully exposing flesh.

I want to throw up, scream, and pass out all at the same time. A small whimper escapes Jenny and my mother snaps her head to us. Now that she's seen how bad the wound is, her face pales as she tenses.

"Go upstairs," she says, pointing at the steps.

"I don't want to leave him," Ash says defensively.

"Go!" my mother snaps.

I reach forward and curl my fingers around Ash's wrist, tugging him toward the steps. The three of us go upstairs and I take them to the second floor where my bedroom used to be. Attached to my room is a small bathroom and we try to clean up the best we can. Ash is the worst of us, and I let him shower while I find Jenny and me something to wear from the clothes I had left behind in my closet. I can't believe my mom didn't throw them out. I find something of my dad's from the laundry room for Ash. Once we're all as put together as we can be, we sit in a tight huddle on my bed, but none of us speaks as our minds continue to live somewhere else right now.

CHAPTER 17

Ash

hen I wake up, I'm extremely disoriented. The light blue walls of Emma's room stand around me. I had fallen asleep at the foot of her bed. Emma still sleeps at the other end, curled up on a pile of pillows. I blink hard and rub my eyes. Jenny was here last night, but now she's gone.

"Em," I whisper, gently shaking her leg.

She lets out a groan and slowly opens her eyes. She scans the room, last night's events coming back to her in the same rush that flowed through me. Suddenly, Emma jumps from the bed and races out of the room. I follow her, knowing we're on the same page now. We start to head for the stairs, when I hear whispers coming from a room at the end of the hall.

Emma pushes the door open and the first thing I see is Wren propped up in the bed, smiling as if he'd just played a perfect scale on his trumpet.

"Wren, you're alive," I breathe and hurry to his side. He raises one hand to me and I match his gesture, pulling us together for a quick hug. "How are you feeling?" I ask and take a seat on the edge of the bed.

His color looks good and the white shirt that hangs from his shoulders is a stark difference from the blood-soaked garment from last night.

"Pretty weak," he admits, and I can tell even those two words require more energy than they should.

When the shock of seeing Wren fades, I notice Jenny is curled up next to him, resting her head on his chest. Her bloodshot eyes blink slowly. She doesn't look like she slept at all last night.

"I'm so glad you're okay, Wren," Emma exhales the words, moving to lean against the foot of the bed.

"I wouldn't be here if it wasn't for you," he says slowly, forcing out every word.

"Hey, I carried your dying body seven miles!" I protest and he lets out a shaky breath, gasping a bit for air.

"Emma jumped out of a tree and speared a vainder," Jenny reminds me.

I turn over my shoulder and look at her, the blonde girl who was scared to death. She shrugs her shoulders like it was nothing, and I grin at that. So humble, but surely she knows what her actions mean to me. She saved all of us.

The floorboards in the hall creak as someone approaches the room and our conversation falls quiet. "Oh, good, you're all here," Emma's mom says, coming into the bedroom.

I have the sudden urge to thank her for helping us last night. She didn't have to do that, and I know how much she risked for us.

"Mrs. Delany," I say, crossing to her. "Thank you for saving Wren's life. He's my best friend and I don't know what I would do without him."

When I say the words *best friend,* I realize, for the first time in years, I don't put the phrase *old* or *childhood* in front of them.

She gives me a sympathetic smile and lays a gentle hand on my shoulder. "He's lucky to have a friend like you," she says softly before moving her attention back to the others. "I wanted to let you all know that Wren will be fine, but he's going to need some time to recover."

I think back to the cards and the situation we're in. We don't really have time on our side.

"I don't know what you four were doing outside the gate in the middle of the night," she begins to scold us. Emma tries to speak up, but her mother puts up a hand to stop her. "And I don't want to know."

The room falls quiet, and the stiff woman who greeted us last night comes back.

"Wren needs three days of rest before he can move again. After that, I want you all out of my house. He'll need at least another week to fully recover, but after the first three days, he should be strong enough to walk."

Her harsh expression scans past each of us. I can hardly argue with her orders. She did save Wren, after all. We put her in a difficult situation. If the Patrol finds out she hid us here, she'd be joining us on execution day.

"Your bandages will require changing every five hours, and you'll need lots of water and vitamins to get your strength back up. If you need me, I'll be down in the study. I took the next few days off in case something changes."

Without any parting words, Mrs. Delaney turns and leaves the room.

"Your mom was incredible last night," Wren says once she's back downstairs. "She's as talented as a doctor!"

Emma lets out a small laugh. "She'd be a doctor if she could afford the diploma. She's already acquired all the knowledge from years of watching and assisting at the hospital."

"Did you know she left last night and went to the hospital to get Wren blood?" Jenny asks softly.

"She did what?" Emma hisses, thinking she must have heard my sister wrong.

Jenny nods, her eyes wide. "I couldn't sleep, so I was going to go down and check on Wren. When I got to the first floor, I heard her talking to herself in the kitchen. She was walking herself through the plan she had and then she left. I sat at the top of the stairs and waited for her to come back. If she didn't, I was going to go out after her. Eventually, she returned with bags of blood and a crate of medical supplies."

"Shit, how much trouble could she could be in if she gets caught?" I ask.

"She risked a lot to save me," Wren says through a tight throat.

"We can't stay any longer than we have to," Emma decides. "She's done too much. More than I'll ever be able to repay her for. As soon as you can move, Wren, let us know."

Wren nods, agreeing. I start to get a little fidgety, thinking about hiding here for the next three days.

Jenny must notice because she says, "Ash, there's nothing we can do until night time, anyway. And I'm not ready to go back out there until we have a better plan."

I nod, knowing she's right. She lets out a tired yawn, the bags under her eyes getting bigger.

"You should get some sleep, Jenny," I say, but she softly shakes her head.

"I'm not moving. I'm fine, here."

She nestles closer to Wren's side. He smiles softly and catches me staring. When did they get so close?

"We'll leave you both to get some rest," Emma jumps in, heading toward the door.

"I'll be back to check on you soon," I offer and turn to follow Emma.

She leads me down to the kitchen and asks if I want anything for breakfast. She mumbles something under her breath about not wanting to eat her mom and dad's food, but decides she'll try to replace it later.

"Where's your dad at?" I ask as Emma places our bowls of oatmeal on the dark wooden table. I realize he wasn't here the last time we came, either.

"Probably at work," Emma says, blowing on her steaming bowl. "He does research with the Patrol. Sometimes he'll be gone for weeks. If it's something really urgent, they make him stay in the lab all the time."

"That sounds intense," I admit.

I lift my spoon and blow on the hot oatmeal. I almost melt at the taste of it. No offense to Emma and the beans she's served us, but it's nice to eat something with flavor.

"That must be where you get your passion for engineering," I add, but Emma just nods quietly. "Are you mad at me for making us stay out there?" I ask, dropping my voice. "I know it was my idea, but..."

She's quiet as she stirs her oatmeal. Emma lets out a sigh and lays her spoon against the side of the bowl. When she looks at me, her eyes are glassy.

"I was at first," she admits. "I mean, it *was* your idea. But I agree that the only way to complete this card is to be out there at night. Otherwise, we'll never know where the stars are moving to."

"I'm really sorry," I say, though I don't know why I'm apologizing. It just feels like the right words to say right now.

"There's no one else I'd do it for," Emma says lightly, but her words carry the weight of the feelings I've been wanting to talk about.

Somehow, with Wren recovering upstairs, and the knowledge that we have to go back into Infinity Forest, I don't think now is the right time to mention how much her words mean.

"I can't believe you speared that vainder," I say, scraping out the bottom of my bowl.

Emma tries to laugh about it, but I can tell she's still shaken by the whole incident. Once she finishes her bowl of oatmeal, she leans back into her chair and I realize I've been staring at her. She tilts her head a little, a single blonde curl falling into her face.

"Em, do you remember how you said you always feel like you have to be brave?" She nods and pushes the stray hair behind her ear. "I think you're so brave all the time, because that's just who you are. It's not a defense mechanism. It's you."

Her eyes hold my gaze and she smiles. A real, genuine, no-teeth smile.

"And you must get that from your mom," I add, and get up to rinse our bowls in the sink. "She was fearless last night. There's no way I could have saved him."

Emma doesn't respond, but the smile on her faces grows a little. She sits there, leaned back in the kitchen chair, and watches me stand over the sink cleaning our bowls.

The rest of the day moves in a series of sleeping, games, and stories. No matter how many naps I take, I always seem to wake up tired. Sometimes, it's because the vainders arrive to scare me out of sleep. Other times, I'm back at home, and those are the hardest to wake up from. I find myself trying to rush back to those dreams.

Wren seems to be recovering well. His sense of humor returned almost immediately, and he claims the worst part about the vainder attack was that the creatures destroyed his shirt featuring his favorite superhero from Space Zone. I know he meant it as a lighthearted comment, but I think it upset him to see one of the few things he has left from home get destroyed.

Jenny and I washed our clothes in the laundry room and, if only because it reminds us of the comfort of home, we continue to only wear them.

"Tell me about your first soccer game," Emma says, staring up at the ceiling. She's lying across the foot of Wren's bed.

Jenny shifts a little, still curled next to Wren. "It's actually not that great of a story," she confesses.

I've found my place in the window seat overlooking the backyard. It's nothing special. The white picket fence wraps around the lot. There's a small garden near the door with watermelons tangled on vines. In the far corner of the yard lives a large tree with a tire swing tied around its highest branch. It really isn't anything special, and yet, it's perfect.

"Oh, Jenny. Tell me!" Emma groans, shoving Jenny's foot.

"I actually sat on the bench the whole game."

"No, you didn't," Wren says, thinking Jenny must be lying.

I honestly can't remember Jenny's first soccer game. I've watched so many they just run together now. She's told this story enough that I don't question how she remembers her past.

"I did too," Jenny says. "It taught me a lesson. If I wanted to get play-time I had to be the best. And look at me now." She smiles to herself. "I'll be playing at Berkley next fall."

"They haven't offered you a position yet," I say.

"They will," Jenny pushes confidently.

My sister's lucky her fall in the woods was really just a sprained ankle. Emma's mom checked, and after some medicine, wraps, and an entire day off her foot, the swelling has finally disappeared.

"Ask another question, Emma," Jenny prompts her.

"Oh, but I asked the last two," she says.

"I know, but the three of us already know everything about each other. We can't keep attacking you with questions."

"All right." Emma sighs and searches the ceiling for a question.

After a minute, she slides back on the bed so her head is hanging over the edge and she's looking at me upside down.

"Tell me about your first kiss, Ash."

I look at her, frozen for a second. *What did she just ask me?* Surely that's not what she asked.

"Ohhh," Jenny sings, leaning over Wren to look at me.

She *did* ask me that.

"I can't say," I quickly stammer. "Not with my sister in the room," I add.

"What!" Jenny wails, insulted. "Why not?"

Why? Because I haven't had my first kiss yet. Yes, I'm not a total nerd and I am about to be a freshman in college, but people in band don't get the girls, and I also don't really like putting myself out there.

"Wasn't it with Sally Temple?" Wren asks, glancing my way. He lifts his arm and props it behind his head.

I almost laugh out loud. Sally Temple plays the flute. She's talented, pretty, and poised, but she's never spoken a word to me in the four years we've been in band together. Surely Wren knows that. I catch him give me a small wink. Yes, he knows that. He probably also knows I've never had my first kiss. He's trying to throw me a raft while I'm drowning in silence.

"Um, yeah. Yeah, that's right," I cover.

"Well, tell me about it," Emma says. Still batting her upside down eyes at me.

Tell her about a kiss that never happened? I completely blank. I stutter over my words and try to tell the lie, but nothing comes out coherently.

"Oh, just act it out!" Jenny teases, sitting up from Wren.

Emma cackles a laugh, but Wren tries to come to my rescue.

"Yeah, I'll be Sally," he offers.

This sends both girls into waves of laughter. When Wren attempts to wiggle himself out of the bed, fully intending to go through with this, Jenny pulls him back.

"Wren, you're not allowed to get up."

"Oh, I'll do it!" Emma says, somersaulting backward off the bed, blonde curls exploding in a cloud around her head, and landing in a sitting position on the floor. "Where should I go?"

And suddenly the laughter pauses and all eyes are on me.

"Oh, I don't—" I start to deny, but the three of them groan and beg me to play along. "She was sitting next to me on the bleachers at the football game," I blurt out.

Out of the corner of my eye, I see Wren's face concentrate. *Does he actually believe that?* Okay, maybe I *can* pull this off.

Emma comes over and sits next to me on the window seat, tossing my feet out of the way.

"And then what?" she asks, her blue eyes sparkling in the afternoon sunlight.

"And then," I draw out my words. "And then I just kissed her." I say, trying to let this go.

Emma wrinkles her nose and Jenny snorts a laugh. "You just kissed the poor girl?" Emma asks.

"Well, no," I backpedal. "It was cold, one of the last games of the season. We finished our halftime show, and I was trying to keep her warm."

I lift my arm and wrap it around Emma's shoulders, her head resting against my tense muscles.

"She had her hand like this," I add and lift Emma's left hand up to grasp my fingers that dangle over her shoulder.

The room seems to slip away the moment Emma's fingers tangle in mine. I become extremely aware of how the sunlight makes her skin glow, those faint freckles like glitter on her cheeks. How her hair smells like cinnamon, and how her breathing is so still, I think she may be holding it.

I slip my right hand beneath her chin and tilt her head up, now so close our noses brush. A thin breath catches in my aching lungs and my entire world freezes around Emma and those sky-blue eyes. I can feel her pulse pick up between our locked fingers, and I can see the heated blush tint her cheeks.

My gaze slips down her face to her slightly parted lips.

"And *then* I kissed her."

My words are airy, but Emma shivers at their sound. I dip my head forward, erasing the breath of air between our mouths, and—

SMACK!

A pillow knocks me in the face and my head hits the window. Jenny lets out a wild cackle.

"Aw, so romantic," she cries, holding her stomach from laughing so hard.

"You know, I think I remember that's how it actually went," Wren adds, making a throwing motion toward me. "The other school's quarterback hit you right in the face with a wild pass."

"Ha, ha. Very funny," I say and lean back into the window. I unwrap my arm from Emma's shoulder and I realize how fast my heart is beating. It thunders in my chest, pounding against my ribs so hard it hurts.

The game continues, but no one asks any questions quite as personal as that one. Emma's mom makes us dinner—a pasta casserole with cheese and chicken—and I think it may be the best thing I've ever eaten. I'd never tell my mom that, of course. We eat up in Wren's room since he can't come downstairs. The best part is that she made so much there are leftovers for tomorrow.

Jenny and I decide to camp out with Wren for the night. If he can't leave his bed, then we don't want to go anywhere either. That and the fact that we can't go anywhere and risk the Patrol finding us.

I find my place in the window seat and Jenny takes her usual spot curled up by Wren, hardly ever leaving his side. I have no idea how to process my sister's new closeness to Wren. Sure, the two were friends before we came to Pintura. Wren spent so much time at our house, him and Jenny had their own friendship. I never knew Jenny would want anything more with Wren. Of course, I've always known how Wren feels about Jenny. Hell, I'm sure *Jenny* knew all along what Wren's true feelings were.

But after everything we've been through, the fact that I saw the two of them smiling the entire day is reason enough for me not to question it.

I slept for most of the day, so it's hard for me to find it now. Up in the window seat, I trace the moon as it travels through the sky. When my eyes find the linked ring of stars far out in the distance, my stomach tightens. They just hang out there and taunt me late into the night.

A low creak rings into the room. I pull my eyes away from the stars and look toward the door. Emma was staying in her room tonight, but I guess she couldn't find sleep either. She crosses the room with silent footsteps, a soft blue blanket draped over her shoulders. She takes a seat on the floor next to the window seat.

"Can't sleep?" I ask, and she shakes her head.

We share a whispered conversation about the memories she has in this house. After a while, she stretches out on the floor next to the window seat, snuggling into the white carpet. The night passes in silence, and I think she may have drifted to sleep.

"Ash," I hear Emma whisper.

I glance down at her; surprised she's still awake. The moon is sending a single beam of light across her face. Her eyes look heavy and her voice is slow and soft, like she's about to give in to her dreams.

"Yeah, Em?" I ask, trying to get her words from her before sleep takes them.

"You're a great actor." She swallows and blinks against her heavy eyelids. "I really thought you were going to kiss me."

Her words hang in the air, finally pulling mine to the surface.

I watch her eyes close and her breathing slow, but I think she may still be awake. I think she may hear me, because after I say it, her lips curl up into the faintest smile.

"I did too."

The next day is terrible. More sitting, more time wasted. I can feel the pressure of being locked inside heating my blood. We try to play games and tell stories, but the games stop being fun and we run out of stories to share.

It's probably just me. The others seem okay. I don't know how they're managing it. Wren is doing better, and that's the only positive.

Not even the left over pasta casserole at dinner makes today any more bearable. Emma either truly cares or is tired of my sour attitude when she addresses me.

"Ash."

That's all she says. That's all she needs to say for me to know. Alone in the kitchen, cleaning up our dishes, I finally speak my annoyances out loud.

"Em, we're wasting time," I say harshly.

"I don't see it that way," she says, scrubbing the soapy water around in the casserole dish.

"I can't be trapped in here," I spit, but I regret the words.

I know Emma's mom has been so nice to let us stay here. She could have turned us into the Patrol. But I need something to be mad about, because ever since I saw those linked stars last night, I've been trying to keep a thought out of my head.

The longer I'm in here, though, the harder it's getting.

Emma rinses out the dish and dries it off. "Follow me," she says, putting the casserole dish on the counter and extending her hand to me.

I take it loosely and she leads me to the set of double doors that open to the backyard. The sun has drifted down below the horizon. Vibrant orange streaks shoot up into the deep navy sky. Late evening hugs the world outside.

Emma opens the door and leads me across the yard. Fresh air hits me instantly, helping to restore some clarity in my head.

"We shouldn't be outside," I whisper, glancing at the neighboring houses that are pressing in a little too close to the white picket fence for comfort.

"Shh," Emma hushes me, pulling me across the yard to the large tree. "Sit," she says, letting go of my hand once I'm standing in front of the tire swing.

I let out a breathy laugh. "Em."

She raises a hand. "I said sit, Ash." She's stern, but her lips curl into a small smile.

I roll my eyes, but my own lips form a smile. I slide into the large tire and grip the sides. Emma comes up behind me and pulls back on the swing.

"Ash, you have one job in this world," Emma says.

"What's that?" I ask, trying to see her over my shoulder.

"Enjoy being a kid."

She pushes hard and the tire swing moves forward, and then back. Emma gives the swing another shove and, with each push, I go higher and higher. Each new height helps me leave the anxious energy I've had all day on the ground. I laugh and suck in the night air.

I need to be higher. Higher and higher. Further and further from the problems on the ground.

But when I get high enough that I can see the tops of Infinity Forest, it all rushes back to me.

The vainders, the cards, home, Wren. I know it doesn't matter how high I swing, I'll never get away from what I'm about to do.

When Emma quits pushing me and I finally drift to a stop, she leans in front of me. "Well, Ash, did you accomplish your one job?"

I look at her happy face. I don't want to lie to her, but I want her to stay happy. I want her to stay this happy forever.

"I did," I say, and force a smile.

She does a little victory dance and we go back inside. While the three of them continue to aimlessly pass the time, my mind is elsewhere, planning for what I'm about to do.

"You know what I just realized?" Wren asks no one in particular.

"What?" Jenny prompts him as she brushes her hair at the foot of the bed, carefully braiding it before going to sleep.

"Tomorrow marks an entire week of us being gone."

Silence answers Wren. Even the sound of the brush working through Jenny's hair disappears.

Emma props herself up on her elbows, already stretched out on the floor beneath the window seat I'm perched on. "Has it really already been a week?"

"That doesn't seem possible," Jenny mumbles, shaking her head.

I bite my tongue to keep from snapping that we'll be here even longer if we continue to sit around and do nothing.

"I'm supposed to make a sale to the men at the Weights Ring tomorrow," Emma says with a sigh. "Hopefully, I can circle back to them later this week."

Jenny and Wren ask Emma about the sale, but I can't keep my focus engaged enough to follow along. All I can think about is how suffocating it feels to be hidden away in this house. All I can hear is the ticking of the second hand on Emma's watch as time continues to pass us by. Still, night does come faster than I wish it would. I wait until everyone else is asleep, and the moon is already deep into its descent before I move.

I gently tip-toe around Emma, who has again chosen to sleep on the floor instead of her bed, and head to the door. I pull on the jacket Emma let me borrow, fling my backpack over my shoulder, and tie the velvet bag of cards around my wrist. *Don't look back.*

I quietly pull the bedroom door closed behind me, but my eyes flicker up just as the door catches. The last thing I see is my sister asleep on Wren's chest, rising and falling with his breathing.

I feel my way down the dark hallway and find my shoes where I left them at the bottom of the staircase.

I can't wait any longer. Someone needs to get to the end of this game so we can go home, and I can't wait until Wren is finally recovered. I can't sit still anymore.

I head for the front door, but something steers me back to the kitchen. The block of knives by the sink catches my eye and I pull two of them free, each the length of my hand. I tell myself I'm just borrowing them. I'll bring them back. I can't go out there without something to protect me.

When I walk back to the front of the house, I pass the double doors that look out into the backyard. In the far corner of the yard, the tire swing is illuminated by the moonlight. It makes me think of Emma and I hope she can forgive me for what I'm about to do.

Silently, I move to the red front door. I slide back the locks and ease it open.

"You're not doing this alone."

Her voice makes my heart clench.

I turn and see Emma walking toward me, boots laced up and her backpack hanging from her shoulders.

"Em, stay here," I whisper.

Her eyes radiate with pain and anger.

"Ash Bane, you do not get to go off and be the hero. You don't get to leave me behind."

We hold each other's stares for a passing minute. I know she isn't going to back down, so I nod and offer her a smile she doesn't return.

"Emma Delaney, we all know you're the true hero."

CHAPTER 18

Emma

I can't believe he was going to leave without me. I knew something was wrong all day. I tried to get him to tell me about his plan. I gave him the opportunity to ask me to go with him, and he didn't.

Frustration still burns through me as we slide through the quiet streets of Artmith, heading for the loose spot of metal in the wall. I'm scared, of course, but I still want to be involved in this game. I've been getting around these streets late at night for years. It's better to sell your illegally engineered tools when no one else is looking. What would he have done if he were ambushed on his own?

The knife he took from my parent's kitchen is fastened against my hip. We each have one, like this will make a difference. After what happened the other night, I can only assume the vainders will be staying in bigger packs now.

No extra Patrol seem to be out, but Ash still walks with the hood of the jacket draped over his head just in case. Every once in a while, we'll pass a billboard with their faces on it.

"They definitely got my nose wrong," Ash jokes, leaning in to examine a picture of his face on the side of a building. Bold black words claim Lord Neko will give a hefty reward in exchange for the three of them. It's a year's worth of allowances. I'm actually surprised my mom didn't want to try and get the money.

"Let's keep moving," I whisper, and pull him along.

When we reach the loose flap in the wall, Ash and I crawl through and hike toward Infinity Forest. I keep glancing and checking our directions with the stars above. The grey clouds still spin in the dark cyclone that spit them out, but the stars shimmer through.

We stop in the middle of the Golden Field and reevaluate our path. It takes a second for me to realize this was the spot I first found them. In the middle of the night, it looks different, like it's balanced in a parallel universe. Rising Salvation soars up to our left and the linked stars hang directly to our right.

"Are you ready?" I ask. The next step will be to head into the dark forest and it all feels too soon for me.

Ash swallows and knocks back his hood, his focus trained on the stars. Finally, he looks down at me.

"Yeah. Ready."

"Remember, we'll be in and out as fast as we can."

That's the last thing either of us says until we reach the edge of the forest. Once we're there, all the words Ash must have been thinking surface.

"Em, I can't." Ash freezes at the edge, his eyes searching the dark shadows of the woods. His chest rises and falls with shallow breaths, sheer panic taking over, and I think he may hyperventilate. "When I was up in that tree," he forces the words pass quick breaths, "and Wren was bleeding out, and Jenny was screaming, and you were on the vainder's back, I was more scared than I've been in my entire life. Everyone I cared about was on the brink of dying and I was *frozen in a tree.*"

"Ash." I grip both of his arms tightly, my fingers wrapping around the muscles he's built from years of drumming. "It's okay to be frozen in a tree."

His eyes move from the shadows to me.

"Wren, and Jenny, and me, we're all fine. You and I are going to finish the second card tonight. *You unfreeze tonight.*"

I watch my words process on Ash's face. Finally, he blinks away his frozen stare and nods. Before he can freeze up again, I tug him forward and we melt into the dark shadows.

We start at a steady jog, trying to pick a pace we can maintain. Ash watches our right and I watch our left. As far as we can see, the woods are empty. After what feels like hours, I tell Ash to stop and check our progress.

"Climb up, and see how much farther it is," I whisper, gulping down my water. It's one of the few things we've dared to speak aloud since entering Infinity Forest.

Ash pulls himself onto the lowest branch and begins to climb. I return my water to my bag and feel the nerves settle in. It's easier to ignore them when I'm running. Standing still makes me feel like an easy target. I pace in a circle around the tree, scanning the area. The whole time Ash is away, a nauseous wave crashes around in my stomach.

Come on Ash, hurry up.

No matter how fast I spin and scan the area, my back is always exposed. My fingers tap on the handle of the knife, ready to draw it at any second. I keep thinking I see black fur shining in the moonlight. I swear I hear a branch snap just over that hill. How many of them are probably watching us right now?

There's a sudden *thud* directly behind me and I *scream*. An ear-piercing shrill that shatters the quiet night.

"Shh!" Ash hisses angrily, as I spin to face him. He clamps his hand over my mouth.

We don't move. I stare at him and he stares at me. My loose scream echoes out into the forest. I follow the sound, praying nothing else heard me.

My heart beats hard, pounding in my ears.

Thump thump. Thump thump.

I can feel Ash's pulse as he presses his body against mine.

Thump thump. Thump thump.

And then there's the unmistakable sound of a *howl*.

Tears rush to the edges of my eyes. They're coming.

"We need to climb," Ash urges, practically throwing me against the tree.

My hands find the branch and I pull myself up higher and higher. Ash stays right behind me, pushing me upward and showing me which branches he used.

We get to the thinnest of the branches before the sounds of the pack reach us. Yelps and howls ring out through the woods. Ash and I find a forked branch surrounded with deep green leaves, and we let them conceal us as best as we can.

Ash presses his back against the trunk of the tree and pulls me into his chest. It's not until Ash has his arms around my waist that I realize how badly I'm shaking.

Through the maze of branches, I see slivers of the vainder pack pass beneath our tree. Their paws pound into the dirt as they race past. *Please keep moving.*

I think we may be in the clear when the last few vainders slow under our tree, turning their noses to the sky.

I flinch back into Ash, my cry muffled behind my locked lips. For a second, the world balances in silence. My eyes stay trained on their glossy black fur. One of them lets out a loud, long, bellowing howl and I flinch into Ash again. He tightens his arms around me, trying to keep me still. I tighten my throat and choke on a suppressed cry.

Then, the few that stopped take off again, following the rest of the pack. I wait until the sound of the pounding feet has finally ceased before I speak.

"I'm so sorry," I blurt out in a hushed voice.

"It's okay," Ash assures me, rubbing a comforting hand on my back.

"Do you think they're going to come back this way?" I ask.

"Probably," Ash admits. "But we won't be here when they do."

His words are the only hope of possible relief right now.

"How much farther?" I ask, knowing he's waiting for me to prompt him.

"We're almost under them, just a little off to the left."

"Do you think we can get there through the trees?" I ask. "I feel safer up here."

Ash looks in the direction we need to go, considering the idea. "I think that'd be smart. I can lead if you want."

I agree to follow, and Ash finds us the best path through the tree branches. We haven't heard another howl from the vainders, so I continue to hope that they stay away until we can get out of here.

"We're close, Em," Ash says over his shoulder. "Keep your eyes peeled of anything out of the ordinary."

But once we cross to the next tree, the thing we're looking for is right in front of us. The large oaks separate around a small clearing. A thin string hangs in the space in front of us, and it looks like it's tethered to the stars above. At the other end of the string, just a couple of feet above the forest floor, is a clear bottle. A piece of parchment appears to be rolled up inside.

The sight of the bottle coming from the sky above makes me once again think of the magic that is rumored to fuel this world. A place I've lived my entire life with this power I never knew truly existed.

"Oh my gosh, Em," Ash says. "We found it!"

He starts to quickly descend through the thick tree branches when I stop him.

"Let's review the card again," I say and nod to the velvet bag tied around his wrist. "We can't be down there for long. We don't want to risk another vainder attack."

"You're right," Ash agrees. "Let's make sure we know exactly what we need to do."

Ash pulls the velvet bag off his wrist and shuffles through the cards. In the slim rays of moonlight, he finds the second card and we read the riddle.

LOOK ABOVE TO THE STARS
TO FIND WHERE YOU MUST GO

THE CIRCLES LINK ON THE CARDS
WILL LEAD YOU WHERE IT HANGS LOW

IF YOU TAKE WHAT THE STARS PROVIDE
BE PREPARED TO LEAVE SOMETHING ELSE BEHIND

192

"What are we supposed to leave behind?" I ask and watch Ash take in the words.

"I have something," he says distantly, re-reading the riddle to make sure we don't miss anything. "I'll get it. You cover me, okay?"

I see a sense of urgency and passion fill Ash's eyes.

"Okay," I say and draw my knife. We climb down the branches and before Ash descends to the ground, we double check that the area is clear. I balance myself on the lowest branch and keep my eyes locked on the shadows.

Ash drops to the forest floor and runs to the hanging bottle. When his feet hit the dirt, an internal clock starts ticking in my head, counting every second he spends exposed to the vainders.

Quickly, he reaches the bottle and removes the parchment, gripping it tightly in his hand. Ash reaches into his pocket and unclips something on a short chain. He pauses for a moment, running his finger over the small object.

My gaze snaps to the rustling leaves across the clearing, and a clammy sweat blooms on my cheeks. A pair of beady, black eyes peers into the clearing. The vainder pulls back its gums, showing its long, metal teeth.

Before we entered Infinity Forest, I told Ash that it's okay to be frozen in a tree. I remember those words now as I crouch on my branch, a kitchen knife gripped beneath my stone-white knuckles, with lungs refusing to hold in my gasping breaths.

It's okay to be frozen in a tree.

It's okay to be scared.

The vainder inches a single paw forward, bending its weight back in preparation to launch itself through the air.

Toward Ash.

Toward the boy who almost kissed me last night.

Toward the boy who has nearly consumed my every waking thought.

It is okay to be scared, but I can't afford to be that right now. I have to fight. *Fight, fight, fight. Do something. Anything!*

That adrenaline that sparked in my blood the night Wren threw himself at a vainder to save Jenny ignites once more.

"Ash, get down!" I scream.

Ash whips his head to me and sees my knife flying through the air. He drops into the underbrush and my knife whizzes past him, striking the vainder. It lets out a painful howl.

"Ash, let's go!" I yell, already starting to climb the tree, knowing more of the vainders will be here soon.

Ash drops his object into the bottle and hurries back to our tree. We climb and leap from branch to branch, not once looking over our shoulders.

"What happened to being quick?" I huff.

"Sorry, I just—" Ash starts to say, but he cuts himself off. "Thanks for saving me."

"Don't thank me yet," I mumble.

We continue at this pace until my legs are aching so badly I have to slow down. Besides our heavy breathing, the woods are quiet. No other vainders are chasing us right now.

The branches bounce under our weight, but their thick centers never give way. I finally stop to reassess our location when we haven't heard any vainders.

"I think we lost them," Ash says between deep breaths.

"We should stay up in the trees," I admit. "We can't travel as fast, but it's definitely safer."

Ash agrees and we take a short break to drink some water and check our direction. Now that we're high enough to feel somewhat safe, we begin to maneuver from tree to tree at a more manageable pace, slowly working our way back to Artmith. I let Ash lead the way now, and follow the path he takes through the twisting tree branches.

"What'd you leave behind?" I ask when I think it may be the right time.

"I left my drum key chain," he says softly. "My dad got it for me when I first joined band in fifth grade."

"Why'd you choose that?" I ask curiously. It seems like something important and sentimental.

"I was ready to part with it."

"Can I ask you why?"

"It kind of feels like I've been holding on to drumming for too long," Ash explains. "For the last year, I only stayed in band for my parents."

"But aren't you supposed to continue playing in college?" I ask gently.

Ash lets out a heavy sigh. "That's the thing, Em," Ash begins. "I can't actually ever let it go. So, letting go of the key chain was the closest thing I could think of."

"You don't like drumming anymore, but you're going to keep doing it?"

"I love drumming," Ash clarifies. "I hate playing music I don't like. I spend so much time at band rehearsing for concerts I don't want to be at and feeling like I always have to prove myself to the other drummers. I love drumming," Ash repeats. "Rhythm is something that has always been beating inside of me."

"I think that makes a lot of sense, Ash," I offer.

"You think so?" he asks, ducking under a low branch. He turns around and helps me crawl under it.

"I do, and I think it's something you should tell your parents."

Ash shakes his head and turns to keep moving across the branches. "Too late now, Em. I have to keep playing to pay for my education at Coastal University."

"I'd like you to play for me sometime," I say.

Ash glances back over his shoulder.

"You know, when we're not running from vainders and trying to unlock a portal to another world," I add.

He laughs and says, "I'd love to."

Silent minute after silent minute passes until they stretch into at least an hour. In the quiet, my mind wonders what would have happened if I didn't throw that knife at the vainder. What if I hadn't seen it? What if I hadn't stayed awake to make sure Ash wouldn't leave? Would he be dead right now? It makes me really stop and think about what Ash means to me.

In the short time I've known him, I feel like I'm closer to Ash than any of my classmates. The fact that I've never had a real friend is probably the reason I jumped at the chance to have three.

I was close with Jake. I mean, I thought I was. Once the relationship was over, I realized how little of our relationship was built around friendship. He just wanted someone to come listen while he practiced for band. Someone he could use as an excuse to skip out on projects and parties he didn't want to go to. And I just wanted someone to be with who didn't laugh at me. Someone who didn't know my parents and didn't know me.

But with Ash, it's *so* different. He not only knows me, he knows *all* of me. For the first time, the real reason we are following these cards finally hits me. When we get to the end of this game, they're going to go home. I'm going to have to say goodbye.

"Ash," I say softly, breaking our silence. "I'm really going to miss you when you have to leave."

He stops and spins to me. I'm sure he can hear the sadness in my voice, but I hope the night conceals the tears in my eyes.

His face seems shocked by my words. Either he's surprised that I'll miss him or he hadn't given the end of this game much thought.

"I don't know how I'm going to say goodbye to you," he admits, letting himself speak unfiltered.

"Do you think I can mail you letters from Pintura?" I offer as a joke, shrugging my shoulders.

His laugh is sad, but he says, "If anyone could find a way to do it, I bet it would be you."

I smile at him, but I don't let myself speak. I hold back my words because right now, the only thing I want to do is tell him how much his friendship means to me. I want to tell him how much I like him, how I think my feelings are quickly moving past friends.

But I keep my mouth shut. If I speak those words, then the feelings are *real*. And if the feelings are real, that means we'll have to deal with them, and for what? Just to have him leave in the end?

I don't want to go through another heartbreak, especially when I know one with Ash would be so much worse.

He moves closer to me and pushes a piece of blonde hair behind my ear. He's always doing that, and I've come to expect it now. I even wish for him to do it.

"I mean it, Em," he says. "You're the smartest person I've ever met."

I almost laugh out loud. How could someone so smart let their heart want to do something so stupid?

"You don't have to say goodbye to me now." He whispers the words and tilts my chin up, knowing I'm avoiding eye contact. "You don't have to say anything."

His last words come out slow, and I wonder if he means something else by them. Does he mean I don't have to say how I'm feeling because he already knows?

"But I'll have to say goodbye soon." My voice is so weak, the words are almost too quiet to be heard.

"Then we'll make the best of our last days." Ash offers me a smile. The kind of smile that tells you it's all going to be all right and you have no choice but to feel that way, too.

"Promise?" I ask, my lips curling into their own smile.

"Emma Delany, these are about to be the best days of your life," Ash says, backing away from me. "Starting when we get back to your house," he clarifies quickly, brushing this predicament off like it's no big deal.

I continue to follow Ash across the branches, and when we finally make it to the edge of the forest, daylight already streams down on the Golden Field.

I hadn't realized how late in the morning it already was. The forest is still grey, holding on to its shadows.

The gate will be opening soon. Ash comes to the same realization as me. Daytime means crowds and the Patrol. Both of which we can't be around.

"Do you think we can get through the gate undetected?" Ash asks, helping me down the tree and onto solid ground.

My legs throb and I'm a little unbalanced. I work on pulling leaves out of my hair and say, "I think we'll be too noticeable. Everyone will be going out and we'll be going in."

"So, the loose spot in the wall is our only option?" he asks.

I sigh and nod, and we start heading toward Artmith. I don't particularly like using this entrance during the day. It's more likely someone will see me sliding inside and if I lose my secret entrance and exit, it becomes a lot harder to sneak my supplies in from the scrapyard. Once we get closer to Artmith, I see the growing crowd at the iron gates. The amount of Patrol has tripled. No longer are people yelling and forcing their way through the gates. The crowd stands in five silent single file lines.

Ash and I stay in the tallest parts of the field until we make it to the loose piece of metal in the wall. With everyone lining up at the gate and triple the Patrol stationed there, we slide into the city undetected.

It's harder to get through Artmith in the daytime. The narrow alleys aren't as dark and the streets are busier. Ash pulls up his hood and takes out the scarf from his bag, tying it tightly around his face.

"You lead the way, Em," he says, pushing me out in front of him.

I'm honestly not sure which way to take us. I keep moving toward home, but every time we get to a street with other people shopping or going to work, I branch off into the closest empty alley I can find. I get so turned around I end up at the University, far past my parent's house. The campus is quiet, so we hurry across the green quads and down University Boulevard.

"Emma?" a voice calls from behind me.

Pretend you don't hear him.

I continue moving with Ash, keeping our heads down.

"Emma!" he yells louder. "Hey! Stop, please!"

I'm not sure where he comes from, but his hand grips my wrist, yanking me back and making me face him.

"What do you want, Jake?" I ask harshly, ripping my wrist from his grip.

He's the last person I want to see right now. Ash stops but keeps his body angled away from Jake. I wish he would have kept going.

"I've been trying to get a hold of you. When I saw the wanted posters of those trespassers, I remembered you were with them. I thought they did something to you," he begins to ramble, but his words are muffled in my ears.

Crap, I forgot we ran into Jake in the band room. He saw Ash, Wren, and Jenny. For the second time, I quickly remember. The night they got into a fight with the Beast at the arcade was the first time.

"Did you tell anyone you saw them with me?" I ask, cutting Jake off when he starts talking about what his first impressions were of my friends from Earth.

"No... I—" Jake's words get lodged in his throat and he changes their direction. "What are you getting yourself into, Emma? Where have you been?"

"I've been staying at my parent's," I say, though I'm not sure why I need to explain myself. Ash shifts his weight behind me, clearly growing uncomfortable. I cross my arms to cover his movements.

"I was hoping we could hang out sometime. I'd like to catch up." Jake drops his head a little, tilting it ever so slightly to the right.

I blink fast. *What did he just say?*

"You're joking, right?" I ask, huffing a harsh laugh.

"Em, I'm sorry about Tammy."

I cringe at the nickname. "I never want to see you again, Jake," I say, my voice low as I shake my head.

"Is this your new boyfriend?" Jake asks, his pleasant personality changing to jealousy.

He reaches out and shoves Ash around. Ash steps back from his grasp, keeping his head down.

"What a coward," Jake says, reaching out to shove Ash again. "You steal my girl and you can't even look at me."

Ash's head snaps up, his crystal blue eyes peering over the red bandana.

"He didn't steal me," I interject and step between Jake and Ash, hoping to block his view. "I'm not yours."

Jake tries to look at Ash over my shoulder, his eyes in narrow slants.

Please don't recognize him. Please don't recognize him.

Finally, Jake looks down at me and says, "I'll be in the band room tonight at seven. Meet me there and let me explain myself."

I open my mouth to deny him, but he puts up a hand to stop me.

"Don't say no. Just think about it."

I snap my lips together. Before anything else is said, I spin around and pull Ash along with me. When we reach my parent's house, my blood is still hot with anger. At this point, I think I'd rather have seen a vainder than Jake. I imagine him alone in the band room tonight, getting stood up, and that makes me feel better.

When we enter Wren's room, Jenny is pacing back and forth in front of the bed. Wren sits with his legs hanging over the edge, trying to put on his shoes.

"Where have you been?" Jenny shrieks, hitting Ash hard on the chest. "Don't you dare tell me you went into those woods last night."

"Guilty," Ash says sheepishly, untying his bandana and pushing back his hood.

Jenny lets out a groan of anger. "Ash, I'm so mad right now I could, I could—"

Before Jenny can finish, I interrupt. "We found it!"

The anger in her face eases away.

"You did it?" Wren asks.

I nod and Ash reaches into his bag to pull out the rolled parchment.

"Well, what did you find?" Wren asks, excitement already chasing their worry away.

"We haven't opened it yet," I say. We move to the bed and sit with the rolled parchment in the center of us. "We wanted to open it together," I add.

"Oh, you want to do *this* together," Jenny grumbles.

"Jenny, I just didn't want to waste any more time. I wasn't doing us any good sitting here," Ash says.

"Why'd you let Emma go with you?" Jenny questions.

Ash laughs at that. "I didn't let her go. She caught me leaving."

Jenny presses her lips together. She doesn't like his answer, but she doesn't know how to counter it.

Instead, she turns her glare to me. "Your mom noticed you were gone this morning."

"What did you tell her?" I ask, knowing I'd never hear the end of it if she knew I was outside the gate in the middle of the night again.

"I just said you and Ash went back to your house to grab some things."

"Thanks," I say, relieved that she covered for me.

"Yeah, well, your mom told Wren and me to be gone before lunch. Our three days are up."

I sigh. Well, my mother's kindness was short lived, as usual.

"Can you walk?" Ash asks.

"Yeah, I'm moving all right. Running isn't happening. No jumping from trees and spearing vainders either," he jokes, looking at me. "Open this thing already!" Wren says, nudging the parchment.

Carefully, I remove the small black tie. The parchment roll loosens and I slowly spread it flat. My eyes sweep across the paper, back and forth, taking in the details.

"It's a map," I say, my voice breathy.

Printed in thick, curvy, black ink is a clear picture of Pintura. It's a twisty circular shape. Stretching across the entire tan page. Artmith is labeled at the bottom of the map. That's where the dashed line begins. I trace the path with my fingers. It goes through the Golden Field, across the lake, and stops right at the base of Rising Salvation.

"Is that where the portal is?" Jenny asks excitedly, completely forgetting the anger she had just moments ago.

"Well, we're only on card three," Ash says hesitantly. "It can't be the portal."

"Emma, you should read the card again," Wren offers.

Ash removes the velvet bag from his wrist and hands me the card labeled with a three. I see that it's titled *X Marks the Entrance.*

THE STARS ABOVE HAVE ALL THE ANSWERS
THEY'VE GIFTED YOU A PATH TO FOLLOW

LET IT LEAD YOU IN THIS CHAPTER
AND YOU WILL FIND WHERE I TURN HOLLOW

GOLDEN BLOCKS IN THE SUN
WHERE THE WATER RUNS

As Jenny and Wren prepare themselves to leave, I steal a moment to go find my mom. She's quietly perched in her favorite chair, tucked away in the study. A book with a deep maroon cover is propped against her knees, her eyes scanning the words. When I enter, she snaps the book closed.

"I know I'm not supposed to bother you when you're in here," I say, the lectures she's had with me are enough of a reminder. "I just wanted to let you know we're leaving."

My mom nods, and I see words are caught in her throat. I stay silent, knowing that if I let the quiet hang long enough, she'll speak.

As I suspected, she breaks the silence. "Should I be worried about you?"

Her words sound like a hundred different phrases in my head. *Are you going to die helping them? Will I see you again? Why are you risking your life for them? Why can't you just be normal?*

"Mom," I say, my voice quivering. I cross the room and sit in the matching chair next to her. "I'm going to show you something, so that you know what I'm doing. I don't want to bring you into this. I don't need your help or a lecture. I just want you to know, so you don't worry."

The tight muscles in her face relax and she nods. I take out the velvet bag of cards and open it. When I fan the maroon cards out in front of her, her eyes register that she recognizes them.

"I'm helping them get back to Earth. These cards are instructions to find a portal," I say softly. I expect her to laugh at me or rip them from my hands. Instead, she smiles.

"Emma," she says with a sigh. "I don't know what lies they've poisoned you with, but this is a children's game. Don't risk your life trying to force them to be anything more."

My throat tightens. I didn't expect her to believe me. I just wish, for once, she would give me a chance. I stack the cards and tuck them into their bag. I don't say anything else to her. I have nothing else I want to say. I stand and walk across the study, clicking the white double doors closed behind me.

CHAPTER 19

Ash

Are you sure you don't want to rest more?" I ask Wren as he walks next to me. Our hoods are pulled up and the scarves have found their places around our faces.

"I'm fine, Ash."

"You were about to die a couple of days ago."

"The medicine they have here is different than at home," Wren says. "Look." He pulls up on the hem of Emma's dad's jacket and shirt—the only spare clothes Emma could find for him after his were ruined in the attack. The vainder slash is now a wrinkled scar. It looks like it happened days ago.

"Wren," Jenny hisses, snapping her hand out to pull his arm and clothes down. "Don't draw more attention to us."

My sister's right. I peer over my bandana and see a few curious glances already flipping in our direction at the jackets we're wearing. In this summer heat we look extremely out of place, but I think it's better than having nothing to conceal us. Once we're on the other side of the sheet metal wall, we can shrug our disguises off.

We make it to Emma's house easily. Most of the streets in Shadow Village are deserted. Emma wants to grab some supplies before we follow our map. Mainly, she wants to get her prototype night vision glasses. Chances are, this map is going to lead us to some kind of cave in the mountain. That's what Emma thinks, anyway. I keep the knife I borrowed from her parent's kitchen tucked away in my backpack.

Emma leads us back through the streets of Artmith and toward the loose part of the wall. I know it's riskier to go there during the day, but this is a challenge we can complete in daylight, so we're taking advantage of that.

She does her best to lead us away from the busier streets, but that means she ends up leading us down random alleys all around the city. The map we retrieved this morning shifts in my backpack. I've already engrained it to memory. Emma promised us we wouldn't run into any vainders now that it's daytime, and since we're staying away from the Infinity Forest, we are even less likely to encounter them.

"Go back," Emma hisses, spinning sharply.

I snap my focus up and my eyes land on the red helmet of a Patrol officer standing at the other end of the alley.

"Stay calm," she whispers, and we turn with her, branching off into another side alley. When we take our next turn, I glance behind us.

"He's following us."

"Run," Emma says, still keeping her voice down and we take off, trying to clear the alley before the Patrol officer turns. I hear the crunching of quickened footsteps on the gravel behind me. *He's definitely following us.*

"Do you have a plan?" I ask and Emma nods her head, blonde curls flying back from her face.

Wren pants hard next to me, but he keeps pushing himself.

"Here," Emma says, racing through a quick series of turns and we come out in front of the wall. She pulls back the loose piece of metal and we hurry through it, snapping it back into place once we're on the other side. I push my back to the wall and listen to see if the Patrol officer saw us come through the wall. I hear his footsteps stop on the other side. He twists left and right, trying to decide which way we went and eventually, he decides on right.

"That was too close," Jenny says, pulling her scarf off face so she can suck down deep breaths.

"Wren, are you okay?" I ask, seeing him bent over, gasping for air.

He sucks in a large breath and straightens. "Yep, all good," he wheezes in a tight voice and then releases the air.

We take a minute to peel off our jackets and tuck them away in our backpacks. Jenny and I still wear the shirt and shorts we put on the day we fell through the painting, and I've noticed the torn hem on her black shirt has started to roll.

My own clothes aren't holding up that well after the week we've been through, but I refuse to trade any of them in for something of this world. It's the only thing I have left that ties me to home, and I know Jenny feels the same.

Out of all of us, Emma seems the most out of place. For once, she's not wearing her navy overalls. A lavender short-sleeved shirt hangs from her shoulders, long enough to reach the center of her thighs, and nearly covers her black shorts that are belted low on her hips.

"Next stop, Rising Salvation," Emma says, extending her hand to me, asking for the map. I take her hand in mine as a joke and her eyes widen a little.

"Oh, I was," she stumbles over her words. "I was asking for the map."

I laugh and let her hand drop after giving it a tight squeeze. I fish out the map and pass it to Emma, noticing her cheeks are flushed a light pink.

After last night, I've pretty much confirmed that, what I feel for Emma, she feels for me. In all actuality, it's a messy situation, but it's also the only thing that seems to make me smile anymore.

"Something going on here?" Wren asks, smirking.

"You're one to talk," I say, shoving him lightly.

"Let's go," Jenny groans and rolls her eyes.

"This way," Emma directs, holding the map out in front of her.

I know she's mastered her way around Pintura. She just wants to use the map so we take the exact path that's drawn out. She leads us into the Golden Field that sits in the valley between Rising Salvation and Infinity Forest.

Some people are out here harvesting wheat, but they keep to themselves. We maintain a healthy distance between us and them, continuing to stay on our path. Seeing the people of Artmith working makes me realize how much money Emma is probably losing since she's been absent from the scrapyard for a week. I wish there was something I could do to help her.

"So, you and Emma finally hit it off," Wren says, his voice hushed.

I glance up at Emma and Jenny a few paces ahead of us. Jenny has taken the hem of Emma's long shirt and tied it up in a little knot at her right hip like a lot of the girls back home wear it.

My mouth parts, trying to find the words I want to say. "Not really," I offer and shrug. "We're just friends."

"But you obviously like her," Wren says.

"Is it really that obvious?" I ask and Wren laughs softly.

"Jen and I were betting on how long it'd take for you to admit it."

"This doesn't count as me admitting it," I say quickly. Emma's words from this morning come back to me. "Wren, we're going to leave at some point. She's from an entirely different world. I *can't* like her."

"Yeah, you don't want to go down that road," he agrees.

It makes me a little sad to say that out loud. My throat tightens and silence hangs in the air between us. I realize this is the first time Wren and I have talked alone since arriving in Pintura. My thoughts turn to our friendship, and after years of avoiding this conversation, I finally want to bring it up.

"Wren—"

"Ash—"

We speak in unison, the silence taking both our minds to the same realization.

"Please, let me," Wren says. "I'm sorry I stopped hanging out with you. I didn't mean for it to happen."

"It's okay, Wren," I say, shaking my head. "I didn't put in the effort to see you either."

"No, it's not okay," Wren retorts, and his voice has grown very serious. "You were my best friend, my sidekick, my wingman. I shouldn't have drifted."

"Well, I'm sorry I got you dragged into all this," I say, gesturing to the world around us. If I hadn't asked him to help move my grandma's things, he would never had fallen into this mess.

"I'm not," Wren says. He glances sideways at me and smiles. "It reminded me how big of a mistake I made letting our friendship go. I wish I could have that time back, Ash. I'm glad I jumped into that painting. I wouldn't take it back, because it's helped us become friends again."

My chest throbs at his words. How many years have I waited for him to say that? How many nights did I imagine texting him or calling him to try and restore our friendship? "When we get back, we'll make up for the lost time." I say and Wren's smile splits, white teeth grinning at me.

He throws an arm around my shoulder and pulls me into his side. "Ash, when we get home, we'll make the best of our last summer before college."

The mention of college, a future of drumming, and endless hours of school makes my stomach drop, so I change the subject. "So, you and Jenny."

I let the statement hang in the air and Wren visibly tenses with a bright blush blooming on his cheeks. I shake my head and roll my eyes in disbelief.

"I can't believe she actually likes you. Like, in *that way*. I guess after all these years of you trying to get her to like you, all you had to do was almost die saving her life."

Wren laughs at that. I glance at him and see he's biting his lip.

"What is it?" I ask, seeing he's holding in his words.

Wren glances at me, wondering if he should tell me the words he's keeping secret.

"Come on, Wren," I push.

"I don't know if I should tell you this," he says cautiously. "Jenny probably doesn't want you to know."

My jaw drops open and I furrow my brows, giving him a look that says he's going to have to tell me now. He understands what I'm saying and sighs.

"Over winter break, I was at Sally Temple's house. She hosted that big Christmas party for the senior class, remember?"

I nod, remembering the annual party Wren and I agreed to *never* go to. It wasn't that we didn't want to go to *this* party. We didn't go to *any* of them freshman year. I liked to spend my free time trying to draw or learn more rudiments for our band tests. I knew Wren had taken to the social scene, and I know that was a part of why we drifted.

"Well, Jenny was at the party and she seemed so out of place. I don't know who invited her to a senior party, but she didn't seem to know anyone there. She kind of stuck with me most of the night. Later, we played this game." Wren pauses, taking in a deep breath. I glance up at him and see his cheeks are burning bright red now.

"See, Sally Temple lives out on the edge of town near Lover's Lake. I mean, it's practically in her backyard. Anyway, one at a time, each guy was taken out to Lover's Lake and there would be one girl from the party there. You either had to either kiss the girl or jump in the lake. I mean, how stupid were we? It was December! I bet it was forty degrees that night. I couldn't imagine how cold that water must have felt—"

"Wren, you're rambling," I interrupt, and I'm suddenly very aware of the words he's saying. Something important happened that night and he's kept it from me for six months. Friends or not, I would have wanted him to tell me. I would have listened.

"Well, they paired me with Jenny," Wren says.

"You kissed my sister *months* ago?" I ask. I don't know what shocks me more, that they kissed or that he really didn't tell me until vainders and Pintura brought us back together.

"I didn't want to say anything because Jenny seemed so embarrassed by the whole night. I think she just wanted to prove herself to the senior girls, and I was the safest choice."

We're quiet for a moment, because I'm not sure I understand everything. Wren and my sister have had this secret for months? I think back to how Jenny had spent most of her weekends with her teammates. She went to prom with a baseball player, and she never, not once, ever mentioned Wren to me.

"You haven't asked her about the kiss? She just pretended it didn't happen?" I ask.

Wren shakes his head. "For a couple of weeks, I hadn't heard anything from Jenny. Then, I started getting these secret letters in my locker talking about the kiss and how she didn't know how to feel."

Suddenly, all the folded pieces of paper I caught Jenny shoving into her drawers and backpack make sense. It reminds me of that piece of paper she was reading in my car on our way to our grandmother's house. Was that a note from Wren? *How could I have missed all of this?*

"We just wrote each other notes. One or two a week, nothing too obvious, but we hadn't actually talked about it at all. I don't know why I just didn't ask her or text her. I guess I felt like we finally had *our thing* and I didn't want to ruin it."

"Why didn't you tell me?"

We may not have been close at the time, but this is something I'd expect Wren to tell me. I mean, he's liked her *forever*.

"Ash, this is your sister we're talking about," Wren says, shrugging his shoulder. "I don't really want to talk about how I'm falling for Jenny. I guess I didn't know how you'd feel about it."

I can't argue with that. I don't know how I feel about it. Him and my sister. The whole thing is weird.

"That's the whole story, Ash. We don't have to talk about it anymore," Wren says quickly, feeling the awkwardness in the air.

"What do you think is going to happen when we get back to Earth? Are you and Jenny going to continue this?" I ask, imagining how weird *that* would be. Wren wouldn't be coming over to play video games with me, he'd be coming over to watch a movie with my sister.

"Just trying to get home first, Ash." Wren brushes off my question in the easiest way he can think of.

I let out a sigh. "Wren, if you hurt my sister," I say, knowing in the end I have to choose family over him.

Wren laughs and shoves me lightly on the shoulder. "You don't have to say it, Ash, I know."

I nod, but can't ignore the pinch in my chest as I glance sideways at Wren. I don't think it's Jenny I'm worried about getting hurt.

"And Ash," Wren starts, pausing to meet my glance. "If acting is really your passion, you should go after it. I'll always support you."

I'm too surprised by his words to say anything right away. I want to ask where that came from, if it's something he's been thinking about since the day we went looking for our tokens, but our conversation is interrupted.

"Are you guys ready for a swim?" Emma calls back to us.

I look past her and over the tops of the golden wheat. In the distance, deep blue-green water shimmers. Rising Salvation towers above us on the other side of the water. Its tan, rocky surface stretches in jagged peaks, reaching for cyclone of clouds above. The air in my lungs is thin as I stare at it in awe. I have to wonder how Emma could

214

ever doubt the existence of magic when something this magnificent is a part of her world.

When we get closer to the lake, the sounds of splashing water and casual conversation grow. Groups of kids are laying out on the bed of the lake. Some are in the water, treading in the small currents.

"Popular place," Jenny mumbles.

Emma nods. "It's the place to be in the summer."

She leads us to a part of the bank that is empty. "The path ends on the other side. Ready?" Emma pulls out the plastic container she swiped from her parent's kitchen and seals the map inside with her night vision glasses and the playing cards. "Come on," she teases when she sees our hesitant expressions.

Emma backs into the water, boots, shorts, shirt, and all. We follow her, the muddy lake bottom sucking at my sneakers. The water is warm, soaking my shorts to my legs. As we get deeper, the sheer weight of the soaked clothes and my backpack pull me down.

We go at a slow pace so we don't wear ourselves out. I can walk through the goopy bottom of the lake longer than Emma, her shorter legs unable to reach solid ground anymore. Eventually, I have to give up on trying to tip-toe my way through the warm lake when it gets too deep, the water lapping against my lips. Uneven and awkward strokes pull me across the lake. Every muscle in my body tenses and works against my weight in the currents.

"Not much of a swimmer?" Emma asks, finding my twisted facial expression funny.

"Not in a lake," I say, the murky, dark green water keeping me on edge. "I'm used to crystal blue waves in Cali."

Emma's eyes go distant, trying to imagine what that could look like. Right, no oceans in Pintura.

"Emma, do we need to be worried about anything living in this lake?" Jenny asks, barely keeping her head above the water.

Emma chuckles at that and I think I see her shrug her shoulders. "I've been swimming in this lake my whole life, so I don't think so."

"Great," Jenny mumbles, kicking her feet hard to stay above the water.

Wren stays at her side, and when her arms get tired, he pulls her along with him.

Emma and I do well on our own. We try to keep some form of conversation going so we don't notice the aching in our muscles.

"I think we're halfway," Emma pants, trying to look back over her shoulder.

I follow her gaze and see the group of people on the bank are small dots.

"So, are you going to see Jake tonight?" I ask, keeping our conversation going.

Emma gives me a crazed look that screams she can't believe I just asked that.

"Absolutely not," she says, her voice curling up at the end. "Also, aren't I a little preoccupied?" She tries to gesture around herself and splashes her arms through the water.

"Do you *want* to go?" I ask, trying to reach a different angle with my question.

"I just said no," she denies.

"So, you don't still like him?"

"No," she quickly snaps, but I see her eyes are still processing the question. "I don't like him," she mumbles. "But I don't like being alone either."

I don't know why she actually decides to tell me this. Maybe out in the middle of the lake with no one else around, she feels safe admitting her desperation to be with someone.

"You have me," I offer.

"I don't," Emma says, her voice growing frustrated. "You're going to leave. He's offering to be with me and I'd be lying if I said I haven't thought about the offer, just so I'd have someone."

We fall quiet for a moment, just the splashing of our strokes speaking. I don't know what happened between Jake and Emma. This morning he mentioned something happening with Tammy—the girl who'd been with him that day at the band room—but I don't think it's my place to ask Emma to tell me that story. Still, my next words come easy and I don't doubt them.

"You deserve better than him, Em."

She doesn't hesitate when she says, "I know."

Our conversation changes to the food I like back in California, and what Coastal University is going to be like. Each second closer to the other side of the lake, makes it harder to push forward. The waterfall has grown so loud it's a steady downpour and the currents it's creating are working against us as we swim.

When we finally make it across the lake, we all let the water wash us in the last couple of feet, and lay on the bank. I don't think it was really that far of a swim, but the extra weight didn't help and I haven't slept in probably forty-eight hours. Emma's the same as me. Jenny too, worrying about Wren, and Wren is so weak. It's pathetic, actually, but at least we made it.

CHAPTER 20

Ash

By the time we have enough strength to stand, my shirt has already started drying. Emma pulls out the map to check where we are in respect to the end of the dashed path.

"We drifted a bit. We should head that way," Emma says, pointing to our right and speaking over the sound of crashing water.

We carefully walk along the rocky bank between the lake and Rising Salvation. The edge of the mountain juts out into the water, and, when we walk around the rocky slab, a roaring waterfall is on the other side.

"Where the water runs!" Jenny says, and the words of the riddle come back to me.

"That's it, Jenny," I agree, and we move a little quicker toward the streaming water.

There's a large bay area where the lake laps against the edge of the mountain. The foaming white waterfall pours down from the very top of Rising Salvation into the shimmery lake.

"Let's walk the perimeter," I say, and Emma and I lead.

The slippery rocks and muddy ground don't make hiking the edge easy. Besides the occasional fallen boulder, nothing seems out of place. When we get closer to the waterfall, I finally see what we're looking for.

"There it is," I announce, and I point behind the waterfall to something sparkling in the misty air.

Emma can't help herself and she takes off, picking up her pace. We run along the edge and behind the roaring waterfall, mist tickling our faces. I wipe away the droplets when we get to the other side. The sound of rushing water echoes, and a chilling breeze sweeps past us.

Behind the waterfall is a shallow cave. Pressed into the tan stone is a giant, golden slide puzzle.

It's a perfect square, two of me tall. Stuck inside the puzzle's outline are eight blocks with the numbers *one* through *eight* carved into them. The bottom right corner is left empty so the pieces can be moved.

"A puzzle?" I ask the group, and I'm unsure if I should be nervous or not.

I walk up behind Emma and unzip her bag. The plastic container rests on top and I fish it out, finding the cards dry inside. I review the riddle, trying to better understand this.

"So, finding this puzzle was card three," I say, confirming the riddle ends with this destination. "We're onto card four."

I flip over the next card titled *Numbers and Light* and read the riddle aloud.

NUMBERS ARE A TRICKY GAME
BLOCKS OF GOLD MAKE YOU STAY

THE CODE INSIDE IS HOW YOU CAME
TO FIND THE PUZZLE IN THE BAY

YOUR ENEMY'S LIGHT WILL REVEAL
THE WAY INSIDE WHAT I CONCEAL

"I guess let's try to solve it," I say, flipping the card over in my hands.

"How?" Emma asks. "It's already in numerical order. There's obviously a code we're missing."

"Where do we get the combination?" Wren thinks aloud.

The code inside is how you came to find the puzzle in the bay," I repeat the second stanza of the riddle.

"The only other thing we used is the map," Emma mumbles. She pulls it out from under her arm and unfolds it. "I don't see any numbers," she admits. "Read the line about the code again, Ash."

The code inside is how you came to find the puzzle in the bay," I read again.

"Well, the map brought us to the bay," Wren says, nodding his head like he's figured something new out. "The code is there somewhere."

We all take our turn examining the map and flipping it over in our hands. I try to hold it at different angles in the sunlight, but there's nothing visible.

Emma starts reading the card aloud again, trying to find what we're missing.

"It has to be the part about the enemy, right?" Wren asks, pacing and listening to Emma repeat the riddle.

"Who's our enemy?" Jenny asks.

"The Patrol," I offer.

"No," Emma says, and I hear fear inching its way into her words.

I turn from the map to her.

"The enemy of Artmith has always been the vainders."

My stomach clenches at her words. This has something to do with the vainders?

"What are you thinking, Em?" I ask, watching her facial expressions change.

"I think the vainders have something that's going to help us read the code."

"It said they have a light, right?" Wren asks.

Emma nods, rereading the final lines from the riddle.

"The code is probably written on the map and the light will reveal it."

"But where do we get the light? I'm not going anywhere near the vainders," Jenny says.

"I don't know. I'm assuming somewhere over in the forest," Wren says.

"So, we swam over here for nothing?" Jenny huffs, looking back across the lake.

I follow her gaze over the water, and in the distance, the lush green forest calls to us.

"The vainders must have a camp somewhere. Some kind of headquarters they go to when they're not hunting," Wren says, continuing to work out the puzzle.

"It could take months to find that," Emma says, trying to imagine us walking every inch of Infinity Forest.

"Not if we have them lead us to it," Wren offers. "We just have to follow them back,"

"Did you not hear me?" Jenny yells, her words ringing in the cave. "I'm *not* going anywhere near the vainders."

"I don't think we have a choice," I say sternly.

"Sure we do. We can just guess," she says and walks swiftly to the golden slide puzzle.

None of us have touched it yet. I think we're all a little too timid to do what Jenny is proposing. She reaches up to the number six block and pulls it down. It scrapes along the other blocks and the side of the puzzle. The pieces are big and heavy. It takes all her strength to move one block. She continues pushing pieces, grunting as they scrape along the track. Emma, Wren, and I watch, frozen. I know we're all hoping the door just opens for us. Reality hits when Jenny steps back from the puzzle, heaving deep breaths, and the wall is still very much sealed.

"I'll just try a different combination," she huffs and goes back to rearranging the blocks. "There can't be that many combinations."

"Thousands, actually," Wren says softly, not wanting to push Jenny into an argument.

"Just let her try," Emma whispers. "We can take a break before we have to swim back. There won't be any vainders to follow until it's dark, anyway."

I sigh and nod. Even though it's the last thing I want to do, I say, "Let's work on a plan."

Emma and I move out to the edge of the cave and perch ourselves up on a large, flat slab of rock. Wren helps Jenny work out different combinations. She's just exhausting herself, but no one wants to argue with her.

As Emma and I plan out tonight's events, the sun tracks higher in the sky, time seeming to move faster than normal. By early afternoon, we've decided on the best plan we can come up with. One that will hopefully keep us all safe.

"You should try to get some rest," Emma says, squinting up at me. She's laying back on the slab of rock we've been sitting on, just behind the waterfall. I imagine I must look pretty wrecked for her to mention sleep. In all honesty, that's the only thing I've been thinking about since we stopped talking an hour ago.

"It could be a long night and you didn't sleep yesterday."

"And hardly any the night before that," I mumble.

"We still have a few hours before we need to go. Get some rest." She pats the warm stone next to her.

I lean back and lower myself onto the rock, propping my head on my bag.

"I don't do crazy stuff like this back in California," I say, and let out an exhausted sigh.

"Really?" Emma teases. "I was getting the feeling that maybe crazy just followed you everywhere. I mean, you did fall through a painting."

A tired laugh easily passes my lips and I rub my eyes that are burning with exhaustion. "I guess I have my grandma to blame for that. It was her painting."

After a few quiet minutes pass, I turn my head and look at Emma, noticing she's silently staring at me. I want to ask her what she's thinking or what words she's itching to say right now, but I don't. I just hold her silent gaze.

Emma's sky-blue eyes are the last things I see before the world disappears. My heavy eyelids close, and eventually, exhaustion numbs my brain, letting me finally sleep.

CHAPTER 21

Ash

Distant hushed voices slowly pull me from my quiet dream where I stood on an empty stage in a dark auditorium. I think I had lines to say, but I can't remember them.

"You promise we're going to be okay?" Jenny's voice says through my hazy state.

"I can't promise that, but I think we'll be fine," Emma tries to comfort her.

"You and Ash survived last night," Wren says encouragingly.

"They weren't following vainders!" Jenny snaps and I can feel her nerves building.

My eyes crack open, the late afternoon sun blinding me for a moment. Slowly, I prop myself up on my elbows, digging them back into the hard stone. My back is stiff, and it takes me a minute to slide to my feet.

"Is it time to go?" I ask, and the three of them turn around, not noticing I'm awake.

"Yes, we need to get started," Emma says, pulling her bag onto her shoulders.

"I don't want to go," Jenny says stubbornly, crossing her arms.

"Just this morning you were mad I didn't bring you with me last night," I say, growing annoyed with her.

"No, I was mad that you went at all!" Jenny yells.

"We have to go or else we'll never get home," I say and shake my head at her stubbornness, refusing to raise my voice and lose myself in her anger.

"I can keep guessing. I'm sure I'm close," Jenny gestures to the slide puzzle behind her. My eyes follow her hand and I see all the numbers have shifted while I slept. I wonder how many wrong attempts she's already wasted her time on.

"Then you stay and keep guessing. I'm going to get the actual combination." I don't wait for her to argue with me or for Wren to speak up. I trudge through the shallow part of the lake and start swimming. Emma is quickly at my side, matching my strokes. She offers me a soft smile through the ripples of water.

I hear Jenny and Wren continue to bicker behind me until, eventually, the splashing sounds of them running into the water reaches me. I glance back and see that they're both hurrying after us.

The swim across the lake seems shorter. My body is already used to swimming with the weight of soaking clothes and now I've finally slept a little. We stumble up the muddy bank and wring out our shirts and shorts. My white shirt is probably forever going to be a muddy cream color now. The group of kids that were here this morning are gone, the sun in a deep descent. The gates are probably already closed.

We trudge our way across the Golden Field and into Infinity Forest. Already, darkness hugs at the trees. As the sun continues to sink, taking the warm temperatures with it, the chilling evening bites at my wet hair and damp skin. Jenny pulls out the jacket Emma lent her and zips it to her chin.

We move quickly, trying to cover as much ground as we can before night fully sets in. We don't know exactly where to go, but we do know the vainders haven't been near the edge of the forest. Emma leads the way, following a trail that goes in the same direction we traveled yesterday. Jenny flinches at every snapping branch or rustling leaf. I glance back and see her fingers are intertwined with Wren's, gripping the life out of his hand.

"This should be far enough," Emma says, coming to a stop beneath a tree with an enormous trunk. We climb up the tree's rough branches, putting as much distance between us and the ground. We distance ourselves across two branches that interlock with the trees next to it, and settle in. We don't have to wait long for night to finally fall. We're probably six or seven miles from Rising Salvation. Of course, now my stomach wants to remind me that I haven't eaten anything since this morning, but that's going to have to wait.

"Are we ready?" I whisper, the first of us to speak since we climbed into the tree. There's a mix of nervous nods and I count down from three on my fingers. When I put my last finger down, the four of us explode in a chorus of screams. I clench my eyes shut and my throat throbs. I put every frustrated, fear-filled second into that scream, and then we cut off our siren wails and listen to the screeching song fade into the shadows.

This time, when I hear the howl of a vainder, I actually feel relief. Just like last night, when I scared a scream out of Emma, the vainders respond. We may have overestimated our lookout spot because the howl seems too close. The pounding sound of paws comes almost instantly.

From our right, a vainder emerges below us, pacing around the base of the cluster of trees we're in. He stands on his hind legs, steel claws drawn. I take quiet breaths and try my best to stay calm. The trees haven't disappointed us yet and they offer the camouflage we need. Like we suspect, the vainder falls on all fours and begins to head back the way he came.

I give Emma a quick nod that says to move and we hurry along the branches, following him. He runs a good distance ahead of us, but when he stops to survey the area, perhaps still trying to find us, we catch up.

When a second vainder leaps out from behind a tree, I flinch back and lose my balance. I cling to the trunk of the closest tree and steady myself. They exchange a series of yapping barks, standing on their hind legs. I hold my breath and stay as still as my wobbling legs can manage. Eventually, they move on together, continuing down the same path. We unfreeze and keep on their trail.

I lose track of how long we follow them. Thirty or so scrapes along my arms from stray branches tells me it's been miles. I can see the words of retreat are hanging on Jenny's lips, begging us to turn around. I almost do, because this is much farther than I'm comfortable going, but the thought of getting Jenny and Wren back home keeps me moving. Emma has hurried almost two trees ahead of us. My path's blocked by both Jenny and Wren. I regret bringing up the rear, but I think it's the only reason Jenny hasn't completely stopped climbing.

Emma pauses up ahead, her chin tilted toward the ground. I think the vainders we've been following may have stopped again, or maybe another vainder has intersected their path, but when I see the rocky craters replace the dirt forest floor and the trees thin out, I know we've made it to their headquarters.

It's exactly where you'd expect vainders to live. Deep chambers are dug into the ground, making the forest floor look like Swiss cheese. It stretches to our left and right for miles, but my focus is stuck on the void of black in front of me. I mean, it's just *black*. There's a stretch of rocky rubble that ends in a sharp cliff that drops into darkness.

The edge of Pintura.

I suck in a breath, and I don't think it's my imagination that makes the air seem thinner. We're all the way at the edge. Emma was right. There's nothing but this land. Just a vast sea of black.

Shiny fur reflecting the moonlight finally pulls my focus from the edge of Pintura. Vainders are everywhere. Hundreds of them in sight, probably thousands hidden below the surface in the deep channels. We settle on the fork in the tree and survey the area, taking in every detail that I can. We have to know exactly where we need to go before starting this suicide mission.

Below us, the vainder's camp buzzes with yapping and howling. The two vainders who led us here melt into the pack and they all bleed together. We probably sit here for another hour, silently studying the area. Most of the vainders stay around the camp. A few venture into the woods and come back with their kill for dinner, hunting the other members of the forest.

Emma stiffens next to me and her chilled fingers reach for my hand. I've been able to ignore the cold of the night—unlike Jenny, whose chattering teeth threaten to give our location away. I didn't realize Emma was so cold.

She tugs a little and nods to our left. I move my eyes in that direction to see what she's noticed. A tall pile of stones opens up into a cave-like home. After watching the area for a while, I've decided the stone buildings are businesses or trading posts and the tunnels are where they live and sleep during the day.

Coming out of the stone building is a smaller vainder carrying what looks like a massive iron tray. A larger vainder stands across from him, his metal torso injured. There's a wide chunk of metal ripped back, but I can't see much else. The injured vainder pushes down on the ripped torso, closing the gaping hole.

The tray that the smaller vainder grips suddenly glows purple, the light so bright I almost have to shield my eyes.

When the lights on the tray go out, the injured vainder runs his black paw over his now healed torso. He lets out a victorious howl and leaves the smaller vainder to return his healing tray back into the stone building.

"That's the light," Emma whispers, pressing her lips to my ear.

I consider it for a second. It's the only thing we've seen that could work. "Okay, how do we get it?" I whisper, my words hidden in the wind.

"We could wait until morning. When they're asleep," Emma offers.

I shift on the branch, my legs already stiff. We probably still have another four or five hours left of the night. Being uncomfortable in the trees sounds better than being shredded by the vainders. I pass the plan down to Jenny and Wren. Once we're all on the same page, we move from our current perch toward the trees closer to the stone hut.

Just to be safe, we climb back a couple of feet to help conceal ourselves. Jenny and Wren move to a branch below Emma and me, attempting to stretch out their stiff muscles while we wait for the night to pass.

"Hey Em," I say softly. I sit with my back against the trunk of the tree, my knees pulled to my chest. Emma perches near my feet, her legs hanging over the branch, twisting the little knot her in shirt between her fingers. Neither of us have talked much while we're waiting for morning to rise. We also haven't dared to rest our eyes or racing minds. Wren and Jenny sit beneath us, and the last time I checked, they were both sitting in silence as well, eyes trained on the vainder camp.

"Ash," Emma says, but she doesn't look at me.

"You missed your date with Jake," I say.

She tilts her head back and I think she rolls her eyes and muffles a laugh.

"Why is that funny?"

"I'm just imagining Jake sitting in the band room where I saw him kiss Tammy. Now he's being stood up, and I hope he feels at least an ounce of the pain I suffered through for weeks."

"I didn't know he cheated on you. That makes me hate him even more," I grumble, my heart gripping together in my chest, that pang of hurt I know she must have felt vibrating through my whole body. Why would Jake ever do something like that? To someone as good as Emma. I can't even begin to wrap my mind around what Jake must have been thinking.

In the silence that settles between us, I remember how Emma confessed to giving Jake a second chance. That desperation to have someone is even more heartbreaking now. I sit up straighter and straddle the large branch.

"Come here," I whisper.

Emma turns to look at me and I see her eyes are glossy with tears. She slides toward me on the branch and leans her back into my chest. My muscled arms wrap around her waist and they hold her tightly against me, the thin material of her lavender top providing little barrier between our bodies.

That's when I realize how cold she is. Icy fingers spread across my chest and to my fingertips. "You're freezing, Em," I say softly and she shrugs. "Here, you should wear my jacket." I flip open the flap of my bag and carefully tug it free with one hand.

"We can share it," Emma offers as she takes the slick material from me. She turns it inside out and pulls down on a zipper I had missed before. The back of the coat expands as a hidden panel unfolds. The corner of my mouth kicks up, knowing this must be one of her inventions. I drape the jacket over my shoulders and Emma pulls it around her front, zipping the jacket and sealing us inside together. I let the arms of the jacket fall limp at my sides and wrap my arms around her waist. The rest of the world slips away with her in my grasp, and I want nothing more than to keep her safe from all the things that haunt her thoughts.

I rest my chin on Emma's shoulder and lean into her soft, blonde curls, still a bit damp from the lake. She shudders beneath my breath on her neck and her arms wrap over mine, hugging herself in my grasp.

Emma's soft fingers curl against my skin, her thumb brushing back and forth. With each pass of her thumb, warmth travels up my arm and all across my skin. The smell of tree bark and earth clings to her and me.

The tears I saw building in her eyes silently escape, and they drop onto the jacket and seep between our pressed together cheeks.

The aching in my chest deepens, shifting from the horrible thing Jake did to the unthinkable thing I'm going to have to do soon.

"I know I have to leave when this is over, but while I'm here, you do have me, Em." I take in an uneven breath, my words threatening to fracture in the tense air. "You have every single piece of me for as long as I can give myself to you."

Emma relaxes in my grasp and she takes in a raspy breath. I think she may be trying to form words, her mouth still agape, but she gives up on them. Instead, she nods and tilts her head back onto my shoulder, still sweeping her thumb across my arm.

For a second, I wish I didn't have to leave. I wish I could stay here with Emma and lose myself in this world. I want to be here for Emma. I want to hold on to her and this feeling of being understood. I just want to save her and be something good for her.

We don't say anything else. I just keep holding her and she runs her fingers along my arm, breathing slowly. She rests against me and we hold on to this moment. I think I'll hold on to this moment for the rest of my life.

The pounding of paws on the ground erupts suddenly. Emma sits up, alarmed, and I tense behind her. A pack of vainders runs beneath our tree and toward their camp, returning from their hunt. I notice weak rays of sun are breaking through the sky. It's time to make our move.

Wren and Jenny stand, alerted by the sudden pack of vainders. They look up at Emma and me, their faces asking if it's time to go. I nod and, after Emma and I free ourselves from the jacket, we all close in on the vainder's camp. I lean over a thick branch and watch the vainders retreat into their tunnels. All of them have moved away from the stone buildings and the camp is clear.

I lead us down the tree as quickly as I can, closing in on the ground. We'll be in and out as fast as possible. Before I leap to the forest floor, I pull out the remaining kitchen knife I took from Emma's parents.

Then, we drop to the ground and sprint for the stone building where we saw the smaller vainder take the purple glowing tray. As soon as my feet hit the forest floor, an internal clock begins ticking in my head, matching the pace of my racing heart. I leap over the rocky ground and skid to a stop at the mouth of the stone building. Grey morning light illuminates the inside. I grip my knife and enter the building.

It's one small room. Racks of ripped metal and wires outline the cave. A large blade hangs on the far wall and I think it's for sharpening the vainders' claws. Emma follows me into the building while Jenny and Wren stand guard near the entryway. I give Wren my knife and help Emma look through the space as fast as we can.

We fling sheets of metal and electric tools out of our way. Finally, we find the tray on the bottom of a self in the back of the room. It's so heavy Emma and I have to lift it together. It's a rectangular slab of metal with little light bulbs screwed in across the surface. We place it on the table in the center of the room and I find the switch on its side. When I flip it, blinding purple light fills the stone room. My heart pounds in my chest, flooding my veins with a kind of nerves I've never felt before. Emma pulls the map out of her bag and holds it over the purple glowing tray.

"There it is!" she says through her excited smile.

I look down at the map and I see black numbers on the back of the parchment, shifting in the purple light.

"Do you have something to write the code on?" She looks at me and the nerves tighten in my throat. The relief of seeing the code appear on the back of the map is short lived.

"No, let me find something," I say, but one quick scan of the room tells me there's nothing in here. *Why would vainders need a pen and paper?*

"Just memorize it," I say, and come back to Emma's side.

She concentrates on the eight numbers glowing on the back side of the map. I see tears of frustration cling to the rims of her eyes and her hands begin to shake.

"What is it?"

"I can't memorize them. I'm too nervous. I can't calm down." Each word she says drives more fear into her voice.

"You can do it, Em," I say.

"No, I'll forget them by the time we get back. It's like, two hours to Rising Salvation."

She's rambling, her words fueled by fear. I try to put the numbers to memory too, but I struggle the same way Emma does. The tiniest bit of doubt inside my head is saying I'll forget these numbers and we'll have to come back here.

"What is taking so long?" Jenny hisses at us from the entrance.

I know the only way we're going to get this code right is if we take the decoder. "Let's bring it with us," I say.

"It's too heavy, Ash," Emma reminds me, clearly having already thought of this, but I see another idea turning in her eyes. "Hold this," Emma says, handing me the map.

She rummages through her bag and pulls out her glasses with the flashlights on either side. I see the engineer in her come to life and I know she has a plan. Quickly, she unscrews the two white bulbs from both flashlights. Her hands find the switch on the metal tray and she turns off the purple light. With quick fingers, Emma twists two purple bulbs out of the tray and she installs them into her glasses. She flips on the two flashlights and now they glow purple.

"Put the map down," she orders, and I spread it out on the table. She holds her glasses over the map and the numbers glow once again.

"You're a genius," I say. I want to cheer and celebrate and tell Emma again how smart she is, but Wren's voice snaps my head to him.

"Ash, one of them is coming."

Wren and Jenny retreat inside the stone room, and the four of us share a quick glance before Jenny says, "We need to hide, hurry!"

I scan the room and head toward the back corner, wiggling behind a storage shelf. The others follow me and we crouch behind shelves full of scrap metal.

The sound of heavy feet sends soft pounds through the floor of the stone building. Between the pieces of metal on the shelf, I see the vainder come into view. Up close, the creature is much larger than I thought it was from in the trees. So large, in fact, that it fills the entire entryway.

Black fur moves in flashes as it paces around the room. It looks like it may be in a hurry. Like it's trying to find something before it returns to the tunnels. From a shelf to our right, it picks up an electric drill. It presses the trigger and the tool sequels in its paw.

The vainder turns to leave and its eyes find the tray on the table. It stops, narrowing its beady black eyes into slants. My breath catches in my throat, my pulse beating so hard in my chest it fills my ears with nervous pounds.

The vainder moves closer to the workbench, examining the two white bulbs Emma had taken out of her flashlights.

My grip tightens on the bars of the storage shelf.

The vainder seems to have lost his sense of urgency, now curious if someone's been in here. It re-installs the two white bulbs in the tray, its paws moving like human hands, carefully twisting the glass into place.

My beating heart pauses. I know as soon as the vainder turns on the tray and the bulbs glow white, it'll confirm someone's been in here and it'll find us.

I need to do something.

Its paw moves for the switch. I brace myself on the shelf. When purple and white light flood the room, I shove all my weight against the shelf and it rocks forward. Emma, Jenny, and Wren catch on to my plan, and they throw themselves against the rack, pushing it over. The overstuffed shelves screech in protest and collapse on top of the vainder. It lets out a howl that could make my ears bleed, and squirms under the fallen rack and debris.

"Let's go!" I yell and stumble toward the door, dodging scrap metal and wires on my way out.

My feet guide me past the entryway and toward the woods. When we reach the trees, I realize I had grabbed Emma's hand, pulling her along with me. Jenny and Wren are right behind us and we run, looking for a tree with low enough branches to climb, but there aren't any. These trees are too tall, and I know we're running out of time. The vainder will outrun us, so we need to get to higher ground. I find the best option and turn to Emma.

"You go first," I say, nudging Emma toward the tree. I link my fingers together and ready myself to hoist her up to the lowest branch.

"Ash Bane, you better be right behind me," she says, her words panicked.

"Climb, Em," I say, gesturing for her to give me her foot.

She swallows and then places her foot in my grasp, the leather bottom of her boot digging into my palm. I hoist her up and she pulls herself onto the closest branch. Jenny doesn't hesitate, placing her foot in my hands and reaching up to Emma, who pulls her onto the same branch.

"Wren, your turn," I say.

His eyes are still trained on the vainder camp.

"Wren!" I snap at him, and then he faces me.

His breaths are heavy with panic and I can't imagine how he must be feeling, standing that close to something that tried to kill him. He already knows what it feels like to have those silver claws rip through his skin.

"Okay, I'll pull you up," Wren says, finding his voice.

I hoist Wren up, my arms shaking under the weight, and Jenny and Emma pull him the rest of the way. A screaming howl roars behind me and I snap my head around to see the vainder stumbling toward us. Patches of its fur are damp with a black liquid. *Vainder blood.*

The creature limps on its hind legs, and those beady black eyes lock onto me, honing in on its target. Silver blades shoot from its paws and the vainder's knife-like teeth gleam in the early morning sun.

"Ash!" Emma shrieks, pulling my attention up to her. Her blue eyes are wide and wild, tears flooding her stare. I glance back at the vainder and see it pick up its pace, crashing through the forest toward me.

"Give me the knife, Wren!" Emma yells, but Wren's focus is

locked on the charging vainder.

Emma reaches over to Wren and rips the knife from his pocket. Without pausing, she flings her arm back and launches the knife toward the vainder. It flies through the air, grazing its left arm. The knife doesn't even faze the vainder. The creature keeps charging toward me, its claws set to find my throat.

"Ash, grab my hand!" Emma screams.

I look back up and see Wren is holding Emma over the branch, her hands extended to me.

Looking up at her, at the massive gap between us, I know I can't make that jump. It's too high. But when my eyes drift to my sister's horrified expression, to my best-friend giving everything he has to hold Emma, and then finally to Emma's tear filled gaze, I know have to try. I brace myself and leap toward her. Toward the blonde hair, blue-eyed girl that has taught me so much about myself in the short week I've known her. I swing my arms up, screaming and stretching my reach as far as I can. My right hand just misses her, the tips of our fingers brushing each other, but somehow my left hand locks into her grasp.

She has me.

"Pull him up!" Jenny screams at Wren.

With my other hand, I reach for the branch, knowing if I could grab it, I could pull myself the rest of the way up.

The sound of cracking underbrush intensifies and my eyes betray me, looking over my shoulder. The vainder is so close I can see a thick line of inky blood running down its face. He jumps toward the tree, claws slicing through the air. I curl my knees to my chest, barely avoiding the blades.

There's a hard yank on my arm as Wren pulls me up. My free hand finds the branch and I'm able to hoist myself to safety, standing on wobbly legs. A sweat trickles down my neck, and my heart wants to explode.

I look back at the vainder who watches us intensely, waiting to see what our next move will be. I have no doubt it'd follow us all the way to Rising Salvation if it wasn't already morning.

Large rays of sun finally break through the grey morning haze and the vainder stumbles back from the tree. Its glossy black eyes flicker from the sky to us and then back to the sky. When another ray of light streams through the branches, the vainder finally makes its decision and staggers back toward its camp.

"Ash Bane, I swear if you die!" Emma shrieks at me, her voice splitting on the word *die*.

I turn and see her clenched fist throbbing, pointing a shaking finger at me. Tears stream down her face. Jenny is rocking so badly Wren's holding her steady against the trunk of the tree.

"Em, I'm fine," I say and reach for her hand, but she flinches back.

"I swear, Ash," she says, sobs escaping her.

"Em, I'm right here," I say and this time I lay a hand on her cheek, forcing her to look at me. To see that I'm okay. I wipe her tears with my thumb and that seems to calm her.

Her blue eyes blink rapidly, finally aware that the threat is over and I'm standing in front of her. "You're my partner," she says weakly. "I can't finish this without you."

"I'm right here, Em," I say again.

Something has changed between us. We've gone from cautious strangers, to friends, to two teenagers with hesitant crushes.

But now it's more. The feelings are deep in my chest. Holding her this morning showed me what I'm going to lose. The way she's looking at me now, like she's not ready to let go yet, like she may never be ready to let go, means the feelings between us are *real*.

My heart beats in my chest, telling me I'm alive, telling me the vainder did not kill me. But I didn't jump on my own. My sister and best friend screaming at me, begging me to live, kept me from giving up. Those blue eyes staring back at me are the reason I jumped. She's the reason I'm alive.

CHAPTER 22

Emma

I hold Ash's hand until we get to the Golden Field and are out of Infinity Forest. I stopped crying, but the tears still stain my cheeks. I thought I lost him, and I'm not ready to lose him. The thought of Ash dying broke me. It broke all of us.

Jenny's fear quickly turned to anger, screaming that she knew we shouldn't have gone looking for the vainders. But we got the code, and after the shock of almost losing Ash passed, we were quickly reminded that we still have a game to finish. They still need to get home.

My tight fingers uncurl and I release Ash's hand. I don't realize how tight my grip is until my stiff fingers have to be forced open. No one has said anything since we started hiking. All of us are still thinking about what would have happened if Ash had died. We're thinking that it could have easily been any one of us.

"All right, enough of this," Ash snaps.

Wren, Jenny, and I share an exchange of sad glances.

"I'm fine. I'm not dead. Stop acting like I could be gone at any second." Ash is trying to be angry, but his voice shakes. "I'm fine," he says, but it's only a whisper.

I think he may start crying. His wet blue eyes meet mine, but he doesn't let the tears fall. He's so strong. Too strong for his own good. I take in a shaky breath and force myself to relax with the released air. Finally, I nod, making myself to let go of the fear of Ash dying.

"Let's finish this card," I say.

Jenny and Wren glance at each other, waiting to see who'll speak first. Wren lets out a sigh and nods to Ash. "Let's do this."

"Jenny?" Ash asks, seeing her eyes are still a storm of fear and anger.

"You have to promise to be more careful," Jenny says.

Ash rolls this eyes and I wince when Jenny snaps.

"Don't roll your eyes, Ash!"

"I'm just trying to get you home," Ash argues.

"It doesn't matter if you die! Then, *you'll* never get home!" Jenny screams.

Ash is silent, pressing his mouth into a thin line. Finally, he says, "Okay. I'll be more careful."

Jenny still doesn't seem pleased, but she gives a stiff nod. "Okay, then let's keep going."

I lead us back to Rising Salvation. It's still fairly early in the morning. The gate hasn't been opened, so Pintura is quiet. The lake is deserted and we swim across with no curious eyes watching.

Our shoes squeak with water as we balance on the slippery rocks at the shore of the lake. The waterfall roars as we near it, blasting us with a chilling mist. On the other side, the golden slide puzzle

242

shimmers in the early morning light.

"Jenny, can you hold this?" I ask, handing her my glasses with the new purple bulbs. I pull out the map and press it flat on the ground. "Shine the light here," I instruct. She does and the eight number code reveals itself.

Ash and Wren work together to slide the numbers as I read them. "Top left should be five."

The stones scrape together and they place the number five block, moving the others out of the way.

"Next is three," Jenny says.

"And then six," I add when I catch Wren trying to move the number six block to the bottom. He stops himself and moves it to the top right corner.

"Okay, next row?" Ash asks.

"Two, four, eight," I say.

Ash steps back, looking at where those pieces are and where they need to be relocated. "And the next row?" he asks, trying not to lock himself into undoing the puzzle to fix the bottom row.

"One and seven."

Ash points out a path to Wren and he nods. The two boys move faster, scraping the blocks up and down, left and right. The blocks start falling into place and finally, Wren slides the seven block to the left, locking in the puzzle.

My ears ring in the silence that follows. All of us stare at the golden puzzle, afraid that if we blink, we may miss it. Just when I'm about to drop my gaze and double check the combination, I hear several soft clicks. The stones begin to tremble and the slide puzzle *descends* into the ground, revealing a dark tunnel into the mountain.

A flash of excitement sparks in my veins that it worked, until I realize I'm going to have to go *into* that tunnel. I reach for my bag and shuffle through the cards.

That's when I realize we're halfway through the game. Only four cards left.

"What does it say?" Ash asks.

I glance up from the cards and see the three of them are staring at me. "We're halfway," I say, holding up the set of four cards we've completed.

This instantly cheers Jenny up. "We're almost done!" she says, standing up to pull on her bag. "What do we do next?"

I organize the cards and find number five, titled *Checkered Steps*.

A TUNNEL OF PUZZLES JUST FOR YOU
TO PROVE THE KEY IS EARNED

A GRID OF STONES JUST TO LOSE
EACH STEP LIMITS THE LEARNED

TRY THEM ONCE OR TWICE, BUT NEVER MORE
LOSE YOUR BALANCE AND YOU'LL FALL THROUGH THE FLOOR

I read the riddle twice, because the first time I get lost after a tunnel of puzzles. I look back up—past Ash, Wren, and Jenny—and take in the ominous tunnel. The three of them follow my gaze to the dark, gaping hole and we watch it like it may come to life and lurch out at us. Ash is the first to break his frozen stare, stepping up to the wide mouth of the tunnel. My feet unfreeze before my mind does, quickly moving to Ash's side. I lace my fingers with his.

"We do this together," I say.

Jenny takes my other hand and offers her other to Wren. He steps in line with us at the opening of the tunnel, locking his fingers with

Jenny's.

Over and over again, we've been reminded just how dangerous this game is, and the ominous black void in front of us only proves that further. But with my hands linked with theirs, a sense of protection warms my skin. I would do anything to save any one of them, and I know they would do the same for me. I glance to my right and left, taking in the faces of the friends I never knew I needed, but am so grateful to have.

"Together," Ash agrees.

He nods forward and we enter the tunnel as one unified group. The sunlight streams into the chamber and we follow its path deeper into the mountain. The air is cold compared to the humid summer day outside, and my damp clothes raise bumps across my skin.

We're still holding hands, taking each step together, when the ground starts shaking beneath our feet. Fear returns, clutching my throat. The patch of sun beneath my feet shrinks. I spin around and see the stone wall with the slide puzzle is *rising* out of the ground, locking us inside.

Jenny screams and races back toward the entrance, but it's too late. With a soft *thud*, the world goes black.

In the darkness, Jenny continues screaming. I think I hear her pounding on the stone wall. Wren urges her to calm down, trying to find her in the pitch black.

"Em, your light," Ash says, his voice still calm and right at my side.

I'm already ahead of him, the two flashlights in my hands. I flip them on and we become illuminated in an eerie purple glow.

Jenny whirls around at the sudden stream of purple rays, her eyes wide. "We're stuck!" she screams.

My skin chills when the echo of her voice doesn't seem to end.

"We're not stuck," Ash says sternly.

Jenny actually gives a sarcastic laugh to that. "Do you see a way out?" she asks, throwing her arms out to the side and walking back to us.

"We play the game and we'll get out. Maybe the portal is in here." Ash, again, is the calmest of the group.

Jenny goes still. She realizes she's jumped to fear too quickly. She presses a hand to her forehead and takes in a slow breath.

"Sorry, you're right."

"Em, do you want to lead?" Ash asks, looking at the glowing glasses.

I look down at my prototype, seeing a better use for it now. I undo the straps that hold the flashlights to the glasses and hand one to Ash. I keep the other and we continue into the tunnel.

The stillness of the air makes me claustrophobic. The lack of a breeze solidifies Jenny's statement that we are indeed stuck. Our purple lights dance along the tunnel walls and the rough slabs of stone glitter in the light.

"I think our first puzzle is up ahead," Wren says, pointing to an uneven hump on the ground in front of us.

When we get closer, I realize it's a pattern of square stones. They're large, each of them two or three feet wide, and they fit together in a checkered grid. I hold Ash's arm next to me to keep my balance and stick out a tentative foot, somehow knowing not to trust the patterned floor.

When my foot graces the top of the stone, it crumbles away. A dark void takes its place. Ash pulls me back, shuffling away from the grid. My heart skips a couple of beats, but I keep my mind calm. *It's just a puzzle.* I walk up to another stone and slowly lower my foot again. A crack slithers across the stone and I stumble back, but the stone holds and doesn't crumble. Even slower this time, I lower my foot onto the same stone and another crack snakes along its top. The stone stays in place, until I pull my foot back, and then it gives way, falling in to the black void.

"Once or twice, never more," Wren says, and the words from the riddle come back to me.

Each square on the grid has a different breaking point. They'll either crack after one touch or after two. I look over the grid and bite my lip. There are only five stones in each of the eight rows, narrowing the number of paths we can take.

"We have too many people," I say, glancing over at the others. I've run the numbers in my head. "Only two people can use the same path. There's not going to be enough stones for us to all walk across."

Ash nods next to me, coming to the same conclusion only seconds after me.

"So, two of us get across and the other two wait here until when?" Jenny asks. It's clear she won't agree to be one of the two who stays behind. Lucky for her, I know how we can get around this.

"If you two," I say, pointing to Ash and Wren, "carry Jenny and me on your backs, we can all go across."

"We have to be careful," Wren says, nearing the first row of the grid. "If you step on a stone and it crumbles, you have to keep your balance. If you step on the one that holds, you can't back off or we lose one of the two steps."

"So, keep your weight on your step, but still recover if the floor falls out from under you," Ash says sarcastically. He surveys the grid again. Then, turns to me. "You're my guide, okay?"

I agree, and Jenny and I combine Ash and Wren's backpacks with our own. We tighten the straps around our shoulders and Ash hands Jenny his flashlight so each pair has a light.

Ash drops to one knee, letting me climb on his back. He hooks his arms behind my knees and stands, lifting me as if I weighed no more than the snare drum he's used to marching with. My arms wrap around this neck for support and I pull myself close to his back so I can rest my head against his. His hair is still damp from our swim across the lake, the earthy smell clinging to him.

"All right, Em, where should we start?"

I look down at the first row of stones. Only three are left to pick from.

"Far right corner," I say, and Ash moves that way.

Wren lifts Jenny onto his back and they follow us. Ash lowers his foot onto the first stone and a crack forms on the top, but the stone holds.

"Good choice," he says, bringing his other foot onto the first space.

Even though the floor holds, I feel like we are floating over the void, no solid ground beneath our feet. Perhaps that's because I'm clinging to Ash's back.

"Next step?" he asks.

I look at our options. One to the left, one forward, or one diagonal to our left. Each stone looks the same. *How am I supposed to know which ones are safe?*

"Em?" Ash asks when I don't give him an answer.

"Go forward," I decide.

When Ash lifts his foot, I tighten my arms a little.

I suck down a breath of air.

And the floor falls through.

CHAPTER 23

Ash

I'm surprised I don't scream. I'm surprised Emma doesn't scream. The floor crumbles beneath my feet and I'm falling forward. My foot is going through the hole. Emma tightens her grip around my neck and she braces herself for the fall.

The sharp tug on my back sends me gasping for air.

"I got you!" Jenny says, her fingers gripping the sleeve of my shirt and I regain my balance.

"Perhaps a different tile," I say, trying to push the fear down and keep my words light.

Everyone has been so on edge today after the vainder attack. I know that what we're doing is dangerous, but if I get caught up in my fear of dying or not succeeding, I just feel nauseous. This *is* a game, right? At the end of the day, that's all this really is. My sanity won't make it if I keep being afraid of everything.

"Try the one diagonal to the left," Emma says, her voice shaking.

I rub my thumb across the side of her knee, trying to give her some comfort. Jenny keeps her grip on my shirt, not taking any chances now. I slide my foot to the next tile, holding my breath. I fight the urge to close my eyes and I press my weight down on the stone.

It holds.

Jenny releases me, and I move my other foot across the grid.

"Breathe, Ash," Emma whispers in my ear.

I let out the breath I was holding, feeling my skin tingle at her words against my neck. Jenny and Wren take the place we were previously on, ready to follow us across.

"Next step?" I ask, and Emma moves her head to look at our options.

"Diagonal to the right."

Jenny's fingers find my sleeve again and I try the next stone. When the tip of my shoe touches the tile, a tiny crack forms in the center.

"Don't pull back," Emma says, reading the muscles in my legs.

I *was* about to pull back. Her voice forces me to keep my foot there and the stone holds. Jenny releases me, I move forward, and Wren takes my spot. When he moves, the tile he was previously on crumbles away.

A chill creeps across my neck. I just realized we can't turn around. We'll be stuck on this checkered floor forever if we don't get across. Or worse, we'll fall into the void.

Emma must be thinking the same thing because her chest presses into my back with a deep breath. She lets it out in a slow sigh, the warm air surrounding my neck. Again, I rub my thumb on the side of her knee. *It's okay, Em.*

"Go to the left," she says.

I don't hesitate or second-guess Emma's directions. I trust her, even though I also know this is only a guessing game. But she's right, again. This tile holds.

Wren moves forward, and the previous stone falls away. Emma is quiet for longer than normal.

"Forward?" she says like it's a question. "Lightly," she adds.

Jenny's fingers seem tighter on my sleeve this time, not liking the hesitation in Emma's voice. I barely rest my foot on the stone when it explodes into dust.

"Nope," I say, bringing my foot back.

"Diagonally to the left," Emma says quickly.

There's a lot more confidence in her voice now. Still, I move my foot tentatively to the next tile.

It cracks.

It holds.

"I've got the pattern," Emma says as I move us to our new space.

"Okay, then what's next?" I ask.

Confidence returning, I look ahead and see we're nearly halfway. Emma calls out my next move, sounding surer this time, and I start to pick up on the pattern, too.

"Diagonal to the right," she says.

My feet move.

"And then to the left."

I do, each stone holding and confirming the pattern.

"I see it now," I say and move my feet diagonally to the left, then diagonally to the right, and then directly to the left. The path snakes from one corner of the grid to the other.

I lift my foot to go diagonally to the left one more time when Emma throws her right hand out.

"Stop!"

I balance on one foot for a second, and then pull it back. There's only one row left now. That should be my last step.

"Go forward," Emma says.

I squint in confusion. "Are you sure?" I ask.

"Go forward," she repeats.

"Em—" I start to say, trying to tell her that every time she told me to go forward the tile fell.

"Ash," Emma cuts me off.

My eyes flick between the two stones. Jenny's fingers curl into my shirt and I step forward.

The stone holds.

I hurry across and onto the solid ground, now on the other side of the puzzle. Wren races to the solid ground as well, thankful to be off the puzzle floor. Jenny practically leaps from Wren, so happy to be on something sturdy.

I lower Emma off my back and she gives me a scowl through her fallen blonde curls, the purple flashlight enhancing her faint freckles.

"What?" I ask.

"Why didn't you believe me?"

I watch as she backs up toward the last row of the grid.

"I was just following the pattern," I admit.

Emma lifts her foot above the stone I was going to move to. Her face tells me she's trying to prove a point.

"Do you want to see what would have happened?" she asks. And although she's scowling at me, I know she's not actually mad. She just wants to show me that I was wrong. I join her at the edge of the grid.

"Sure," I say and I actually hope I'm right, too. Maybe both were the correct option. I think I actually just want her to be wrong for once.

Emma lays her foot down on the tile and quickly pulls it away. The tile crumbles and falls into the black void. Then, the one next to it does the same thing, and so does the next one, and the next one. The entire grid floor turns to rocky ash and disappears into the vast crater.

I glance at Emma and see she has a smug look on her face. "How'd you know?" I ask, my mouth agape.

"We started the puzzle by stepping straight on. We needed to end the same way," she explains.

"No, how did you know the whole grid would crumble?"

She lets out a sigh. "Because that's how this game works."

Her blue eyes look at me through the purple rays of her flashlight. I think she expects me to be mad that I was wrong or that she was right. But really, all I want to do is *kiss* her.

"Why are you so smart?" I say, my voice much softer.

Gently, I push a blonde curl behind her ear. I realize I do that a lot, actually. Her smile grows and I think I see her cheeks darken with what appears to be a purple blush, thanks to our limited lighting.

"It just seemed obvious to me," she says, filling our silent space.

She starts ruffling through her bag for the next card and the moment passes. She's really too smart for her own good.

"Card six?" Wren asks when Emma and I cross to them.

"Card six," Emma confirms and reads the riddle.

It's titled *The Black Mist*.

THE DARKEST FEARS HIDE DEEP INSIDE
CROSS THE SMOKE WHERE SHADOWS LURK

THEY MAKE YOU SCREAM, THEY MAKE YOU CRY

IT'S ALL IN YOUR HEAD, THEY'RE NOT REAL
ONCE YOU BEGIN, YOU CANNOT KNEEL

I think I'm going to be sick. My eyes scan the riddle again, hanging on the written words. *Fears. Scream. Cry.* I look up and see the color has drained from everyone else's face as well. Maybe it's the purple light playing tricks on me, but I don't think so.

"That doesn't sound good," Jenny admits softly.

My eyes focus on the dark stretch of tunnel in front of us. I swallow, not sure what I should be preparing myself for. Nothing in this riddle sounds good. I remind myself that *it's just a game.*

"We have to keep moving," I say, watching Emma stuff the cards back in their velvet bag. She hands them to me and I tie them around my wrist. "We can't go back the way we came, obviously."

Jenny looks like she wants to slap me. She knows I'm right, though. She can't be mad that it's our only choice. I didn't push her into the painting, Wren did. If she want's anyone to be mad at, it should be her new boyfriend.

Instead of releasing her anger, Jenny spins quickly and starts heading deeper into the tunnel, the flashlight still tightly gripped in her hand. Wren follows after her, and Emma and I bring up the rear.

"You should go easier on Jenny," Emma says softly. "She knows she has to do this, but that doesn't mean she's going to enjoy it."

"I know," I say and sigh. "I just want to move as fast as we can. I just want to get out of here."

There's a heavy silence that falls between us. The stillness of the tunnel air makes it even more unbearable. In the quiet, the words I just said echo back to me.

"I didn't mean out of Pintura." I try to correct myself. "I meant out of this tunnel."

Emma looks up at me, the purple light casting shadows on her face. "I know." Her voice breaks, and I wish I could take my words back. I didn't mean to upset her.

"We're here," Wren calls back to us.

A solid rock wall comes into view after a few more paces. At first I think it's a dead end, until Emma sweeps the purple beam of her light back and forth. The rays catch on the stone surface, and then they disappear through a dark void that runs from the floor to the ceiling of the tunnel. A crack that's shoulder width apart creeps deep into the stone wall, so dark the light from Emma's flashlight is swallowed by its grasp.

"It says we have to enter one at a time," Jenny says, pointing to something carved next to the ominous split in the wall. I walk up to her and read the message scratched in the stone.

"I'll go first," Wren says. He leans his head into the dark crack in the stone, sending his blonde hair tumbling in front of his face.

"Are you sure?" I ask.

"You and Emma are always making the calls and leading us. I think it's time I do something first." Wren steps back and starts stretching out his legs like he's preparing for a race. I want to tell him that Emma and I have been leading because he was lying on his death bed not even forty-eight hours ago, but I bite my tongue. I don't want to be first, but someone has to be.

"Read the card one more time," Wren says, looking back at us.

I pull it out again and read it once more. Both Wren and I seem to focus in on the last two lines. *It's all in your head, they're not real. Once you begin, you cannot kneel.*

"So, whatever lies in there isn't real?" Wren says, still stretching out his arms and neck.

"That's what it says," I offer.

Wren nods to himself. "Okay. I'm going."

And then, all of the sudden, he runs into the black split in the stone wall. There's no goodbye or encouraging words. He just *goes*. Once he vanishes into the darkness, the wall begins to move. Rocky bars jut out across the crack in the wall, like a gate. I assume we wait for it to be each of our turns, and then the gate will open back up.

"How long do you think it'll take?" Jenny asks, wringing her hands together. Her eyes train on the barred gate like she may see Wren reappear there.

"I'm not sure, Jenny," I say gently.

For a minute, we just stand there, a hundred different thoughts running through my head. After Wren doesn't reappear, and the bars across the split in the rock don't retract, I figure we could be waiting for a while.

The three of us sit together on the cold floor of the tunnel and wait for it to be our turn. Emma and Jenny each hold a flashlight, distracting themselves with the how the stone wall glitters beneath the purple light.

A couple of minutes pass, and the cave is still silent. I want to call out for Wren and see if he's okay. I want to know what he's seeing in there. Would he even hear me if I yelled? How far has he gone?

I get the answer to my thoughts when a wild howl echoes off the rock wall. *A vainder's howl.*

With the tense silence broken, we all find our voices.

"Wren!" I scream and run up to the barred entrance.

"Ash, that was a vainder, right? What are they doing in here?"

Jenny asks, her eyes wide.

"That's his fear," Emma says, her voice trying to stay calm.

"He's locked in there with vainders?" Jenny screams.

"They're not real, remember?"

"That sounded real, Emma!"

The wall begins to shake again and the bars across the split in the wall pull back.

"He got through, Jenny. It's fine," I say.

"Or he died!" she yells, and tears find her eyes.

"Only one way to find out," Emma says and then she walks into the black split. She stops on the other side and the bars reappear, blocking her from me.

"Em," I call out her name on instinct, and reach through the bars for her hand. A rush of anxiety courses through my veins at the idea of her leaving me. What if Jenny's right? What if Wren did die and now Emma is about to face the same fate?

"It's okay, Ash. We all have to go through at some point. Remember, *it's just a game*." The purple light illuminates her face, and she looks *calm*. Standing deep underground, holding that purple flashlight, Emma Delaney looks *calm*.

My lips part slightly, but my mind can't find any words. I don't know what I want to say to her. I just don't want her to go.

Emma lifts my hand to her lips and brushes a kiss across my fingers. "I'll see you on the other side."

Then she's going and my hand falls limp. I stand at the gate the entire time she's gone. My feet are rooted here in case she comes back or needs my help.

Silent tears roll down Jenny's cheeks while she sits, leaning against the rock wall. When she sniffles a cry, my frozen trance at the split in the rock finally breaks and I lower myself next to my sister.

I wrap an arm over her shoulder and let Jenny rest her head against mine. It's been a long time since I've held my sister like this.

"So, you and Wren," I say, forcing my broken voice the fill the tense air around us.

I think Jenny means to huff a laugh, but more tears break from her eyes. "Ash, if he's gone—"

"He's fine, Jen," I say, tightening my grip around her shoulders. "Wren is fine, and so is Emma. We're going to take our turns, face whatever fears this enchanted crevice has in store, and then we'll move on. We'll complete this card just like we did all the others."

Jenny nods, her head brushing against mine. A sense of confidence builds in my chest and I didn't realize how much I also needed to hear those words.

My sister and I are quiet for a moment until she dips her head out from under my arm, sitting up on her own. "I know Wren told you about Sally Temple's party," Jenny admits.

I pull my knees to my chest, locking my arms around my shins, and I look at my sister. "He did," I say, and she drops her gaze from mine.

"I don't know what any of this means," she fumbles for her words, gesturing between herself and the barred crack in the rock, implying Wren is on the other side. "I don't know what we'll do when we get back home."

"And you don't have to worry about it until then," I say, cutting her off from any more rambling.

Jenny looks at me, round eyes full of questions I know she wants to ask. I'm surprised when she voices them. "Is that what you and Emma are telling yourselves? That you don't have to worry about the inevitable goodbye until it's here?"

My heart aches in my chest at the reminder. "Something like that," I mumble, tightening my fingers in my grasp around my knees. "By the way, just so you know, I'm not upset about you and Wren," I say, pulling our conversation away from Emma and me.

I think I see Jenny fight a small smile before she says, "Yeah? Well, just so *you* know, I'm not going to judge you if acting really is your passion."

I flip my gaze up to meet hers, taking in the purple glow around her black hair and pale face. It's at this moment that I realize how much of the last four years I've missed spending with my sister. Once I went into high school and we both grew up, we didn't do the things we used to. Didn't say the things we should have. I wish I would have told Jenny the truth about how excited I was to be in the play. I don't know why I doubted it then, but I know Jenny would've been the one in the front row screaming the loudest.

I want to tell her that I'm sorry I kept that a secret from her. That I actually like the idea of her and Wren together. That I trust Wren not to hurt her, and I know he's liked her for a long time. I know our parents like Wren, and it wouldn't be awkward if he started being around more. It'd be like old times, in a way.

Before I can say any of that, the stone bars retract and the split in the rock is open again. I glance over my shoulder at the ominous black void, the eerie silence raising the hair on my arms. There were no vainder howls or screams.

"I'll go next," I say, since the presence of the open crack shattered the conversation we were just having.

Jenny doesn't argue and just nods. The wet streaks on her face still shine in the purple light that's gripped in her hands. She shouldn't be alone in the dark, so I leave her with the flashlight. I'm hoping if I go in without the light, it'll help keep me from seeing what fears this game has prepared for me.

I don't say any other parting words to Jenny. I enter the crack in the stone and the bars lock behind me.

I move deeper into the black void and hold my hands out in front of me to feel where I'm going. It's so dark I can't see them. I can't see anything. I slide my feet across the tunnel floor, too afraid to lift them. My heart speeds up. The darkness fuels my fears. And then a blinding white light streams down on me.

I blink fast, trying to adjust to the light. Slowly, things around me start to come into view. There's soft green grass beneath my shoes. A warm breeze hugs my face, and a bright blue sky glistens above. Everything shimmers in the sun, glittery and overly saturated in color.

It registers to me that the shimmering world is not real. None of this is real. I know I'm still deep inside Rising Salvation, but that's not what I see. I see a bright world and while I should feel relaxed, I feel tense. This is far from scary. What fears are here?

"Ash, are you coming?"

My head snaps to the right. *Emma?*

The glittery green grass rolls in the distance, going on forever.

"Ash?" her voice sings, followed by a small laugh.

My feet move through the grass, its shimmery points tickling my ankles. "Em?"

When I get to the top of the grassy crest, I finally see her. At the bottom of the hill is a red and white checkered blanket. Emma lies on top of it, a bright yellow dress draping over her shoulders and spiraling around her body.

"Em, what are you doing here?" I ask and hurry down the hill to her. Something isn't right because Emma's not wearing the lavender top and black shorts she left her mother's house in. I've never seen Emma in a dress at all, or this relaxed.

Emma's blonde curls blow in the warm breeze. A soft, pink blush glows on her cheeks, and her smile is blinding. When I reach her, she jumps up from the blanket and throws her arms around my neck. I hug her back and I begin to lose my mind in this pretend world.

When she steps back from my grasp, I notice her skin is glittering like the rest of this pretend world. It confirms that this isn't real. She's not really here.

"Are you ready to go?" she asks and looks at me like I should know what that means.

"Where are we going?"

Her eyes sparkle and her smile tightens. "Come on," she says and her fingers lace with mine.

We move through the grass, walking in the glittery world as if it were any normal day. It's hard to force my mind to remember the tunnel and the cards and the game. I'm not walking through a grassy clearing with Emma. I'm walking through a cold cave. But I *wish* I was walking with Emma in a grassy clearing and that is what makes it so easy for my mind to start believing that this is real.

After a couple of minutes, I stop looking over my shoulder for the vainder attack or spiders or any other fear I expected to face in here. Maybe we just misunderstood the riddle.

In the distance, a single tree grows out of the grass, the only tree I see at all. When we get closer to it, I recognize it as the tree in Emma's backyard with the tire swing.

"You wanted to bring me here?" I ask when we reach the tree.

Emma leans on the rope of the swing, resting against the tire. "I just wanted to be somewhere happy when it happened." Her eyes grow glossy and I think it's the world's glittery finish, but then I realize they're filled with tears.

"What are you talking about, Em?" I ask. My heart squeezes in my chest at the sight of tears in her eyes. They start to fall and streak across her cheeks.

"Why are you crying, Em?"

My heart beats hard in my chest, trying to figure out what's going on. She raises a shaking hand and points behind me. I turn around and see a dark maroon door rising out of the ground. Two golden circles are painted on the wood and I recognize it as the design on the Ending in Cadence cards.

There's a loud crack of thunder and a bright flash of lightning. When the white jolt of light fades, the world around me has changed. Dark grey clouds loom over the grassy clearing. Heavy raindrops pour from the sky. Another rumble of thunder makes my body throb like it's inside of me.

"It's time to go, Ash," Emma says, stepping away from her swing. Tears mix with the raindrops on her cheeks.

My soaked clothes hang heavy on my body. Pieces of my brown hair plaster to my face and my breathing is quick and shallow.

"What do you mean?" I ask over the pelting rain.

"You need to go home. You need to leave me."

And suddenly, the fear the game had been trying to target builds in my heart. *Saying goodbye to Emma is my fear.*

"I'm not ready," I say. The words are soft under my shaky breaths. "Em, I'm not ready to go!" I say, louder now.

I want to scream at the world. I want to run and hide. I want to do *anything* but say goodbye to her.

262

The maroon door swings open and a black void is on the other side. A force begins to pull me toward the door like a strong wind.

I try to walk against it and back to Emma.

"Em, help!" I say, reaching my hand out to her. "I don't want to leave!"

My own tears fill my eyes. The cold rain washes them off my cheeks. Emma breaks into a heavy sob, falling to the muddy grass beneath her feet.

"Don't cry, Em," I gasp, my heart crumbling in my chest at the sight.

I did this to her. I'm *hurting* her. I knew I had to leave. Why did I get attached? She just wanted to help us get home, and I let my heart fall for her. *What have I done?*

I can't breathe.

I can't do this.

My hands clench against my chest.

I. Can't. Breathe.

Tears keep falling and the wind yanks me closer and closer to the door.

"I'm sorry, Em!" I yell as the last gust of wind pushes me through the door and I'm stumbling backward into the dark room.

Tears burn on my cheeks. I suck down air, forcing my lungs to breathe. *I need to breathe.*

My heart beats so fast I'm sure it's going to explode. It aches in my chest, hurting from the fear, and the pain, and the sadness that floods my veins.

"Ash," her voice breaks through my panic.

I turn around and there she is, standing in a blanket of purple light, her lavender shirt still tied up in that little knot at her belted hip.

"Em," I say, her name breaking in my voice.

I run to her and take her into my arms, squeezing her against my chest. She wraps her arms around my waist, her fingers gripping my shirt. I put my hand on her back and then in her blonde curls. I have to be sure she's real. I pull back and brush my hand across her soft cheek. My clothes are dry, her skin isn't shimmering. She's real.

"You did it. You're through the crack," she says softy. Her fingers find my damp cheeks and they wipe my tears away. "It's okay, Ash."

I swear, this time I'm going to kiss her. I press my forehead to hers and close my eyes, taking in this moment of relief and comfort. Finally, my breathing relaxes. I anchor myself to the warmth that radiates from every point of contact between Emma and me. To the metallic smell of Artmith that lingers on her. To every single piece of Emma that I've discovered in the last eight days.

I slowly open my eyes and see Emma is peering up at me, our foreheads still touching. I see her concern swimming in her blue gaze. She's worried about what I just went through, but all I can think about is the overwhelming joy I have now that I'm back at her side.

Until all that warmth turns into icy fingers around my neck.

An ear-piercing shrill ricochets through the tunnel.

Jenny.

CHAPTER 24

Emma

I know the card said the fears inside the split rock weren't real, but Jenny is screaming like she's being shredded by a vainder. It's been ten minutes straight of constant screaming.

"Jenny, it's okay!" Ash yells to her.

He's sitting at the edge of the stone wall. Wren and I had to hold him back from running in to get her. The game was specific that only one of us could go in at a time. I don't know what would happen if we didn't follow the rules, and I don't want to find out.

"Ash!" Jenny shrieks, and Ash's face tightens at his sister's call for help.

"Jenny, it's okay! It's not real," he yells back to her.

"Ash, I don't think she's going to make it through. She's already been in there longer than the rest of us," Wren says.

Ash shakes his head. "She can do this."

Another shriek from Jenny sends shivers along my skin.

"*Please*, someone help!" Jenny yells.

"Jen, we can't come in. You have to do this on your own," Wren hollers back to her.

"I can't. *I CAN'T!*"

She's losing her mind in there. Here screams are making *me* lose *my mind* out *here*.

"Jenny!" I yell back to her. "It's not real!" My call to her probably doesn't help. I'm not her brother or her boyfriend. I'm also sure I sound very annoyed.

Another glass-shattering screech rings throughout the cave. It's so loud I have to cover my ears. When I drop my hands, I hear her crying sobs. Ash stands and I think I may have to keep him from going to get her, but he doesn't move into the rock crevice. Instead, he starts to *sing*.

Blue is for the swimming sky
Yellow glows in the morning rise
Here your dreams are alive
Here no worries will survive

We will run away
Where the sun is always shining for you

Green are the trees reaching high
Red feathers of the birds that fly
Here your dreams are alive
Here no worries will survive

We will run away

Where the sun is always shining for you

And when black like smoke comes to try
And block the yellow morning rise
I will be here to always say
That here your dreams will live another day

He starts so softly I doubt Jenny would even hear him. But after the first line, her sobs stop. The tunnel is quiet except for Ash's voice. It's slow and soothing and so beautiful. His tone is rich as he gets louder, his voice growing stronger. I can tell the melody is familiar to him.

It feels like something he's sung a thousand times.

Wren and I don't dare to interrupt him. When he sings the final lines of the song, Jenny stumbles out of the split in the rock.

She looks terrible. Her usually slicked-back black ponytail is half yanked off her head, her cheeks are red and raw, her puffy eyes burn with tears, and her entire body is shaking. When she sees Ash, she collapses into him.

Still shaking, Ash carefully lowers Jenny to the ground. She curls against her brother and he sings the song again, taming the wild pieces of her hair. It's something he's probably done before, because he knows exactly how he can calm her down.

I will be here to always say
That here your dreams will live another day

Jenny finally gets in control of her breathing and the shaking subsides. I'm surprised when she's the first of us to speak.

"You're going to hate me." She draws in an uneven breath. "It was snakes."

There's a moment of silence as we process her words and then Ash is rolling his eyes and Wren is laughing so hard he's crying and now *I* want to scream at Jenny.

"Jen, you were screaming like there was a dragon or a three headed demon killing you," Wren says through another round of laughs. "I had to face vainders!" he adds.

"You couldn't just ignore them?" I ask her and she shakes her head, but she's laughing now, too.

"Gosh, that was awful," she says, her voice scratchy from all her screaming. Jenny presses the heels of her hands to her eyes and takes a few more deep breaths that seep out as exhausted laughs.

We sit here in our huddle, laughing and letting the weight of those fears fade. Wren swipes the tears from his eyes and Ash ruffles a hand through his sister's hair. When our laughing quiets and our breathing settles, I realize we've finished the challenge. "Card six is done," I announce softly.

"Ash, what does the next card say?" Jenny asks, unwrapping herself from her brother's grasp.

He pulls the velvet bag of cards off his wrist and takes out the seventh card. It's titled *The Twisted Journey*.

"Only two left," he says, exhaustion making his words sound dreary.

"Can I read it?" Jenny asks, peering over the top of the card.

"Sure," Ash says, and he hands the card to Jenny. For some reason, his eyes lift and lock on mine. They look awfully sad, or maybe just tired.

Jenny clears her rough throat and reads the riddle aloud.

LEFT AND RIGHT, EAST AND WEST
TURN AROUND, UNWIND, AND LOST AGAIN

KEEP YOUR SENSE OF DIRECTION AT ITS BEST
ENTER WHEN THE CLOCK STRIKES TEN

FIND THE MAP TO GUIDE YOUR WAY
BEWARE OF MONKEYS THAT HIDE AT BAY

A lot processes through my head when Jenny reads the riddle. This is the seventh one we've had to decipher, so they're starting to make more sense to me.

"It's a maze," I say.

Wren and Ash are nodding their heads, seeing how I've drawn that conclusion.

"What time is it?" Jenny asks. "It says to enter at ten."

I turn my wrist and my watch glows. "Seven," I say.

"So, we need to be at the maze in three hours."

"Do you think you can move now?" Ash gently asks Jenny.

She nods and pulls herself to her feet.

"All right then," Wren says, taking Jenny's hand in his. "Let's move on."

We continue down a straight path, deeper and deeper into the mountain. My feet have started throbbing, but I try to ignore it. We left my parent's house a little after nine, *two days ago.* That makes me realize how far we've gone since then. We swam all the way to Rising Salvation and then went to the vainder's camp only to travel all the way back. Last night, I slept in a tree, and I'm tired and hungry.

I sip on my water—the last bottle in my bag. I don't think anyone else has even considered our food and water supplies. What if we never get out? We'd die in here.

"Hey, it's a dead end!" Wren says, his voice suddenly louder than the whispered conversation he was having with Jenny and Ash. I had lost myself in a haze of a nightmare where we starve down in this cave. My attention snaps to Wren, the purple lights reflecting back a solid wall in the distance.

When we get closer, I see that the tunnel opens up into a shallow square chamber. I spin around, letting my purple light glide along the walls. When the light glistens across a sword, I flinch back. I slide the light back and forth, and more weapons come into view.

Swords and knives and spears hang on the wall. The weapons have caught the others' eyes as well.

When I step up to the wall, I notice a tight seam running from the roof of the cave to the floor.

"I think we found the maze," I say. I turn my wrist to look at my watch. Eight. "We still have two hours. Then, this should open up to the maze."

"Are we going to need these weapons?" Jenny asks, her hand resting on the hilt of a slender sword.

I bite my lip, considering it. "I mean, I don't think it would hurt to have them."

"So, now we just wait?" Wren asks, and I nod. "Honestly, I could use some rest," he says and plops down against the wall.

"We should go through our food and water supply," I offer cautiously. I don't want to startle anyone with the crazy thoughts I was having, but I know I'd feel better if we took inventory.

The others agree and we dump our bags into a collective pile. I'm relieved to see Jenny has hardly touched her own supplies. I wonder if that's why she had such a hard time wrapping her brain around the fact that the snakes weren't real.

In total, we still have sixteen granola bars, four for each of us. There's four full bottles of water and a couple half drank ones. With our supplies re-divided I feel better about our chances. Though, after we all eat a granola bar for our dinner tonight, I realize that leaves me with three sources of food. But we only have two cards left. Surely it won't take us more than a day to finish these off.

"The first thing I'm doing when we get home is sleeping," Jenny says between a large yawn. She and Wren both lay down with their heads resting on their bags. My own eyes start to feel heavy. Now that we've finally stopped moving, my adrenaline has ebbed away, leaving exhaustion behind.

"Em, you should rest," Ash says softly. He pats his lap, motioning for me to lay head there. I'm so tired, I don't bother to give it a second thought before I rest my head on his legs.

Silently, he runs his fingers through my blonde curls and somehow, he makes me feel safe here in this enchanted mountain.

"Hey, Ash," I ask, my eyes trained on the ceiling.

"Yeah, Em?"

"What fear did you have to face?" When he doesn't answer, my eyes flicker from the dark ceiling to his face. His eyes don't meet mine. He just keeps running his fingers through my hair.

Finally, he says, "It wasn't vainders or snakes." He sighs and stops running his fingers through my curls. I wish he wouldn't. His blue eyes meet mine, glittering in the purple light. "I had to say goodbye to you. That was the fear I had to face."

Now my eyes can't meet his gaze and they move back to the dark ceiling. I remember how panicked he was when he came out of the slit in the wall. The tears on his cheeks and his shaking breaths engraved in my memory. He broke at the idea of saying goodbye to *me*.

"I had to watch you die," I whisper. Flashes of the fear infested tunnel come back to me now. Of all places, we were in a hospital, like the one my mom works at. He was just lying there, dying, and I couldn't do anything to help him.

Ash's soft fingers dance across my cheek, wiping silent tears away. My breath threatens to give out, but I tame it. It wasn't real.

"At least you won't ever have to face that fear," Ash says, his voice thin.

My eyes move back to his face and I see he's staring into the dark void in front of us.

"You didn't look very happy when you said we only had two cards left," I say.

"My heart's fighting with my brain," Ash admits with another sigh.

"I bet you didn't plan on falling for a girl from Pintura," I say with a forced humor in my voice, even though nothing feels funny about this.

"I never could have planned on you, Em." He lifts his hand and returns to running his fingers through my hair. "I need to admit something," Ash says after a silent minute.

"Yeah?" I prompt him.

"I never actually kissed Sally Temple."

My eyes meet his, and I let out a breathy laugh. "I know, Ash."

He looks at me, shocked. "How do you know?"

"I know you've never kissed *anyone*," I say, and his confusion grows. I think a deep blush settles on his cheeks.

"Why do you say that?"

"Because you would have kissed me by now."

Our eyes lock in a silent, heated stare. He knows it's true. The moments we've come close are endless. He's never kissed anyone before, and that's what keeps him from kissing me. My heart aches as I look into his blue eyes, almost a silvery color in the purple light. I wish this game didn't exist. I wish Earth wasn't real. I wish he was able to be mine, and I wish I could be his.

To keep the moment light, I force the corners of my mouth to turn into a stiff smile.

"It's cute, Ash."

His lips crack into a grin and he leans his head against the wall. "It's embarrassing."

I close my eyes, hoping to keep my tears at bay.

"Get your first kiss right, Ash," I say. "I feel like so many people get it wrong. You still have a chance to get it right."

We don't say anything else and eventually, sleep consumes me.

The ground beneath my body shakes me awake. I roll onto my side and scramble to my feet. The maze is opening.

I turn my wrist to check the time. Ten.

Wren, Jenny, and Ash are as disoriented as I am. I rub my eyes and try to force my brain to wake up. "We only have sixty seconds until the maze closes," I say.

I pick up one of the purple flashlights and start to pull weapons off the wall. I place three knives in my bag and take down one of the smaller swords that's sheathed in a leather scabbard. It feels heavy in my hands, straining my wrist. I loop it around my hips and let the short sword rest against the knot in my shirt. Wren and Ash also take swords, both buckling the scabbards around their waist. Jenny looks at the wall, trying to decide what to do.

The ground begins to shake again and the stone wall starts to close. Panic surges through me. We're running out of time. I race into the maze and Ash and Wren follow close behind me.

"Just pick something, Jenny!" I yell.

She settles on a pair of daggers that are tucked into two holsters. She straps them to her arms and runs toward us. The gap in the rock becomes thinner and thinner, and at the last second, Jenny slides between the stones and makes it into the maze. We share a chorus of deep breaths and quickly regroup, Ash and I each taking a flashlight and agreeing to lead.

Rocky slab walls reach up, nearly grazing the ceiling. They tower so far above us that I feel like a mouse in a cage. We walk down a straight and narrow path for a couple of feet, and then we're tasked with our first choice of either right or left.

"Anyone have a guess?" Wren asks, turning his head both ways.

"I think we just have to pick one. Let's go left," Ash says.

We keep our lights trained on the ground, watching the steps we take. The path twists and turns and I know relatively quickly that we picked the wrong direction because we aren't faced with another choice.

"Dead end," Jenny says, confirming the feeling I had.

"Not off to a great start," I say.

We turn around and head back the way we came. This time, we continue in the other direction. The path continues straight for a while before splitting into a crossroads. Left, right, or straight. Ash, Wren, and Jenny all say something different, and my stomach drops.

"There has to be a better way to figure this out," I say.

"We could split-up," Wren offers.

"Absolutely not," Jenny says.

"Didn't the card mention a map?" Ash mumbles to himself. He reaches into the velvet bag and pulls out the card. He holds the seventh card under the purple light. "Yes, there. It says to find the map to guide our way."

I pull out the map that led us to the cave entrance behind the waterfall and see if we missed something. "I don't see how this helps," I admit.

Nothing on this map matches anything about this maze.

"Okay, then maybe there's another map," Wren says.

"Well, I hope it's in here. Otherwise, we won't be able to get it," Ash says. He furrows his brows together, trying to figure this out.

"We didn't miss anything between the split in the rock and here," Wren says.

"Just the wall of weapons," Jenny adds.

I pull the sword from its sheath and turn it in my hands. I examine the hilt and the blade to see if there are any markings I might have overlooked. Nothing jumps out at me. The others check their weapons as well. I hope we didn't leave the one thing we need outside of the maze.

The sound of metal clattering to the stone floor makes my heart leap in my chest.

"Sorry," Jenny stammers. Her daggers hadn't been hooked in their holsters all the way.

"Jen, be more careful," Wren huffs, the sudden noise making his nerves jump too.

I shine my light at Jenny so she can see where her daggers had fallen. She kneels down and picks them up. My purple light follows her as she stands, and that's when I see the shimmering marks on the wall, just behind her shoulder.

"Look at this!" I say and point to the wall that branches off to our left. There's a glowing dashed line, revealed by the purple flashlight.

I turn back the way we came and see the dashed line continues back that way.

"It's like the numbers on the map," Ash says, moving to stand next to me.

"I'm guessing we go that way, then," I say, pointing my light down the tunnel to our left.

I keep the flashlight trained on the wall and follow the glowing dashed line. The path continues around two more turns, and now I'm sure this will lead us all the way out.

Before relief can settle in, the glowing line on the wall seems to fade.

"Em, my flashlight died," Ash says. I turn around and see his light has gone out. Now the fading dashed line makes sense. It's my light that's dimming.

"It's okay, I have spare batteries," I say before anyone starts freaking out.

The light in my hand glitches. Spurts of purple light strobe the tunnel and then darkness engulfs the maze.

"I'll get them, hold on," I say into the dark void.

A high-pitched screeching makes my heart stop.

"What was that?" Jenny's voice quivers to my left.

"Em, hurry with those batteries," Ash says, trying to hold his voice steady.

I drop my bag to the floor and fish through it. My fingers graze across a granola bar, another granola bar, a bottle of water, some bandages, and then, in the bottom corner, I feel the box of batteries.

The screeching grows louder and Jenny begins to whimper.

"I've got them," I say, but my nerves are getting away from me.

I take the top of the box off and pull out two batteries. They fall through my shaking fingers and rattle on the floor.

"Emma!" Wren snaps at me.

"Sorry," I say and feel around on the floor.

More high-pitched squeals join in and a chorus of animal calls rains down on us. My fingers curl around the batteries and I pick them up. I twist off the top of the flashlight, tipping it over to dump out the dead batteries, before trying to guide the new ones into place in the dark. They fumble in my fingers, not wanting to go in. The screeching is so loud I know our attackers have closed in on us.

"Em! Hurry!" Ash screams to my right.

Ash's distressed voice sends a sense of urgency through my mind. My hands steady and the batteries fall into place. I quickly twist on the top of the flashlight and flip the switch.

A jolt of purple light streams from the bulb, igniting the world around me, and I watch as two crazed monkeys pull Ash up out of the maze.

CHAPTER 25

Ash

I'm rising up from the ground as hard claws dig into both of my arms. The purple light below me sinks away. My sister, Emma, Wren... they all shrink until I can't see them anymore.

"Help!" I yell and squirm against the two giant monkeys that are pulling me to the top of the maze.

Their grip tightens on my arms and I scream in protest. The dead flashlight I have gripped in my hand falls. Glass shatters on the stone floor below.

The monkeys reach the top of the stone walls, hauling me over the edge and across its flat surface. They run along the smooth finish, dragging me behind them. The blood drains from my face when I see the complexity of the maze. It stretches on for as far as I can see in every direction. We are just a pin in a sea of channels.

Emma's purple light is bouncing in the distance, and I think I hear them yelling at me. She's not able to keep up with the monkeys and I lose sight of her. I twist and turn in their grasp, hoping to break free. In my frantic movements, the sword at my hip comes loose and clatters to the floor of the maze.

The two monkeys screech back and forth. The sound feels like nails in my ears. I yell back in frustration, and yank hard. Their grips on my arms rip free.

I roll across the stone top, skidding to a stop at the edge. The rock scrapes the skin on my cheek. It burns and warm blood stings at the surface. I try to scramble to my feet, but one of the monkeys pins me down, my chest and face digging into the stone.

Its teeth pierce the skin on my neck and a raging cry escapes me. Warm venom seeps into my skin. It burns in my veins. The venom crawls through my entire body. Hot liquid coursing its way through me. My head throbs and the world around me starts to go fuzzy. I feel like a weight pushes down on my head and then, I lose consciousness.

CHAPTER 26

Emma

hat the hell were those things? My brain is in overdrive, trying to grasp the fact that two seconds ago Ash was standing by my side, and now he's *gone*. Ripped from the ground by those disgusting looking monkeys.

"*ASH!*" Jenny, Wren, and I all scream his name at the same time as his body disappears over the top of the maze, and the screeching from the monkeys fades.

"Where are they taking him?" Jenny gasps between her deep breaths.

"I don't know," I admit the obvious, barely keeping in my fear and frustration from lashing out at Jenny for asking such a dumb question.

"What's that?" Wren says, throwing his arm wide as something small and black spirals through the air.

I close my eyes at the sound of it shattering on the rock floor. "That would be our second flashlight," I say. Another chorus of screeches erupts from deeper in the maze, back in the direction to captors are taking Ash. I make the realization that the monkeys must be taking him back to some sort of headquarters or camp. "We can follow the sound of their screeching," I say and snap my bag closed, slinging it over my shoulders and tightening it into place. "Let's go!"

The three of us turn and take off at a full sprint down the maze. We know we're going in the right direction when we pass the shattered flashlight.

"Ash, we're coming!" Wren yells into the void where my purple flashlight can't reach.

The unmistakable sound of a *CRASH* rattles my ears.

"What was that?" Jenny screams over the sound of our shoes pounding into the stone floor.

"I don't know!" I snap back at her, once again growing frustrated at her aimless questions. It sounded like metal clanging and ringing in the chamber.

We continue racing ahead and find the source of the sound after a few more seconds. *Ash's sword.* Any hope I had of him being able to fight back and free himself vanishes at the sight of it.

Wren doesn't miss a beat as he leans over and picks up the sword, keeping his pace and running on into the darkness. Jenny and I only falter our steps for a second before we're back in line with Wren and continue on our course.

We'll find him. We have to find him.

"This way," Wren pants as he slides Ash's sword beside his own. I follow the sound of the monkey's chattering and howling off to our left and nod, agreeing with Wren.

"What do you think they're going to do to him?" Jenny whimpers as we make the turn and sprint ahead.

I bite my tongue and this time, choose not to respond to her at all.

"How would we know, Jenny?" Wren says my exact thoughts, but his tone is much gentler than mine would have been. "We don't know anything more than you do."

A soft sniffle escapes Jenny, and when I glance at her out of my peripheral, I see tears streak her cheeks.

"I know you don't," Jenny whispers under her hard breathing. "I just don't know what else to do in this moment." A harsh sob threatens to choke her, and she shakes her head hard, fighting her thunderous heart against her tears. "I can't lose my brother."

My chest aches at the hurt in Jenny's voice. Ash is important to all of us, but to Jenny... He is truly unreplaceable. He's someone she's known her entire life. Someone who has been by her side every day for sixteen years.

As we run into the unknown, I reach over and sweep her hand into mine. She looks at me, continuing to race alongside me, hand-in-hand.

"We'll find him, Jenny," I say. I may not know the answers to any of her questions, but I do know this. I know it because I will not stop until I find him.

CHAPTER 27

Ash

Whatever was in the venom sends my brain into a spiral. It brings up memories I don't even remember. My first words, the day Jenny was born, our first family vacation. I watch myself grow up in a haze of flashbacks. Jenny and I when we were little, and the song I sung earlier is in many of the memories. I spent every night singing her to sleep because she was afraid of the dark.

Some things that I remember differently re-surface in my unconscious state. In the third grade, I got in trouble and I thought it was because I forgot my homework in my room. But it was actually because Wren stole it. I completely forgot he did that. Back before he knew who I was and before we ended up being friends.

When I joined band in the fifth grade, I actually wanted to play the trumpet, like Wren, but my dad said he wanted me to play the drums. He said that I would like that more. All this time later, and it wasn't even me that had wanted to play the drums.

My life unfolds in flashes of drumming sessions and Jenny's soccer games. I met Wren at band camp, going into sixth grade, though I had already known of him the year prior when he was the first chair trumpet player.

I failed my first test in eighth grade science class. I cleverly lost it on the bus and couldn't show it to my parents. Wren's old comic books I used to spend my summers reading speed by me in fast-forward. All the summers I spent with my grandma come back. The first summer she taught me how to draw. She was so happy I finally put my phone away.

A certain afternoon at her house seems to linger with me, its importance lost until now. It's the one time I went into her art studio. The door was left cracked open and I remember leaning in to tell her the timer on the oven went off. She was crouched over a pried up floorboard in the center of the room, her long, grey braid that she always twisted her hair into draped across her back. After quickly putting the board back in place, she hurried out of the room, pulling me with her.

Wherever my body lays now, there's a pain that blooms in my chest. I miss her so much. I wish my grandma was still alive. I wish I could walk back into her house and smell the sugary sensation of whatever dessert she made for our visit. She'd open the door, her eyes so blue they were silver and glittering at Jenny and me. I wish I could still balance myself on a stool with her in the kitchen while she taught me how to paint; her wrinkled hands guiding my brush along the canvas.

I just wish I would have spent more time with her while she was alive.

Freshman year homecoming shows me as an outcast on the gym floor with Wren at my side, swearing we weren't going to any more school dances. But the next year, Jenny was a freshman, so Wren had to go in case, maybe, Jenny would ask him to dance. Which meant I had to go with him so he didn't have to sit by himself on the side of the dance floor when Jenny didn't ask him to dance. That was one of the last nights we talked before our friendship fell apart.

High school comes in waves of sleeping in study halls, rolling my eyes at the cheerleaders bickering in English class, marching band performances at football games, cheating in algebra class, and countless afternoons at practices. Every single memory is flying through my head and I want to laugh and cry and scream all at the same time.

Senior year, when I lied about going to calculus tutoring to actually attend the auditions for the play, hits me hard. The director was my history teacher. I remember how he had me read for the lead role more than anyone else. I should have known I had the part then, but it didn't dawn on me until I saw my name printed on the cast list the next day.

Jenny thought it was a joke I was playing on her. Mom and dad were just confused, but I was so happy. Opening night was an actual dream, and I beg the venom to flow slower so I can relive it a little longer.

The first night I was on a stage. Hundreds of eyes on me. Hot spotlights illuminating the set. The sounds of the audience clapping for me. Cast photos and parties. Late nights spent together at the snow cone stand. It was a sense of community and belonging I didn't realize I was missing.

And then I have to relive all the lasts. The last night of the play, the last halftime show, last homecoming, last prom, last band concert, last physics lab, and the last of my rehearsals. And it doesn't stop with my time on Earth. My grandma's funeral plays back and I realize how much of it I spent in a haze. I didn't remember my mother talking or Jenny crying. I didn't remember that my drunk Uncle Wes decided to show. I didn't even remember that I was crying after I played my snare.

And then Jenny, Wren, and I are cleaning out my grandma's art studio. We fall through the painting and into Pintura. I see those blue eyes peering at me through the tall grass in the field. The moment I met Emma. Her quick remarks make me laugh and make my heart ache at the same time.

The memories here in Pintura move faster, flying in colorful blurs in front of my eyes. I think it must be because the venom is wearing off. The last few memories I have of the maze flicker weakly in my head and finally, my mind rests. My head is quiet. The visions have stopped.

My eyelids crack open. Dusty rocks meet my gaze. My face rests on the stone floor. Grey and black shadows stretch in front of me, and I strain to adjust my vision to the darkness. My body is stiff and aches with every movement.

Slowly, I push myself onto my knees. I raise my head and my eyes scan up the metal bars of a cage. Panic swells through my entire body, my heart skipping in my chest. I sweep my eyes back and forth. Stone walls surround me on three sides. The fourth being the barred door.

I reach for the bars, and my fingers curl around a cold slime that coats their metal surface. My stomach lurches at the disgusting feeling, but I grip the bars and shake them hard. The sound of metal rattling startles a black creature on the other side of the cell. The monkey uncurls itself and his yellow eyes find me. His stained teeth glow in the dim light.

I expect him to lurch forward and bite me again, but he scampers out of the chamber, screeching down the tunnel.

This is my chance to escape. I shake the bars harder, but they don't give. The rattle of a latch in the top right corner draws my focus. A bolt is wedged through the latch of the cell at the top of the bars. It's far too high for me to reach. I grip the slimy bars of the cell as tightly as I can and try to pull myself up. It reminds me of climbing a rope in gym class. Even with every muscle in my drummer arms clenched and engaged, my grip slips through the goop on the metal bars and my shoes hit the ground. I wipe my hands on my dirty shorts and jump, gripping a higher spot on the slimy beams. This time, I try to use my feet to keep myself up.

The screeching from the monkeys grows and three of them crawl back into the chamber, yapping to one another. When they see me up on the bars, they break into mayhem; screaming and crying out. The two additional ones spin back around and race out of the chamber, probably going to get more of their kind to restrain me. The single monkey that guards me now lunges forward and I drop so I can scramble back into the cage. My heart pounds in my chest as the monkey screams at me, ear-piecing shrieks ricochet around the cage. Its crazed yellow eyes follow my every move. Thick, goopy saliva hangs from its snapping jaws. It's not as terrifying as the vainders, but it's a close second.

I don't scream when it snaps its teeth and lunges at me. I don't even scream when its claws grip the metal bars.

I scream when the end of a sword flies through the monkey and muddy yellow blood coats the blade. The sword retracts, and the monkey falls to the floor. Emma is standing in a pool of purple light in its place.

"Em, you found me!" I say and run to the bars. The slayed monkey lies still on the chamber floor.

"Of course, I did. Are you okay?"

I nod and rub the back of my neck where the monkey had bitten me. My fingers brush across two scabby bumps on my sore skin. "It bit me when I tried to fight," I explain. "I think the venom has worked its way out of my system, though."

"Venom?" Emma questions and her eyes widen.

A chorus of screeching in the distance rings out.

"The latch is up there," I say and point to the top right corner of the cage.

Emma's eyes turn up to the latch. She stretches her arm into the air, using her sword to hook the pin. She pulls it out and frees the latch. I lean against the barred door and it eases open.

"You've got to stop saving me all the time," I say, and Emma smiles through the fear on her face.

"Maybe you should stop needing saving," she counters.

The ricocheting screeches grow louder, closing in on the chamber.

"This way," Emma says, leading me out of the stone room and into a dark hall. We go to the left, running as quickly as we can manage in the narrow space. The squeals subside now that we're moving in the opposite direction, and the narrow hall opens up into a stone clearing. Large walls slither in different directions. We're back in the maze.

"Oh, thank goodness you found him!" Jenny has her arms around my neck before I can even see her.

"Let him breathe, Jen," Wren's familiar voice says, pulling Jenny off of me, just so he can pull me into a quick hug.

"I didn't think you'd come for me," I say.

"Why would you think that?" Jenny asks.

"Well, I just didn't think you'd find me," I admit.

"Those things haven't shut up since they took you. It was easy to follow the screams," Emma says, placing her stained sword back at her hip.

"I lost my light and sword when they took me," I say.

"We saw," Wren says, pulling a second sword from his belt. "I found your sword, but the light was shattered."

I return the weapon to my hip, feeling better now that I have some kind of protection.

"What happened to your neck?" Jenny asks when her eyes find the scabs.

"The damn things bit him!" Emma exclaims, shining her light on my neck to get a better look. "It doesn't look infected, actually," she mumbles. "You should still let me bandage it."

Ear-piercing cries ring into the maze.

"Maybe after we get away from their den," I say and am already backing further away from the narrow tunnel Emma and I ran out of.

"Right," Emma says. "Follow me."

She takes off at a jog, using her purple light to guide us through the maze. The dashed line glows back on the wall and we follow it around the bends. I'm completely turned around now. I have no idea where we are since I went unconscious. It seemed like the monkeys were taking me to the right of the maze, but I can't know for sure.

"Ash, you're bleeding," Jenny says after we've been jogging for nearly thirty minutes.

My hand flies to my neck. The scabs at the spots it bit me have split open.

"It's fine. We can bandage it when we get out," I say, though the warm blood already trails down my neck and across my shoulders.

Another thirty minutes goes by and the back of my shirt is soaked with sweat and blood. My head is throbbing and I'm having a hard time staying upright. As we run, I keep thinking about the memories that coaxed their way through me, my entire life playing out in my head. I didn't realize how much I've lived through until I saw it all unwinding inside of me.

And it *hurts*. Every memory from my childhood rakes itself across my heart with a searing grip that makes me wish I was still a kid. That I wasn't running from crazed monkeys or having nightmares of vainders. But it also reminds me of the world I'm currently trying to return to, and the one I'll have to leave behind. How I'll have to say goodbye to the blue-eyed girl who peered at me through the wheat field.

I've already lived through all of my lasts back home. I'm on the threshold of a new chapter in my life. I can see that—*feel that*—now, and this new world, this fierce and unreadable girl in front of me, she—

"There it is!" Emma screams, shattering my thoughts.

I lift my heavy head and see the opening in the maze. The purple dashed line leads us all the way to the end. When we cross through the exit, I collapse on the ground. I think the venom must be working its way out of my system because my mind still clings to those memories. Emma and Jenny are at my side, but I'm having a hard time knowing which world is real; the one in my head or the one beneath me.

"He's lost a lot of blood," I hear Emma say.

"Gosh, he's so pale," Wren adds.

"Here Ash, drink some water," Jenny says, and a bottle is pushed against my lips. I take slow sips of the warm water and it helps. I'm able to sit up and my head stops spinning.

"We need to take his shirt off so I can add bandages," Emma says.

With sluggish arms, I pull the shirt over my head and feel the warm blood smear in my hair and on my face. I suck in a sharp breath when the water pours over my cuts.

"Hold still, Ash," Jenny says soothingly.

Emma takes another bottle and pours the water down the side of my face. She uses a wrap to wipe the streaks of blood from my face and out of my hair.

"Okay, his back is cleaned too," Jenny says when she's seen Emma's cleaned the rest of me up.

Emma pulls out two large rectangular band-aids. The kind my mom would put on my knee when I'd wreck my bike.

"Finish off this bottle," Emma says, shoving a half empty bottle of water into my hands.

I lift it to my lips and sip on it, forcing myself to lift my head. Through the purple rays from our single light by Emma's feet, I see Wren staring at the wall across from me. I furrow my brows and my eyes sweep along the wall.

"Is that a map of the maze?" I ask, my voice weak.

Emma and Jenny look up from my wounds and turn their eyes to the stone wall. Deep grooves are carved in the stone wall, snaking across its surface. It stretches for at least ten feet. On the far left side, halfway up the wall, a wooden shaft sticks out of the stone. Wren reaches up to it and slides it in the channel. He tries to pull it from the wall, but it's pinned beneath the stone.

"I think I have to slide this down the path we took to release it," Wren says. He moves the wooden piece in stiff movements, going straight, and then down, and then straight again.

"That could take hours," I say, gulping another mouthful of warm water.

"Good, you need to rest," Jenny says. She stands and moves to help Wren, who seems to have forgotten if we went left or right after the zig zag of channels.

"Your sister's right," Emma says, reading the scowl on my face.

I finish off the bottle of water and hand it back to Emma. My mental tally on our resources says we probably only have two full bottles of water left. Plus, the half one I have in my bag. I wish they hadn't used any on me. I feel like I'm wasting our resources.

"Eat this," Emma says, placing a granola bar in my hand.

"You don't need to take care of me," I say, trying to make my voice sound strong.

"Ash, don't push me away," Emma says softly and a pang of guilt ignites in my chest.

I take the granola bar and eat it slowly. I didn't mean to make her feel like I was pushing her away. I'm just tired and actually, hungry. I look back up at Wren and Jenny and see they're about halfway done, not taking nearly as long with the puzzle as I thought they would. Who knew memory games and mazes were Jenny's thing?

Jenny goes to the other end and starts to work out the path backwards so she can take over when they intersect.

"Vainders and evil monkeys all in the same week," Emma mumbles next to me.

She leans her head against the wall and watches Jenny and Wren solve the puzzle. "Do you want to go over the eighth card while they complete the puzzle?" Emma asks, pushing away her comment about the vainders and monkeys.

I nod and finish the granola bar. Emma reaches across me to my left wrist and pulls the velvet bag free. Her arm is warm against my bare chest and her fingers gently brush against my skin. I become very aware of the fact that she's never seen me without my shirt on and my face flushes with heat.

Emma opens the bag and pulls out the eighth card. The *last* card. The end of *this card* could be the portal. I have to go home once we finish *this card*.

I keep the light trained on Jenny and Wren so they can see their puzzle, but Emma's able to make out the riddle in the soft purple glow. She reads the riddle to me, but I find it hard to focus on her words. My heart so badly wants to block out the fact that I have to leave. I ask her to read it again. She does, and this time, I force my brain to listen to the riddle.

NOW IT'S TIME TO RETRIEVE THE KEY
IN A BOX LOCKED WITH A ROUND

BURIED UNDER THREE FEET DEEP
INSIDE, THE KEY WILL BE FOUND

TAKE IT TO THE HIGHEST PEAK
WHERE BRANCHES REACH AND THE AIR GOES WEAK

"It's not even a riddle," Emma says, tapping her fingers on the card. "We just have to dig up the box."

"There's that part about a branch," I say, rolling the words in my head.

Emma nods and scans the riddle again. I know she's thinking the same thing as me. This card is going to be easy. It's straightforward. It means the end is that much closer.

"Almost there," Jenny says, her voice breaking my train of thought.

My tired eyes sweep over and I watch her slide the wooden peg out of the puzzle.

"Let me see that," I yell to her and extend my hand.

She walks across the clearing and hands the wooden piece to me. The grip is a rectangular block of wood, but the end that had slid beneath the channel of the slide puzzle is a round disk. My thumb rubs over the edge of the peg. *In a box locked with a round.*

"Keep this in your bag," I say, and hand it back to Jenny. "We'll need it for the last card."

"Did you already read over it?" she asks, tucking the wooden piece away in her bag.

Emma recites the card once more for Jenny and Wren and even in the dark purple light, it's hard to miss their excitement.

This is it. These are my final moments in Pintura.

CHAPTER 28

Ash

Jenny and Wren have me on my feet quicker than my head would like. It still throbs a little, but nothing is stopping them. I pull my shirt back on, a bit disgusted by the damp patches of crimson blood.

While my heart is hurting at the idea that I'm so close to leaving all of this behind, it's hard not to let Jenny and Wren's excitement overtake me. It's contagious.

The beam of purple light dances along the tunnel walls while Jenny practically skips in front of me.

"Wren, we're almost home!" she beams for the third time.

"I'm still taking you to get that burger," Wren reminds her.

"Fine, as long as I can sleep on the way there."

"I hope mom and dad aren't mad," I say and Jenny actually laughs.

"I'm sure they're going to be *furious*, but at least we'll be home!" Her response is practically sung, the happiness ringing on the walls around us.

Emma is even smiling, though it looks a little forced. I know she's happy for us, but her eyes tell a different story. Sadness clings to their blue depths.

"Look!" Jenny calls.

She's a couple of feet ahead of us now. We jog to reach her and I see what's got her all excited. The stone floor changes to soft, dusty dirt. Two linked circles are drawn in the loose ground, and the tunnel is sealed at the other end, closing us in.

"I'd say this is where we start digging," Jenny says.

Without giving any of us a chance to say anything, she drops to her knees at the spot where the rings cross and she starts scooping up dirt with her bare hands. We join her, mixing up the dusty dirt in the air. It's soft, like sand, and that makes it easy for us to sift through.

"Ash, don't reopen your cuts," Wren says, gently pushing me back.

I want to argue, but I already feel my shoulder aching. "All right," I say and step back.

I take the flashlight and hold it up so they can see where they're digging. Emma moves her arms so fast there's a cloud of dust around her, coating her face and getting in her hair. Wren heaves armfuls of sand out of the way, raking large piles off to the side. In a matter of minutes, they've dug deep enough that when Jenny jumps into the hole, she's down to her knees.

"We're getting close," she says, though I have no idea how she can conclude that. She sticks her arms into the soft sand, sinking to her elbows. "I feel something!" she says, her mouth hanging open. She yanks back on her arm, but whatever she's got her grip on stays stuck beneath the sand. "Wren, help me pull it out," Jenny grunts, pulling back again.

Wren pushes his hands into the sand, finding the buried object. "On three," he says.

He counts up and they pull together. Wren yells, straining backwards and slowly, the sand on the surface shifts and a box comes into view.

"That's it!" Emma gasps.

She lunges for the other end and helps push it out of the sand. It's a dark, chocolate wood with gold metal brackets and handles. On the front of the box is a round key hole. They get the box up on level ground and dust off the sand. Jenny shifts through her bag and pulls out the wooden peg she freed earlier. She pauses, twirling the key in her hand.

"Well, go on, Jen," Wren says.

Jenny looks nervous, or maybe anxious. She licks her lips and crouches in front of the box. I lean over her shoulder and shine the purple light on her shaking hand. She pushes the round end of the key into the hole and there's a soft *click* inside the box. Emma takes in a sharp breath. Jenny's eyes flip from her hands, to us, and then back to the lock. She slowly turns the key and more soft clicks echo in return. Once the key has rotated one-hundred and eighty degrees to the right, the golden clamps on the front pop open.

Emma and Wren reach for the top of the box at the same time. "Together?" Emma says.

Wren nods and they pull up on the chest. Its hinges squeal in protest. The purple rays of light stream into the box and a piece of wood is lying inside. Jenny reaches in and lifts it out. It's thin like tree bark and about the length of her forearm, so she cradles it in the hook of her arm.

I take out the last card to review the riddle. "That's supposed to be the key."

Jenny twists the piece of bark over. The corners of her mouth spread into a toothy grin and I think I see tears well up in her eyes.

"It's the key," she whispers.

We lean in and look at the piece of wood, and sure enough, the symbol of two linked rings is carved on the back.

"Ash, pull out the golden card," Emma says.

I do, remembering Emma had called it the winning card when we had played nine days ago. *Nine days...* I shake my head before the thought can settle. There, printed on the reflective card, is a picture of the wooden slab of wood in Jenny's arm.

"It's the key," I say, showing the group.

There's a round of victorious hollers and claps before Emma speaks up. "What's the last part of card eight?"

I look back at the card and read the last two lines.

"It says to take it to the tallest peak."

As the words leave my mouth, the ground beneath my feet starts to shake. I shine the light around the chamber and see dust falling from the ceiling of the far wall. Wren, Jenny, and Emma stager to their feet on wobbly legs. The wall across from us sinks into the soft sand and hot rays of sunlight stream in.

CHAPTER 29

Emma

My hand flies over my eyes to block the bright beams of sunlight. A warm summer breeze blows in and I realize how suffocating the still cave air is. Once my eyes adjust to the sudden light, I finally rejoice at seeing the outside world again. If I'm being honest, I wasn't sure we'd ever make it out of here.

My excitement steals my feet and I race out of the cave. I'm greeted by a thick, green forest, ascending from all sides. Rising Salvation encircles the valley, making me feel like we're in a crater. The others find their feet and join me outside; equally as confused as to where we've been let out. I spin around, suddenly feeling very trapped.

Every five feet is a small wooden post next to a narrow path. I approach the nearest one and see that there are five random letters carved into the wood.

"Why do I feel like we aren't quite done with this game?" Jenny questions cautiously.

I watch her swallow away her anxious nerves.

"One of these paths will lead to the highest peak," Ash says.

I turn and see he's still studying the card.

"Any hints on which one?" Wren asks.

Ash shakes his head.

"Anything on the wooden piece?" Wren asks, turning to Jenny.

She rotates it in her cradled arms, but the only markings are the linked rings.

"Well, I don't think we should go down any of them until we figure out which one's right," Ash offers.

"You just want to sit here?" Jenny asks.

Just the other day, she was making Ash swear he would be more careful, and now she wants to be reckless because we're so close to the end.

"Ash is right," I say, breaking the tense silence. "We don't know what might happen if we choose the wrong path."

"Okay, then let's go over everything it could possibly be," Wren says. "That purple light has revealed more things than anything else." Wren takes the light from Ash, not nearly as bright in the summer sun. He joins Jenny and they examine the piece of wood.

"Anything?" I ask.

Wren just shakes his head. Then, he works his way to every single wooden post and tries to see if there are any hidden messages on them. Each one results in a more frustrated grunt. In case he missed something, Wren goes around to each one of them a second time. I'm more of a sit-and-think kind of person, instead of a pace-and-think person. Ash has found a spot in the shade to sit, also preferring to work out the puzzle this way. I go and join him, sinking into the soft dirt at the edge of the trees.

"T E O T L," Ash mumbles to himself.

"What's that?" I ask.

"The letters on this sign." He lifts his hand and taps on the wooden post next to us. I turn to my left and read the other post.

"R U L A M."

"Maybe if we unscramble the letters they mean something," Ash says.

"Gosh, my brain can't do that," I admit.

I close my eyes and rub my forehead. All that we've been through has taken a toll on me. Something that might have been an easy puzzle, like unscrambling letters, is an impossible task now.

"I know, I can't either," Ash says, letting out a loud sigh.

Just like that, he lets the idea go. Something feels very forced about his words, and he doesn't seem all that concerned that we're stuck.

"At least we're out of the mountain," I offer, trying to find something positive about our current predicament.

"I don't mind a few more minutes here," Ash admits softly.

I wonder if he really means here in Pintura, or another minute with me. Has my world really grown on him? After all they've told me about Earth, I can't imagine any world being better than that.

"You'll be home tonight," I say.

"You think we're going to figure this out?" Ash gestures to the puzzle around us.

"I think we've solved harder puzzles before," I say. A moment of silence passes between us and I let my next words boil over in my head. "Ash, I know you've already figured it out."

His eyes fall closed. "What makes you say that?"

"You're the only one not trying to solve it." I'm quiet, waiting to see if he's going to admit it. He doesn't, but he doesn't deny it either.

I reach over and lace my fingers through his. I remember the first time I felt his hand in mine. We had been dancing in the auditorium, right before he found his token. His skin is rough now, his grip stronger.

"Tell me about your home," I say softly.

"What do you want to know?"

"Everything."

I let Ash talk for a while. At this point, it couldn't hurt anything. I can't imagine what he's feeling right now, and if he just wants to sit here a little longer, I won't take that away from him. Plus, I love hearing him talk. I'm not ready to let him leave either. We're both probably being selfish about this, but what's another hour?

I get lost in Ash's stories about growing up with Jenny. How he used to sing that song to her every night to help her fall asleep. How he started playing the drums because of his dad. How he traveled all over the world with his aunt and uncle before they became alcoholics. He tells me about his first slow dance at his junior prom and how he stepped on the girl's dress and ripped it. He talks a lot about the summers he spent with his grandma. She sounds magnificent. Especially all the stories about her being an artist. I wish I could paint. Ash makes it sound like her work could be in museums.

"This one time, Jenny and I told our parents we were going to run away," Ash says.

I'm stuck somewhere between dropping my jaw, shocked, and laughing. Ash glances over at me and sees the mixed emotions on my face.

"Why'd you say that to them?" I ask.

"Because we were kids, and that's what you do."

"Did you ever run away?"

Ash laughs. "Yes. We camped out in the backyard for an entire weekend."

"Got too hungry?" I ask.

Ash shakes his head and I see his tired blue eyes find Jenny. "I went back because Jenny wanted to go home. I could've stayed out there forever. I actually liked being on my own."

Ash is quiet, so I fill the silence. "That's probably why the allowance at twelve here works so well. You won't find many kids who don't want to do their own thing."

Ash nods, thoughtfully. We sit here for a long while in silence. So long my grip on Ash's hand goes numb. Tears brim my eyes twice, but I pull them back each time. Crying isn't going to make this any easier for him.

"Ash, I think it's time," I whisper.

As if to drive my point further, Jenny lets out a frustrated scream, pouting like an exhausted child.

Ash sighs, knowing he has to do this for Jenny, just like he did when they were kids, because he needs to get her home. I wonder, if Jenny and Wren weren't here, if he'd stay. I hate myself for even thinking it. Of course, he wouldn't stay here. He has his own world and life to live. I stand up and pull Ash to his feet.

"One last puzzle," I say.

He takes a steading breath and repeats, "One last puzzle."

We walk over to where Jenny and Wren have slumped over, defeated, against the opening of the mountain.

"Let me see the flashlight," Ash says.

Wren hands it over and scrambles to his feet. "I've already checked everything."

"Not everything," Ash says.

He pulls out the eighth card and shines the light over the riddle. Random letters down the card light up in a neon purple glow. Wren sucks in a sharp breath and Jenny hurries to stand so she can see the card, too.

"How'd you know?" Jenny asks.

"It's the only thing we have with letters," Ash lies.

I know when he figured it out. When we were digging for the chest, he had read the card under the purple light. He's known since then that those letters meant something. I don't think Jenny or Wren remember that. They're both too excited to even question it now.

"Read me the letters," Wren says, and he starts pacing around the clearing, looking at all the wooden posts.

"H P R A."

Wren repeats the letters to himself and then stops. "That's only four letters. All of these signs have five."

"They spell something," I mumble, finally putting the final piece together. We walk around the clearing, placing our four letters in between the five letters on the sign. I'm not sure what they should spell, or how we'll know what the correct decoded word is.

"There!" Wren announces.

He pauses by the post directly to the right of the cave opening. His smile fills his entire face. We race over to him and I realize it was the post Ash and I had been sitting next to. We were right there all this time, and by the look on Ash's face, I can assume he knew that, too. When I combine the four letters from the card with the five on the sign, I take in a sharp breath.

THE PORTAL.

"Let's go!" Jenny squeals and she pulls Ash along before he even has a chance to put the card away.

Suddenly, everything starts to move insanely fast. Jenny and Wren are racing up the trail and now I'm longing for that still hour we spent under the tree. This was our last test. We've flipped the switch and now it's all tumbling to a close.

CHAPTER 30

Ash

I want to tell Jenny and Wren to stop. I want to slow things down, but the day keeps moving too fast. I knew as soon as I told them about the letters on the card that it would be the end of this journey. And while I'm hurting at the idea that in a few moments I'll be saying goodbye to Emma, I can't help but feel Jenny and Wren's infectious excitement pulse through my veins.

I'm going to be home soon. My mom and dad can stop worrying. I can sleep, shower, and eat a home cooked meal. Home is just a moment away.

The trail starts to incline, and we hike up a steep, rocky path. In the cave, I got used to the dark and the cool air. Out here, the thick humid breeze chokes my throat. The sun has started its descent, but it's early afternoon and still very hot. Sweat rolls down my back and my hair is damp on my forehead. But home is at the top of this mountain. Goodbye is at the top of this mountain.

Every once in a while the trail will branch off and we'll have to decide between two posts, always being sure to follow the one labeled T E O T L. Now we know we could have chosen incorrectly and probably still found our way to an intersecting path.

I know I should have told them when I first noticed the glowing letters on the card. I think Emma is the only one who's realized I've known longer than I admitted.

She's surprisingly upbeat right now, letting Wren tell her all the things he's going to do when he gets home. She has him tell her the history of Earth again so she can write it down and sell books about it. Gosh, I love that about her. She's always thinking ten steps ahead. Maybe I could do that about Pintura. I shrug the idea away. I'd rather keep this world my secret.

Finally, the ground levels out and we make it to the top of the trail. It continues to snake on level ground to our right, but we freeze at the crest. The trail lets us out at the very edge of the peak of the mountain. I can see all of Pintura from up here. I mean, *all of it*.

"Let's take a quick break," I say through deep, heavy breaths.

The others agree, the steep incline taking all of our energy. On wobbly legs, I lower myself to the ground and take in the view. To our right, Artmith gleams in the afternoon sun. I think of the swing in the backyard of Emma's childhood home. I think of the theater we found my token in. The streets we walked down, the Center of Technology building we snuck into, Emma's little shack in Shadow Village, and the secret engineering lab under her house. I even think about Billy's Salon and the Penny Arcade we wandered into on our first day here. That city has become so familiar to me.

My eyes shift to the Golden Field nestled between Rising Salvation and Infinity forest. The tops of the emerald trees sway slightly in the summer breeze. Why does the thought of leaving a world with creatures like vainders make me upset? Those things will haunt my dreams for the rest of my life. But moments with Emma up in the trees fill my heart. I've never really been someone who loves nature before, but I know when I go back I'll have to find time to hike and climb trees. That way, maybe for a little bit, I can pretend I'm here, and in a few seconds Emma would swing down from a higher branch and we'd be together again.

My eyes dampen, and I tilt my head back to hold in the tears. The grey clouds still turn in a lazy cyclone overhead. I guess when we go back, that will go away. Maybe then, everyone else will forget we were ever here. I look back at Artmith. No, those papers with our pictures will still be here. That's all they'll have left of us. Drawings of people from another world. That's all they'll remember.

Movement near the wall draws my eyes to the scrapyard. I imagine Emma spending her days there. Tomorrow, she'll probably start working again. She needs to earn back quite a bit of money after the time she's been away. I wonder if she'll catch herself glancing at the clouds, hoping we fall through again. I wonder if I'll look at paintings and imagine she's on the other side of them.

A sudden flash of red to the left of the scrapyard catches my eye. A flood of Patrol officers flows through the gate. I had forgotten about them.

"You guys," I say, breaking the silence.

They follow my gaze and see nearly fifty officers making their way into the Golden Field.

"They're still looking for us," Jenny breathes.

The officers form into five lines and they begin to sweep through the field.

"They're going to search every inch of this world," Emma mumbles.

"When we go back, we'll close the portal," Wren says. "Then the clouds will go away and they'll know we're gone.

And then they'll forget we were ever here.

"Ready to go?" Jenny asks.

We rise from our lookout point and continue along the trail. It stays on the edge of Rising Salvation, so I watch as the Patrol below searches for us. It's easier to look down there than at the end of the trail ahead.

I wish I could slow down time or make this path longer. Isn't there one more card we need to complete or riddle we need to solve?

Much too soon, I hear Jenny squeal and Wren gasp. The half of me that's excited to go home draws my eyes away from the Patrol. The narrow dirt trail finally comes to an end. Near the final wooden post is a large weeping willow tree, right at the top of Rising Salvation, nestled next to the roaring, glittering waterfall.

When we approach the tree, I see that a chunk of its bark is missing. My eyes flip from the tree to the piece of wood in Jenny's arms.

"Can I do it?" she asks, glancing at all of us, and speaking above the sound of the rushing water.

"Go ahead," I say.

She steps forward and lines up the edges of the wooden piece to the hole in the tree's trunk. They form a perfect and snug fit. She presses it into the groove and steps back.

Bright yellow beams of light spray out of the groove around the wooden piece in the tree. At first, I just think the branches are blowing in the wind, but they rustle faster. Light brown limbs stretch out and begin to braid themselves together. The wind picks up as the arms of the tree shift faster and suddenly they start to rise. A spiral staircase of branches forms, twisting into the sky. I crane my neck back and watch the limbs ascend all the way up into the cyclone of clouds we fell from.

The olive leaves shiver and change to a beautiful gold confetti. They explode from their branches and we're rained on by a storm of glittering leaves. After all this time, and everything we have seen, this pure act of magic still leaves me in awe.

We won the game.

Jenny's hand flies over her mouth and an excited laugh bleeds between her fingers. Wren looks like he may cry, and the corners of my mouth tug at my skin, a smile so wide it hurts. *I'm going home.*

The distant sound of a siren catches my attention. I pull my eyes away from the spiral staircase of branches and see that the Patrol is moving their unit toward us. They've seen the staircase, but I don't worry. They still have to cross the lake and find the right trail up here. I'm not even sure they could get here without solving the cards and going through the tunnel inside the mountain.

"Emma, thank you for helping us," Jenny says, pulling my attention away from the Patrol. She gives Emma a tight hug and Emma tells Jenny she hopes she gets her soccer scholarship.

"You saved us, Emma," Wren says, moving in to hug her next.

"Thank you for telling me your stories, Wren," Emma says, and both Wren and Jenny move to the tree, leaving their bags and weapons from the maze on the ground. The only pieces of this world they take with them are the clothes Wren was given after the vainder attack. Their gleaming eyes look back at me, understanding glistening there.

"Don't be too long," Wren says, and he nudges Jenny up the

staircase. Emma and I watch them ascend until they move out of sight.

Then, her light blue eyes are on me. Her blonde curls spill around her face. She's wringing her hands together, already dreading this just as much as I am. My heart beats faster in my chest and it feels like I'm back in the tunnel of my fears.

Everything comes back to me so fast I almost stumble backward. The feeling of her hand in mine. Her smile that could lighten every day. That fire that burns inside of her, making her the bravest person I've ever met. Her breath on my neck, her arms around my back, her tears on her cheeks. The metallic smell of Artmith and the citrus aroma of oranges. Everything about her forces its way into my head, and I realize there's no way I can be without her.

I can't say goodbye to Emma Delaney.

My feet guide me to her, and I reach for Emma, pressing my palms to either side of her face. Wild blue eyes stare back at me and I take in every inch of her, the faded freckles and rosy cheeks, before I press my mouth to hers.

I kiss Emma Delaney with the passion and fire that has licked my skin since the first second I met her. Every pulse in my chest explodes, and it's like gravity is pulling me into her. Her lips are soft and damp against mine. I slide my hands to the nape of her neck and run my fingers through her blonde curls.

All of the moments where I almost did this flash in my head; dancing with her in the theater, telling her stories of my past, holding her in the dark of her home, and seeing her face at the other side of my fears.

Emma's hands find my chest and her fingers curl into the collar of my shirt, pulling the kiss deeper. Her words come back to me, spoken before the maze and before the crashing end of this game threatened to suffocate me.

Get your first kiss right, Ash.

I couldn't think of anything more perfect than this. Than her.

I break my lips from Emma's, and my words rush out before I can stop them.

"Come with me."

Her blue eyes shift, confused.

"I can't be without you, Em. Come back with me. Let me show you my world. I can take you to the ocean and show you all the technology Wren told you about and you can study to be an engineer." I take a breath, my lungs begging for me to slow down. "Please," I whisper.

Her eyes shift from me to Artmith in the distance. She takes a step back, her hands falling from my chest. Emma's cheeks flush bright red, her breaths short.

I never should have asked her to come. This is her home. I want to pull back my words, but then I see her smile.

"Yes," she says and looks at me. "Yes, I'll go with you!"

I want to ask her if she's sure, but she's already pulling me onto the spiral staircase. Her hand in mine, racing up toward my world. We leave our bags, the Ending in Cadence cards, and weapons on the ground below. I even pull off my blood-stained shirt because I don't want to begin to explain that to my mom.

This is our way of leaving the game behind us.

Emma stops just below the swirling clouds and turns to me. The entirety of Pintura fades below us and I have enough common sense not to look down to see how high we are. I think Emma may have changed her mind, but then she kisses me again, smiling against my lips and sending my heart racing against my bare chest.

"Thank you, Ash."

With only a breath of air between our faces, I look at her and lose myself in her magnificence. She is like nobody else in either of our worlds and she is mine. I get to be hers. We are staying together.

I grab Emma's hand, and hold on to her like my life depends on it. We turn around and continue up the staircase and into the cyclone of clouds together.

CHAPTER 31

Emma

I'm not sure what I expect. The world around me goes grey as we pass through the clouds. Wind rips at my face, making it hard to catch my breath. I squeeze Ash's hand and keep moving forward. I guess I expect to fall through the sky like they had, but one second I'm walking up an enchanted staircase, going through a grey cyclone in the sky, and the next, I'm rising up into a wooden room. I look down at the painting I'm standing *through*. I step out of it and onto the tan wooden floor.

"Emma!"

I snap my head up and see Jenny and Wren. They both tackle me in a hug while Ash comes through the painting behind me.

"You're on Earth!" Jenny squeals when she and Wren release me.

I laugh because it's obvious. I'm here, aren't I? "You're my family now. This is where I want to be."

Jenny lets out an excited squeal and squeezes my hands. "We have so much to show you!"

"First, we need to get rid of this," Wren says, nudging the painting with his foot.

Ash kneels next to it, running his hand along the golden frame.

"So, this is the magical painting you fell through," I say.

I've been with them for over a week now, but it still amazes me that it's true. I tilt my head and examine the painting. It does resemble Pintura. The city and the Golden Field, bordered by Rising Salvation and Infinity Forest.

Ash's fingers catch on a loose piece of the frame. He rotates it back into place and then lays his hand on the now solid canvas.

"That must have been how I unlocked it," Ash says.

"Should we burn it?" Wren asks.

I glance at him and see he's actually scared of the painting.

"Wren, it's her only way home," Ash says gently. "If we leave it closed and put it somewhere safe, then it's not doing any harm."

I can see Wren and Jenny want to disagree, but they don't feel they can in front of me.

"I don't want to go back. Wren's right. This isn't safe to have. We don't want it falling in the wrong hands," I say. I meant it when I said they are my family now.

"So, fuel for our bonfire tonight!" Wren cheers.

I think Ash may want to push back, but the slam of a door beneath our feet stops him.

"Ash!" a woman's voice calls.

"Are you and your sister ready for the truck?" a man's voice says next.

"*Mom?*" Jenny asks, her voice weak.

The sound of muffled footsteps on hardwood rings out, and they step through the door.

"What on earth happened? You guys look awful," the woman says.

"Moving truck is downstairs if you're ready to help," the man interjects.

"Moving truck?" Ash asks, confused.

"Yes, I told you today at the funeral that we'd come by." The man shakes his head. "I know it's been a long day. You probably just forgot."

"Today," Ash says under his breath.

When Ash, Jenny, and Wren landed in Pintura, Ash told me that morning he was at his grandma's funeral. Over a week has passed in Pintura, but it seems like little time passed here.

"Byran, look at them. Is someone going to explain why you're missing a shirt— Wait, is that blood?"

"Paint!" Jenny interjects the moment her mother's voice pitches up, horrified. "Ash made a huge mess with the paints," she further explains. We're lucky the only bits of blood left on Ash are faded and smeared from our best attempt to clean him up after we exited the maze.

The shock on their mother's face shifts back to confusion as her attention turns to Jenny. "Why are you covered in sand? Wren, it's good to see you, and—"

The woman stops when her eyes land on me, taking in my lavender top and long, black cargo shorts.

"Who are you?"

My throat tightens. This was *not* how I wanted to meet Ash's parents.

"Mom, dad, this is Emma," Ash says, moving next to me. He puts a gentle hand around my waist. "She's my girlfriend."

I refrain from laughing or pulling out of his grasp. I mean, yes, I guess Ash and I are dating. We hadn't really discussed that, and the term *girlfriend* feels awfully childish for what we really are to one another. After everything we've been through, Ash feels like so much more than my boyfriend. He's my person. He's everything to me.

"Girlfriend?" his father says and then sticks out his hand.

I take it and give a quick shake.

"It's nice to meet you, Emma."

"And you never mentioned her before because," Ash's mom prompts him.

"She goes to Central West. We met last week at that band contest," Ash quickly covers.

"I see," his mother says. I think she may not approve, but she offers her hand and gives me the same greeting. "Well, it's nice to meet you. Maybe you could join us for dinner tonight and we can get to know you better."

"Actually—" Ash starts, but I interrupt.

"I would love that."

"Perfect. Let's finish packing and we'll get some food," Ash's mother says. "Is that one of grandma's paintings?"

Our eyes move down to the painting of Pintura.

"Uh, yes. I was just taking it down," Ash says, hoisting the painting up into his arms.

"Looks like you're just about finished up here. We'll go down to the kitchen," Ash's father says.

"I'll still want an explanation on your appearance," Ash's mother adds as she turns to follow her husband downstairs.

"Did we time travel?" Jenny whispers as soon as the sounds of their footsteps have left the upper level.

"No, I think," Ash starts to say, pausing to squint as he processes his thoughts. "I think time just moves slower here."

"A lot slower," Wren adds.

"Right, because we still had four hours or so until they we coming with the moving truck after you pushed me into the painting," Jenny says.

Suddenly, Ash drops the painting of Pintura and hurries across the room.

"Ash, what's wrong?" Wren asks, and we all follow Ash.

He kneels down on the tan wooden floor and drags his hands across the planks of wood. "When I was infected by the venom from the monkeys, I saw a memory of my grandma moving one of these floorboards."

"Ash, who knows what kind of toxins were in your system," Jenny says, trying to calm him down.

When the board beneath his hand wiggles, loose in the floor, we all freeze. "No, it was a real memory," Ash says. He pries up the floorboard and we drop to our knees to peer inside.

Ash lowers his hand into the dark void. When he pulls his hand back, a black velvet bag is in his grasp.

"Is that—" I start to say, but the words get lost in my throat.

Ash pulls open the bag and a set of Ending In Cadence cards tumbles to the floor. An exact match—except for the age—to the cards I left on the top of Rising Salvation.

Jenny sucks in a sharp breath. "Grandma knew about the painting."

The cards are old; the colors more faded than the deck we played with. I pick them up and the material is softer, worn with age and use. Most of them have folded corners or rips along their sides. I imagine

Ash's grandma going through what we've just experienced and I can see the wear of that journey on these cards.

"Are you kids coming?" Ash's mom calls from downstairs.

"We should burn those with the painting," Wren says.

I hand the cards to Ash and he packs them back into their velvet bag. I want to ask him what this means and what we should do with this information, but I can see he doesn't have an answer for me.

"We can hide the cards and the painting up here. Tonight, we'll come back and destroy them," he says.

We stand and store the painting under some old drop cloths with the cards. When we make our way to the door, I feel the need to say something.

"You didn't have to lie," I speak up, still playing back how I meet his parents.

"I couldn't tell them the truth," Ash says.

I know he's right, but I hate that I'm this big lie now.

"I'm sorry, I just panicked," Ash adds.

"It's like when you lied about us to your mom," Jenny comes to his defense. "The less they know, the better. My mom just buried our grandmother this morning. The last thing we need to do is try to explain to her that she had a portal to another world in her art studio."

"So where do I live?" I ask. "In this lie, where am I from? What do I do at Central West?" I say, pulling the name Ash had used and pressing it to memory. We hadn't thought this through. I don't have anyone here to go to, just them.

"Well, you can stay here," Jenny says. "The house won't sell right away." I must look angry because she adds, "Or not."

"We'll figure it out later," Ash says. "Maybe at dinner we can tell them the truth."

I take in a deep breath and shrug it away. We'll figure it out. This isn't nearly as difficult as what we just went through. We grab the final things in the art studio and follow Ash out of the room.

His grandmother's house is enormous. Definitely outdated, but I love the character it has. I help Ash load the stacks of his grandmother's paintings into the moving truck. He really did describe them well. They're absolutely beautiful.

"Gosh, your grandmother was so talented," I say as I place the last one inside the truck.

"Yeah, she was," Ash says, and he helps me down from the truck bed.

It doesn't take us very long to move the rest of the larger items into the moving vehicle. I try to avoid questions from his parents because I don't want to dive deeper into this lie. For the most part, they don't ask any. Ash and Jenny's mother is still more concerned with their appearance and has Ash clean off what remains of the blood—*paint*—in the bathroom.

Once the truck is loaded and the house is locked up, we meet by their vehicles out front. I've been a little distracted by them since I've only seen our Patrol trucks and they look nothing like these.

"That's mine," Ash says, coming up behind me.

"I've never seen a vehicle like this," I say.

Ash laughs. "If you weren't from Pintura, I might take offense to that."

"Wren, will you be joining us for dinner?" I hear Ash's mom ask behind us.

"I'd love to," he says.

"All right, does Burgerville sound good?" Ash's father asks.

The corner of Wren's mouth turns up. Looks like he's getting that

320

burger after all.

"Works for me," Wren says.

"Okay," Ash's mother lets out an exhausted sigh. "Why don't you guys head there? We'll take the truck by the storage unit first."

"Are you sure you don't want us to help you unload it? We still need to run the things in my car and Wren's truck to the house," Ash says, fishing his keys out of his pocket. I notice he's crammed tons of boxes to the bursting point in his back seat.

"We'll put that stuff in the basement after dinner. The pier gets really busy at this time in the summer. You should go ahead and get our name on the waiting list."

"We can do that!" Jenny says and follows Wren over to his truck.

"Do you trust me to drive you?" Ash asks, a teasing tone in his voice.

He reaches for the door and it squeals as he opens it. I cringe at the sound and he laughs at me. He leans over the passenger seat and pulls out a wrinkled white shirt he had crammed in a bag on the floor of his car. He pulls it on and sees I'm still hesitant about getting in the car.

"Why does this seem worse than facing the vainders?" I joke.

Ash laughs and nods his head toward the car. "Come on. I'll let you pick the radio station."

From there, it's just one unbelievable thing after the next. His car is one giant mystery that I can't wrap my brain around. The fact that he can drive is another. When we pull away from the house and past the gates, my eyes land on the blue water in the distance.

"Is that the ocean?" I ask, amazed. It stretches on forever, fading to touch the sky.

"Oh, you'll be able to see it up close soon. The restaurant we're going to is right on the beach," Ash says.

Other cars of every shape, color, and size fly by us as we pull onto the street. Ash cranks his window down, so I do the same, and the afternoon breeze whips my hair around my face. The sun is in a deep sunset now, the sky a dark purple and rosy pink. Lights twinkle all around us. They're on strings above us, in buildings next to us, and flashing on the cars in front of us. Everything moves by in streams of yellow and red light as Ash flies down the road.

"I can't believe I'm here!" I yell against the strong wind, sucking down the salty air. I blink fast against the tears of joy that seep into my eyes when I realize it all smells like Ash, that tropical scent that clung to him beneath the metallic grime of Pintura is all around me.

Ash laughs at me again, but his smile is so genuine. He drives us along some more roads, moving a little slower now. Shiny glass store fronts line the sidewalks. I peer inside and see clothes and furniture. One store has large monitors all over the wall, flashing with harsh clarity.

People are everywhere, milling about on the sidewalks. Bags line their arms as they move from store to store. I face the front again and see the ocean inch closer. Ash turns down another road that runs right along the coast. The air is thicker here and I can smell the salt in the breeze. The sound of lapping water fills the car. My eyes are caught in a trance by the white waves.

"It's amazing, Ash," I breathe.

"I knew you'd like it," he says, smiling sideways at me.

He pulls into what he calls a parking garage and finds a place to leave his car. He grabs what looks like a very small computer screen from the center of the car.

"I'll tell Wren to go ahead and get the table. I want to take you down to the water," he says.

The screen in his hands lights up and he taps on it with his thumbs. When he sees I'm watching him closely, he chuckles.

"This is my phone." He hands it to me and I stare at the thing like it might attack me. Ash shows me how he can send messages to Jenny and Wren. He says we'll have to get me one, too. For some reason, the fact that I don't have one is a major sign that I'm not from this world. Ash laughs at that, so I do too. It's all a little overwhelming, but I'm just trying to absorb every detail.

Ash leads me out of the parking garage and we cross the busy street we were driving on. His fingers lace through mine and he points out different things as we walk. The air is warm and the beach is so inviting. Everyone is glowing with happiness. He points over to the pier and says that's where the restaurant it at.

Instead of going that way, he leads me onto the soft sand. I sink into the tan dust and we trudge our way toward the water. Most people are leaving the beach, heading toward the restaurants and stores, so we have this strip of coast to ourselves.

When we get close to the water, Ash slips off his shoes and socks. He lets my hand fall and runs toward the water. I leave my shoes behind and follow his lead.

The cool water swallows my feet and a joyful scream escapes me. Ash wraps his arms around my waist. He pulls my back to his chest and spins me around.

"Em, I can't believe you're here," he breathes into my hair, his words tickling another laugh from my already weak lungs.

He puts me down, and his lips are on mine again. My heart leaps in my chest. Ash's strong drummer arms pull me tight against him and his warmth radiates across our skin. This is everything I've ever wanted. I am free of Pintura, I have real friends, Ash is mine, and I have a future to look forward to. I have never been so happy.

A deep roar above my head causes me to pull back from Ash. I look up at the long metal machine flying in the sky.

"Is that a plane?" I ask, remembering Wren's stories.

"Yep," Ash says, but his eyes aren't on the plane. His glittering blue gaze never looks away from my face. I lift my hand and tuck a piece of hair behind my ear, and I look down from the plane to meet his stare.

"How do they work?" I ask, not able to keep the engineer in me at bay.

"Here, I'll show you something," Ash says, leading me from the water to where we left our shoes. He sits down and I join him in the warm sand. He pulls out his phone and turns on the screen.

"You can ask phones anything," he says and types *how does a plane work?* The screen changes and text runs down the phone.

Ash hands it to me and my eyes skim the screen. I take in the diagrams that depict airflow and talk about turbulence. There are symbols I've never seen before. All the information is right at my fingertips. There is so much more for me to be a part of here.

"What else can this do?" I ask, knowing it's probably an endless question.

"It can do this," Ash says, taking the phone back.

He holds it out in front of him. The screen has changed to a direct reflection of the two of us. He leans his head against mine and says, "Smile."

He taps the phone and the screen freezes.

"That's the clearest photo I've ever seen!" I say and snatch the phone from his hands. It's not that we don't have this technology in Pintura. We do to some degree, but it's rare that anyone besides the

Patrol or more important personnel get to use it.

"Will you take more?" I ask and hand it back to Ash.

"Sure," he agrees.

Ash takes more pictures of us together and then he has me stand at the edge of the water and he takes my picture with the sinking sun behind me.

I flip through his phone, still shocked that they're real. My favorite is the one of both of us when he poked me in the side and I leaned into him, laughing. My blonde curls brush against his tan cheeks. Those blue eyes glitter as he looks at me. His smile is tight on his face. I can almost hear myself laughing.

"We should probably head to the restaurant," Ash says, slipping the phone out of my hand.

He stands up and pulls me to my feet. I stumble backward and feel my head pinch in protest.

"Are you okay?" Ash asks, steadying me.

"Yeah, just a little dizzy."

His hands press against my cheeks and forehead. "Maybe you just need some water," he says.

I laugh it off and stand up straighter. "I'm fine, Ash. Let's go."

We put on our shoes and dust the sand off as best as we can. He leads us across the beach and onto the pier. Now that we're back in the crowds of people, I stick to Ash's side and we work our way past the groups of strangers. Up here, the smell of food is overwhelming. My stomach begs me to eat anything and everything right now.

We enter a building on the right of the pier, and one of the workers escorts us to a round table at the back of the restaurant. Jenny, Wren, and Ash's parents are already there. We fill in the two empty seats across from his parents. Behind them, a wall of windows captures the vibrant sunset over the ocean. Sparkling lights from a roaring city in the distance dance on the coast.

"Did you take the scenic route?" Ash's mother asks.

I want to gush about how spectacular the ocean is, but I think someone that lives here probably wouldn't say something like that.

"I had Ash take my picture," I say instead. "Show her," I tell Ash.

He pulls up the photos on his phone and his mom instantly softens at the sight.

"I love this one," she says, turning the phone so I can see. It's the one of Ash and me laughing that I like too.

"That's my favorite," I agree.

She hands the phone back to Ash, and a waiter walks up to the table with glasses of water for each of us. She starts to take everyone's order, but I haven't even looked at the menu yet. Ash's hand finds mine under the table. He squeezes lightly, feeling my nerves. I relax as he recommends what I should order. Once the waiter is gone, the questions start coming. I'm thankful they're not directed at me, but at our appearance when they found us. Ash and Jenny feed them a story about how dirty the basement was and how they didn't even see the worst of it when they came to help. His parents eat it up and the conversation moves along. Now that they're back with no time lost, Ash, Jenny, and Wren start talking about finishing their classes.

I sip on my water and try not to draw any attention to myself. My head still hurts, and I'm a little disoriented.

"Are you okay, Em?" Ash asks when I place my glass down on the table, but almost knock his over.

"You look pale," his mother adds, and everyone turns to look at me.

"I'm fine," I say, but my head throbs with each word.

A saving grace comes when the waiter shows up with our food. Burgers and fries circle the table. I start with the fries and hope the food makes me feel better.

It doesn't.

My head continues to pound and my neck dampens with sweat. My stomach swoops uneasily and my lungs tighten in my chest. I heave in a deep breath and my whole body aches.

"Em, what's wrong?" Ash asks, his hand on my back.

"I—" My voice cuts off. "I. Don't. Know." I force out each word.

My eyes lift to find his face, but everything is blurry. The room is spinning. Flashes of purple sunset and water glasses swim by my eyes and then my weight shifts. I fall from my chair, hitting the floor hard, and everything goes black.

CHAPTER 32

Ash

"Em?" Her name leaves my lips as she falls to the ground. I slide my chair back and hurry to her side. "Em!" I say again when she doesn't respond to me.

I roll her onto her back, her body limp and unresponsive. Her eyes are closed and her face is so pale. I press my hands to her cheeks and they feel *cold*. They're not feverish like I anticipated.

"Ash, is she okay?" my mom asks. She appears at my side and her eyes grow wide with worry.

I try to find a pulse in her neck. It's there, but it's very weak.

"You need to call an ambulance. She's barely breathing," I say, words rushing from my mouth in a panic. "Em, can you hear me?"

There's no response.

"Em, please wake up. Please, Em."

My mom stands and pulls her phone from her pocket. There's a mix of voices in my head, but nothing sounds clear. I keep shaking Emma and begging her to wake up. Jenny and Wren join me on the floor, both of them as desperate to reach her.

"The ambulance is on its way," I hear my mom tell my dad.

Other people in the restaurant ask if we need help, but I don't know what to do. She won't wake up, her pulse is weak, and she's so cold.

"Em, it's Ash. Can you hear me? You need to wake up. Em, *please*."

Time moves undetected by us. I hear the sound of the sirens grow louder and I know she just needs to hold on until they get here. They will help her.

Two paramedics are pulling me to my feet and away from Emma. They check her pulse like I had done. I try to tell them it's getting slower, but they aren't listening to me. Orders fly between the two of them and a radio clipped on their belt beeps. Another pair of paramedics approach the table with a stretcher. When they lift Emma, acid from my stomach burns my throat and I think I'm going to be sick. Her body is limp. She looks dead, but she *can't* be dead.

CHAPTER 33

Emma

S irens echo in the distance.
I'm bobbing on water.
My head hurts so bad.

CHAPTER 34

Ash

My mom drives all of us to the hospital. Wren and I fill the back row of the car, with Jenny wedged between us. I want to ride in the ambulance with Emma, but I can't get the words out fast enough before she's gone.

"Is she allergic to anything, Ash?" my mother asks, glancing at me in the review mirror.

My brain races in my head, and I try to remember if Emma ever mentioned allergies. "I don't know," I admit. "I don't think so."

I realize how stupid it is that the girl who followed me from a different world never even told me if she has allergies.

The city passes in a flash of color. Jenny won't stop talking about how Emma is probably just dehydrated and how she didn't drink any water while we were packing up grandma's house. Lies and more lies.

What if that's not it? What if Emma is really sick? What if this secret kills her?

My gaze trains on my mother and father at the front of the car. I'm going to have to tell them the truth.

Before I can speak up, we're pulling into the parking garage at the hospital.

Let's find out what's wrong, first, and then I'll decide what I need to tell them and the doctors. I don't know what they'd do if they found out the truth. Emma's not a citizen. She's not even American or any other nationality. She's not going to have a driver's license or health care or money—

Jenny is pushing me toward the door of the car and my mind releases the thoughts. All of that is coming later. Right now, I need to get back to Emma.

"You should call her parents," my mother says over her shoulder, hurrying ahead of us.

I share a glance with Jenny and bite my lip. I wish I could call her mom. She's a nurse that saved Wren's life after a vainder attack. She could actually help Emma.

We walk quickly across the parking garage and through a set of sliding glass doors. The blinding white floors pull me to a stop. My breath gets caught in my throat.

I hate hospitals.

Too many times, I walked through these doors to see my grandma.

Too many times, I was told it would be the last time.

I can't go in there.

I don't want to be here.

I hate hospitals.

CHAPTER 35

Emma

Muffled voices speak to me, but my mouth won't move.

A cool breeze prickles my cheeks.

I'm rolling somewhere fast.

Hands are touching me.

Needles pierce my skin.

A beeping in the distance tells me I'm alive.

Barely.

CHAPTER 36

Ash

When I was ten-years-old, I was brought to the hospital for the first time. My mom had just picked Jenny and me up from school. She said we were going to see my grandma, but brought us here. I'd never been to a hospital before then, but it was still terrifying. I remember I felt like I was choking on the air that smelt like chemicals. There weren't other kids here, either. Just a bunch of nurses hurrying around the halls.

My dad was already here with my grandma. They had been here all morning. My dad had told us grandma wasn't feeling well, and I had never seen her look so weak. She didn't remain in the hospital then, but she was in and out of them for years after that day.

Every time we'd visit, I hated it more and more. Every time I thought it'd be the last time I'd ever see my grandma. It got so bad at the end that I just stopped coming. I either had band practice or tutoring. Sometimes those excuses were real, but most times it was a lie. I wasn't even there when she died. Thinking back on it, I can't even remember my last time with my grandma. I haven't been in a hospital since those visits.

But I'm here now.

My feet guide me down the bright hallways. I have to be with Emma. I won't leave her here alone.

My mom finds someone who finally knows where Emma is, but we're told we can't see her right now.

"Ma'am, you'll need to wait here. She's not stable right now."

The first word that sticks out to me is *Ma'am*. She's being formal, which means this is serious.

The next words that stand out are *not stable*. That means she could die. At any second, Emma Delaney could be gone.

"Ash, have a seat," my mom says quietly.

I forgot that about hospitals. Everyone's always whispering and hushed.

I sit between Jenny and my mom, my foot tapping nervously against the floor. Wren flanks Jenny's side, as pale as the tiles on the floor.

"Did you get ahold of her family?" my mom asks me.

I shake my head, not able to get my mouth to form anymore lies right now.

"Well, keep trying. They must be worried sick."

My foot freezes.

Gosh, I bet her mom is worried sick. The numbers start running through my head. We've been back for nearly three hours. That's almost a week in Pintura. I lean back in the chair and close my eyes. *Breathe Ash*. I try as hard as I can to imagine that I'm anywhere but here.

The late afternoon shifts to night in a haze. Nurses walk through the halls, but none of them come to talk to us. Other families wait in the neighboring chairs and the room is filled to the brim with nerves.

My dad gets us all some water and snacks, but I don't have the stomach for the food. None of us got to eat our dinner tonight, but I'm not even hungry. Or maybe I'm so hungry that I'm not anymore.

I take the water and sip on it. Every time I see the flash of blue scrubs, I fight the urge to jump to my feet.

Another hour goes by and I've just about reached my breaking point. I don't care if she's unstable. I just need to be with her.

When a woman finally approaches us, I've already convinced myself to expect the worse. It's been too long. When she introduces herself as the doctor, I know this is going to be bad. They never send the doctor unless it's bad news.

She's about my mom's age. Her green eyes scan over our tired faces through her glasses.

"Are you here for Emma Delaney?"

"Yes," I say quickly, pushing myself out of my chair. "Can I see her, please?"

The doctor nods. "She's stable now, but very weak." I expect her to lead us to Emma's room, but instead, she lowers herself into a chair across from us.

"You should have a seat so we can discuss what's happened in the last couple of hours," the doctor says.

I slowly sit on the edge of the chair.

"I won't use the term diagnosis now, because we haven't identified what's wrong with Emma. She came in with a very low pulse, incredibly dehydrated, and malnourished. Her organs have been slowly shutting down since she arrived. We had to use the defibrillator to shock her heart back to a normal pace, but I'm afraid it's not steady. I've already spoken with her and she has no record of any other medical conditions." The doctor pauses. "I've never seen someone with these conditions that doesn't also have some kind of physical injuries. I'm nervous there could be an underlying issue we haven't found yet. Because of that, we're going to perform some more tests."

"But I can see her now?" I ask, pushing past her comments about Emma's health.

"Yes, you can see her." The doctor stands and leads us away from the waiting area.

Rooms with other patients and anxious families pass by until we reach the end of the hall.

"She's in here," the doctor says, standing out of the way.

I hurry through the propped open door. Monitors surround a bed to my left. One of them rings with a slow beeping. Bright lights and green lines blink and flash on the screens. Too many tubes to count are filled with a clear liquid. They run down from the machines and toward the bed.

"Ash."

I turn my face from the monitors to Emma. For the first time, tears find my eyes.

"Em," my voice breaks.

She looks so frail, the dressing gown they gave her hanging limp around her body. I prop myself on the edge of the bed and my left hand finds her right. I link our fingers together, and I can't help but notice how small they feel. I move my right hand to her face and push back one of her blonde curls like I always do. She leans her head against the palm of my hand and slowly blinks her tired eyes. She sucks in a shaky breath and fear courses through me as if it could be her last.

"Em, what's going on?" I ask her softly, hating that the quiet whispers of the hospital come from me too.

"I don't know, Ash. I was fine this morning."

"Emma, we've been trying to get ahold of your parents. Do you have a better way we can reach them?" my mom asks.

"I already told the nurse how to contact them," Emma says softly.

Her eyes meet mine. Even now, she's trying to keep the lie going for me, because I'm the one who didn't want to tell my parents the truth. Emma sucks in another unsteady breath. The monitor to her left beeps faster.

"Em?" my voice quivers.

"Oh, I don't feel good," she wheezes.

"What can I get you?"

Emma pushes herself up and reaches through the air toward the trash can in the corner of the room. Jenny grabs it and once it's in Emma's hands, she heaves dry air and stomach acid into the can.

My whole body starts shaking. I feel so useless. I want to make her feel better. *How can I fix this?*

She leans back in the bed and Jenny takes the can from her weak grasp. Suddenly, her eyes fall closed and her head rolls to the left. The monitor lets out one even tone.

"Em?"

Her body starts moving in quick jerking motions. She's seizing.

"You need to leave!" The doctor and a team of nurses rush in, pushing buttons on the machines. A nurse rolls Emma on her side and yells orders at the other officials in the room.

Amidst the mayhem, this horrifying scene reminds me of the tunnel of fears on Pintura. Emma said the fear she had to face was watching me die in a hospital bed where she couldn't do anything to help me, and that's exactly what's happening now. Except, the roles are reversed, and it's me who's watching Emma.

"Get them out of here," the doctor orders one of the nurses.

Hands are on my shoulders and I'm being pushed out of the room and guided back to the waiting area. *What am I going to do?* How long can Emma survive like this? She's not getting any better.

When we get back to the quiet waiting room, the high-pitched ping of an elevator draws my eyes toward it. Four red helmets on the shoulders of black uniforms gleam under the hospital lighting.

Pintura Patrol officers.

I almost think I'm hallucinating, my mind confused what world I'm in, but Jenny and Wren see them too. The four Patrol officers flank two individuals, a pair on each side. One of them is in a similar uniform, but much more extravagant. A gold helmet, red stitching on the black leather, and gold medals make him stand apart. *Lord Neko.*

The other individual is familiar, though she looks much more exhausted than the last time I saw her. Emma's mom stares straight ahead, dark bags under her eyes. None of them even look our way.

When they reach the doors to the patients' hall, a brave and fearless nurse tries to stop them. The four Patrol officers pull out large, black guns with glowing blue liquid canisters at their sides.

Everyone in the hospital waiting room starts screaming and ducking behind chairs. Absolute mayhem breaks loose at the sight of the weapons. My dad pulls me toward the edge of the room, reaching for his phone with his other hand.

"We will pass," the Patrol orders and then continues down the hall and out of sight.

"Dad, what are you doing?" I ask when I see him typing on his phone with nervous fingers.

"Calling the police."

"No, you can't," I say.

I break free from his grasp and head back toward Emma's room. I try to follow the Patrol, but the nurses pull the doors closed behind them. The sound of electronic locks click into place as the security system in the building takes over, putting us all on lockdown. I explain to the nurses that one of them was a patient's mother and not an intruder, but they still refuse to let me go after them.

"Ash, where are you going?" My mom and dad pull me away from the doors, their voices hysteric.

"That was Emma's mom," I say, letting the truth break free.

My words leave my parents in disbelief. I swallow, knowing everything just got so much worse. There's no lie I can tell them that will make this any better. I know I'm going to have to tell them the truth.

CHAPTER 37

Emma

When I finally gain consciousness, I'm confused where I am. The harsh white lights and subtle beeping are a sudden reminder. My throat stings with a wretched taste. I blink slowly and take in a shaky breath. My lungs feel like crumpled paper burning in a fire.

Shrieking coming from outside my room startles me. My tired heart tries to beat faster, aching in my chest, and heavy footsteps enter my room. I swear my heart actually stops when the red helmets turn the corner. If I wasn't already pale, the blood would be draining from my face.

Four Patrol officers enter and stand stiffly at the far wall of my room. When the fifth officer enters, I think I may be sick again. I've only seen that golden uniform a few times and from much further away.

Lord Neko is standing in my hospital room. *On Earth.* The ruler of

Pintura, the communicator between mortals and magic, is right in front of me.

I didn't realize coming here would be illegal. Actually, I'm certain that it's not, because there would be no point in making a law about something that is thought to be impossible.

So, why are they here? *How* are they here?

"Emma."

My head snaps toward her voice, forgetting the Patrol and Lord Neko.

"Mom?" The word crumbles in my mouth, tears finding my eyes. She rushes toward me and wraps her arms around my shoulders, pulling me close to her.

"I'm so glad you're okay," my mom says.

"I'm not," I say and choke back a sob. "I'm really sick and I don't know what's wrong." I pull back from her embrace, and she lays a gentle hand on my damp cheek.

"Emma, you're lucky you're still alive. Someone like you can't survive in this world."

Her words pull me out of my emotions and I stiffen. "What do you mean?" I ask. "Why are you here?" My eyes flicker to the Patrol and Lord Neko, the hospital room reflecting off their tinted helmets.

"The Patrol came looking for information on where you were. I told them about the cards you showed me in exchange for their help to bring me to you. I can't believe you'd follow those people back to Earth." My mother's tone has changed after the shock of seeing me alive has worn off.

"I'm not going back to Pintura. I want to stay here," I say through a scratchy throat.

My mother rolls her eyes at that. "You can't, Emma. You will die if you stay here. Our world moves faster than Earth. Your body can't adapt to the change in time."

My brain tries to comprehend what she's saying. I know days are faster in Pintura. Four hours here is over a week there. My slowing heart and dying organs suddenly make sense. Hot tears return to my eyes.

"But Ash, Jenny, and Wren didn't get sick in Pintura," I say defensively.

"The body can adapt to speeding up better than slowing down. It's like running a race," she says. I'm reminded of all the times she taught me different things about the human body, hoping I'd adopt her interest in nursing. "The body is a muscle that gets stronger when it's pushed harder."

"Wouldn't that mean I'm so strong I can survive here?" I whisper, begging for this to be the truth.

"You're too strong," my mom says. "Your body needs the speed of our world. It wants to move faster."

"Mom, I can't go back." My thoughts turn to Ash and our moments on the beach just hours ago. The cars and planes and ocean. I have so much more to see. Ash and I were supposed to have more time.

"Emma, you don't have a choice," my mom says sternly.

"How much time do I have left?" I ask, the tears escaping.

My mom looks at me, puzzled, until she realizes what I'm asking. "You are not dying here. I'm taking you home!"

I shake my head hard. "I don't want to go with you."

"Emma!" my mom snaps.

"Mrs. Delaney," a robotic voice underneath one of the Patrol masks interrupts. "You cannot force her. We brought you here to advise her."

My mother pulls back from me and her face hardens. "Ash won't let you stay once he knows the consequences."

My heart sinks, pulling hard on my chest. She's right, and I hate it. If Ash knows the only way I can live is if I return to Pintura, he'd throw me through the painting himself.

"We're running out of time," another robotic voice says. I locate this sound coming out of Lord Neko's helmet. "You had your chance to advise her. Now, I need to go over the legality of this situation."

The room falls still as Lord Neko steps toward my bed.

"Leave us," he commands.

My mother's desperate stare lingers with me a moment longer and then she rises from my hospital bed and exits the room without saying another word. The four Patrol officers walk stiffly behind her, leaving me alone with Lord Neko.

I sink further into the pillow that props me up. I can only imagine what he wants to tell me. He probably wants to kill me before I can expose Pintura to the people of Earth.

He takes another step toward my bed and slowly lowers himself onto the edge of the mattress. I try to hide my nervous flinch at being so close to him. His hands raise to his golden helmet and he *removes* it.

A long, chocolate brown ponytail flutters down to meet the shoulder pads of the uniform. Young, dark, glowing skin shimmers in the hospital light, and long lashes, thick with makeup, blink over grassy green eyes. I suck in a breath.

"You're a—" I stop myself when *she* raises a finger to her lips. My mind tries to race and find a way that this makes sense, but my brain pounds in protest.

344

"Yes, I'm a girl." She smirks at my shocked face.

"How?"

It's the only word my tired lungs can form. I know Artmith has never had a female ruler. Absolutely never. It's always been the sons of the Stelling family. There have been Ladies and female siblings, but our ruler has always been male. I almost want to ask if she killed Lord Neko and stole his uniform, but I'm too afraid of the answer to form the question.

"My identity has been kept a secret my entire life," she says softly. "My mother was very sick when I was born. She died days later from a rare disease."

"Textra," I say, remembering learning about the disease that killed the Lord's mother in school.

She nods her head. "My father was so upset that our reign would come to an end because she died before she could give him a son to be the heir to the position. He'd rather hide my identity than marry someone else. My father sworn me to secrecy and I've been living a lie ever since."

I think about the election that landed her in this role. Had the public known they were voting for a daughter of the Stelling family, I know she wouldn't have been elected. Actually, I don't think she would have been allowed to run at all.

"Why are you telling me this?" I ask, nerves crawling up my arms. What does this have to do with me or Earth? It sounds like she's just given me another secret she has reason to kill me to keep.

"Because I'm not going to hide under this helmet much longer. Things in Pintura are about to change, and I want you to be there when they do." Her translucent green eyes study me carefully.

She wants me to return to Pintura, and she doesn't want to kill me.

"I want to stay. I can't leave Ash," I say weakly.

"Emma," she says, taking my hands in her gloved grasp. She looks deep into my eyes, and I know her next words are important. "I told you who I am, so you know that change is coming. When we came for you, we had to complete Ending in Cadence ourselves because the game reset when you left."

"You came through the painting?" I wheeze out.

"Yes, and we'll return the same way. I admire what you did to get here. I have so much respect for you, and I think the two of us could be important allies to the other. You have a friend within the chain of command in Pintura."

She drops my hands and pulls back. My head tries to decipher what that means. Could she be talking about helping me with money? Could she know about the illegal engineering business I've been running? Is she offering to let me keep doing that?

A memory from the night Zane came to my house returns to me. He told me my friends from Earth would be executed when the Patrol caught them. I suck in an uneven breath. Lord Neko sees the realization cross my face.

She's offering to let them come back with me.

"When you get to the other side, I will come find you. I think we're going to be equal partners in this change." She rises and moves toward the door. "The painting needs to be destroyed after you return. See to it that someone here does that. I'm going back with my officers and your mother now. We've been gone too long."

I don't get a chance to respond before she pulls the golden helmet over her head, tucks her brown ponytail inside, and leaves the room.

The tears I'd been trying to hold in fall free and I crumple forward. *I'm dying. I have to go back to Pintura.* I know Lord Neko said she'd let them come with me, but I know I could never ask Ash to do that. Jenny and Wren would never return, and Ash would never leave them behind.

I won't be the reason Ash is separated from his family and the life he has here. I'm going to *have* to leave him.

A desperate sob escapes me, rattling in my chest. My heart tightens and rips apart inside of my body.

"Em," Ash's voice mixes with my cries as he runs into my room. His arms are around my shoulders, trying to comfort me, but all it does is make my heart ache more.

"Em, what is it?" he asks, running his hand through my blonde curls. "Shh, Em. Breathe," he soothes, pressing his forehead against mine.

I force my lungs to pull in a deep breath and I try to stop crying.

"What happened? What did they say to you?" Ash asks when I pull out of his arms, trying to put some distance between us. My body shakes with my suppressed sobs. I try to hold my breath to keep from crying. Ash can see so clearly how much I'm hurting.

"Is your mom here to help you?" he asks.

My heart throbs. She didn't tell him. But I know I can't keep this from him. I wish my mom had told Ash the truth, because now I have to do it and I don't know how to form those words.

I shake my head and release the tight breath, and a shaky sob escapes with it. "I'm dying, Ash," I say. "I'm dying because I'm here. I have to go back to Pintura."

His face pales to match my own.

"I'm sorry, Ash," I cry. My tears seem to unfreeze his shocked state.

"It's okay, Emma," he says softly, pulling me in for another hug.

"It's okay."

But it's not okay and I know he's only pretending so he can help calm me down. I want to tell Ash about how Lord Neko is a girl and how she wants to be allies in the changes for Pintura, but none of that seems to matter right now. What's the point of sharing any of that with him?

So, I don't say anything. I just let Ash hold me and tell me that everything is okay, even though it's not.

CHAPTER 38

Ash

I 've never been the type to hide in the bathroom and cry, but that's where I find myself now. The nurses sent me away while they prepared Emma to be discharged. I can't believe she's leaving.

The security system did little to keep them from leaving, though they did have to take the stairs since the elevators stopped running. I can only imagine the commotion they're causing down on the streets right now.

I haven't told Jenny or Wren or my parents about what needs to happen with Emma. Once I left Emma's room, I was going to find them, but I couldn't make it back to the waiting room before the tears came.

I press the wet paper towel to my eyelids and try to ease the puffiness. My chest throbs with each breath, but I can't cry anymore. These next few hours are going to be unbearable, but I need to hold myself together for Emma.

She's already so sick and weak. I need to try and make this as easy as I can for her, but my heart threatens to explode. Why did I have to fall for her? Why did my heart choose her? I thought we had survived the hardest part. We were supposed to have more time.

The restroom door swings open and Wren walks in. "There you are," he says, approaching the counter I'm leaning against. "What's wrong?" he asks and I curse the paper towel for not wiping the evidence away faster.

I suck in a deep breath, feeling my throat tighten up. I know I'm only going to be able to get these words out once.

"I'll tell you all at the same time," my voice rakes out.

Wren nods his head cautiously, keeping his worried eyes trained on me. For as long as Wren has known me, I don't think he's ever seen me cry.

He follows me out of the bathroom and I find Jenny and my parents still sitting in the waiting room chairs. My father stares out the nearest black window, still processing everything I told them about Pintura. My mom wanted to argue what I was saying, but when the Patrol came back through, she found it hard to come up with another explanation.

"Is she okay?" Jenny asks in a hushed, worried voice.

Wren takes his seat next to Jenny and I place myself across from them.

"They came to tell Emma that she has to go back to Pintura. She can't survive on Earth. If she stays any longer, she'll die." My voice cracks on the last word, but I keep the tears in my eyes.

Jenny shakes her head hard in protest. "Ash, I'm so sorry."

"The nurses are discharging her now. We need to get the painting and open the portal," my words form faster, trying to rip off the bandage. Jenny lays a gentle hand on my knee.

"Wren and I can do that. You just need to be with Emma."

Now the tears fall, slowly and silently down my cheeks.

"I know you don't understand," I say with a shaky voice, looking at my parents' confused and distant faces. "But Emma means a lot to me. She—"

But I can't find the right words to describe what she is.

"I love her and I thought—"

My mom finally speaks, moving to hold me. "Ash, it's okay. She's just one girl."

I shake her off. "No," I say and stand. "This isn't just another breakup. She isn't just any girl. She's my person. She's who I'm supposed to end up with."

My father turns this gaze back to the dark window.

"Just because I'm seventeen doesn't mean I don't know what love is. You assume that, since I'm young, I don't know anything, but you're wrong. I know everything. I know that I love Emma, I know that I'm tired of playing the drums, I know what death looks like, and I know how lucky I am to be alive right now."

We're the only ones left in the waiting room, and the silence makes my ears ring.

"I know everything," I say again and I slump back in my chair, feeling defeated by the universe.

What good is it to know all of this and have zero control over your life?

Another hour passes without anyone saying a word. The weight of my outbreak resonates in every quiet second that follows it. I wish I could make them understand what I want. I wish, for once, they would listen to how I actually feel instead of forcing what they think I'm feeling onto me.

A nurse comes by to tell us that Emma will be ready to leave soon. My mom is the first of us to speak. "Bryan, I think we should tell him—"

"Elaine, don't," my dad says, his voice finding a sense of urgency that contrasts the empty stare he's held for the last hour.

"Tell me what?" I ask when my mom presses her lips together.

"Ash," she starts to say before my dad interrupts her again.

"Think about what you're doing, Elaine." His stare is so sharp it could cut glass. "Think about the promise you're about to break."

My mom holds his gaze with equal fire in her irises. "He already knows the worst of it."

"What are you talking about?" My heart beats uneven in my chest at their cryptic conversation.

"Did you know?" Jenny asks, her voice dropping. "Did you know about Pintura?"

My mom presses her lips together once more.

The ground falls out from under my feet. *How did they know about that?* "You just tried to deny everything I told you!" I snap, anger leaping into my voice before I can tame it.

"I know," my mom breathes. "I thought I could hold on to the secret a little longer, but..."

Silence hangs over us while I process her words and the truth behind them. "What changed your mind?" I ask, the question hesitant to form.

My mom looks at me, bright blue eyes that match my own, taking in my surely puffy face from crying. "How you feel about Emma," she says softly. "You deserve to know the truth about that painting."

"Elaine, we haven't talked about this—"

"What more is there to discuss?" she quips, snapping her head around to meet my father's wide eyes. "He's seventeen. He can know the truth and make his own decisions." My dad's face softens as he looks at me.

"Will someone please tell me what's going on?" I nearly beg.

My mom faces me once more, and with a deep breath, leans back in the chair. "Your grandma fell through that painting when she was a little girl," my mom finally explains.

I want to tell her that I already know that. I figured as much once I found the playing cards under the floor of the art studio, but I bite back the words. I can tell there's more my mom needs to say, and I don't dare interrupt her now that she's finally telling me the truth.

"She told me stories of what she saw on the other side, swore me to secrecy," my mom continues. "Made me promise I would never go through that portal."

"So why did she keep the painting?" Jenny asks, unable to help herself from speaking her thoughts aloud.

My mom's eyes grow distant and her gaze falls to the floor. She takes in a shaky breath and steadies herself before she looks at me once again. "She had a sister who fell through the painting with her. Emersim was her name."

"Grandma had a sister?" Jenny gasps. "Why haven't we met her before?"

My mom's gaze never leaves mine.

"Because she chose to stay in Pintura."

I'm not sure how much time passes as I sit here and process everyone's words, so shocked about everything I just heard.

"Jenny and Wren, we'll take you back to your truck at the pier," my mom says, her throat sounding raw. "Dad and I will bring you your car, Ash. We'll meet you and Emma out front so you can take her home."

She stands and the rest of them follow her out of the waiting room and toward the parking garage. I sit alone in silence for another thirty minutes, waiting for the nurses to discharge Emma.

Finally, she emerges into the waiting room, fighting a nurse who wants her to be escorted out in a wheelchair. I notice someone returned her lavender top and black shorts, both looking dirtier than I remember in the crisp hospital light. My phone vibrates in my pocket, telling me my mom and dad are out front.

The world keeps us moving in sync, continuing to hurry this along. For once, I don't want it to slow down. I want this to be over.

The nurse tells Emma she shouldn't be walking right now, but Emma pushes forward. Even at her absolute weakest, she is being everything I love about Emma Delaney. So strong, always brave, with a fire roaring inside that refuses to go out.

I cross to her and lend her my arm. She hooks hers with mine and leans on me.

It's time to take her home.

CHAPTER 39

Emma

Ash leads me toward the front of the hospital in silence. I lean on him for support as we walk, and I wish I had the right words to say at this moment. When the front doors slide open, hot California air chokes my weak lungs. Ash's green car is parked in front of us; his mom and dad stand waiting outside their own car.

My throat tightens. I've ruined their night. Gosh, his mom just buried her mother this morning and I've sprung this mess on them. Ash said he explained the truth to them when the Patrol showed up. I bet they'll be glad to be rid of me. I wish I hadn't ruined everything.

Ash leads me to the side of his car and I lean against the metal frame when he goes to get the car keys from his parents. His mother embraces him in a hug. She whispers something to him and hugs him tighter. She probably hates me for hurting Ash. Surely she knows I didn't mean for this to happen.

He pulls away from her and wipes his eyes. She hands him a bag that he throws over his shoulder and his car keys. When he moves to his dad, I look away, not able to see them all hurt because of me.

A gentle hand on my arm startles me. Ash's mom looks at me carefully.

"Get home safe," she says.

I swallow, my throat gripping back a cry.

"Thank you for saving my son," she adds.

I'm shocked when she pulls me into a hug. She steps back quickly, her eyes wet with tears. Pain is engraved on her face. Ash clearly over emphasized my role in our journey here. He probably did that on purpose, trying to make his parents not hate me.

Ash walks away from his dad and meets me by his car. His mom steps back further and Ash opens my door. He helps me into the seat and once the door is closed, I let out the tight cry I'd been holding in. Just one, sad sigh, and then I suck it back in.

The door on his side of the car opens, and he gets in behind the steering wheel. If he sees me crying, it's just going to make all of this that much harder.

He turns the key in the ignition and the car rattles to life, mirroring how I'm feeling. Ash slowly steers the car away from the curb. Small raindrops tap on the windshield when we come out from under the awning. Even the sky is crying tonight.

"I really would have loved it here," I say softly, not wanting my last moments with Ash to be spent in a tense silence.

"I know you would have," Ash says. He sighs and leans back into his seat as he drives.

The radio isn't on, but a song still plays in my head. A series of notes and rhythms that make up the soundtrack of my memories from the last week. I once asked Ash if he would play the drums for me one day. Now I realize we've been creating our own song all along.

It started with the crash of a cymbal when I first saw Jenny fall through the sky. The mysterious melody that came next warned me of where the song would go. The drums are quick, matching the pace of our feet as we ran from vainders and the Patrol. Choruses of trumpets and flutes ring at each moment we finished one of our cards.

Our song echoes in my head as we drive in the silent car, and I relive it all. I train my eyes on the window, determined to remember every piece of this world. The ocean is dark now and moonlight reflects off the rippling surface. The white and red lights on the cars around us are much fewer than before. In the distance, the rising city still glistens.

I memorize the feeling of riding in a car, so I can imagine what it would be like if I were still here. If I could ride with Ash and go to the beach. If he could take pictures of me in the ocean and I could always look at the twinkling city lights.

"Ash, can you promise me something?" I ask. "Two things, actually."

He glances at me and then returns his eyes to the road. "I can try," he says cautiously.

"Promise me you'll really try to be an actor." I stare at the profile of his face and his eyes grow sad. "You should do what you love, Ash."

He nods and lets out a breath he had been holding. "Yeah. I promise." He shakes his head, a weak smile forcing its way onto his face. "What's the other thing?" he asks.

"Promise you won't forget me."

The words are a whisper, shattering the air between us. His face settles in sadness and his eyes are dark with the shadows of the car when he looks at me.

"I promise I will never forget you, Em."

Em. I'm going to miss hearing him call me that. I tell myself to hold on to that, too. I nod, wishing those promises made me feel better, but they don't.

"You have to destroy the painting once I'm gone," I say, remembering Lord Neko's orders.

Ash just gives me a single hard nod.

I turn back to the window and continue to let our song sing me back the memories I know I'll never forget. When the car turns onto his grandma's driveway, the melody slows in my head, telling me our song is about to come to an end.

Ash parks the car in the circle drive and tells me he'll help me out. He pops his door open, the metal scraping together, and grabs the bag his mom gave him.

I want to ignore him and get out by myself, but sometimes it's okay to not be strong and brave. It's okay to let someone help.

My door groans when Ash pulls it open and he helps me to my feet. He swings the door closed and we hurry under the white porch and out of the rain.

"I had Jenny and Wren set the painting back up in the art studio. I don't want to risk doing this any other way. The portal should be open now," Ash says as he leads me inside.

I force a weak smile and nod. In the daytime, his grandmother's house had looked extravagant. Now, cloaked in a dark rain shower, it's haunting.

We climb the stairs slowly. Mostly because I'm so weak, but also because I'm trying to fight this as long as possible. When we reach the landing and the art studio comes into view at the end of the hall, my heart starts to beat faster. It pounds in my chest with each step I take, racing with fear. Ash must feel it through our hooked arms because he squeezes my hand lightly.

We enter the art studio and Jenny and Wren flank the painting that's on the floor. I haven't seen them since the Patrol came and the tears are fresh in my eyes.

"I'm so sorry," I say, as if I meant to cause any of this.

Jenny's cheeks are stained with tears, but she doesn't cry now. "Don't you apologize, Emma," she says and embraces me in a tight hug. "I wouldn't change a thing."

I want to believe her, but I bet if she had the option to go back, she never would have come through the painting. I hold Jenny tight and wish I had gotten to see her play soccer. I wish I could see if her and Wren stay together. In the version I'll dream up in my head, I know they will.

Wren wraps his arms around Jenny and me. "Don't forget to write my stories down, okay?" Wren says, his words tight in his throat.

"Of course, I will," I agree and when we pull apart, I know I only have one goodbye left.

The tears are still tracking down my cheeks and my heart rips in my chest. Jenny and Wren back away, and Ash's arms wrap around my shoulders. He pulls me in so tight, I feel safe against him. I press my face into his shoulder and try to remember everything I can about Ash Bane. I remember how his strong arms from years of drumming hold me, his wavy brown hair, and ocean blue eyes. I remember how he smells like warm California air.

Ash steps back slightly, not letting the embrace break, and his lips meet mine.

It's not like our kiss when he was leaving Pintura. This one is soft and gentle. This one is wet with tears and it breaks my heart. This kiss is goodbye.

When I step back from him and his arms fall to his side, the heel of my shoe brushes the frame of the painting. Ash's blue eyes are wide. His breathing is quick. His face is begging me to speak to him. He's waiting for me to say something. *He wants me to ask him.*

"I won't ask you to come with me."

His face settles, his lips pressing into a thin line. I won't rip him from his world. I won't take him from his family. *I won't.*

I take in one final breath of California air and step back into the painting.

A strong wind erupts against my face, making my blonde curls fly in a wild storm around me. I gasp for breath at the sudden shock of falling. The bright afternoon sun is a harsh change from the darkness of the night on Earth. Every instinct in my body wants to scream as I fall through the sky, but I don't have the energy. In my head, the song I had been hearing rings with the final crash of a cymbal and a loud crescendo. The symphony of instruments roars together, the final notes melting into one final, triumphant chord.

A pocket of air, inches from the ground, catches me and then releases me to meet the Golden Field of Pintura. I pull myself to my feet, and already my body feels stronger.

Rising Salvation is to my left, its waterfall streaming into the lake below. Infinity Forest sways to my right, bright, lush, and green. I turn around and Artmith rises in the distance, the setting sun reflecting off the jagged metal buildings.

I'm home.

The wind has dried the tears from my eyes, but my heart still aches in my chest. My feet move before my brain can command them to, navigating me back to my city. My head throbs in the silence of the song, reaching out for more notes.

Thud.

My feet freeze for a moment and I hold my breath as I slowly turn around.

Ash Bane stands in the field.

A soft pattern of drums beat in my head. Our song wasn't over.

"Ash Bane, you didn't," I say cautiously, crossing the field to where he landed.

He can't be here. His home is on Earth. Jenny and Wren and his parents… He left all of them. A nauseous ache warns me that I'll have to complete Ending in Cadence all over again to take him home.

The corners of Ash's mouth stretch across his face into a wide and glorious smile that makes my breath catch. I haven't seen him smile in what feels like weeks.

"Of course I did," he says, watching me approach him like he's simply not real.

"Do you realize how hard it's going to be for you to go back home?" I say, as if I need to remind him of that. My steps are hesitant and finally, I reach him, leaving a gap between us.

"It won't be hard at all, Em," Ash says, stepping forward and filling the gap I had intentionally left. "I'm already home."

He stretches his arms wide and my face splits into a smile of its own when I register his words.

Ash Bane is home. Pintura is where he wants to be, and I'm who he wants to be with.

I throw myself into his embrace and squeeze my arms around his shoulders, letting him sweep me up into his strong arms. I wrap my legs around his waist and relish in the fact that I feel him against me, that Ash Bane is holding me right now after everything we've been through.

I lift my head from his shoulder and press a strong kiss against his lips. His mouth moves against mine as he hugs me tighter to his chest. And then I kiss him again and then I kiss his cheeks, and his forehead, the tip of his nose, I just pepper him with kisses until I'm laughing so hard I'm crying and he's spinning me around so fast I can't see straight.

"I love you, Em," he breathes into my hair, stilling his feet.

My chest rises and falls with rapid breaths, but when I lock my gaze with his eyes—eyes that I can now say remind me of the ocean— my heart stills. "I love you too, Ash."

Suddenly, his mother's whispered goodbye and the bag over his shoulder make sense.

They told him he could leave.

"You're really here?" I ask when he puts me back on my feet. I lay a hand on his chest, making sure he's real. I feel his warm skin beneath his shirt, his thunderous pulse. *He is real.*

"This is where I belong, Em. With you. In Pintura."

His hand reaches up to mine and he brings it down to his side, lacing our fingers together. We walk, hand in hand, toward the gate that surrounds Artmith, the song we had been playing finally ending in cadence.

EPILOGUE

Moments before the end...

Jenny looks at her brother like it could be the last time she ever sees him. Her chest shakes as she takes in a deep breath and tucks her black hair behind her ear.

"I can't believe you're leaving," she whispers, unable to support her voice. Ash's face crumbles at the words, so Jenny sucks in a steadying breath and adds, "But you need to go, Ash. I understand that."

Before his sister can say anything else, Ash pulls her to his chest, wrapping his arms around her tightly.

Holding her like it could be the last time he ever holds his sister.

"I know that's where I belong, Jen," he says into her hair that smells like the rain tapping on the windows outside. "I knew it the second we landed in that field. The entire game was always about getting you and Wren home, but I was already there."

Ash feels Jenny nod against his shoulder, squeezing him tighter in their embrace before stepping back and aggressively wiping the tears from her eyes. "I'll keep the painting somewhere safe. You can always come back, Ash."

"I'll see you again, Jenny," Ash says. "Don't worry. I'll be back." His lips tighten in a forced smile, and even though he tries to be convincing, Jenny can tell that Ash has no intentions of coming back to Earth anytime soon. Especially when the only route home will be completing Ending in Cadence all over again.

"Man, you're both going to make me cry," Wren mumbles, fanning his damp eyes.

The gesture makes both Jenny and Ash burst with laughter. Wren and Ash have never been the kind of friends to show their sentiments through hugging. But right now, in a moment that feels like their very last together, neither boy hesitates, before they spread their arms wide and embrace each other.

"I'm going to miss you, Ash," Wren says softly.

Ash nods his agreeance and angles his head to whisper, "You take care of my sister while I'm gone." His words are too soft for Jenny to hear. When Ash steps back, his serious stare meets his best friend's, unwavering and waiting for confirmation.

Wren clamps a hand on Ash's shoulder and squeezes. "I promise."

"Okay. I think it's time," Ash sighs, picking up the bag his mom had given him at the hospital and slinging it over his shoulder.

"Emma's going to lose it," Jenny teases, her voice curling up. "I can't believe you didn't tell her."

"Where would the fun be in that?" Ash says, placing his toes against the frame of the painting and looking over his shoulder at Jenny and Wren.

"I'm glad you found her, Ash," Jenny says, her voice finding that serious tone again.

Ash's dark blue gaze sweeps across the faces of his sister and best friend before he says, "I think we all found who we were looking for."

A soft blush creeps across Jenny's cheeks, but she doesn't shy away as Wren steps beside her and wraps an arm around her shoulder, pulling her into his side.

"Do you think you'll find her?" Jenny asks, resting her head on Wren's shoulder.

Ash doesn't have to ask. He knows Jenny is talking about their grandma's sister. He turns back around and looks down into the painting that is a perfect replica of his destination. "I think we may have already found her," Ash says, his voice even and soft.

Jenny and Wren step toward Ash, each laying a hand on his shoulders. "You can go now, Ash," Jenny says, memorizing the sight of her brother standing in front of her in case she never sees him again. Like her grandma never saw her sister again.

"Good luck, Man," Wren adds, squeezing a reassuring burst through Ash's shoulder.

Ash looks up to the ceiling of his grandma's house and takes in a final deep breath. Then he lifts his foot, lets it hover over the painting of Pintura, before he rocks his weight forward and drops through the canvas.

Jenny and Wren's arms fall to their sides as Ash drops through the magical painting, not nearly as shocked as they were the first time it happened. They stand there a second more, staring at the normal-looking piece of art—as if Ash or Emma could reappear any second now.

Jenny kneels and finds that loose piece in the metal frame. She carefully twists it until it's back in place, locking the portal from her side. She wonders if closing the portal would keep Ash from returning, but she decides it must only stop her from traveling through the canvas. Ending in Cadence, on the other side, could still open the portal. He could still have a way home.

"So, now what do we do?" Jenny asks as she lifts the heavy artwork.

Wren scoops the old deck of Ending in Cadence cards that they found under the floor of the art studio into his hands. "We put these in a safe place."

Jenny hums her agreement, examining the painting in her grasp. "I was thinking about finding a new piece of art for my bedroom."

Her words are half-teasing and half-truth. She hadn't really been thinking about hanging any artwork in her bedroom, but the idea of keeping Ash close gives her some comfort.

"So, now we'll take this back to your house," Wren says, answering Jenny's question.

"And then what?" Jenny asks, her voice dipping into that dangerous territory of sadness.

Wren steps closer to her, taking his hand and brushing loose strands of her hair behind her shoulder. He lets his touch travel up her neck until his warm hand cups her cheek.

"And then I'm taking you to get that burger."

READ THE FIRST CHAPTER

FROM THE SEQUEL

BEGINNING

IN

UNISON

CHAPTER I

Ash

The afternoon sun shimmers against the black metal sides of University Hall like flames licking the inside of a fireplace. That same sun raised a sweat on my brow when I ventured to this side of Pintura this morning. If it weren't for the shade of the tree hovering overhead, I'd be burning from its warm kiss. Summer here is really only beginning. Though, I suppose that's true for Earth as well. Odd, right now, our worlds have almost lined up.

The grass beneath my feet has taken on the shape of my sneakers after the hours I've spent standing here. If I could just get myself to move, the anxiety from waiting would be over, but it's taken me all morning to even take a step. This is as far as I always get before I turn around and go back to Emma's home in Shadow Village.

Because what happens if I go in there and I'm wrong? Or worse, I'm right and I don't get the answers I want.

What answers do I want?

The steel doors at the front entrance of University Hall open just a sliver, and I flinch back at the sudden movement. Nothing in this building has moved in the week I've been coming here, though I knew she'd be inside. Somehow, I had a feeling she was waiting for me.

Professor Sim's small, round face peaks out of the front entrance, eyes so light a blue they appear grey in the bright summer sun. She extends a frail hand and waves me across the front lawn of the university.

How did she know I was out here, contemplating walking into her classroom? Has she known I've been out here every day for the last week?

Finally, after delaying this conversation as long as I can, I move forward, leaving my padded grass behind.

Professor Sim doesn't wait for me to reach her and reenters the school building without me. I climb the marble slab staircase, and when I slip between the heavy steel doors, I see Professor Sim dip into her classroom beneath the grand staircase in the entryway. She leaves the wooden door open behind her, a clear message that I'm supposed to follow.

A knot forms in my throat, my heart picking up its pace in my chest, even though my steps are painfully slow. When I finally reach her classroom, I find the old woman sitting behind her desk at the front of the space. The board behind her is clean of chalk smears. Classes have been over for a while, but the room looks as it did that day Emma brought me here with Jenny and Wren. The wooden beams creak beneath my white shoes as I walk to the front of the classroom. That day from weeks ago flowing in parallel beside me. Except Jenny and Wren aren't here this time. No, they're back in California. Back with my mom and dad and the life I knew before.

"You sit out in that heat much longer and I'll have to call the Patrol to come take you home," Professor Sim says, her throat bobbing with the words.

Though her voice is soft, it makes my skin tighten with anticipation for the conversation we're about to have.

"So, Ash, what can I do for you?" She looks at me intensely, like her grey gaze could see into my mind and try to figure out why I'm here.

I take another steadying breath and separate my dry tongue from the roof of my mouth. I've played this conversation over enough times in my head that I know what I want to say first.

"I want to talk about you."

"About me?" The old woman leans back in the chair she's perched on. Her wrinkled arms cross in front of her chest, and she waits for me to clarify.

I nod, my long brown waves brushing my jawline. They stay slicked back from my face with sweat. "I think I'm about to ask you something crazy, but the longer I think about it, the more it makes sense."

Professor Sim gesture to me. "Well, go on and ask it."

My eyes drift from hers to the faded olive green walls around us and the old glass windows before coming back to her crinkled gaze. "Are you my grandma's sister?"

If I wasn't already watching her, I may have missed the corners of her mouth pinch together. The room is silent as I hold my breath, and the stillness of the air feels heavy on my shoulders. My mom had said my grandma's sister's name was Emersim. I couldn't help but pair the slight similarity to Professor *Sim*.

After another unbearable silent minute passes, Professor Sim's eyelashes flutter in a rapid series of blinks. "I apologize for my silence. No one has asked about my sister in years."

"So you are..." I trail off, too many realizations crashing through my mind at once. "My aunt?"

"Technically, I'm your grandaunt, but an aunt all the same," Professor Sim says as our eyes lock, and all of the pieces fall into place.

"I'm sorry, I'm just having a hard time processing this," I admit and let my weight fall forward so I can brace myself on her desk. "I know I came here expecting you to confirm that, but I still can't make sense of it."

Professor Sim—my aunt—walks around the desk, her steps small and slow. "Ash, why don't you sit?" Her touch is like a feather on my arm as she guides me to one of the chairs in the front row. She sits across from me, taking a minute to adjust her old bones to let her sit comfortably. "How did you figure it out?" she asks, sounding a bit out of breath.

"I remembered seeing my grandma placing a floorboard back into place in her art studio," I explain. "When we made it out of Pintura, I found an old deck of Ending in Cadence cards beneath the floor. That's when I started wondering about her connections to this world, and then my mom explained the rest."

She takes in every word I say, living off the small details I have from Earth. "Did Alice not tell you about Pintura?"

I shake my head, still feeling as insulted as Professor Sim looks. There was this family secret buried away for years. Had Jenny, Wren, and I never fell through that painting, I don't think my mom would have ever told me.

"No, my mother only told me the other day because I decided I was coming back here with Emma."

Professor Sim's grey eyes widen as if she just now realized that I not only escaped Pintura, but chose to return knowing how impossible it would be to ever go home. "I can't believe you'd want to stay here."

"You did," I retort before I realize what impact my words could have.

Her expression saddens, but she nods, agreeing with my proclamation. "I'm sure Alice still hates me for that decision."

My chest tightens at the clear tension that spreads on Professor Sim's face. Does Jenny hate me for coming back? Were her optimistic parting words an act? Did she cry after I left? Curse me for abandoning her in California?

No, she's not alone. Wren is there. Our parents are with her.

"If you ever do return to Earth, will you tell her I miss her?"

I suck in a sharp breath, snapping my eyes back up to meet hers. "She's dead," I say, the loss of my grandma still fresh. "Her funeral was yesterday," I add, after doing the math in my head on how much time has passed here compared to on Earth.

"Oh, Alice." Professor Sim lifts a trembling hand to her chest, tears rushing to her eyes.

"I'm sorry," I say, the instinctive words fleeing from my tongue and I reach across the space between us, laying a reassuring hand on her knee.

Professor Sim squeezes her eyes closed and shakes her head, taking in a deep breath the steady her emotions. "It's okay. I'm okay," she says, though her voice shows the opposite. After another deep inhale, she opens her eyes and swats away the few tears that managed to escape. "I said my goodbyes to her years ago when I chose to stay in Pintura and she left. It's just, seeing you had me imaging seeing her again. Something I haven't thought about in a very long time."

I pull back my hand when I'm sure she's steady and wring my fingers together, unsure of what to say now. The silence lingers in the conversation and I let my eyes wander around her classroom while my mind drifts to other places; to my sister, to Wren, to my parents. How will I ever know what happens to them? What about if something happens to me?

"I still don't know the specifics on how you and my grandmother came here," I say when I'm ready to break the quiet. Our gazes lock once more, and I ask, "Would you tell me the story?"

A weak smile finds her mouth, and it lifts the excruciating weight that had landed on my chest. I wasn't sure if talking about my grandmother—about her sister—would be something she'd be willing to do, but I see a light find her silver eyes. Joyful memories with her sister surely running through her mind, and in this world, I'm the only person who could understand those tales from Earth.

"We came here when I was only sixteen. Just a year younger than you," she says and settles back into her seat. "Alice and I were tasked with cleaning out the prop room at our high school when she found the painting."

"It was just lying in a storage room at a school?" I ask and Professor Sim nods.

"Buried with a dozen other pictures used to decorate sets for theater productions. Your grandma loved being on stage."

I can tell Professor Sim's focus drifts as her mind goes back to that day. She's no longer looking at me, but through me. I think about interrupting her and telling her that I share that love of acting, but I'm too curious about where her store will go next that I don't risk stopping her.

She reaches up and reveals a silver chain to a necklace that was hidden beneath the collar of her shirt. When she pulls it free, I notice a ring hangs in the center. A simple gold band with tiny four-point stars carved in the metal. "I was wearing this the day we were cleaning out the storage room. It belonged to Alice, but I always took it even though it was too big for my fingers at the time. The ring slipped free as we hovered over the painting and fell *through* the canvas. That was how we discovered it was a portal into this world."

"Into Pintura," I say softly, if only to clarify to myself how this all comes together.

Professor Sim's face scrunches and she tilts her head to the side, pulling her focus back from the place it drifted and to me. "Not exactly," she whispers.

I lean forward to catch her words and immediately need her to speak more.

"When we came through, this world was very different from what you see now. The portal was open all the time. We didn't fall here and become trapped. We stepped through the painting and onto a spiral staircase of tree branches from a weeping willow."

I instantly know the tree she's talking about. It's the one that we ascended at the end of completing Ending in Cadence. What she's saying now is that the bridge to our world used to always be open. The staircase stood for all time, not just for the winners of the game. I want to hear more about the way the world was when she first came, but Professor Sim jumps through her story to the part my mother had told me.

"I'm sure you understand exactly how we felt coming through that portal. How magical this world felt when our simple lives on the other side had gotten so ordinary. Alice entertained the incredible discovery for a few hours and insisted we return home before mother and father got worried beyond repair. But those hours were all it took for me to fall in love with a place that wasn't supposed to belong to me."

My chest dips at her words, a heavy ache taking root there, because I felt the exact same way. I knew early on that I loved Pintura. I denied that I'd ever call it home until the night I was about to lose the one person who has ever understood me.

"I refused to return with Alice. I begged her to let us stay just a week and then we could go home, but Alice was always the responsible one. Even at eighteen, she had her life together. A boy she was engaged to and a plan to make a family. Back then, Ash, that was how women were expected to live their lives. That was how they were deemed successful, and in a few short years, I knew it would be my turn to do the same. That is partially why I didn't want to leave here. I could feel the difference in the world, the freedom it would give me. Much like the freedom I'm sure you feel it's giving you."

I only nod so I don't interrupt her story even for a second.

"Alice went back through the portal that morning and I promised her I'd follow a week later." A hint of a smile pulls at Professor Sim's lips. "Obviously I didn't do that."

"You never saw your sister again?" I ask, hating that my grandam lost her sister on a broken promise. *I'll see you again, Jenny. Don't worry. I'll be back.* My own words to my sister echo in my head. I only said them to make my leaving easier for her, but I know I'll keep my promise. I have to.

"I saw her once more after that," Professor Sim says.

The tone of her voice sharpens, and the hairs on my arms stand in anticipation. My mom never said anything about grandma coming back for her sister.

"As I'm sure you just figured out, time on Earth and here moves at different speeds," Professor Sim says.

My head naturally begins to spin as I try to grasp that thought once again. One week here is only four hours on Earth. I've already been back in Pintura for days, but to Jenny, to Wren, to my family, it's only the day after my grandma's funeral.

"Alice didn't realize that until she got home and discovered the hours we spent in this world wasn't how much time had passed back home, but by that time the school was closed and she couldn't get back to me to warn me. Not until the next morning." Professor Sim finally releases her grip on the necklace and the ring falls back against the fabric of her shirt. "When Alice came back, so much had changed here," she whispers. "The portal was no longer open all the time. Soon after she left, this world broke apart and the magic that fueled the portal drew back into the world."

"Is that why you couldn't keep your promise to my grandma? Because the portal closed?"

Professor Sim nods. "I really was going to go back after a week, but when the tree branches receded from the sky and the swirling grey clouds faded, the relief I felt was frightening. I loved it here, but I would have gone back. If only to say a proper goodbye to Alice."

"But then she came for you," I say, bridging the gap in her story.

"She did. Much like you had. She only wanted to warn me of how differently time moved, but she found herself trapped here." Professor Sim shifts her weight and reaches for the belt around her waist.

Clasped there is a black velvet back I know well.

"These cards only exist because of her." Professor Sim frees the bag and pulls out an identical deck of Ending in Cadence cards that I used to return home. "There's a lot you don't know about the history of Pintura, Ash. How the magic that lives in this world can only be communicated to through the Lord. But I had to get my sister home, so we prayed to the magic, tried to communicate with it for hours. Since that day, I'm the only other person besides the Lord in power that the world has answered."

My mind races to keep up with the pieces of her story that she's revealing. Emma had told me about the magic here and Lord Neko's duty to communicate on the people's behalf. For years, Emma and everyone else in Pintura believed the magic had died.

"The world reopened the portal?" I ask.

"The world gave us Ending in Cadence." She fans the cards out, letting the sun send the gold paint on their backs shimmering. "That was how the game was born. We played it just like you did, and I sent Alice home. That was the last time I saw my sister."

"After all that, you still didn't want to go home?" I ask Professor Sim, my aunt, *my family*. There are people on the other side that loved her.

"After all that, you still jumped back through the painting," she says, bringing her grey eyes up to meet mine.

While she puts the cards back in the velvet bag, we sit in silence and I digest her story. I take in each word again and put it all together with my family's past.

"Ash." Professor Sim says my name hesitantly. "I'm afraid you may not have thought through your return to Pintura."

A wave of nerves begins to coil around my stomach. "Of course I have. This is where I want to be; with Emma and with this freedom. Just like you chose it."

Professor Sim shakes her head and folds her wrinkled hands over each other. "You have not thought about the time difference enough."

"What do you mean? I have. I understand that time moves faster here," I say, explaining what we've already discussed.

"But you are only thinking about a day, Ash." Professor Sim leans forward, bringing her face closer to mine. "You are not considering your years. Your age. You will be old and wrinkled like me before your sister starts her freshman year of college."

Icy fear curls around my throat at her words. My brain races to do the math in my head. I hadn't even considered the fact that I would start aging faster than Jenny. If I stay here... "Oh my God," I breathe with my realization.

"That is what Alice came to warn me about," Professor Sim says as she sits back in her chair.

When she speaks, it fractures my frantic thoughts and I focus back on her. On the woman who sits across from me that appears to be my grandma's age.

"Why didn't you age any faster than my grandmother? You've been here for... for nearly 65 Earth years. That would mean—"

"I've been living on Pintura for over 2,800 years."

My mouth hangs open as her words cut me off. "Holy hell." She should not be alive. There is no way she could live that long. "How is that possible?" I finally ask when I've had a minute to absorb that fact.

"Magic."

Professor Sim says the single word that seems to always be the answer here in Pintura.

"When Alice left after completing Ending in Cadence, part of me always wondered if she'd come back for me. I didn't want her to return and find me... Well, like this." She gestures to her wrinkled face and a brittle laugh escapes her. "From the moment she left, I prayed to the magic once again and begged there to be away that I could live here, but not age. A possible fatal mistake in my wording."

I wish I could know what she means by that, but my mind can no longer run alongside her story and decipher its meaning. "Explain, please. Because I don't want to die before Jenny can start college."

Professor Sim stares at me for a long minute, and the soft features in her face harden. "I prayed every day until my 77th birthday. On that day, the magic in this world finally answered my prayers. The ground in front of me opened and revealed a shallow puddle of water, a single glass bowl beside it. It allowed me one drink of the water before the world pulled it back and my aging stopped. It didn't slow, like I had wanted. It *stopped*."

"That is how you've lived for 2,000 years?"

"It's how I'll live for another 2,000, and 2,000 after that. I've lived under many names in my time here. I've seen generations of Lords come and go," Professor Sim says. "And my sister never did come back for me."

The fear that had tightened itself around my throat pulls back when Professor Sim's voice begins to tremble, tears resurfacing in her eyes. I lose sight of my own panic and take Professor Sim's hand in mine.

"Maybe you were never supposed to stop aging for Alice. Maybe you were supposed to be here when I fell through that painting with my sister and Wren. You gave us the Ending in Cadence cards. You're the reason I was able to get them home." I squeeze her thin hand gently, wishing I could do more to comfort her. To comfort the only family I have on this side of the painting.

"I don't know if the world would listen to you, Ash," Professor Sim finally says after she takes a moment to rein in her tears. "But even if it did, and you could slow down your aging so the ones you love on Earth don't lose you, you'd be giving up that time with Emma."

At the mention of Emma, my heart begins racing again, that fear lurching out at me. I recede my hand and squeeze my eyes shut. Of course, if I try to age slower for Jenny, Emma will continue to get older. Either way, I'm giving someone up. Part of me knew that when I jumped back through that painting. I thought I'd made my decision then, that Emma was my choice, that this world would be my home. But until this moment, I still felt like I could change my mind. But I can't. If I choose this world, I am giving up my home and my family forever.

And it's only a matter of time before Jenny does the math and realizes that. Maybe my parents already understood, but I find that hard to believe.

"It's an impossible choice, Ash." Professor Sim pushes against the chair and slowly rises to her feet, extending a hand to help me up. "But it's not one you have to make today."

I take her bony fingers in mine and rise, letting her escort me to the door of her classroom.

"At least now, you know you have family here in Pintura," she says when I swing the door open. "Don't linger outside under that tree any longer. You are always welcome to come see me," she adds. Before I walk away, Professor Sim lifts her hand and offers me the bag of Ending in Cadence playing cards. "In case you need to go home."

Her words are light and meant to help ease the ache that's raking through me, but they do little to relax the tension. One glance at her steel gaze tells me she isn't going to budge until I accept the cards. I take them since I left the original deck I played with at the top of

Rising Salvation, and Professor Sim steps back from me.

I'm going to have to make a decision soon. Do I try to find a way to age with my family, or do I let that entire part of my life go and fully accept the new world that surrounds me?

I think I already know what I want, but I fear it will break my family's heart. As if my leaving wasn't enough.

ORDER YOUR COPY OF

BEGINNING

IN

UNISON

AND CONTINUE READING

THANK YOU!

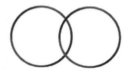

LEAVE A REVIEW TODAY
YOU CAN MAKE A DIFFERENCE

Thank you so much for reading ENDING IN CADENCE! It would mean the world to me if you could take a minute to leave a review for my book. In a world with millions of amazing stories, reviews are how books reach new readers, how authors connect with their target audience, and how distributors know which books to recommend their users. By spending just a minute leaving a review, you are impacting lives of hundreds of people that love to read and were involved in the publication of this book!

ALSO BY CATHERINE DOWNEN

DON'T READ THE LAST PAGE

THE MARKINGS TRILOGY

COMING SOON:

BEGINNING IN UNISON (Book 2)

SPELLBOUND LIES (YA Fantasy Retelling)

ABOUT THE AUTHOR

Catherine Downen is a Young Adult author in both fantasy and contemporary romance. She graduated from Bradley University with a degree in Mechanical Engineering. Currently, Catherine is working as an engineer in St. Louis while writing her books.

Connect with me:

Book Playlists on Spotify

OTHER SOCIAL MEDIA:

CPSIA information can be obtained
at www.ICGtesting.com
Printed in the USA
BVHW042314290422
635743BV00016B/381/J